NIGHT

PART 1 OF THE ALL THROUGH SERIES

K.R PRINCE

YELLOW TREE PUBLISHING

For information address publisher at:

Yellow Tree Publishing

Instagram: yellowtreepublishing

Cover Design © Tullius Heuer

Photo copyright: © Olies/Deposiphotos.com, Carlodapino/Depositphotos.com, Sciencepics/

Depositphotos.com, Akinshin/Depositphotos.com

Font copyright: Requiem/Christopher Hansen

Publisher's Note: This is a work of fiction. Names, characters, places, and incidents are a product of the author's imagination. Locales and public names are sometimes used for atmospheric purposes. Any resemblance to actual people, living or dead, or to businesses, companies, events, institutions, or locales is completely coincidental.

Book Layout ©2017 BookDesignTemplates.com

All Through The Night/ K.R Prince. -- 2nd ed.

ISBN 978-0-9990255-2-9

TABLE OF CONTENTS

DEDICATIONS

*This story is a work of fiction born from a place that
wishes for beautiful things.*

For

*Anyone who has ever felt forgotten or unable to see
themselves reflected in the world
around them.*

Acknowledgments

I would like to honor those who encouraged me when things got tough and stayed for the smiles as well. Thank you Vivian, Eve, Angel, Abrie, Lio, Maria Joaquina, Yajaira, Nubia, Valery, my parents and all of you who started reading this story when it was just a baby; you know who you are, without you guys this book wouldn't exist. Your support has been invaluable and inspiring.

Please never stop reading, never stop dreaming.

EPIGRAPH

"Human hearts are underrated at best. They have eyes that see through our eyes even when we are blind. They will beat more than two point five billion times in a lifetime while enabling the tireless and the ineffable living inside our minds. It is necessary to often think of what those restless walls must harbor; sometimes in silence, sometimes alone. Because it is rather altering to realize that stories cling to what is left of us after we go. All the uniqueness, weakness, and strength, just like a fingerprint, leaving behind a piece of our individuality, something that only another heart can see through those special kinds of eyes. The feeling kind."   Ed Hawthorne.

PROLOGUE

"I will never forget the day I met Emily Knight. It was my first day at Clearwater University; I had left Mr. Carlisle's office feeling relieved, he seemed genuine. Specific plans for the day crossed my mind when suddenly, I collided with someone. Every book I held went flying up and then to the ground. The second my hand touched the rugged material of my 'Coalesce' collector's copy, something shifted in me, and I was yet to look up. I recall that morning I had finished page 122, Elliot's and Clara's conversation fresh in my mind... 'Can you remember all that, darling?' ... 'Yes. How could I ever forget? ' Ed Hawthorne had a way with words.

Coalesce was my second book since I had arrived in San Francisco, but nothing, not even the story that had me completely enthralled for weeks could have prepared me for what I found when I looked up and saw her unforgettable eyes. Emily was an exquisite being. Right in that very moment, I knew she was capable of great and deep loyalty. She was good; she was so good. I would remember her forever, I was sure of it.

Coalesce was also the last book I read for the following four months. Emily had managed to turn the structure of my emotional and mental system upside down. When she said those first words, regardless of them starting with 'Shit' I knew I had found my first true friend. —How?— I am not certain I could answer that; at the time it made no rational sense to me. My world ever since I could remember had been one of order and science. Those two went hand in hand; they held logic —my parents always reminded me to be logical, to be practical; I liked it that way, but what

I felt in my chest blew my mind; it made more sense than science, and that scared me.

By the way, my name is Helena; I am an eighteen-year-old girl from San Francisco. Most of my life I have been considered to be an outsider; I like horror film magazines and classic fashion, the latter being the only thing I could possibly have in common with most girls my age. I have spent the last twelve years of my life at a boarding school in Germany, where all of the above didn't necessarily place me on my peer's good side. I am a loner, have always been a loner and before returning home, I thought I'd be one for whatever amount of living time I had left. Meeting Emily Knight changed my life forever; but before we get to that part, this is how everything started..."

1

COALESCE

A COLD SEPTEMBER NIGHT GUARDED the robust walls of an opulent mansion overlooking the fresh waters of San Francisco Bay. The exclusive edge of Pacific Heights' billionaire's row was the lavish home of Katherine, Santiago Millan, and their children. Bold and misunderstood, Maddison, nineteen, offspring from Katherine's first marriage; she had icy blue eyes and auburn hair like her birth father, though just as her mother she was beautiful and straightforward —far too witty for her own sake. Warmhearted and handsome, Caleb, nineteen, was Santiago's son and also the product of a failed marriage. And lastly, their youngest, Helena, eighteen, the gorgeous brunette was the only one to be born of their union. She had thick long hair and heart-rending dark eyes. Many would say Helena's eyes bore the intensity of her soul for the whole world to see, leaving anyone enamored with the kindness and mystery they exuded. Her olive-toned skin was as flawless as the way she spoke.

San Francisco had been their home for generations preceding them, old money and well-known family names.

However, both successful surgeons were keen on giving their progenies the best life could offer, even if that meant sending them to boarding schools far from each other at a young age. Maddison and Caleb had returned from their respective schools in England and Switzerland years prior and were attending Clearwater Private University. Helena had just returned from her all-girls school in Germany and would be joining them at the prestigious institution.

The light sounds of expensive silverware and china cut through silence as the family sat and ate dinner. Katherine sipped on a delicious glass of red wine while eyeing her three spawns. Helena and Caleb seemed to be having some sort of telepathic conversation while a visibly annoyed Maddison played with her food.

Caleb and Helena had borrowed greatly from Santiago's beautiful and exotic Argentinian gene pool, making them look strikingly similar; they were also close despite the distance while growing up and that never sat well with Maddison.

"Maddison, dear, what is it?" Katherine asked.

The girl rolled her eyes, ignoring her mother and continued pushing brussels sprouts around her plate.

Moved by her daughter's challenging silent attitude, Katherine gently tried again, "Maddison, I am talking to you, please regard me as I do so, it is incredibly disrespectful to roll your eyes and play deaf."

"Insufferable," Maddison muttered to herself between teeth. Helena and Caleb stopped chewing, awkwardly shifting in their seats. Maddison's English accent was thick and shone through even in whispers. It always made her feel like an outsider since none of her family members had one. She had tried to be quiet, but everyone clearly heard the comeback.

Katherine raised a brow and put down her fork, exhaling deeply. Helena slowly began chewing again as she scratched the back of her head uncomfortably; Caleb cleared his throat and went back to his food.

"Excuse me?" Katherine challenged, collected.

Maddison shrugged and rolled her eyes. "This situation is… insufferable." she said.

Nice save. Helena and Caleb eyed each other, they continued eating.

"Whatever do you mean, love? I thought you'd be pleased to be moving to campus. It's all you've talked about for the past year." Katherine tried.

"Right, I was not talking about that part, Mother." Maddison sassed, unamused.

"Then what are you referring to?"

"This…" She looked at her siblings and then back at her mother. "Going to the same college as them!" she said, sneering as if it were the flu.

"Need I remind you that your grades are suffering, Maddison, and you are on the verge of expulsion; Clearwater is one of the most prestigious universities in the state; you should be grateful Mr. Carlisle gave you another chance!" Katherine chided.

"Who bloody cares?!" she grunted.

It was Santiago's turn to intervene serenely; he looked her way. "Watch your tone with your mother, Maddison."

Blue eyes barely acknowledged her father; Maddison loved him deeply since he had never made her feel like the result of Katherine's first marriage, but at the moment, she was utterly pissed. She turned back to her mother.

"*That* is exactly my problem, Mother; Clearwater *is* prestigious and incredibly suffocating! It is impossible to go by unnoticed there! Everyone knows everyone —I can imagine how delightful it will be when they all find out I'm the idiot of the Millan clan. They all know Caleb is a jock with stupid dimples and a pretty face; and now, you add 'Evil Genius' here to the mix, so smart, sweet and perfect —forgive me for feeling a little apprehensive about becoming the laughingstock of the entire stinking place! I swear I'd rather go to community college, I would gladly take it over this humiliation!" Maddison whined, growing flushed and upset.

Helena furrowed her brows and interjected, "So your problem is with me."

Maddison rolled her eyes and ignored her sister's words. She continued facing her mother. "And now you tell me I have to share a dorm room with her?!"

This wasn't new for Helena, though the bruising ache in her chest was always there. "Mother, I don't have to move to campus… I can stay here; it makes absolutely no difference to me." she said.

Caleb swallowed a bite and sneered at Maddison. "God, you're so thoughtless!" he said.

She glared at him. "Shut up."

Katherine exhaled. "Stop it, both of you. Maddison, I want you all to spend more bonding time together —now that…" The churning in her stomach was something she was still getting accustomed to. Nothing hurt the strong woman more than the thought of losing Helena. She gathered herself as any physician would. "You *will* share a dormitory with your sister on campus, and I hope you both see value in the experience."

They all knew why Katherine said what she had, so everyone averted their eyes except for Helena. She simply sighed and returned to her meal. Resenting her very own anatomy for turning on her was frustrating.

Katherine smiled and regarded her three children with genuine affection; gleaming hazel eyes lingered on Helena, who matched her soft smile.

"The white Mercedes outside is all yours, dear," she regarded her youngest.

Deep down, Helena dreaded what would come of her mother's extravagant gift. Her mouth opened and closed. "I— thank you, Mother, but you didn't have to do that..." she said, and smiled uncomfortably.

"What?!" Maddison said, seemingly appalled, her eyes widened as she drew back sorely. "That car is for her?! Then what the hell am I supposed to drive?" she protested.

Katherine frowned. "Language, Maddison." She had always been the mouthy one. "You will continue to drive the hybrid." Katherine informed.

"Oh, boy..." Santiago mumbled quietly and shifted in his seat while Helena looked around awkwardly and Caleb grinned challengingly; perfect dimples formed on his lightly tanned cheeks. He was gloating, and Maddison was fuming.

"What?! Are you kidding me?" she said, tightening her fists with frustration. "This is beyond unfair! This is bloody blunt predilection towards them over me!" she protested.

"*No*, I told you last year that if you were to raise your grades, you'd get the Audi you wanted. However, if I recall correctly, the complete opposite happened, Maddison."

"This is crap!"

"Maddison!" Katherine scolded while feeling a puncturing

headache coming along; she pinched the bridge of her nose.

"What?! This is incredibly horrid parenting. Oh, but of course! The jock son drives his 'perfect boy' sports car, and she, who's barely out of diapers, gets a freaking Mercedes?! While *I* get an egg shaped car?! Why are you treating me like a child?!" Maddison argued, growing flushed.

"Because! You *are* acting like a child!" Katherine slammed her palm on the table and glared at her daughter.

Helena spoke up, attempting to smooth the ridges of the uncomfortable argument. "I can drive the hybrid," she regarded both her parents, "she can drive the new car, or I can ride with either one of them, I honestly don't care." She looked at her brother and then over at her oldest sister who rolled her eyes.

Maddison huffed. "You are such a martyr... Christ!" She crossed her arms; eyes bound to the ceiling.

Helena shifted uncomfortably and looked at Katherine. "Mother, it's just a car, definitely not worth fighting over." she finished, feeling foreign to the group, wishing for the night to end —wishing to go back to being with herself.

Katherine looked at Helena softly; it was a silent plea. This wasn't about predilection; she had it under control. "Maddison, raise your grades, and the arrangement will change... you have the power to shift things if you don't like them. Do it. I know you can." she encouraged.

"Ugh! Whatever..." Maddison huffed and stormed off the table.

Helena felt like shit and uncomfortable as she usually did when they were all together. She loved her sister, of course she did. However, Maddison seemed to hate her for no reason she could remember. For breathing? Existing? She wished she could change it.

After dinner was over, Helena went upstairs to her room feeling inadequate. It was strange to be back home after two years. Two years ago was the last time she had spent a couple of weeks with her family over Christmas and then back to her boarding school. Back to her lonely life, the one she had grown incredibly accustomed to. Helena wasn't a girl who made friends easily, she was gorgeous, sinfully smart —which made her sometimes awkward to others and maybe difficult to understand, but Helena was kind and independent; traits she kept to herself and those who gave her the time. She kept to herself and her books, her family and a couple of acquaintances back in school. She had never had a real friend in spite of having so much to offer. Life seemed unfair, but Helena didn't see it that way. To her, this was just the way things were; she knew no different; she had no other perspective to compare it to, but still, her young heart yearned for more. She knew there had to be more.

***

Morning had arrived with peach-colored clouds smeared on a bright blue sky. Both Helena and her brother sat in her sleek new car, parked by an empty street on Pacific Ter. The comfort of the driver seat didn't make her immune to feeling her brother's gaze. Ready for a tennis match with his little sister, Caleb took his racquet from the back seat when he noticed a pensive Helena. Perfectly manicured hands gripped the wheel as brown eyes stared at the horizon, lost in thought.

"What is it, Lena?" he asked, something had her longing focus.

Oxygen bruised her lungs, and gleaming eyes found him. "I just… I don't want this to create an even worse rift between Maddison and me, Cai —I feel terrible."

"Look, I know where you're coming from and why you'd feel like shit after Maddison's little show at the dinner table last night, but whatever made her so unhappy all these years has absolutely nothing to do with you. Do you understand?" he finished softly and fixed deep brown eyes on even deeper ones.

"You can't let her ruin your time, Helena, I know she's not all bad, but she's a spoiled brat, and you didn't deserve to be blamed for her discontent with mom's decision. You don't have to lower your head and take her bullshit, sis."

"I know that, and I am not. I mean —I'm not stupid, but I wish things could be different between us; I wish she'd give me a chance." Sentiment stung her eyes. "She's my sister… I just," Helena shook her head and found an invisible oblivion in the distance. "There's so much I'd like to share with her if only she would let me. We can't blame her attitude, Caleb; she had it far worse than us, she has practically lived away from Mother and Daddy since she was five."

Caleb smiled; he loved Helena. Helena was special; she was lovely and unique —she was his baby sister even if they were only a year apart. "She'll come around, Lena… just give her some time to adjust, and you'll see." His gentle touch against her shoulder was grounding.

Helena nodded and stalled, "So, please tell me all about Clearwater!" Her smile was as bright as those secret eyes.

Caleb grinned. "Like Maddison said, it's not your typical large campus, so the vibe can be a little segregated; a ton of brats like her —if you ask me, I think she fits in nicely." he said, chuckling.

Helena bit back amusement. "You know, technically, we are often unfairly branded as spoiled brats, too, so..." She winked.

Caleb grinned at his sister's comment. "Ha-Ha —well, it's totally true. Clearwater is filled with rich snobs and your occasional asshole. You should really be more excited about our tennis match and not worry about that." he joked.

Helena mused him with an arched brow. "That is a rather general statement, and it can't be that terrible —can it?" she said, and almost dreaded.

"I mean, not everyone is like that of course, but that's the general feel of the place. Nothing too different from the spoiled girls you went to school with, I assume, only here there are guys, too, and of course, it's college... you get to have freedom, but still, you won't escape the bureaucratic, bullshit feel of it all." he said with a smirk.

She furrowed her brows. "Are you serious?"

He laughed. "See, I told you. You should be more excited about our game, Helena."

***

Two weeks passed and the day had finally arrived. Helena was bursting from her seams with excitement despite Caleb's obscure perspective on the place. Aesthetically, the structure was grandiose and impeccable. The air of longevity and collegiate gothic architecture on the building was majestic. The vibrant green grass was crossed with sidewalks and mossy stone benches. But the best part and Helena's favorite was the lush Yoshino cherry trees. They arched in a magical canopy of downy pink flowers for the walker by.

She didn't expect her luck with making new friends to change, but part of her welcomed the different experience in a schooling environment. No stuffy uniforms and a co-ed system. However, the best part of it all would be something she was far from expecting.

Helena sat opposite Dean Carlisle. Her eyes read from the shiny nameplate sitting on his expansive desk.

"Your records are impressive, Miss Millan; I sincerely hope you find your first semester at Clearwater University to be most rewarding and fulfilling. It is a pleasure to have you join us," he said with a brief smile on his usually blank face. "I understand it will only be temporary?"

"Well, I have taken a test and applied for the advanced program at Ravenford Medical School —I am still not sure if they will allow me to skip the complete undergraduate program. We will have to wait and see." she informed.

"With your records, I don't see why not. You are far ahead for someone your age; that is quite rare, congratulations on your achievements, Miss Millan."

Helena smiled and stood; she straightened the invisible wrinkles on her simple dress and extended her hand. "Thank you, sir, for your kind welcome and—" Her smile evaporated slowly. "I am sure my mother has already discussed my illness with you— I... I would greatly appreciate your discretion in the matter." she requested politely.

He caught a gleam of sadness in her eyes, perhaps embarrassment. "I have indeed spoken to Mrs. Millan, and you have nothing to worry about; only the necessary personnel has been advised in case anything sudden should arise. However, I assure you, your wish for privacy will be respected." he said politely with hands held together behind his back.

"Thank you." Helena said with an awkward smile. "I should get going… Mathematics awaits." she said

"Of course… please." He nodded and watched her exit his office. Dean Carlisle felt sorry for the beautiful girl. It was a shame.

Past the dean's door, scattered sounds of rushing steps and distant voices found Helena. Holding the designer bag on her shoulder, she read directions on how to get to the classroom where her first subject of the day would be held. Juggling her newly acquired books while making sense of the confusing place wasn't necessarily ideal. She scanned the space full of people with a seemingly set goal —they all knew where to go. —*Where the hell is Caleb?* She hated being late. Helena hurried her pace, and in the blink of an eye, crashed against the warmth of a body that smelled spellbindingly good. There was hair... long blonde hair and books on the ground. Both girls instantly reached down.

"Shit!" The voice matched the delicious perfume. Brown eyes rose from pale hands to a beautiful, big white smile and deep dimples piercing carmine cheeks.

Helena was smitten. Gleaming brown found two. No, no... —three tiny moles following each other like constellations on her chest. Green… definitely green eyes that looked like bright precious stones. The color of beryls; *yes...* the most beautiful person Helena had ever seen.

"I'm so sorry," Emily tried genuinely. "I am such a clutz," she added while collecting Helena's books from the floor. "Here…"

A gaping Helena closed her eyes and smiled, realizing she must have looked like an idiot. Cold sweat claimed hidden skin and oxygen fled from her lungs.

Emily blushed and held a contemplative smile. This girl had class, the effortless kind of class. —*She's stunning.* Emily thought. The gorgeous stranger looked like she had just walked out of a high fashion magazine. Magical green drank her. Those dark eternal eyes made Emily feel things she didn't know existed, things that moved inside her stomach. That heart-shaped face and exquisite jawline; pale fingertips itched to caress it and every inch of breathtaking... like her provoking lips. Emily shook herself off the trance and took in what she could, including gentle hands and black fingernail polish. —*Class with a twist...* The brunette was a walking paradox made of softness and edge.

"Thank you, and it's not a problem, I wasn't paying attention to my surroundings." Helena tried with a deep breath.

Emily's smile faded. —*Is she shaking? She seems pale.* "Hey, are you all right?"

Helena composed herself. "I am. Thank you, I must go or else I will be rudely late for my first class." she said, smiling, and quickly gathered everything to move forward. The way she spoke was so proper and adorable; most would have believed she was awkward, but *God...* Emily had never seen anything so endearing and challenging at the same time.

"What classroom are you looking for? You seem lost." she asked.

Helena shamelessly canvassed red chucks, tight jeans, a lanky and gorgeous frame... her edge. —*Is that a soccer jacket? Yes... it definitely is.* It had the university crest on the right side of her chest. Helena swallowed hard and questioned her involuntary reactions. —*Are these symptoms or am I just... nervous?* she thought.

"Um... Are you sure you're okay?" Emily insisted.

"Yes, I..." Helena snapped out of her trance and shook her head. "Yes, I am... thank you." she managed, feeling lame. "Umm... right —classroom 801." she read from the paper and handed it to the girl.

Emily took it and grinned. "Ah... well, lucky for you, we have the same class; sadly for me, though, this is my third time taking this course." Green eyes looked up and found the increasingly adorable girl.

Helena was nervous, but sighed in relief —she could deal with nervous. "That is most certainly convenient."

Emily chuckled, enraptured. "I bet it is."

Suddenly realizing how that must have sounded, Helena smiled and closed her eyes. "I am sorry— I didn't mean—"

"It's totally okay, I was kidding, and Math isn't my forte— that's why I'm here... again."

Helena blushed. "Well, we are—" She looked at the costly watch on her wrist. "Four minutes tardy." she announced.

Emily furrowed her brows and grinned. *—Did she say tardy? Definitely adorable.* "Right... well, I'm always *tardy,*" She laughed at how weird that sounded coming out of her mouth. "We can be late together, come on." Emily beckoned, and Helena followed.

The large door opened and Emily motioned with her hand. Not used to getting such attention, Helena smiled and walked in —Caleb was right. The classic and rich structure of the place was impeccable but indeed reduced. She counted roughly seventeen heads in the classroom.

"New face..." the professor said. "And of course... Miss Knight, we meet again." She frowned.

Helena froze at the woman's attitude but soon found her quirky charm and extended a hand. "I sincerely apologize, Professor Spencer —on both my peer's and my behalf," She glanced over her shoulder at the girl behind, who was completely unfazed by the woman's taunt. "I assure you, it will not happen again."

Professor Spencer arched a brow and shook Helena's hand. —*Captivating and awkward.*

"My name is Helena Millan; it is a pleasure to meet you." she added.

Emily bit her lip and burned that name to her brain.

"All right… Miss Millan," She spotted Emily and frowned condemningly yet again. "And Miss Knight… please find a seat." She motioned to the last row, only three seats were empty.

Helena accepted while Emily rolled her eyes at the woman's smirk, she knew Professor Spencer didn't like her. She sighed and focused on that beautiful sound, Helena… —*I love her name.* she thought while Helena walked to the back of the classroom. Emily quietly followed and sat next to her, unable to tear those green eyes away.

"Please open your books on page seven;" Professor Spencer walked to the whiteboard and scribbled. "We will start with Biostatistics: Introduction to probability and statistical inference." The screeching sound of dry marker matched the strong smell permeated by silence.

Helena found the requested page. She dug through her bag, pulled out a mechanical pencil and a spotless notebook —every item placed in perfect symmetry.

Emily smiled faintly and continued to find the beautiful, geeky girl captivating. She opened her book on the same page, instantly noticing the all too familiar, highlighted portions of paragraphs. *Patrick Knight* sloppily written with blue ink on free spaces. '*This class sucks*' and '*I'm so bored*' She had completely forgotten about the stupid dick-stamped book. To Emily, this was nothing new. She was the youngest one of three. Hand downs were keywords in her world. She found Rhys' signature dicks drawn all over the bottom of the page —a blush claimed her cheeks. She cursed her brothers in her head and shifted in her seat, shielding others from seeing the worrying amount of penises tightly drawn on the page of her 'new' old book. —*Assholes.* Emily loved her brothers, but yes, they were real assholes. They were both out of Clearwater and knew Emily would be using these. —*Ugh! Royal assholes.* she mentally cursed.

The class finished, and Emily didn't get to see Helena in her next few ones, which sucked. Judging by how lost Helena seemed, she figured it was her first year. It looked like her archenemy Mathematics would become her new favorite addiction if she got to see the girl and all her cute geeki-ness. In only an hour she learned that those delicate hands loved to color code everything; that Helena was incredibly smart and *nice;* Helena was kind and polite. She was defi-nitely unreal… —*Stop it, Knight; she's so out of your league.* Emily thought.

***

Lunch was the same when that time of the day came around. The Vine was a low-key café on campus and the place to find good food, decent coffee, and underground music without having to leave Clearwater. Emily was of course, ready to eat the entire food display. While she sat at the empty table with her beautiful cheeseburger, green eyes searched the room for her face, but the place was filled with the usual and a few new ones. Emily was like Helena; she didn't have many friends. She was well-known for entirely different reasons than just her athletic achievements. Emily was a sports goddess just like her brothers had been to the university. She was Professor Shepherd's daughter, and she was different in a way that had always made her feel like an outsider —not that she wanted to be part of a crowd that was so incredibly dense and narrow —not that the whole crowd was the same, but whatever. People talked… they talked *a lot*. They assumed and judged, but that was the way things had always been for her. She didn't give a fuck about what everyone else thought. She felt lucky to have the family she had; Emily was somewhat happy with herself, still fighting to stay afloat within a sea of self-loathing, but really... —*Who isn't?* she thought.

Emily had a lot of worthwhile things, including her childhood friend, who was approaching the table. Big blue eyes and blonde hair, familiar warm smile —Etta was as delightful as her honey-kissed skin.

"Hey, Em,"

"Hey, Etta," Emily said, and smiled at her best friend Henrietta Andersen, who placed her salad and bottle of water on the surface. Etta smiled and pushed a bag of cookies next to Emily's cheeseburger much like she had done since they were in Elementary School. Emily's eyes widened at the sight. Words weren't needed between them, but something was off. Etta studied her unaware friend, who continued to ignore her prized burger *and cookies* only to scan the entire café. "Em…?" she asked.

Green eyes found familiar blue ones nonchalantly.

Etta skimmed over her shoulder and scanned the place herself; she turned with furrowed brows. "Have you lost something?"

Distracted eyes were caught again. "Um, what?"

Etta chuckled. "Okay. What's up?" She was officially curious.

Emily blushed and stalled, feigning bravado. "Nothing's up. What are you talking about?" She took a sip of her water.

Etta arched an inquisitive and unsatisfied brow. "You look like a dog in labor; something is definitely up."

Taken off guard, Emily coughed and dodged the liquid spilling from her mouth; she laughed. "What?! How the fuck is that?"

Etta rolled her eyes. "Like you're in distress."

Emily cleared her throat and scanned her water-stained clothes. "Why not just say that from the beginning? Much less gross." she said, chuckling, and brushed off the droplets from her black soccer jacket.

Etta's shrug was conceited and playful. "Because... Where's the fun in that?"

Knowing her friend all too well, Emily scoffed, amused. Loving Etta was easy.

"Okay, so spill," Etta pressed.

Emily blushed and sighed. "Nothing's up, okay?" she said, growing annoyed.

Two hands rose in mid-air like a peace flag. "Okay, okay... nothing's up." She retreated from the subject, knowing Emily would come to her when ready.

***

Theater, the last class of Emily's day, had begun, and she was more than ready to go. Not even the tapping of an impatient foot on the hardwood floor of the stage soothed her. "I have to go to practice, Professor Silverstein! The coach is gonna kill me," Emily urged as kindly as she could manage. "I'm so sorry, but I really can't take theater this semester."

The eloquent Professor Silverstein was an avid lover of the performing arts, but she was also a caring counselor. The blonde girl had a special place in her heart. "No, Emily... I know that this class gives you no credits, but sweetheart, you need this; it will aid you on so many levels! I promise you may return to your soccer practices only if you accept my offer."

Emily slumped her shoulders with furrowed brows and whined, "Professor Silverstein, I'm *begging* you, I don't beg... please don't make me do this; I'm not an actress!" She cared deeply for the woman and letting her down was tough.

"Emily, it's a very small part, I am not asking you to be Juliet! God knows you'd faint if I made you spend that much time on stage," The woman's face fell with a longing sigh. "I have yet to find my perfect Juliet."

Emily shrugged and exhaled; that kind gleam visible in her eyes, she gave up. "All right, so... this Rosaline, I never heard of her."

Professor Silverstein clapped excitedly. "Oh, honey, fantastic! Thank you, Emily, you will not regret it." She couldn't wait to watch her shine as Rosaline.

Both the professor and Emily turned around to the sound of a voice approaching from behind. The blonde male playing Romeo, and a few other key characters turned as well.

"Excuse me... I am looking for Professor Silverstein's class, is this perhaps it?" Helena asked, feeling the clutter of gazes on her skin.

The professor drew in an inspired batch of magical air while Emily's heart pounded hard inside her chest. Helena's brown eyes meet with green ones. The gleam in them, undeniable —that slightly low and dulcet voice seduced Emily's composure.

"Helena... hey," she said with a shy, tight-lipped smile.

Helena saw dimples, those perfectly symmetrical dimples again. "Hello," Her contentment didn't overshadow the odd sensation in her stomach. —*What is that?* Helena thought.

The enthralled professor beamed. "Oh, you sweet, beautiful girl, you *are* in the right place —you have indeed found Professor Silverstein's class, and I have just found my Juliet..." she said, enamored with Helena's face and everything surrounding her. Two hands cradled carmine cheeks, and Helena tensed, awkwardly looking around.

"Oh..." Brows knitted softly. "All right," Helena said.

The hour flew, and Emily forgot about missing soccer practice. Staring at Helena was painless. The words, those weird Shakespeare words and the way they made everything seem complicated in a beautiful way —Helena spoke them as if she understood them; somehow they made sense to Emily's heart even though her brain was confused. —*What kind of language was that?* From the red velvet seats, all Emily could see was **her** —until obnoxious blonde hair approaching Helena's face interrupted the trance. Emily's brows crashed, and something shifted inside her. —*What the hell is that loser doing?* She rushed off the chair.

"Stop!" Emily blurted out, startling Helena, the blonde

Romeo and every single head that turned to look at her. —*What the fuck did I just do?* Awkward wide eyes scanned their faces. "Um… I uh…" she tried, pushing a hand in her soccer jacket's pocket.

Helena cocked her head to the side and quietly studied her.

"Yes, honey?" the professor asked.

"I uh… well, Rosaline wouldn't want Romeo to um—" Emily darted to the script and cleared her throat. "You know, to do that with other girls, right? I mean…" She flipped through the pages, mocking interest in them.

"Emily, Rosaline is a silent character, and she doesn't return Romeo's affections." Professor Silverstein explained.

"Oh…" Emily faked. "Wait…" She drawled, genuinely confused. "Why would you give me a character with no lines?" she asked.

"Because, Rosaline is a vital part of the story, your presence and what you convey with it will be your performance."

Emily scratched the back of her head. "Okay…"

Helena took everything in with a slightly heaving chest; two fingers ghostly brushed her own beautiful lips, and a smile broke. Brown eyes shone, they glowed yearningly. They were like open windows to her soul and how deeply it ran. —Emily —*That is her name… Emily.* Helena thought.

***

After theater class was over, both Emily and Helena walked through campus and found the parking lot while invested in conversation. The stroll had been a breeze and most certainly not long enough. They stood next to Helena's new car; brown eyes scanned the ground shyly and moved to green ones. She blushed and smiled. "Well, I should get going," Helena said while holding onto the strap on her shoulder.

The wind blew gently against Emily's skin and long hair. —*Helena, you're so beautiful...* The thought stung her. —*What are you doing?* she scolded herself. Emily's smile died. She had been obsessing over a girl who wouldn't want her if she knew. Emily was aware of the thing between them, but Helena didn't know the truth.

"Are you all right?" Helena asked, genuinely searching her eyes and noticing the change. Defeated sadness.

"Yeah... yeah," she lied and pushed a smile. "I'm fine, it's nothing —um... Is this your car?" Emily pointed at the elegant vehicle.

Helena tucked strands of hair behind her ear. "Yes, would you... I could take you home if you'd like." she offered kindly.

"Actually, I brought my motorcycle, and I live on campus most of the week, but thank you for the offer, I might take you up on it one of these rainy days," she said. "Where are you headed?" Emily didn't recognize her suddenly nosey self.

"Pacific Heights... What about you?" Helena asked. The last rays of sunshine hit brown eyes, turning them chestnut as the sun sank.

—*Of course she lives in Pacific Heights.* Emily thought, suddenly remembering she went to college with a bunch of rich kids. "Well, my parents live in Outer Sunset, totally out of your way," she said, and smiled briefly. "But like I said, the dorms are super close, right on campus."

"Oh..." Helena said with a smile, trying to hide disappointment. This blonde girl captivated her. "It would be my pleasure, let me know if you ever do, I certainly wouldn't mind the distance." she offered, questioning her body's reactions.

Emily's smile was big and honest; it made her face feel tight. She blushed. Helena showed sincere interest, and even though she didn't know better, it felt good. Emily enjoyed those seconds and cherished them. "Thank you... That's very nice of you." she said, burning into Helena longingly.

Something twisted in Helena's axis and claimed her like a rooting tree. "Well, at least let me thank you for... you know,"

"What for?" Curiosity conquered Emily.

"For stopping the kiss Nick was going to give me." Helena said.

"Oh, gag—" Emily grimaced. "That wimp," She shrugged. "Sure... no problem, I would totally freak if he were to stick his tongue in my mouth."

Helena furrowed her brows and chuckled. "Well, I would have absolutely hated for my first kiss to be with someone I don't even know or feel attraction towards," she explained.

Genuinely surprised, green eyes rose. "Oh, you've never..."

"I have not. It sounds ridiculous, I know," she confessed, smiling. Carmine blushed her skin.

Emily felt dizzy, and all of a sudden found Helena even more irresistible. Did that make her a perv? *Jeez...* she hoped not. She swallowed and found some words again. "It's totally not. Not at all... but you should talk to Professor Silverstein, though, that wouldn't be right." Emily said.

Helena shrugged. "Well, it is Romeo and Juliet, I think I will have to bite the bullet and go through with it, I'd hate to be one spoiling the play —it's just a kiss anyway... not a big deal, perhaps I should get it over with."

"Oh, **it is**… a big deal, Helena, that's a huge deal;" Emily pressed passionately, "your first kiss should be with someone you choose to share it with, someone who appreciates what it means."

Helena bit her bottom lip, and their gazes met, taking in the very last fleeting glow of the almost sunken sun. "Thank you." she said earnestly.

"I've done nothing." Emily shrugged. "It's the truth; your first kiss should mean something to you, Helena, don't just throw it or give it away lightly —even less because of peer pressure, it's just a stupid play." she insisted.

"I won't." Helena said, and stared deeply into those beautiful, light green eyes. Emily lost her breath, almost tasting what she knew she never would.

"Well…" Helena broke the trance; she needed to collect herself and rest; the day had taken far too much. "I should really go,"

"Yeah, me too…" Emily said, pointing over her shoulder. "Etta must be looking for me." She pulled out her phone and scanned it for missed calls or texts from her friend.

"Etta?" Helena asked with a sinking stomach.

"My best friend and roommate," Emily inspected the almost empty lot. "I was supposed to meet her; I think all that Shakespeare numbed my brain." she said with an honest chuckle.

Helena eyed the device and wanted so badly to have the exact numerical combination that would connect her to the dreamy girl. —*Think quickly, Helena… Think!* And so she did, as it was the very thing she did best.

"I could help you study for the Rosaline part if you'd

like." Helena offered in a blur, and Emily looked up from her phone. She smiled with aching insides.

"But my character has no lines…" Emily mentioned, feeling a little stupid for the ridiculous part she had been given.

"Well, Rosaline is a very significant part of this story, though she is originally unseen —I believe I know why Professor Silverstein chose for her to make a silent appearance. Since she is Romeo's first deeply felt love, or at least he thinks so at the time, she aids to his distress; it drives him to the state he finds himself in when he meets Juliet." Helena explained thoroughly, and Emily felt the heat of blush creep up her cheeks, forming a smile.

—*She's perfect.* Emily thought, and took the time to scan Helena's face in detail; that tiny mole right on the contour of her top lip —*She has a small scar there, too—I wonder what happened...* Emily yearned for those lips and beyond her thinking. She loved how the small mark made them look even more memorable—*God, those beautiful lips—her skin...*

"It's just a thought;" Helena broke Emily's haze and smiled. "You don't have to accept my offer, of course." she said.

"Well, I'd hate to make a bad Rosaline so, I think I would be an idiot to reject your offer." Emily knew this was territory she shouldn't step into, but found it hard to resist Helena; she found it impossible to deny her a reason to smile. This girl breaking Emily's heart could potentially doom her for a good while, but even still, she was so worth it.

"Okay." Helena's gleaming eyes spoke of the things she wanted from Emily. She wanted to touch her skin; she wanted to know her more… she wondered what her lips tasted like. Helena shook her head. —*What am I doing?*

"Do you have a cell phone?" Emily asked.

Pulling out the sleek device from her bag, Helena felt her body's claim.

Emily typed her number, giving Helena complete power. She had earned her respect. Helena was special, the way she carried herself, the kindness in her eyes, that brain… Helena was a once in a lifetime opportunity. She was *more*.

"Call me anytime… Bye, Helena," Emily said, and walked away, glancing over her shoulder with one last smile.

"Goodbye… Emily," she whispered.

2

PARIAH

A COUPLE OF DAYS PASSED, and Helena hadn't used Emily's phone number. She wanted nothing more than to text her, but what would she say? Helena had a terrible track record when it came to making new friends or engaging in prolonged interactions with people her age —with people, period. Helena wasn't shy; she had an internal library of possible topics to dive into or break the ice with. Carrying a mature, prolific conversation with anyone was easy, but people could be cruel. She was far from a stranger to teasing and rejection.

Since Helena's infancy, Katherine would always hold her little girl; reassuring her that people were simply intimidated by her intelligence, that perhaps it reminded them of their insecurities. Even though Helena was very young when this speech started to be recited to her, she understood it quite well.

She had spent the past two days thinking about Emily, unable to get the blonde off her mind. She would catch herself drifting and allowing her imagination to run wild; her body would sometimes react in ways she understood in theory but had never felt with such intensity before.

These things she was feeling when thinking about Emily were new; so overwhelming and primal; even stronger than those moments when sometimes late at night she would explore her very own body.

The cool air of night invaded Helena's room with the scent of chlorophyll and bright stars. Unwinding in the comfort of her bed, she sat against the headboard; those hands Emily adored were thoroughly occupied with two long needles as they expertly interlocked loops of yarn. There was nothing more soothing than the light of a lamp and her favorite songs playing as she knitted.

The intrinsic patterns were the perfect distraction; getting lost in the activity she enjoyed so much had been a good call. Only it really hadn't.

As she looped one more strand to make a perfect square on the basket pattern, brown eyes hesitantly eyed the cell phone resting on the nightstand; it taunted her... Helena felt the urge prickle at her fingers but quickly shook it off. She went back to the halfway-finished scarf in her hands.

Warm eyes seemed to have an agenda; curiosity so bold, Helena looped another stitch, then sighed in defeat and gave in. Biting her lip, she found Emily's number and typed, giving her burning desire a way of release. Helena's stomach filled with swelling sensations and trembled while staring at the unsent message.

The cursor blinked in the text box...

'Hello, Emily; I have suddenly found myself thinking I had agreed to text you a couple of days ago; I hope this isn't a bad time?' Pretty thumbs lingered on the lit screen. Helena chewed on the inside of her cheek and considered what she was about to do.

She was opening herself up to possible rejection.

Sent.

She scanned the room. It was easier to be bare when alone, but it was also scarier and more real. Painful memories surfaced to the expanse of her totality.

"All through my life, I felt things with intensity. I felt deeply, but I never understood that part of me. I didn't know how to express it, so I kept it to myself. My first favorite book was 'A Boy and His Moon' the premise was simple. A writer gets lost in the Swiss Alps and meets a boy whose only dream is to touch the moon. Under the white coat of winter, they become friends; the boy had lost hope, but the writer had a pen.

It resonated with something inside me, as if what it spoke of was somehow real. My nanny used to read it to me every night before I went to bed; she made it sound so authentic, regardless of the reality that I was accustomed to.

Playground gatherings always ended up with me sitting away from everyone else. At first, it was painful; rejection is heavy and difficult to forget, but it got easier over time. I had no ties with anyone. When I was six, that one girl whose eyes lingered on mine longer than anyone else's smiled at me. They were so green and warm. I smiled back, and she said 'Hi.' I remember the following days were the same; she stealthily sought my attention, and I was happy, I had a friend. I now look back and realize it was the first time I had been 'broken' by someone my age; I had been domesticated into complete vulnerability.

We continued our secret friendship until one day I decided to walk up to her and the other girls. I smiled and said 'Hello' but what came after was a choir of mocking laughter and a very clear… 'You can't play with us because you're weird.' —She didn't laugh, but chose silence and followed the others. I felt forgotten like words that got lost in the back of someone's throat. My heart had been broken for the first time. After that, it was scarily easy to conform. I understood that to be my way… the way things were from my side of the world; other humans scared me. They were capable of much with so little, of things just so painful. The thought of a friend… so foreign."

A buzz came, and Helena was startled back into reality; she eyed the phone in her hands, and a thumb swiped the screen. An inevitable smile broke free from her lips. **'Hi, I'm glad you did and no it's not a bad time at all, I was just listening to music. You?'**

Helena chewed on her lip some more and typed a response; she regarded the needle and yarn on her lap. 'I am doing the same and also knitting, not the most paradigmatic pastime, I know… though it certainly helps me relax.'

The buzz bounced back quickly, and that made Helena's heart shudder. Her stomach felt like a mess of black holes and uncertainty principles. **'You knit? I've never met anyone who does that. You're right it's not common, but it's interesting… different. What music?'**

'You are the first person to tell me that; I usually get comments including 'my grandma' as a subject, and to answer your other question, I am listening to Violet Shadows. What about you?'

Emily's responses were rushing in and Helena's painful memories melted; that scared her. It was like jumping with the possibility of falling. **'Ah, Violet Shadows... wicked and beautiful! Which song? Hypnotic Slate is playing for me. :)'**

Another smile formed on Helena's lips. The colon and parenthesis made her feel warmer inside, somehow. She noticed Emily's lines to be concise and reserved. The insecure part of her immediately thought she was inopportune and perhaps Emily wasn't interested, though the more rational part of Helena's mind settled for the alternate; she was simply shy and didn't open up easily. She had gathered that much from reading Emily's behavior while on campus.

'At the moment, Movie... my favorite song from them, and I love Hypnotic Slate ;)'

Buzz... Buzz....

'No way, you know them?! Never met anyone who did, and did you just wink at me? Not that I'm complaining. Movie is wicked good.'

Helena's eyes gleamed, this time the smile had turned into a chuckle, faithfully accompanied by a warm blush on her cheeks. 'I do, I saw them once... This is not one of my proudest confessions, but I was blackmailed into leaving the dormitories of my old school to go to a concert. 'More Of Us' is beautiful... and yes, I might have used punctuation marks to convey playful allure.'

Helena felt bolder by the second, perhaps rushing

hormones were partly at fault, though she credited it almost entirely to the hold Emily had on her.

'Blackmailed? Doesn't sound like a friend, if you need someone to defend your honor... I could settle that for you. More Of Us is my favorite from them... now I have more reasons to send you punctuation-mark-made faces. I hope that's okay.'

Helena beamed and felt the ardor of her soaring heart.

'Worry not, I blackmailed my way out of her infantile wager, she had far too much alcohol that night, and I may have taken a video; thank you, though, for your chivalrous offer, and I will not object to the latter.'

Their texting went on until late hours of the night. They got to know more... and quickly felt more. Emily had been hit just as hard as Helena. Their attraction was undeniably magical and instant.

***

Morning arrived and had proven to be hazy for each girl. Smiling at nothing out of thin air, exuding that deliciously sweet flush. It was magic indeed.

Later that afternoon, Helena sat in the middle row of the bleachers on the soccer field. Brown eyes scanned eleven bodies on the bright, green grass. Eleven black uniforms with white numbers stamped on their backs chased after a checkered ball.

Helena smiled when her gaze found a long, blonde ponytail. With headphones on each ear, she touched her phone's screen and found the familiar reverb of a song. Even though her brother was playing, he was swiftly ignored. — *Emily is the only girl on the team.* Helena noticed. That spoke volumes about the seemingly traditional university.

She followed the agile blonde who had been occupying her thoughts non-stop. Even from a considerable distance, Helena was able to observe the object of her undivided attention. Emily's legs were inviting, voluptuous lines drawn with skin and off focus juxtaposition. Her hips so beautifully shaped; her supple, small breasts complemented her athletic build flawlessly. Helena loved the female form, the mystery it held; the subtle traces, just like those of a painting or the notes of a perfect song. She found humans to be fascinating creatures, but this human seemed to have taken her. —*Emily, you are stunning.* Helena thought. Pearl white teeth brushed against her bottom lip and bit tight. At that moment the player's running came to a halt, and Emily was singled out by the coach. She walked to him with a heaving chest and squinting eyes.

Helena removed her earbuds and tried to make up what they were saying. Emily listened to the man in charge closely and nodded; a loud whistle blow echoed for yards, and they retreated to the water station.

Emily lifted her damp jersey, exposing a taut abdomen, the sight made Helena swallow hard. Curious brown eyes scanned her enticing figure —sports bra completely drenched.

Heat.

Flushing, intense, and abrasive heat claimed Helena's

face. She placed an index and middle finger on her wrist while trying to detect the untamed thumping of a pulse. Her excited heart slammed against her ribs. She imagined Emily's hands on her body, against her skin, perhaps pushing her against a wall. Helena's breathing rushed and suddenly that very thought; having Emily pressed against her body with nowhere to run, made her stomach ache in the most enticing way.

Helena shook the thoughts from her head. She crossed her legs and averted her eyes, slightly embarrassed of her hungry imagination. She felt warmth and a tight feeling in her axis while in the distance, a wincing Emily tried to catch her breath; green eyes turned and met relentless brown.

Helena gasped —Emily was approaching her with that beautiful smile. She had been caught ogling. —*Fantastic... Oh, God...* Embarrassment permeated Helena's cheeks and neck. Part of her felt like she was using her friend for fantasizing about them groping each other.

Emily jogged towards the beautiful brunette. "Hey..." She had been thinking about Helena since their last text the night before.

"Hi," Helena replied, and found her voice within the sea of embarrassment. —*If only Emily knew. God, maybe she would never speak to me again.* Helena thought.

"Thank you for coming," Emily said, unable to keep from smiling.

"It was my pleasure; you are quite talented."

Emily shrugged. "I think it's just luck... It's hard not to love it when you have two older brothers who are savage soccer fans," She chuckled. "Thank you, though, for the compliment," Emily said, gleaming eyes burned right through Helena's heart.

At that moment the sound of the coach's whistle startled them both, breaking their lingering trance. Emily smiled and pointed over her shoulder. "The coach is calling, I gotta go, but um... after practice is over..." she said, blushing, deep dimples pierced her cheeks.

Helena knew where this conversation was going and she was thrilled. Fluttering emptiness made her aware of her stomach.

"Would you like to hang out? Maybe get something to drink?" Emily asked.

Helena's eyes were like constellations, dark and so bright. "Of course."

Fire prickled under Emily's skin. "Okay," she said, blinking softly and jogged back to her teammates. Helena sat there and watched them all play until practice was over. The struggle continued while trying to assuage the effects Emily had on her anatomy.

Minutes dragged like molasses, but after another loud blow of the whistle, each seemingly exhausted body on the field brought their lethargic running to a relieved jog.

Finally.

Emily rushed to her beautiful admirer, still trying to catch her breath. Those dreamy green eyes fought the rays of a blinding sun.

Helena focused on something in the distance and caught her brother watching them from afar; he was drenched in sweat and panting heavily. She observed him, trying to make sense of his expression. Caleb didn't seem mad; he was apparently feeling the heat of the sun, though there was something more, he was pensive... he was debating; something was definitely going through his mind. He longingly stared her way and pushed a faint smile.

She smiled back, only to watch him walk away.

"Helena?" Emily said, shaking her out of the trance. "Hey... Are you all right?" Emily noticed the almost crimson on her cheeks.

Helena nodded. "Yes. I am just incredibly thirsty," It wasn't a lie, brown eyes narrowed and hid from the flares hitting them. "The sun is far too intense."

"Are you sure you're feeling okay? Do you want some water?" Emily offered. "I'll go get you some from the field—" She motioned and looked over her shoulder.

"No, no," Helena said, smiling. "Thank you, but I'd prefer if we could get out of this heat, I need something cold, please... Perhaps we could get something elsewhere?" she suggested.

"Of course, yeah..." Emily nodded. "Come with me; we need to go back inside. I'll shower and change; then we can go, okay?"

Helena relished the warmth inside her chest. "Okay."

***

Thirty minutes passed, and they walked down the oak-dressed hall of the university. Emily was back to her casual clothes. Long champagne waves cascaded over her shoulders, wafting a delicate aroma of vanilla and lavender. The cold air inside made life worth living once again.

"Where are we going?" Helena asked as they walked towards a classroom.

"I need to talk to my mom for a second."

"Oh," Helena said, surprised. "Your mom is here?"

"Yeah," Emily said with an honest smile. "She's a professor here."

"That is just lovely, Emily. What's her name? Perhaps she is one of mine."

Emily blushed with pride over the woman she adored. "Maureen Shepherd."

Brown eyes widened, and that captivating smile spread across Helena's lips. "Professor Shepherd? Sociology?"

Emily grinned with a slight nod. "That's her."

"Oh, I loved her seminar on Tuesday! She is such a splendid educator; I had no idea —I mean, the last name..."

"Yeah... Well, she's actually a Mrs. to my dad," Emily said. "But she kept her maiden name for teaching purposes; she's been working here since before they got married, so..."

"Now that I think about it..." Helena bore into that green gaze and her smile faded. Hyper-awareness tempted Emily's secret. "You two have the same eyes," Helena said.

"Yeah... we do." Emily said while feeling *that* heat. Helena made her burn, so she tried to think of her grandma. —*Oh, my God. Dean Carlisle, Dean Carlisle kissing Professor Spencer. Gross thoughts, not so hot thoughts. Fuck!* Emily was well acquainted with the effects Helena had on her raging body. The most affected she had ever been, and that couldn't happen right now. Emily felt *it,* though she took comfort in knowing it was thoroughly concealed. She swallowed hard, in fact, she had never been happier to see a door in her life. "We are here." Emily stalled and opened it. Her sudden nervousness didn't go unnoticed.

As they entered the empty classroom, Helena decided

to keep a distance and give them privacy. A beautiful brunette standing by the desk turned; her face lit up like a star. Emily's mom was stunning, perhaps in her forties; her skin was like milky porcelain, and those candid, mossy eyes contrasted so boldly with her short dark hair.

"Em, what are you doing here?" Maureen asked, happy to see her daughter. She peeked over Emily's shoulder, noticing a familiar face and smiled at the girl. "Hi…"

Helena swore the woman seemed surprised. *Happily* surprised, she smiled back at the professor. "Hello,"

Maureen acknowledged her daughter and raised a playful brow. "Emily, sweetheart, please introduce me to your friend," she muttered.

Emily glared at her mother with a tight face; she knew what was circling her mind. Helena screamed smart, sweet and polite. Emily knew her mother saw dating potential, *girlfriend* potential. It was incredible how much she had read from Maureen's playful expression. "*Mom,*" she hissed between gritted teeth. "Stop." it was barely a whisper.

"All right, Em, but please introduce us, I taught you better than that." she murmured, looking into identical eyes.

Emily's face relaxed and finally gave her a smile. "Of course, Mom," She turned and locked eyes with Helena, the one person who held her complete attention, both emotionally and physically.

"Helena, this is my mom, Maureen Knight…" she said, smiling. "And… Mom, this is Helena Millan."

Flying over the moon, Maureen beamed and shook her hand —Emily's recent behavior made sense. Lately, it seemed she had a brand new reason to smile more often and wider, drift away in a thinking cloud and chuckle. Of course Maureen was happy; she was beyond delighted. "It is a pleasure to see you again, Helena."

"Likewise, Professor Shepherd," Helena said genuinely. "Or would you prefer I called you Mrs. Knight?" She attentively waited for a response.

"Whatever you'd like, sweetheart, whichever makes you most comfortable I am okay with."

Maureen's indulgence was pleasant. Helena felt at ease instantly; not many made her feel such warmth.

"Well, Mom, we just came 'cause I wanted to tell you that I'll be going out for a drink with Helena and um... I know we were supposed to have dinner together, but I'm not sure I'll be able to make it... rain check?" Emily said, feeling awkward; this was a situation she had never been in before. Her mother had never met anyone she liked, and even though she hadn't mentioned just how much Helena meant, she could tell her mother knew.

Maureen smiled and leaned in to kiss her daughter's cheek. "Okay, have fun girls, and I hope those drinks are virgin ones." she mocked warning. Everything was going so well... —*Damn, Mom. You had to say something.* Emily thought.

Helena overcame her state. "Of course, Professor Shepherd, I understand your concern since we could drink alcohol even while in our underage status. However, you have nothing to worry about, and I am strictly prohibited by my physician to indulge in the consumption of such beverages." Helena finished, realizing the last part of her admission wasn't necessary, she hadn't meant to blurt it out.

Emily didn't think anything of it since she was engulfed in her geeky word-vomit. —*Damn, I love it!*

Maureen took notice of the words and nodded gladly.

"Thank you for the reassurance, Helena —be careful, and well, I'll see you tomorrow, Em." she finished.

"Sure, Mom."

"It was a pleasure to meet you as Emily's mother."

Maureen beamed. "The pleasure was all mine, honey… Thank you." she said.

Helena wasn't sure why the professor had thanked her, but she nodded still.

***

Emily loved the comfort and cold air in Helena's luxury car. Simply knowing they were together made her stomach flip. She wanted to swim into anything and everything Helena but needed to keep her cool intact. Helena didn't know her secret, and well, the entire map of everything Emily Knight hadn't been revealed —just like in one of those real-time strategy games. This, though, was no game.

A couple of hours passed and the weather had transformed; the typical San Francisco evening shift to be more exact. They settled for a quiet walk by the beach. Helena noticed how everyone seemed so relaxed, no status or classes, and besides all that, she was with Emily.

They sat on a lonely bench and watched the salty waters so expansive and bright; the sinking sun made them sparkle like amber-colored diamonds. Away from everything, they studied each other freely. Helena smiled and blushed, holding her gaze while Emily felt the vivid presence of air in her chest. She was the first one to falter and look down; a grin broke free as she opened the paper bag containing her juicy burger.

Helena eyed the giant sandwich and chuckled. "That—

is *a lot*— of food, Emily."

"Well, then maybe you should help me." she said with an earnest shrug, and winked.

Amused, Helena opened *her* brown paper bag. "I think I'll stick to my salad, but thank you for the offer."

Emily laughed. "Are you serious? Not even a little? You should try it, come on," Charming dimples pierced her cheeks and Helena blushed.

"I really can't, medical reasons... I wish I could." she said with a sweet smile.

As the words left Helena's mouth, worry robbed Emily of her ease. "Oh, I'm so sorry —are you okay?" she asked earnestly.

"I am, I promise." That wasn't a lie; in fact, it was the healthiest she had been in the past year.

Emily sighed with relief and nodded. Eating while indulging in small talk was just so easy, it felt natural. "So, um… what made you choose Clearwater?" Emily asked, and bit on a crispy fry.

The sound of waves crashing in the short distance aided the beautiful sight of blonde locks blowing freely in the breeze; the orange and blue in the sky… the peace. Helena felt lucky to witness it. "Well, I had been attending a boarding school in Frankfurt for the past twelve years… after graduation, I came back and took the admission test for an advanced program at Ravenford Medical School. However, I must wait a few months for the results, in the meantime… I enrolled in Clearwater, mainly to be closer to my siblings."

Emily's eyes widened. "Frankfurt, like Germany Frankfurt?"

"Exactly." Helena said pleasantly. "I must say coming

back home to San Francisco has been incredibly nice, I could not have hoped for a better outcome." she finished and looked into Emily's eyes, suddenly feeling braver.

"Um, you have siblings?" Emily ventured, she was never this inquisitive or outspoken. Ever.

"I do..." Helena responded and smiled. "An older sister and brother, they are both nineteen —um... they attend Clearwater also, in fact, you may know my brother," she said. "He is part of the soccer team —he was on the field today, his name is Caleb." she added.

Emily sighed and nodded when realization hit her. How did she not put two and two together? They shared the same last name and exotic good looks, "Caleb Millan."

"Yes." Helena said with a nod.

Emily cleared her throat. "He's one of the nicest guys I've crossed words with on campus."

Helena smiled. "Yes, Caleb is a great person," she said, and frowned, looking slightly disturbed all of a sudden. "Quite the ladies man —I've noticed some girls, unfortunately, engaging in such poor behavior to catch his attention."

"Oh yeah... It's hard not to notice." Emily stalled as her stomach sank; she was certain rumors about her weren't news to Caleb. —*Fuck.* she suddenly realized.

"And my sister's name is Maddison —she, on the contrary, is not so happy about me attending Clearwater..."

"Oh, why not?" Emily blushed, suddenly feeling nosey. "I mean— I'm sorry, I don't mean to pry, I'm just..." She shook her head.

Endeared, Helena smiled. Emily had a strong and beautiful presence; on campus, she seemed to have a tough exterior; she was quiet and seemingly reserved, mysterious and captivating, but when she was with Helena, Emily offered a different side. "We don't get along so well... and in a couple of weeks, we will be sharing a dorm —I am not looking forward to that." Helena said, and smiled sadly, the wind softly blowing dark tendrils of hair that escaped her side braid.

"Oh, I'm sorry, Helena..."

"It's all right," she said, seeming like it truly wasn't.

Emily bobbed her head and frowned, feeling confused. "Wait, you said they are the same age,"

"They are only a couple of months apart from each other. Caleb is my half-brother, and Maddison is my half-sister... we were all raised together since we were babies, so we have never seen it that way —I am the youngest of the three."

Emily took in the knowledge as Helena satisfied her curiosity. "So you're eighteen."

Helena nodded softly as the wind caressed her face. "What about you, Emily?" she asked sweetly.

"Me?"

"Yes," Helena said, smiling. "You —I'd really love to get to know you better." she confessed, cocking her head to the side, and Emily felt it, that gesture... That look hit her right in the middle of her heart. Helena was unlike anyone she had ever met. She was honest and not afraid to speak her mind or feelings. —*This girl is just beautiful.* Emily thought.

"Well... I'm nineteen. This is my third semester at that torture chamber," She chuckled. "I have two older *twin* brothers; Patrick and Rhys, they used to go to Clearwater, too, but hated it and got the hell out of there as soon as they finished their associate's degree a year ago." She shrugged "They're both attending different colleges on sports scholarships —Patrick is in Seattle and Rhys goes to college here in San Francisco."

Helena took a sip of water and placed the clear bottle next to her. "I'm sorry you feel so uncomfortable there, though I must admit, it is so lovely you all attended the same college where your mom teaches."

"That's *the only* reason why we were even able to attend." Emily said honestly.

"What do you mean?"

"Well, we get to go for free because my mom is a professor there. Trust me; my parents couldn't afford the sixty thousand dollars a year tuition —for all of us? Forget it," Emily said. "Not even for one."

"Oh," Helena nodded. It was easy to forget that money wasn't a tool everyone had access to in surplus amounts. Life was a struggle for many people, and Helena never took that for granted, even though she had grown up wealthy.

"I think it is the least the faculty could do for your mom, Emily, she is such a fantastic professor; I was enthralled during her class the other day."

Emily smiled, and her eyes gleamed with pride. The compliment meant more because it came from someone as attentive and detail oriented as Helena. "Thank you; she is an even better mother, believe me."

"Oh, it was so easy to see while you two interacted... she seems fantastic and very caring," she said.

Emily thought of confessing to Helena how amazing her mother had been about her transition, how her parents had done everything in their power to help and enable her to be herself since she was just a toddler —but she didn't, and Emily didn't know why. She knew she could trust Helena; this girl was unbelievably unreal and open. Emily found herself wanting her more and more by the second.

She wanted to smell her, touch her skin; she wanted to tell Helena how she made her feel and how affected her body was by her mere presence or thought. Helena already had her, and even though that was a very scary and open-ended realization, Emily knew it was too late. —*I want her... I want her, and I don't wanna share her.* Not caring how selfish it sounded, Emily wanted to touch Helena in places no one else could; she craved intimacy with her, the warmth of a kiss, wet lips... tongue. —*Stop it, Emily.* she scolded herself mentally.

And well, the way Helena was looking at her, telling her with those profound, dark eyes just how much she wanted the same things didn't help the threatening sensation between her thighs. It was painful, and she didn't know how long she could go without doing something about her constant excitement, rightfully ignited by the unknowing girl.

"My mom has been so amazing to me, to all of us, but she has given me so much, you really have no idea how lucky I feel every day —when I see..." —*Emily, watch what you say.* More internal censure. She cleared her throat and continued, "When I see other parents... who shouldn't even be parents in the first place, you know? So many kids mistreated and without unconditional support from the people who should be there... It sucks." she finished with a lamenting shrug.

Helena was smitten, and could have sworn she wanted Emily more. So sure her lacy underwear was effectively ruined; in fact, it had been ruined for hours. She crossed her olive-toned legs and felt it again. Helena blushed as she thought about it. Heat claimed her cheeks. —*Curse young hormones and their inopportune timing.*

"I wish my mother had been more like yours." Helena

admitted sadly and it broke Emily's heart.

"Helena..." she whispered.

"She loves us, I know, I just... part of me wishes she had been there all along; I would have loved to live at home with my parents, and my siblings versus seeing them once or twice each year."

"I'm really sorry, Helena, you're right, and I wish I could help you feel better about it." She felt useless to this amazing girl's sadness.

Helena shrugged. "It's all right, Emily, but thank you," she said genuinely and placed her warm hand on a soft, pale one. Emily looked down at the touch and felt her heart pound. She almost hesitantly entwined their fingers loosely.

Helena swallowed and tightened their grip, daring to look up and into green eyes. She wanted to kiss Emily so badly. She wanted to be more to her; she wanted parts of Emily others could not get.

If only they knew they were aching for the same things.

At that moment, Helena's cell phone rang, startling them. "I have to take this," she informed evenly and answered the call. "Hello, Mother," she said, and smiled at Emily, who gave her another irresistible grin —Helena felt warmth and her stomach sank lower; her body demanded things from her.

Emily wondered what Helena's mom looked like. What was she like? She wanted to meet the woman who had made it possible for her to get to share with this stunning human girl.

"Yes, Mother, I assure you, I am. I'll be home in a little while; I am with a friend at the moment," she said, blushing.

Emily winked at Helena charmingly, the wind graciously

scattered long blonde hair against the killer view... It wasn't very fair of the universe, or perhaps it was everything.

With rosy cheeks and warning eyes, Helena gently squeezed her pale hand.

Emily bit her lip and stared at her shamelessly, it all felt so easy and familiar, as if they had always known each other, as if they had always wanted each other.

"A female friend, from college —yes, thank you, Mother... I'll see you then." she said, and bit her lip at the teasing fingertips drawing maps on her hand —never breaking that suggestive gaze.

Helena hung up, still blushing purposefully. "You are terrible!" She chuckled, and Emily let out an amused laugh.

"I guess I just can't help it when I'm with you." Emily dared. —*Shit. Did I really just say that out loud? Idiot!*

That was open and direct flirting. Helena swallowed and rolled her tongue on enticing lips. "I can conclusively say that I relate to that." she replied bravely, unwilling to miss the chance to let Emily know she wanted her.

"Really?" Emily asked with provocation and innocence dripping from her eyes.

"Yes. Really." Helena's smile faded. The look turned into a kindling kind of seriousness, the searing kind that made blood rush to places and spread heat.

Emily tried to swallow the desire to breathe harder and felt grateful for how concealing her jeans were. It was getting dark out, undoubtedly convenient.

After a few minutes of silence, they decided to leave. Helena drove Emily to her dorm. They sat inside the elegant car, only the lights from the dash and stereo bounced back on their faces. The casualty of the soft music emanating from everywhere felt life-altering. "Thank you for every-thing, Helena, it was really nice," Emily said while freeing herself from the seat belt.

Helena's eyes glowed with fire; the longing in them so true. Emily bit her bottom lip, wondering how soft Helena's were —dying to show her what it felt like to be kissed on the lips by another. To be kissed by someone who wanted her so much it hurt. *Literally.*

Helena unbuckled her seat belt and gently leaned towards Emily, all the while stealing glances of her green eyes and inviting lips. Fear gone out the window, replaced with valor and want.

Emily's breathing felt like pounding waves against her lungs. The aching below was one thing, and her impending fears were another. Her heart was expanding and the one doing the leading.

"Helena…" she murmured to the girl inches away from her lips and hooded eyes. Helena's soft perfume drugged her, it smelled exclusive, like something she had never experienced before. Her breath was warm and neutral, Emily was already addicted, and she hadn't even kissed her yet.

"Don't you want to?" Helena whispered, suddenly feeling insecure.

Emily almost whimpered at the weakness she felt. She felt weak and grand. "God, yes —so bad," she murmured, looking at perfect lips; Emily swallowed while green eyes studied everything from up close and felt so lucky. Her amazing mouth, the tiny scar that made her seem like an irresistible rebel; those profound and gleaming dark eyes— so much vivid clarity. Emily ran her fingertips on Helena's soft jawline. This was Helena's first kiss, and she had to make it special for her. Helena deserved everything.

"Are you sure?" Emily asked softly, looking into glowing brown. They were so open and genuine.

The torture was delicious. Emily closed her eyes and focused on the feeling in her chest, trying her best to override the one raging inside her pants. Their breathing quickened.

Helena nodded, "I am sure..." she said, breathing out almost inaudibly.

So, Emily leaned in and claimed Helena's lips for the first time; their eyes fluttered closed, and it was indeed perfect.

For Emily, it was sweet demise. Helena's lips were soft and tempting; they were carnal, and they were tender, they were fire, and they were hers, at least in that instant they were.

Helena whimpered and trembled as she brushed her tongue on Emily's lips. —*I want in, I need... in.* Her insides turned and hips burned, ignited by those intimate, wet sounds.

Emily was fighting the fight; she was trying to remain PG-13, begging her body to please be gentle... to please wait, to understand her heart's desires, to understand her fears of rejection. Helena didn't know yet.

Helena moaned as she felt Emily's tongue invade her mouth once, twice...

Fuck.

Helena sensually wrapped a hand around that fair neck. She pulled Emily in and rolled her hips forward against the leather seat by instinct, her aching body begged for some friction to alleviate the burning in her belly. Helena saw stars, Emily tasted so good.

A loud moan broke from Emily's lips as she moved a hand to Helena's lower back. Their breathing grew out of control, and she gently ended the kiss with a delicious, wet sound. "Helena, wait," Emily begged breathlessly.

Helena panted and looked into green eyes, enraptured. "You are exquisite, Emily," she whispered, and Emily felt her entire world cave in. Helena's eyes and words were so honest; they felt and looked honest. She felt so indescribably good. No one had ever made Emily feel so wanted, so special... Ever.

Green eyes glazed with tears she blinked away quickly. Not many got to see the softer and vulnerable side of Emily Knight.

Helena knew Emily was apparently overwhelmed and honestly, so was she. However, Helena understood her plea, she didn't know what it was but felt it be raw and genuine.

"I..." Emily tried to explain.

Helena placed a slender finger on those sweet lips. "Shhh... May I see you again tomorrow?" she asked with endless eyes.

Stunned by her luck, Emily nodded. "Yeah, yes, of course." she murmured.

"Goodnight, Emily."

"Night." Emily barely managed and exited the vehicle.

Helena smiled and allowed her head to fall back on the smooth leather. She felt alive.

"Remembering my first favorite book, 'A Boy and His Moon' always saddened me. The boy never gets to touch the moon. However, the writer gives him a story. Inscribed in the pages, the writer gives him hope. My current book "Coalesce" spoke of letting go. It was about finding bliss in knowing that everything dead and alive simply was. No ending or beginning, therefore, no need for hope.

The older I became, the concept of growing up felt more like absolute betrayal. In the course of my life, I had slowly lost relatability to the word hope. It was a conscious decision; hope was painful, just as the things humans did could be. But Emily Knight had made me rethink my choice. With one look into her eyes, I saw her humanity; I felt it on her lips, on her breath, her warmth, and her touch. Emily Knight made me want to forgive hope and allow it back in."

3

EVERYBODY WANTS YOU

THE DRIVE BACK TO Pacific Heights was a delicious haze for Helena; her face felt sore from the constant beaming. Passing by Broadway Street had never been more beautiful; the trees looked eternal, and the lights adorning the historic walk made the magical feelings coursing inside her materialize to her eyes. Kissing Emily had been the most sublime event she had ever experienced in her life, and she wanted more of it.

While opening the door to the Millan mansion, Helena bit her bottom lip and smiled to herself while replaying the kiss in her mind. She closed it and jumped, startled by her mother's presence. Brown eyes widened and rolled with relief as she brought a hand to her chest. "Mother! You scared me."

Katherine's eyes went wide, she scolded herself internally —sneaking up on her daughter wasn't wise; the brunette doctor placed a caring hand on Helena's arm and searched for her gaze. "Are you all right, sweetheart? I am so very sorry... I didn't mean to sneak up on you."

Helena nodded. "I am."

Katherine gently pulled on Helena's arm and dragged her deeper into the lavish home. The crackling fire burning in the heart of a stone crafted fireplace wasn't enough to soothe the doctor. "Let's get you some water; you should sit down, I—"

Helena's happiness turned into mild annoyance; she resisted Katherine's move instantly. "Mother, I am fine, that is not necessary."

Katherine furrowed her brows while looking into the sweetest brown; the same eyes she had been admiring since the day Helena was born. "Darling, I... Are you sure you are feeling all right?" she tried. Helena's stubbornness when it came to her recently diagnosed condition was new for Katherine.

Helena softened once she caught mild hurt and guilt in her mother's hazel eyes. "I am, Mama, I promise." She looked down at her hands and then up at Katherine. "I apologize, I didn't mean to snap at you —it was rude of me." Helena had hardly snapped.

Katherine eased, "You have nothing to be sorry for, Helena, I didn't mean to overreact."

"I know."

Katherine sat on the sofa, and her daughter sat only inches away. "I just... you know I don't want to feel coddled or pitied." Helena said.

"Oh, sweetheart, I don't pity you —Helena, you know that, darling, don't you?" Katherine's eyes searched her girl's.

Helena shrugged and pushed a knowing smile. "I can see the gloomy sympathy in your eyes, Mother."

Katherine's lips turned up softly; she knew her daughter

was perceptive and clever, but she needed to clarify. "Please, never mistake my concern with pity, I could never pity you, darling."

Helena found her center. "I know you feel guilt, but you shouldn't —what is happening to me isn't your fault." she tried.

Katherine sighed, wishing she could see things the way her daughter did. She smiled with knitting brows and caressed a few of Helena's long locks. She *did* feel guilty.

Helena smiled softly, and Katherine changed the subject. "Now tell me… Where were you so late?"

"It's only seven, Mother." Helena said, slightly amused.

"I know… and I also know it is very rare for you to be out at this hour, that's all,"

"You mean to say; it is rare for me to be out with actual people?" Helena continued to chuckle lightheartedly.

Katherine tilted her head to the side, admiring the beautiful glow in her daughter's eyes. She twisted her face with curiosity and realization hit her. "You seem—extremely... joyful."

A blush crept up Helena's cheeks; part of her wondered if her mother could see what she had just done. She bit her lip and smiled. "I am."

Katherine grinned. "Well, please tell me about these 'people' you were with; I must ask, seeing they have brought you such happiness."

"It's only one person… and her name is Emily."

Katherine took in the information while favoring her daughter's glee. "So you've made a friend, darling, that is fantastic."

Helena beamed, and Katherine instantly knew this friend meant more than that. The way her daughter blushed and her eyes gleamed, she could almost smell the hormones encompassing her.

"Yes, Mother. She is very kind and interesting, and she treats me so well, she makes me feel... I don't know — *seen*." she shared honestly.

Katherine had always admired Helena's valor to be so transparent with her thoughts and emotions; she wasn't one to feel ashamed by things others would. If she felt comfortable talking to someone, she would hold up no walls. Katherine was also surprised by Helena feeling this way about another female; not that it bothered her —she was a woman of science and a forward moving mind. However, anyone getting close to her daughter, she wanted and needed to understand. "I am very glad to hear that, and this girl —Emily... you said she is a friend from college,"

"She is, I met her on my first day at Clearwater."

Katherine wanted to give into boldness and simply ask. However, she didn't want to tarnish Helena's confidence or make her uncomfortable. "And she... feels the same way about you?"

Helena rolled her eyes and grinned. "You can ask Mother; I will answer whatever question you may have."

Katherine blushed; she had been a physician for years, and embarrassment wasn't something she felt often or ever. But this was her daughter; this was her child who had blossomed into a stunning, strong and obviously very open young woman. She couldn't be prouder. "Are you attracted to her, darling?"

Helena took a deep, unwavering breath and blinked softly. "I am... I feel very attracted to Emily."

Katherine nodded, taking in the information. "You hadn't spoken to me about this before, dear... you feeling this way about other women." she said, wondering if she may have seemed unavailable to Helena. She knew the girl was very independent and usually kept to herself.

"I knew you wouldn't mind," Helena shrugged casually. "And I had never wanted to act on these feelings before, I mean, I've always felt attracted to other women, but not like this."

"Well, dear, I am glad you are aware that you can come to me with anything, no matter what it is." She looked into Helena's eyes with searing conviction.

Katherine needed her child to feel the strength and measure of her love. "But Helena... now that you have this friend in your life, you will feel compelled to try new things, to go out more often, and that is very normal. However, darling, I need you to promise me that you will be careful and not strain yourself; please... you need to be responsible and take care of yourself —I know this is new for all of us, but you need to discover your limits and see how much you can do without exhausting your body, honey," She pierced her eyes. "This is very serious."

Helena nodded honestly; she understood her mother's concern. "Of course, Mama, I promise..." she gave Katherine with equal amounts of intensity and softness, pleading for trust.

At that moment they both turned to the young male voice joining them. They had apparently missed Caleb walking down the grand mahogany staircase. "Dad is asking for you, Mom," he said.

Katherine placed a kiss on Helena's cheek. The girl smiled and silently agreed to continue the conversation another time. Katherine stood and walked past her son with a gentle brush on his arm.

"All right. Goodnight, my darlings,"

"Night, Mom," he said as they watched her disappear. Caleb sat next to his sister and turned her way. "So…"

Unknowing, Helena gave him an effortless smile. "What is it?"

"Um… nothing." He shrugged. "Where were you?"

She rolled her eyes and chuckled. "What is it with everybody? Is it really so strange that I could go out like any other normal human being?"

Caleb rose both hands in mid-air. "Hey, whoa… I was just asking."

"If you must know… I was out with a friend, we had something to eat and talked for a while."

"Yeah?" Not knowing how to approach the subject, he cleared his throat. "Hmm... With Emily?"

Helena remembered the look on his face earlier that day at the field and narrowed her eyes. "Yes… Why?" Helena was careful to read his reaction; she wanted to figure out why he seemed to care so much.

Caleb shook his head and shrugged coolly. He stalled. "Nothing… I was just curious, that's all."

She studied him, wondering why he was avoiding eye contact. Unfortunately for her and her desire to figure out what was going through his mind, Maddison walked down the stairs. Helena's eyes followed her sister until she was in front of them.

"Hello, jockstrap…" Maddison said, and smiled falsely while regarding Caleb. He smirked mockingly.

She addressed Helena, "Diapers…" Forced smile in place.

Helena frowned and drew back visibly irked. "Please don't call me that."

"Well, you are the infant of the house, it seems very

fitting to me." she mocked.

Helena crossed her arms and raised a brow, feeling the usual frustration her sister ignited in her.

"So, you've finally decided to stop acting like the ridiculous weirdo you are and came out of your cave... Nice one, Helena, you are on the right track to normalcy." Maddison said curtly.

Helena huffed and stood; she looked at her sister —she wondered why. What had she ever done? It wasn't fair. A red ring of welling emotion pooled in brown eyes, Helena rolled them, pushing back the tears. She was annoyed at herself and why she was reacting this way. Why did she let Maddison get to her?

A steel gaze caught an affected one, and Maddison smiled challengingly. "Oh, honey, you're going to cry?"

Helena inhaled a batch of air that reached into her heart and grasped at the melancholy there; she observed Maddison. Her soulful dark eyes shone with tears that continued to sting, but she wouldn't allow to fall, not yet. "What did I ever do to you?"

"Christ, Helena, don't be so dramatic! —I hope you don't act this way when we share that stupid dorm room." Maddison was indeed one of the few people who shook her core and even though she didn't understand it, Helena cared. With a sore heart and dismissive eyes, she walked away.

Maddison felt as a tiny piece inside her chipped away. "Oh, come on, Helena— I was kidding!" she said, watching her sister rush up the stairs, she turned to her brother and found disapproving brown eyes. "Oh come on! I was only joking with her."

"Why do you have to be such a jerk to her, Maddison? I

don't understand why, but she looks up to you, you know?"
Caleb fumed and left.

Stale blue eyes were left scanning the place, mouth slightly agape with half a sore smile, not feeling so smug anymore. Maddison did often wonder why she acted the way she did, but it wasn't like it mattered, no one cared, not truly. Then why should she? But no matter how hard she tried to show otherwise. She did care.

Helena closed her bedroom door and sat on the bed. Her chest heaved, breathing in and out intensely. Wet eyes closed as she tried her very best to find it. She took a deep breath and let it out again. The thoughts going through her mind when this happened made her want to vomit. Helena tried to find that moment when she knew it would pass and things would go back to normal. She placed a darkly manicured hand on her chest and opened her eyes softly; she got hold of the prescription bottle on her nightstand and took a small white pill —grabbed the clear bottle of water next to it and washed it down. Hoping to wash down her fears as well. Helena tried to go back to her happiness with Emily. That incredible way she felt when they were together, and just like that, she began to push it all to the back. Emily made it all better. So much better.

***

Morning had arrived, and along with it came many things that felt untouched and full of endless possibilities. Wanting Helena was so easy. It came effortlessly, just as the captivating life that shone right through her, right through those eyes.

58

Emily never felt happier about going to theater class. She would've easily traded her soccer practices all together just to be able to watch Helena smile, to have her near. She would've given anything to kiss her lips again. Emily had tossed and turned in bed all night, thinking about how Helena had become her very favorite thing.

Sparkling green eyes were fixed on the stage. Rosaline was a mute character, but she felt so grateful to Juliet's silent foe. From where Emily sat, Helena looked so beautiful and graceful in one of those exclusive-looking dresses. Her shiny, long black hair was flawlessly entwined into a loose braid that fell to the side, touching her warm neck, just like Emily wished she was touching it.

As the lovely and quirky Professor Silverstein spoke, the sounds came to Emily's ears in an incomprehensible language. She was too enthralled and happy —she was far too comfortable looking at *her*. Helena was intensely aware of Emily's gaze and was, in fact, looking right back at her with a smile of her own. Emily noticed Helena was chuckling.

"Emily— Emily—Emily?" The voice faded into her head slowly. Professor Silverstein repeated her name over and over.

She blinked and snapped out of it. "What? Ye— Yeah?"

"You're drifting, honey… I've been calling your name for the past five minutes."

"I'm here, I'm here, yeah;" Emily said in her stupor and Helena smiled, a knowing sparkle in her eyes. It felt amazing to know she had the ability to render the gorgeous blonde speechless. —*If only Emily knew she does the same to me.* Helena thought.

"I was asking if you could please come up here," Professor Silverstein said.

"Yeah." She agilely stood and made her way to the stage. She made her way to Helena, and her stomach was a trembling mess.

"I was just informing everyone that unfortunately, Nick broke his leg and will be unable to play Romeo."

"Oh... that sucks," Emily stalled; glad the guy wouldn't have his paws all over Helena.

"Well, Helena brightly suggested you should take his place." Professor Silverstein said, and smiled maybe too happily.

Emily's mouth opened and closed as she looked for words, something? "I'm... Uh..."

"I know it may sound a bit unorthodox. However..." She lifted a finger excitedly and walked around the students. "The curse of true love never did run smooth, —this will be perfect!" she finished, eagerly hoping for Emily's answer to be a yes.

Helena bit her lip and averted her guilty eyes. She grinned, feeling it all inside.

Professor Silverstein continued to pitch her support of Helena's idea even though Emily had been sold at 'take his place.' "You see... Our tempestuous playwright's work was mostly portrayed by men during the Renaissance. This too shall be impactful, ladies." She looked between them with bright fervor and delight, a couple of girls stood by, silently watching the woman like she was nuts or simply strange. Professor Silverstein eyed Emily. "For never was a story of more woe than this of Juliet and her Romeo." She was inspired.

Emily found Helena's eyes as her lip curled upward. "All right... I'll be her Romeo." she agreed and grinned, Helena's heart ached just as her stomach reverently succumbed to her desire's will. Brown eyes never left green ones while the teacher's excited claps echoed from a faint distance —they stared at each other... into each other.

"Perfect!" Professor Silverstein almost sang with unmatched joy.

***

Emily stood behind Helena as she opened the Millan mansion's rich wooden doors. Nerves were eating at Emily, and suddenly everything turned intimidating. Was this even the right thing to do? She feared being rejected by Helena once she knew the truth, but Helena felt as safe as the warm breath inside her very own lungs. Helena felt as expansive as gratefulness —she felt like the certainty of the voice inside that guides and is objective, not like the one that threatens and feels impending. Helena felt as definite as the best outcome. She felt like the relief of an aching soul.

Awed, Emily gawked at the large mansion. Outside, the place had robust, gilded age architecture's influence. She had driven by the grand and well-known structure so many times. Never did she imagine she would meet the ones living inside, even less being inside.

They both walked in, and wondering green eyes met the beautiful, pristine home.

Damn.

After passing the double-leaf doors of bronze grillework, the mesmerizing high ceilings drew Emily's focus upward. A few steps into the striking place and she spotted large stairs made of marble and mahogany. There were marble and handcrafted details on everything. Rich, dark woods and towering oriel stained windows. Emily had never seen anything so opulent. Ever. The emerald green in her eyes and dark pupils contracted as the bright light from the Victorian chandeliers hit them. Damn, indeed.

Helena closed the door. "Would you like something to drink or eat?" she offered kindly.

"Sure, just some water would be fine. Thanks." Emily said as she hooked two thumbs on the back pockets of her jeans. After scanning each passing square foot of impressive, Emily realized she had been led to the equally refined kitchen. The blonde immediately noticed they weren't alone. Caleb was leaning on the central island, munching on something while another familiar face from the soccer team did the same.

Feeling uncomfortable, Emily swallowed at the twisting sensation in her stomach, but Emily was resilient, she stood her ground.

Helena smiled. "Hey, Cai..." Defined boundaries were placed as she regarded her brother's friend, "Hello, Julian."

They both mouthed their hellos casually and continued chewing.

Emily nodded faintly. "Hey," She found her tough edge while Helena went to the large, see-through refrigerator.

Caleb pushed an honest smile. "Hey, Emily," he said.

Julian cleared his throat and continued to munch on a chocolate chip cookie, awkwardly looking around.

Once Helena was finished retrieving two bottles of water from the refrigerator, she closed it, eyeing her brother and his friend. —*What is going on? Caleb's attitude when around Emily was strange and now Julian, too?* she thought. Helena brushed it off, slightly annoyed and dared she say, harboring a covetous feeling over Emily.

"Excuse us…" Helena said, and walked past the boys. "Come on, Emily," she suggested softly.

Faultless green eyes challenged them in silence and followed Helena. "Bye, guys," she muttered.

"Bye," they said in unison. Emily and Helena were soon out of sight.

Julian grinned. "She's so hot, dude… too bad I'm not into dick." his mockery was heartlessly crass.

Caleb tensed up defensively. "Hey, man… come on, what kind of crap is that to say?"

"You know that shit is true, dude… If I were you, I'd lock Helena away;" He laughed playfully.

"Shut up, man!" Caleb stood protectively and glared at his friend. "Where do you get off talking shit? You must have seen her naked since you're so sure of that, then!"

Julian frowned at Caleb for bruising his virile ego. "Hell no, I haven't." he said defensively, brows furrowed and all.

"Then why do you talk out of your ass?" Caleb challenged.

"Everyone on campus talks about her." Julian's frown was replaced with disdain.

"So what?! What she has or doesn't have in her pants is none of your business, bro, you sound like such a little bitch. What's your problem?"

Julian laughed. "Shit, if I didn't know better, I'd say you liked the freak,"

Caleb clenched his jaw, and flushing irritation bubbled under his skin. "Fuck you, Julian!"

His friend continued to laugh mockingly.

"You know what? I don't feel like playing anymore, man; you need to go." Caleb told his inappropriate teammate.

"All right, whatever, dude." Julian shrugged, taking his soccer ball from the nearby surface and walked off.

***

Helena closed her bedroom door, and Emily walked in while studying every immaculate detail; everything seemed to be perfectly structured and placed. The colors on the walls were light and warm, just like her soul. Everything was so simple and tasteful; so intimate. Emily could breathe easy in her space; she could smell Helena's exclusive perfume lingering in the air. Perhaps it was because she was right there. Emily opened her bag and pulled out the script for her part. "I don't know how I'm gonna learn all this gibberish by heart," she said, and turned to face her.

With a longing huff, Helena clasped the seams of her soccer jacket and pulled her into a searing kiss.

Emily rushed both hands to Helena's lower back and moaned at the softness of her lips.

"Helena..." Emily managed between grazing lips. Helena had become synonym for loss of control —she needed to press pause before things got out of hand.

Helena grinned and walked them backward into a wall. She claimed Emily's mouth again, this time brushing her warm tongue against parted lips. Just when her back hit the wall, Emily felt the halt; she moaned as their bodies pressed against one another and Helena invaded her mouth with sweet and wet possession. Their chests rose and fell heavily. —*Shit.*

Olive-kissed hands crept through the jacket and wrapped around Emily's waist. Helena's small and vulnerable sounds unleashed a blood rush that hardened. —*Fuck. Fuck. No!* Emily thought, feeling hyper-aware of the ache at the axis of her body.

The want in Helena's subtle sounds was raw and needy.

It was beautiful and heated. It was so untainted and inviting. It was open and free; it was new.

The hardening reminder tucked in Emily's pants spoke of ache and the will she needed to find to stop this. It wasn't fair for Helena, but the fight was grand. Emily's arousal told her just to feed on the girl's warmth and reach under that dress... —to run her hand up soft thighs gently. It told her to move lace aside slowly, and graze her fingers on Helena's wet flesh while spreading her legs open. Helena wanted her, and Emily knew it, but her heart and mind begged to do right by *her*, by both of them. "Helena..." Emily whispered, gently breaking the kiss.

Brown eyes opened and looked into green ones wantonly. "I love kissing you," Helena said intimately. Breathless. Enraptured.

Emily softly ran her fingertips from Helena's honey-kissed shoulder down her arm. She touched her as if she were touching a binding promise. Helena's skin was a promise she wished more than anything she could keep and never let go. Emily was gentle; she didn't want Helena to take it the wrong way, she could never dare make her feel rejected, so she placed a sweet kiss on those lips she was already a slave of. "I love kissing you, too... so much," she whispered, eyes gleaming.

They told the truth, and Helena knew. She smiled, cupping Emily's cheek and pulled her into another kiss. A softer... kiss. Emily's need to stop was unspoken, but somehow Helena understood.

Emily was grateful; she didn't feel alone. She felt lucky Helena was the one on the other side of this romance. She was considerate and perceptive like no other. She was vulnerable, and Emily would cherish that vulnerability to the last of her ability. Sweet dimples pierced Emily's cheeks while indulging in Helena's skin. "I really need your help with all this nonsense; I don't speak Shakespeare."

Helena grinned. "It's not a language."

"It is to me." Emily contorted her face and looked down at the paper.

Helena took a pale hand and led her to the bed. "Okay, my fair Romiette. Let's study, then."

Emily's eyes spotted the peculiar and geeky ambiance given by the smaller details in Helena's room, the ones that spoke of what she liked and enjoyed. She was enthralled with the vinyl records on the shelf.

Helena realized something had taken Emily's attention and turned. She smiled. "What is it?"

Emily casually pointed at them. "Those are pretty awesome," The sleek vinyl turntable consumed her focus. "Oh, I love this..."

"Thank you. I bought that record player while on my last trip to Switzerland." Helena said, and walked to her shelf.

Emily gawked over the impressive book collection — so many colors and names neatly arranged. "Wow, this is pretty fucking cool," Emily blurted, and an amused Helena chuckled.

"Thank you," she said with a smile.

A thought suddenly thundered through Emily's brain. "Wait! I have to see your knitting stuff; I still can't believe it."

Helena laughed, slightly amused. "Why not?"

"You are too amazing to be real..." Emily said, and Helena blushed.

"Well, I don't know about amazing —thank you, though, for the lovely intent and..." She opened the drawer on her night table, pulling out her needles and yarn; green eyes sparkled as Emily beamed.

"Holy shit, it's true," she said, and studied the oddly captivating wear.

Helena pulled out a black knitted scarf and handed it to Emily. "It should go well with just about anything; I hope you enjoy it." she said.

Deep dimples pierced Emily's cheeks. "Are you shitting me?"

Helena chuckled; Emily's sailor mouth was fairly new to her, though she felt strangely endeared by the honesty behind it. "I am not." Helena took the garment and placed it around Emily's neck. Brown eyes grew bright. "You look lovely." she said.

Emily caressed the soft, thick material with her fingers; looking at the intrinsic pattern with knitting brows. "This is so beautiful, Helena, thank you... I don't know what to say; I mean, you freaking made this with your hands!"

Helena nodded slightly. "I did, and it is my pleasure." With fading smiles and a long drag of oxygen, eyes lingered.

Ready to give into the sensations burning her newly discovered womanhood, Helena yearned for more, but Emily's earlier desire to move slowly hit her even harder; she smiled and thought a change of subject was in order. "We should get back to the Renaissance," she suggested.

Emily quickly snapped out of her adoring trance. "Oh— um yeah, yeah, of course; we really should..."

They had been drilling the script for the past two hours, and Emily was positively parched. Before leaving, Helena kissed her and promised to return quickly with something to drink.

Emily stood from the bed and stretched her legs. It

was as if Caleb had been waiting for his sister to open the door —almost as if he'd been ogling and hovering on the hallway, because as soon as Helena was out of sight, he entered the bedroom and Emily looked up, startled.

Caleb eyed over his shoulder, hoping Helena wouldn't return as quickly as she had promised.

Green eyes stared at the girl's brother. She swallowed but didn't succumb to dread.

"Emily... I," He blushed and well... it was expected, this was awkward. "Look... I know that this is so out of line, and I hope you know I have absolutely nothing against you. *At all.*" he reassured.

Emily bit her lip and looked down but didn't keep her gaze there for long. She wanted Helena. She was going to try for Helena; eyes rose almost challengingly.

"But Helena is my little sister, and I have to look out for her... I—"

"Just say what you have to say, Caleb." Emily said with unwavering confidence.

"Look, I know that people are cruel... and they talk, they feel as if they have the right to do so —the bottom line is, I don't know your story, and it is none of my business, really, I mean, *this* is none of my business, but Helena is in the middle, and that is where I take issue." he said earnestly.

Emily stood strong while her world crushed inside, expecting for Caleb to trash it all any second.

"I've heard things about you, and I am sure you are well aware —it's not fair, I know, and I am so sorry, but regardless of it being true or not, I really think you have to tell my sister before this thing between you two goes any further." he finally let out, and Emily swallowed. She wasn't expecting **that**, *at all*.

"I know… and you're right; I *will* talk to her." Emily said with a blank face —she didn't deny or confirm anything. He was right, it wasn't his business.

Caleb furrowed his brows. "Don't hurt my sister, Emily, please…"

"I never could." she said honestly.

"Caleb," Helena said from the door, and he closed his eyes. —*Fuck!* Caleb thought, hearing the annoyance in her voice, and even though he couldn't see her face, Emily could.

She stalled and smiled. "Hey… we were just talking about next week's game." Emily shrugged and chuckled awkwardly.

A deep sigh flared Helena's nostrils, lines formed on her forehead. She wasn't stupid. "What are you doing here?" she asked her brother.

"I was just… we were talking about the game, Emily just told you." he tried casually.

Helena raised a skeptical brow and wished for her boiling blood to cool. "We should go, Em… It's getting late, and remember you have dinner plans with your parents." she said, never taking her piercing eyes from Caleb's.

Emily nodded, and Helena glared at her brother, once again feeling protective over the beautiful blonde.

After Emily had left the room, Helena regarded him with a threatening finger, "Please, don't leave —you and I need to talk." she warned.

He sighed and nodded. "All right." Caleb said.

***

Emily closed her parents' front door with a deep sigh. She stood in the foyer, inhaling the familiar soft scent as she gathered her thoughts before going to the kitchen. Her feet came to a halt, and the two familiar voices of her parents engaged in a discussion lured her closer; she quietly listened by a wall.

"She's my little girl, Maureen, of course I'm not going to tell her about this!"

The discussion was about her. Emily continued to listen under a faint shadow of warm glow and darkness. Her insides twisted. A deep breath gutted her and tears stung her eyes.

"She needs to know about it, Ben! I will not lie to her because some bigot feels like terrorizing us!" Maureen was ardent about her stance. She was a sweet and protective mother —Emily loved her, but what was she talking about?

"We're already on it, Maureen; she just started a new semester, and the lieutenant allowed me to work on the case! I don't want to frighten her." he tried.

"*It is* frightening, Ben. It is a terrible and unfair thing, but she has the right to know and be aware of what's going on! I know that you are her father— that you want to shield her and protect her but—"

"Yes! I do! That is precisely my job, and I'm not doing it right!" He threw something at something, and Emily jolted at the loud crash.

"I know, honey, but Emily isn't a child anymore... she's a young woman. We need to trust that she will be strong enough to know this, Ben—she has endured far worse, we all have!"

Emily sighed and felt the usual guilt wash over her. Something that went beyond sadness blurred her vision.

"All right…" he finally agreed with defeat in his voice.

***

For Helena, the drive back home was a blur. She had never felt this vexed before. Questions tasted tart in her mouth; they had been stewing inside her stomach, swelling until they choked her. She closed the door of her parents' mansion and rushed up the grand staircase. She wasn't known for barging into people's rooms without knocking first, but she was livid.

Her brother was comfortably lying on his plush bed, wearing only a pair of sweatpants. He jumped startled by his sister's intrusion. Helena acknowledged the casual words emanating from a large TV on the wall.

"Helena, are you all right?" Caleb asked as he slowly sat up.

"What is your problem with Emily, Caleb?" she questioned sternly as she stood by the door. This side of Helena, her brother had never seen. He knew she was pissed, but managed to stay collected as always.

"I have no problem with her, Lena."

Helena's eyes shone with warm tears as she bit the inside of her cheek. She closed the door and walked further into his room. Caleb knew it was time to talk; he tried a weak smile and motioned for her to sit.

She did. Helena was boiling inside; a tight feeling she couldn't name taunted her. "Do you like Emily? I mean, are you attracted to her… *interested* in her?" Helena asked, still affected, those profound eyes did not lie. She was jealous.

Caleb jerked back, looking surprised. "What? No, no, Helena, I… I think she's gorgeous and nice, but no."

"Then what is it?" she pressed.

He exhaled. "I know *you* like her."

Helena's focus fell to her hands but quickly met his again. "Yes, I do, I like her very much, in a way that— I like her more than I would a friend." she confessed.

Caleb smiled with knitting brows. His sister was too adorable for words. "Yeah... I gathered." Caleb mused.

"And you're okay with that?"

"I am if you are, Helena,"

"I am, yes..."

"Well... then I am, too, but..."

"But?"

"Have you two... talked?" He wondered if Emily had told her anything yet. He didn't want to intrude; it wasn't his place.

"Not really, not in depth or detail." she said.

"Then you need to... Helena, if you're going to be getting into something deeper and more meaningful with her, you should tell her about what you're going through."

"I know..." Helena tugged at her hands and looked down —she played with the ring on her finger.

He aimed for her gaze and found honest, scared gleaming eyes. "Hey, it's only fair, you know? If she's going to get attached to you."

"Yes, I know..." she repeated, her voice so raw.

He placed a soft hand on her shoulder.

"I will tell her tomorrow." Helena said.

4

BLACK AND BLUE

THIS MORNING IT WAS Helena who was suffering the aftermath of tossing and turning in bed all night. She had been thinking of ways, so many ways; countless scenarios lingered from one thought to the next. She had tried to find the 'right way' to tell Emily.

—How do you find the right way to tell someone that your body, the one sacred place supposed to sustain you, to tear itself apart just to keep you thriving —even though sometimes you trash it— that your only unconditional ally is turning on you with each passing second? Helena thought. She *thought* and wrecked her brain until sweat felt cool against her skin and sleep conquered her. How could life be so cruel? How could it be so beautiful and cruel all at the same time?

It wasn't fair, but that was Helena's truth at mere months away from her nineteenth birthday. She only wished to be alive when the next anniversary of her birth arrived, that it wouldn't collide with her expiration date.

73

Once morning came, Helena's eyes felt stiff; she felt disoriented —as if she had just fallen asleep a few hours ago, but the sunshine coming through the window reminded her that Emily was out there, somewhere in that world she wanted so badly to stay in.

She found the strength to get up and shower, to get dressed and smile as she looked at herself in the mirror. Dark eyes sustained a lingering gaze and a brilliant, beautiful gleam. Helena observed the blush in her cheeks. Even though she hadn't applied any makeup yet; the intrinsic flow of life ran through her effortlessly.

At this moment, life was being gentle and kind. To the naked eye, it seemed that she was healthy as ever —that she was developing vigorously and seconds weren't running against her. She gently brought a hand to her face and touched her young skin. It wasn't fair.

She didn't want it all to end. There was so much she wanted, **needed** to do. There was no time to waste. Every breath was precious, every moment was gold, and Helena wanted to spend as many of those as she could with Emily, feeling alive and falling in love.

If only Emily would allow her to —if only Emily were willing to subject herself to that kind of short-lived happiness and subsequent heartache; she could have a chance at tasting the most desired of all promises life had to offer. Love.

***

The better part of the day had passed, and Emily was still counting the minutes to see her Helena again. —*My Helena...* Well, she wasn't trying to sound like a possessive jerk, but Helena felt so hers; she felt hers in a way that was free and good, Helena was a gift; she was the prettiest thing that knew everything. If love had a color, Helena would match its intensity.

Afternoon had arrived, and The Vine was thriving. Emily sat at a table; the languid day was almost over, and she hadn't seen *her* yet. They had no classes together that day, but luckily she shared most of them with her best friend, Etta.

The warm honey blonde kept Emily sane; she had listened to her speak of Helena until her ears bled, but it was more than okay. Etta smiled. Big blue eyes couldn't complain; her friend was so happy, and that meant everything to Etta. If there was someone who deserved to feel this amount of joy, it was Emily.

"You need to relax, Em," Etta said with her usually gentle voice, letting out an amused chuckle.

Emily scanned the place as she tapped her fingers against the surface incessantly.

Etta bit on a slice of green apple and shook her head, still smiling.

"She hasn't returned my text from this morning —it's weird, I mean, I know I sound like a clingy stalker, but she usually answers back; she says it's rude to leave others hanging."

"Emily... Maybe she's been busy with classes," Etta shrugged. "Or maybe she's had a crazy day, who knows? But you really need to relax a little; I don't think I've seen you bite your nails since you were six."

Green eyes turned to meet wide blue ones while munching on a pale fingertip. Emily lowered her hand as her friend's brow arched. "Okay, okay... I won't bite my nails, but what if she heard something? —I mean, what if she hates me now?" Emily said to her friend with a scarier thought in mind "What if something happened to her? Maybe I should call her," She reached for her cell phone on the table without thinking twice. A hand stopped her.

"Em," Etta pierced her friend's eyes, "*Stop.*" she said with a chuckle. "You're starting to panic."

Emily blinked. "Yeah, I know. I thought that much was obvious." She stomped her foot on the floor and whined, "Etta... How am I gonna tell her? I mean, what if after I do tell her she doesn't want me in that way anymore?" she said with knitting brows.

"Based on what you've said about her, Em, she sounds like a pretty awesome girl... nothing I say can be set in stone, because, well... people—" She rolled those big blue eyes. "Some people can be horrible and stupid, but..." Etta pierced her friend's nervous gaze and smiled; she took Emily's hands in hers. "You have to know and believe that there are fantastic and open humans out there, too."

Emily nodded.

"And if she doesn't like you in that way, then you can always be her friend, if that's something you want, of course."

Faint red outlined Emily's welling eyes. The conviction in her childhood friend made her believe in happy endings and things like hope. Emily nodded and blinked back her tears.

"Okay?" Etta asked, searching for a trace of optimism in there.

"Okay..." Emily murmured and drew her hands back, suddenly feeling too mushy and sentimental. "You're gonna burn my badass reputation." she joked and wiped away a tiny tear that had barely escaped the corner of her eye.

Etta laughed and arched a brow. "Now, *that* wouldn't

be too hard to do."

Emily frowned, mocking offense, but her next words got caught in her throat along with her heart. The smitten look on Emily's face urged Etta to look over her own shoulder and see what had caused it. That was the first time she laid eyes on the person that would change her best friend's life forever. Etta turned with her mouth slightly agape. "That's her?"

Smiling like an idiot, Emily shamelessly stared at the girl standing in front of the food line across the cafe. Helena had stolen her heart; that was for sure. "Would you even doubt it?"

Etta turned again and studied the beautiful girl with long black hair. Helena was every bit as breathtaking as her friend had described her to be.

Emily realized this was the first time she had seen Helena wearing jeans. A thin red sweater wrapped her small torso while a black bra flirted with her eyes. But... Helena hadn't noticed her. She seemed distant, as if her mind were somewhere else.

"She's gorgeous, Em..." Etta said.

"Yes, she is." Emily continued to admire Helena.

"Well...?" Etta said with a questioning brow.

"Well what?"

"What are you waiting for? Go get your girl! You were only like ten seconds away from having a meltdown!" she joked.

"You're making me sound like I'm whipped." Emily objected.

Etta raised both brows this time and drew her head back. "Oh, sweetheart, you so are."

"I am not whipped." Emily protested.

"Oh... yes, yes you are."

Emily playfully threw a folded straw wrapper at her friend. Etta chuckled.

Things happened fast, but Emily's senses were sharper, as soon as she saw Helena's step falter, the smile on her face turned into a frown.

Helena lowered her head; hand gripped tightly onto the counter's edge, knuckles white. She was waiting for her herbal tea, just ready to pay, when suddenly her lights blinked, and everything sunk in. Off focus. Strands of black hair fell forward as she took a deep breath.

That was the day the cashier on the other side realized just how much of an asshole the tall, obnoxious guy standing behind Helena was. The clerk deadpanned. This girl wasn't feeling well, that was obvious. His insensitivity was appalling. "Hey, shorty, keep it moving! I have a class to get to, get your money out and pay or move aside!"

Helena was far too busy regaining her composure to take in the sounds around her.

If Emily was sharp, Maddison had been even faster. The blur and speed in which things unfolded were unreal. One second Helena felt like she was about to collapse, completely alone, and the next, her sister's voice rang in her ears. —Is that Emily's perfume? she thought. One deep breath, then another, and she felt those arms around her, so gentle and protective, so opportune and warm.

"Helena..." Emily whispered in the embrace.

Helena managed to grasp onto Emily. With eyebrows still furrowed, she tried to find her center. —Breathe in and out, Helena, find the feeling. she told herself internally.

"You bloody idiot! Who do you think you are talking to my little sister like that?!" Maddison bellowed at the impatient jerk.

Emily's face twisted as the screeching voice and familiar English accent hit her ears. It was the annoying auburn-haired girl from her social and behavioral science class, giving the tall guy behind Helena a run for his money. It was sudden; it was all so confusing, and —*damn, her sister?* Well, that didn't matter; she decided to shut out whatever else was going on —she could still barely hear her blasting him. "Helena, are you okay?" Emily tried again, looking for that beautiful face.

Helena nodded, still holding onto strong, lean arms. Dark eyes met green ones, and Helena saw great worry. She pushed a smile. "I am… It was nothing." She straightened herself out, suddenly feeling more and more alive.

"That was not nothing… It seemed like you were going to pass out." Emily said, concerned.

Helena was looking more like herself and Emily somehow eased at the sight.

Trying her very best to put Emily at ease, Helena murmured, "I'm fine… I promise." She smiled more convincingly this time. She did feel better. It wasn't a lie.

"Are you sure?"

"Yes, I am." Helena reassured once again. A bit more firmly this time, yet still kind.

After successfully finishing off Helena's bully, Maddison turned to her sister and furrowed her brows, slightly taken aback by the intimacy Helena and Emily were displaying. The way Helena held onto her hand, their torsos so close together; the taller girl's hand on Helena's small waist. Overall, Emily was acting like a concerned girlfriend. "What are you doing?" Maddison regarded Emily, seemingly confused and annoyed.

God, Emily wasn't a fan of the spoiled redhead. She raised a defensive brow, still holding on to the girl she already cared so much about. "What do you mean what am I doing? I think it's pretty obvious, isn't it?" Emily bit back.

Unsatisfied, Maddison searched for her sister's gaze. "What are you doing with her, Helena?"

Helena cringed at her sister's obnoxious persistence. "Maddison, please lower your voice, you're giving me a headache." She was not in the mood.

"What's your problem?" Emily asked.

"My problem? *She* is my problem and my little sister! Who the hell do you think you are holding her like that?" Blue eyes widened as Maddison ignored Helena's plea.

Those were a lot of 'who the hell do you think you are' for such a short span of time.

***

Inside the university's sterile health station, the fight continued. "Okay, you need to shut up, I'm serious—" Emily threatened, pointing her finger at Maddison while Etta stood nearby, nervously eyeing them and Helena.

With knitted brows, Helena winced; their bickering was driving her insane. "God…" she whispered and rubbed her temple.

"Like hell, I'm going to shut up! Or let you near my sister for that matter!"

Helena had been growing highly annoyed at Maddison for uttering that term so freely, she finally snapped. "Since when am I your little sister, Maddison?"

The redhead turned in a whim. She found brown eyes and grew silent.

"All you've ever done is tease me, make me feel bad about myself and belittle me… Why do you suddenly care so much?" Helena challenged.

Maddison tried to ignore the small pang of hurt twisting her stomach in knots; she knew she deserved it, after all, she was a bitch to most breathing humans, including her little sister, but that didn't mean she didn't care at least a decent amount —Helena knew she cared deep down, didn't she? "Because!" Maddison shook her head, confused. "Why were you touching each other like that?" she demanded with a scrunched up nose.

"Like what?" Helena questioned with a kind of strength that told Maddison her little sister was now a woman. It was like waking up years later and seeing how much she had missed.

"Like… like a couple! Are you a lesbian?" she asked bluntly.

Helena huffed in disbelief and chuckled lightly. "Actually, Maddison, yes. —*Yes*— I —*Am* —why? Do you have a problem with that?"

Maddison deadpanned. "Of course not!"

Emily took a deep breath and found Etta's dreading eyes; she realized her childhood friend was on the edge of her seams as well. Maddison could blurt out her secret any second, and for the looks of it, that was her absolute intention. Fear stung Emily.

"Are you an idiot, then? Or just greedy?" Maddison asked Helena sarcastically. *Rudely.*

Emily swallowed, and Etta was itching to intervene.

Helena furrowed her brows genuinely lost. "What do you mean by that?"

Maddison turned with wide blue eyes that threatened to

pop out of her face and pierced Emily. "You haven't told her?!"

Emily's face drained of color; her hands were shaking, so she balled them into fists and swallowed hard again. —*Fuck.*

"Told me what?" Helena questioned, looking confused.

Emily's eyes welled up with a gush of pink and sentiment; she bit her lower lip —sadness settled in her usually bright and honest gaze, Helena felt her insides shatter.

"She's a—"

"Okay, stop!" Etta cut in sharply. She had to intervene passionately and put a halt to this bullshit conversation. "That is not your place!" Blue eyes pierced Maddison's glaring ones. They were like rabid dogs facing one another; breaths grew heavier.

Helena grew angry; fire raced under her skin, and confused eyes found Maddison. She didn't understand what was happening, but all her body demanded was to rush to *her*. To console Emily, and try to ease whatever was making her hurt like that. Helena studied Emily with gentle brows. The star in profound brown eyes burned in the form of sadness. In the loudest silence, Helena urged, —*What is wrong?*

A single warm tear ran down Emily's cheek, and she couldn't take it anymore, unable to hold the dam of emotions much longer, Emily rolled her annoying cry off and walked out.

Helena stood there with a hurt and confused look on her face; her mouth fell slightly open as she turned to look at Emily's best friend. She seemed kind, and Helena knew Emily cared for her. She then noticed her sister's chest heaving.

Maddison was so ready to let it all out. So fucking ready and Etta knew it.

"Helena, you need to know she's a—"

"I TOLD YOU TO STOP!" Etta shouted, this time startling them both.

"You can't tell me what to do!" Maddison bit back. "I'll tell her whatever the hell I want!"

"Tell me what?!" Helena demanded for the hundredth time. It was easy to see she was aching to run after Emily.

"That your girlfriend has—"

"Oh, my God. SHUT —UP!" Etta barked. "Helena, go! Just go talk to Emily, please, go find her and speak to her." Etta pleaded as she stalled. Maddison apparently had a big, relentless mouth.

Maddison's eyes were wider than ever. She was annoyed and frustrated. She wanted to drag Etta through the ground by those long blonde locks of hair and relieve the irritation coursing through her veins.

By the time the angry and shuddering girl turned, Helena was gone.

***

Helena looked for Emily all around campus. She called her repeatedly with no success. After an exhausting hour, she was certain Emily had left the college grounds, so she rushed to the dorms.

After knocking on her dorm door for minutes, she realized Emily wasn't there either. No motorcycle. No Emily.

Out of breath from so much jogging, Helena finally found her car. She got in it, cranked the engine, and went off to find the sweet blonde —she had to have gone home. Helena needed to talk to her and make whatever was hurting Emily better. She needed to see her, hold her and kiss her again.

***

A soft knock came from the door while Emily's face was buried in her pillow; swollen and flushed from crying; soaking wet eyes were still so green, though marred with sadness and a blurring dew of pink. "Not now, Mom."

"It's me, Emily… Helena —may I come in?" the familiar voice came from the other side.

Emily sat up quickly and took a deep breath. —*Shit.*

The screeching sound of the door revealed that truths needed to be said.

Helena's heart shattered at the sight, and the pieces cut every inch of her soul. "Oh, Emily…" Her brows knitted together purposefully.

Emily turned and walked back to her bed, but chose the floor instead. She felt the soft side of the mattress against her back. Emily brought her knees to her chest and ran both hands through her lush blonde hair —not knowing Helena would gladly give anything for her... to be with her, to be allowed in. Things were moving so fast, and yes, it scared Helena, but at the same time, it felt so natural. Their connection felt fated.

She sat next to Emily. Helena didn't know what was going on but knew that she was dying to feel her touch again. She dared reach for Emily's hand, entwining her fingers with soft pale ones. Obviously, Emily had something to tell her, and for some reason, she felt like it was maybe too difficult, perhaps she didn't feel comfortable enough? Helena wanted Emily to trust her and allow her inside. So she realized she had to do the same.

Emily had been crying so hard; the warmth and vulnerability radiating from her body were soul-altering.

Helena's empathy ran high in excess —she broke the silence and went first. "I have a deteriorating, life-threatening heart condition." Helena confessed and sought green eyes.

It was like acid had been poured into Emily's chest. She swallowed hard —suddenly her secret seemed minimal. Emily's stomach tightened as she took in the magnitude and meaning of what she had heard. "Helena…" she whispered while feeling her heart truly break for the first time. She thought it had been shattered by cruelty before, but this, this was just... Tears prickled at her eyes, but Emily didn't cry. Instead, she found honest brown; they looked braver than Emily felt inside.

"We recently learned this," Helena said with a shrug. "It is the main reason why my mother brought me back to San Francisco and insisted on me spending more time with my siblings."

"But... —How? I mean —are you okay? I—"

"I am." Helena said, and smiled peacefully.

—*My beautiful girl and her strength.* Emily thought while squeezing her soft hand.

"I was completely healthy until last year when I began to have these intense episodes where I'd lose my breath and faint," Helena explained softly.

She listened attentively while caressing Helena's fingers with her thumb.

Emily felt so warm and perfect, the perfect temperature —ideal. She felt good, so good to touch; it gave Helena strength and hope. —*Hope.* she remembered the contrasting messages of her books.

"A year ago my parents were, of course, called in, and when they flew to Germany they took me to dozens of doctors, none of them could figure out what was causing my heart to deteriorate, but regardless of a definite cause, it was doing so anyway." She shrugged.

"I'm so sorry, Helena..." Emily's tears stung the edges of her beautiful light eyes, but she held herself together.

"They then took me to Switzerland. One of my mother's colleagues examined me and decided to place me on treatment immediately; he later concluded that the anomaly in my heart was congenital —it's incurable." she said, and looked into Emily's eyes. She wasn't going to hide any longer.

Emily shook her head and felt a swelling, bruising breath invade her. She couldn't lose Helena. Why was life so cruel?

"I flat-lined when I was in Zurich." Helena spoke of the scary incident only her family and doctor knew about.

Emily's tears fell, she honestly didn't know what to say, but she tried, "So—you..." she couldn't push it out; the thought seemed to scrape its way from her brain down to her heart, getting stuck in her throat.

"Yes. Technically, I died." Helena said. "They brought me back, and I have been in a very exclusive trial medication since... It has made me stronger and gotten me to the point where I can actually lead a normal life; for now." Helena had to be completely honest.

"So... if there is no cure, then... Where— I mean, what..." Emily tried again.

"What's next?" Helena mused.

Emily nodded.

Helena sighed. "At the moment I am fine. However, there is a chance that my heart may continue to deteriorate at any time —if that were to happen, I would go into the heart transplant list."

Emily swallowed audibly. She felt like falling apart. But maybe there was hope? "So if you got that transplant you could get better? And not…"

"Die?" Helena asked with a small smile.

Emily shrugged sheepishly. "Yeah,"

"If my body were not to reject it —that is in case I could get one… then no, I would not die… or well, technically my chances of living would be better than without it."

Emily didn't know what else to do, she just launched herself into Helena's arms and held her for what seemed like an eternity. Smelling her sweet perfume and feeling her heartbeat. She was warm and alive; Emily suddenly pulled back. "Wait… but today —you almost fainted, does that mean that you're getting sick again?"

Helena shook her head with absolute conviction. "I am fine, I promise. I am being monitored very closely; I was merely tired —I didn't sleep very well last night," Helena played with the thin ring on her finger. "I kept thinking of the right way to tell you this…" she said with those warm brown eyes, and Emily melted.

A pale hand caressed her honey-kissed cheek gently, knowing this could very well be the last time she did. Emily had to come clean as well, and not knowing how Helena would take it was a scary thought. "Well…" She bit the inside of her cheek. "I have something to confess too…"

Helena nodded so kindly and softly; she squeezed Emily's hand and gave her a reassuring smile. "You can tell me anything, Em; I promise I would never betray your trust."

"I know you wouldn't, and I do trust you —I'm just so surprised you haven't heard anything about it around campus."

Helena let out a small laugh. "I have no friends there apart from you —I believe to have crossed words with two different people since I started my semester." She found it amusing and very normal. Helena was used to being a lone wolf, a very self-satisfying and independent one. The fact that people found her odd didn't bring her down in the least.

"That's because they're all idiots. You're too smart for them; it's intimidating." Emily tried a sad smile.

"That is what my mother used to tell me," Helena added.

"Well, then your mom is a very wise woman." She raised a brow and grinned.

Pleased, Helena squeezed a pale hand again. "Thank you."

Emily lowered her head and bit her lip. "Helena, I feel awful —like I wasn't honest with you… I mean, I should have told you this thing about me before I kissed you."

"Nothing you may say would change the fact that I loved kissing you and I would do it again."

Emily blushed. —*Damn.* "Well… This might change the way you see me, completely." Fear taunted Emily's intentions and hopes; her stomach felt hollow and painfully empty.

"You can tell me, and I promise you; I will not see you differently, Em —no matter what it is…" she said so very softly that it made the blonde's heart flutter, it made her axis burn.

"I…" Emily looked down, trying to find the courage and even laughed a little, her face grew hot and flushed. "I'm… I um," She bit her lip; face hardened in concentration, not daring to look into Helena's eyes just yet. "I was born a boy." she finally confessed, and green eyes looked up into brown ones expectantly.

Helena blinked softly and swallowed.

Emily scanned her face, looking for traces of rejection, of an impending freak-out, *of disgust*. She found none of those; she could still see her kind, and lovely know it all. Helena was still there, and she was still holding her hand.

"You were?" Helena asked softly. "I would have never known." She smiled with knitting, gentle brows.

Emily wasn't sure if she wanted to laugh or cry. She smiled instead. It was a confused smile. "I am a woman, though. Helena... I..." She prayed for the words she had always wanted to have access to, the exact words that could convey how she had always felt inside. "Ever since I could remember... I have felt— I've felt like a girl. I just —my parents, they have always been so amazing, they allowed me to transition when I was just a little kid, they..." Green eyes shone with warm tears as she bowed her head. "They allowed me to be me —when they saw how horribly unhappy and depressed I was at such young age. I mean, they listened to me, and paid attention —they are *everything.*" Emily's chin trembled slightly as she chewed on her lip and continued to look down, tears falling freely.

Helena squeezed her hand, making Emily look up with wet eyes and a flushed face. She placed two fingers under Emily's chin, and with a thumb, she caressed her soft cheek. "You are the most beautiful woman I have ever seen," Helena reassured and leaned in to kiss those warm, flushed lips —finally tasting salty tears, tears of truth and lingering ache. Emily allowed her to do as she pleased.

The kiss was short but meaningful. Helena opened her mouth temptingly, and Emily followed. Eyes closed, bound by something sublime.

They parted, and Emily slowly opened her mossy eyes.

Helena was looking at her like she would at the moon or blinding constellations of a far away universe. "You are exquisite, Emily," she whispered with raw honesty.

Those exact words. Emily smiled; she couldn't believe this was happening. Those words meant acceptance; those were the same words Helena had given her right after their first kiss. "Do you have any questions for me?" Emily asked, honestly looking into brown eyes.

Helena nodded and bit her lip with carmine claiming her cheeks.

"You can ask me whatever you need or want to know," Emily added genuinely.

Helena saw in green eyes that it was indeed true; Emily was wide open.

"How did you manage to look... so much like," She didn't want to sound like an ignorant idiot. Helena shook her head softly and felt indeed like a fool for not being able to formulate a concise, sensitive question.

"Like a girl?" Emily said, and smiled, feeling endeared.

Helena nodded. Emily was the most beautiful girl she had ever seen; she was so soft, delicate and strong. The blonde was a waking dream, and her non-threatening, earnest, raspy voice was just so —evoking.

Emily took a deep breath. "Well, it's a long story... but like I said, I've lived most of my life as me— a girl and um... my endocrinologist is pretty amazing." She shrugged, suddenly seeming so much more relaxed; this made Helena happy.

"He's Etta's dad." A faint smile broke from her lips. "That is how we met so young... Anyway, he has been my doctor since I was a kid and well, he has monitored my development, my growth and overseen my transition.

I'm on some trial treatments as well." Emily confessed, realizing just how much they seemed to have in common. "At the right age, a few years ago, he put me on blockers and other things he has been developing, you know, to help me feel completely comfortable in my body —like it matches me, who I am ...if that makes sense?"

Helena nodded. "Of course it does..."

"I can't believe how incredible you are being about this..." Emily said, dumbfounded.

Helena smiled and looked into green eyes, just as enamored as she had done so in the past. "Why wouldn't I be? I feel so lucky to have finally found you; I would be a fool to be anything but."

Emily caught a breath so deep in her chest, and her eyes glazed over. She smiled honestly.

"May I ask you an incredibly personal question?" Helena said, but quickly shook her head, feeling stupid, she blushed; "I don't want to sound like a jerk..." — "You know what? —Nevermind." She chuckled, looking embarrassed, and pinched the bridge of her nose.

Emily smiled. "No, no... please ask, I mean, I said you could ask me anything —really, it's okay." she reassured.

"Do you um... do you... —Do you have a—" Helena blushed deeply, so deeply that it told Emily everything. Helena certainly didn't want to say a word Emily maybe wasn't comfortable with.

"I do..." Emily nodded with a blushing smile.

The corners of Helena's beautiful mouth turned up pleasantly as she leaned in for another kiss. Emily felt so relaxed —it was new. She had never had this kind of intimacy with anyone. Her previous experience never felt right.

Helena's hand caressed her soft, toned arm until it

reached her fingers. Emily shivered into the kiss —having Helena's feather touch on her was like diving into nirvana. Goosebumps claimed her.

Licking Emily's bottom lip, Helena begged to be let in, and Emily did... She opened her mouth and opened herself. Helena's wet tongue gently seduced hers into submission with each delicious stroke.

A weakening moan found Helena's ears. Warm bodies drew closer. A tanned hand traveled from delicate pale fingers to Emily's stomach and thigh. At the burning ache consuming her, Helena whimpered into their brushing lips.

Emily's loud moan broke the kiss with a smacking sound. Green eyes widened. —*Shit!*

Helena chuckled and looked at her as if she were the only thing that existed. Her smile as sweet and addictive as her kisses.

"My... um," Emily cleared her throat and pointed down. "You make me lose my mind very quickly... but my bits have a mind of their own."

Helena chuckled. "Your bits?" The term endeared her.

"Yeah... Um, you know... my penis." She blushed adorably.

Helena's smile was so bright, her eyes glowed; want and euphoria bursting inside. She leaned in and brushed a smooth kiss on Emily's neck. A hand grazed her denim-covered thigh. "Is this okay?" Helena asked so very softly, *thoughtfully*.

Emily nodded. "Yeah... but um, if you keep going, it's going to..." As Emily's finger pointed north, Helena moved her hand to a safer place, adoring every second of intimacy shared. She finally had that part of Emily no one else did. This was only theirs, and it felt incredible.

"Do you feel okay with having it?" Helena asked.

"Yeah… Do I hate it or feel rejection towards it you mean?" Helena bit her lip and nodded.

"No… I actually don't have dysphoria towards it anymore." She shrugged. "I did when I was younger— I mean, it's not the perfect situation, but I have learned to see it as part of my body now, I know it may sound strange to you, but —" Emily's eyes glowed, it was a rushing mix of self-consciousness and ease.

"No, it doesn't…" Helena said. "I feel like it doesn't make you more or less of a woman."

Emily smiled, and a saddened frown reappeared, she had more to share, Helena thought.

"My dysphoria manifests itself differently, I mean, it's not the same for everyone. When I was younger, I hated being called 'he' or 'boy… little man' I felt like my name, and everything else wasn't mine —the thought of growing up and having male features just—" Emily closed her eyes and inhaled deeply. "I have nothing against men; I'm just not one."

Helena's thumb traced Emily's hand. "I believe I understand what you mean; it makes sense— gender and sex aren't the same things."

With furrowed brows, Emily smiled. Her warm lips rushed to the safety of Helena's neck —the soft flesh there, the unforgettable scent of her perfume… "You are so amazing." she murmured against Helena's skin.

A quiet moan claimed Emily's ears. Helena moved her head to the side, giving her better access to do as she pleased. Soft lips grazed the rushing pulse on her neck, and Helena shivered until—

Puzzled brown eyes squinted and zeroed in on something carved on Emily's nightstand; it was barely hidden... She shifted to get a better view of it —Emily, still indulging in her sweet neck.

"Is that a penis?" Helena asked.

Emily stopped her kissing and drew back, confused. "What?" She looked down at herself, and Helena rolled her eyes with a chuckle.

"Not you, there..." She pointed at the wooden piece of furniture.

Emily's face turned into an annoyed frown. "Fucking Rhys—"

"What?" Helena asked, thoroughly confused.

"My brother must have carved it; I can't believe I never saw it before."

"Your brother carved a penis on your nightstand?" Helena asked, looking amused.

"Yeah... He loves to draw dicks everywhere; you should see my books." she huffed.

Helena laughed. "Are you serious?"

Emily reached for her bag that lay smeared at the end of the bed. She pulled out one of her 'old' new books and handed it to Helena who opened it with curious eyes. She chuckled while scanning a crazy display of cartoonish dicks everywhere. "This is a very impressive collection of phalluses."

They laughed together while flipping through the pages marked with memories of Emily's brothers. After a few seconds, Helena's eyes studied the unaware blonde, she closed the book with a grin and pulled Emily in once again; she needed more of this exquisite girl. She could never get tired of this, never.

5

LUST FOR LIFE

THE MILLAN DWELLING WAS architecturally stunning. The history behind it, perhaps fascinating, but this specific morning more current matters unfolded in the home. Katherine had decided to make good use of the secluded terrace with a grand view of the blue San Francisco Bay. She thought breakfast with her three children, surrounded by the vine-covered walls and their gorgeous city, would make the Saturday morning a pleasant one.

The way things were progressing made her sincerely doubt that initial thought. Maddison and Caleb had been going at it back and forth over the breakfast table. Helena remained in her chair, chewing on a grape when Katherine finally had to intervene. "That is enough! both of you." she reprimanded.

Caleb grew flushed, and Maddison fueled her pent-up frustration while taunting her brother back to back.

Katherine's intervention fell right through the cracks, *unheard*. Helena took a deep breath and sipped on some orange juice, feeling rightfully annoyed and uncomfortable.

Katherine's nerves were getting pulled at and the mild pang bullying her head didn't help. She pinched the bridge of her nose, trying to find a small ounce of calm in an incessant sea of bickering. "Christ," she muttered.

Caleb's ego was sore, and Maddison was utterly relentless.

Santiago was out of town at a medical conference in Seattle, and all Katherine wanted a mere hour ago when she welcomed the day was to enjoy a bit of alone time with her spawns. —When? — When between brie cheese and blueberries being spread on fancy crackers did this lovely breakfast turn into an ultrasonic discussion between her children?

"I can't believe you're still whining over that stupid car! I swear, you're such a spoiled brat!" Caleb barked at Maddison.

"Oh, sweetheart, believe me! I will fight my way until I get what is only fair! Why should you two get what you ask for and not me?" she disputed passionately.

"I never asked for that car." Helena interjected, and Maddison rolled her eyes, swiftly ignoring her.

Annoyed, Caleb huffed, falling back in his chair; he threw both arms up in the air. "I give up! I swear, just take mine, okay? I can't listen to your crap anymore; I'd rather walk!"

Maddison drew back offended and scanned him from head to toe. "You have got to be kidding me," She sneered. "That whore-mobile? —No, thank you —I'd like to remain venereal-disease free, darling."

—Shit! Caleb turned bright red and immediately sank into the chair while eyeing his mother.

Katherine sipped on her coffee and put the cup down,

forehead creasing; she regarded them both, "What is that supposed to mean?"

Caleb cursed his sister between teeth and Maddison smiled smugly, turning her gaze from him to Katherine. "Your beloved son uses his car as a motel on wheels, Mother... now tell me, how is it fair that he gets a sports car while I have to drive that tiny hybrid?!— It's dreadful!" she ranted.

—*That bitch!* Caleb thought while clenching his jaw. Helena swallowed a piece of strawberry and her brown eyes widened. She certainly wasn't surprised, but felt awful for the position her brother was put in.

A perturbed Katherine turned to her only son. "Caleb, is this true?" she demanded, obviously appalled.

The poor boy was ready to dig a hole and crawl in it; he couldn't bring himself to look at his mother in the eye and say yes to that, even though it was the truth.

Maddison gloated. "His silence is damning, Mother," she taunted.

"Maddison, please stop. I am talking to your brother." the doctor said without taking her glare from her son.

Helena rolled her eyes at her bitter sister. Maddison smirked. With crossed arms, she fell back on the chair to watch Caleb go down.

Not even the lovely chirping of the birds comforted him. The poor boy's cheeks were red as beets. He scratched the back of his neck, and Maddison arched a smug brow.

"I uh..."

"Caleb, are you serious?!" Katherine scolded, taking his state and lack of words as confirmation.

He finally looked up at his mother. "It's not— it's not like that, Mom," he stammered and turned to his sister with a burning glare. "She's exaggerating; it makes me sound like I'm a pimp or something."

"Oh, no, dear brother, you're not the pimp… you're the WHORE!" she shouted.

Helena's eyes widened. "Maddison!"

"I am not a whore!" Caleb defended, and Katherine shook her head with eyes closed.

Clearly embarrassed and upset, Caleb countered, "Well, you're one to talk crap just because you use Leo's 'whore-mobile' to get yours!"

Helena slowed down her chewing; this was getting more and more uncomfortable by the second. Picturing her siblings engaging in sexual situations was *not* something she needed in her brain.

Wide-eyed, Katherine turned to a gaping Maddison. "You little prick!"

"Maddison! Language! This is incredibly inappropriate you two! I cannot believe you are doing that —God knows where! I raised you better than that!" Katherine felt the pulsating fire of a migraine coming along. "Which Leo is he referring to?" she questioned Maddison.

Oh, it was his turn to smirk. "Blackwell," he said smugly.

Katherine frowned. "What?!"

Blue eyes sneered at Caleb. "You little bastard," she hissed.

"Maddison!" Katherine scolded again.

"What?! What is wrong with me being friend's with Leo?" she asked with heated cheeks.

"I don't want you around Leo Blackwell; he's trouble and not to mention he's a con artist!"

"He is not a con artist!" Maddison bit back.

Caleb mocked, "Hell yes, he is,"

"Maddison, I can't believe you've befriended that—"

"That what, Mother?" she challenged, visibly hurt.

"That… young man."

Blue eyes reddened. "You don't even know him!" She stood from the chair, her heart detaching from the group as always. She felt foreign.

"Certainly I know who he is; I am very aware; I know he put his father in a terrible position after he poached money from a few of his business partners last year."

A heaving Maddison felt not only invisible in this family but also completely rejected. Her heart thumped fast as her lungs filled with oxygen and deflated. Blue eyes grew wider. "Don't judge him without knowing him!"

"I don't want you with him! Period!" the woman demanded sternly.

Katherine knew her daughter was of legal age to make her own decisions, but she had to put a twenty-one and older clause on each their living trusts for a very good reason. This one. She knew they wouldn't be ready for such responsibility, at least not Caleb or Maddison. She knew Maddison would have to obey her as long as she had no access to her money; the blue-eyed girl knew the cost if she didn't. Though in truth, Katherine would've never ripped her children from their inheritance.

"He is not a criminal!"

"This conversation is over!" Katherine shouted in a definite tone that brought her daughter to the edge.

Red, almost crimson, Maddison's seams were about to burst. "Well— Helena's girlfriend has a penis!" she blurted out, and immediately regretted the words.

All eyes on the table widened but Katherine's. The woman was beyond confused.

Helena gasped. "Maddison!" She stood from her chair in

a rush; gleaming brown searched blue with a breaking heart.

"God! You are such a bitch!" Caleb jumped from his chair.

"Caleb!" Katherine scolded and shook her head while massaging her temples.

Sentiment prickled at Helena's eyes; her chest heaving as she challenged proudly. "That is none of your business! I can't believe you just used that to try and make yourself look better before Mother's eyes— you are such a child!" Helena was passionate in her speech.

"OK. STOP! The three of you!" Katherine shouted. "What is Maddison talking about, Helena?" she regarded her with a less scolding tone since technically, she hadn't been making her skull break in two for the past thirty minutes.

"I will not discuss that here, it is... personal." Helena clasped on the plackets of her cardigan and closed it tight, suddenly feeling unnecessarily exposed. "I will tell you when we are alone, *in private*, Mother." she said, blushing deeply.

Maddison noticed Katherine's acceptance of Helena's answer and scoffed; she turned on her heels and left.

Pinching the bridge of her nose, Katherine wondered where she had gone wrong.

Helena swallowed and crossed her arms; Caleb looked at her apologetically. He mouthed, 'You okay?'

She exhaled and nodded, pushing a smile to comfort her brother.

Katherine sighed. "I have to get ready, or I will miss my flight... your father is waiting for me in Seattle; we have a dinner to attend to," she said disappointedly, their family time, ruined. "You two, please... no more fighting, I'd hate to have to go right in the middle of this..."

"It's all right, Mother. You don't have to worry; we will

be fine." Helena tried to reassure her with a smile.

Katherine pushed a smile of her own and placed a kiss on Helena's cheek. Both Helena and Caleb knew the woman was sad. They felt bad. She then moved to give the same attention to her son and walked off.

Katherine turned once at the door, seemingly exhausted. "Caleb, don't ever call a woman that horrid word ever again, please?" she warned, and he nodded, looking embarrassed.

***

Emily and Helena had agreed to see each other that night. Helena had been daydreaming of Emily nonstop. A smile escaped her lips as she finished applying her light makeup and perfume.

Emily's nerves were a wreck. The apparent effect Helena had over her was scary, but she couldn't care less. She had changed clothes five times, settling on her best pair of jeans, a thin white sweater, and a black leather jacket —her signature red chucks weren't amiss. Pale, sweaty palms ran on denim as she rang the doorbell.

A few minutes later, the girl she had been dreaming of appeared. Helena's smile was seductive and innocent. The wind that filtered through blew her dark locks lightly. Emily gave her a persuading and shy smile of her own. The way they managed to look at each other was always filled with such candor; their enamored eyes held a gleam that never went unnoticed by the other.

From Helena's side of the door, the world had just turned a little brighter. Blonde hair blew in the evening breeze. Dazzling green eyes took her breath away once again; Emily made her skin race with a kind of warmth that promised many things. Every nerve-ending within her obsessed over the longing sensation. The heat traveled from her chest to her cheeks, and she smiled.

Helena gave her a wide open pass with that bright, beaming gesture; Emily had to smile back, she couldn't have helped it even if she tried. —*My beautiful girl.*

Effortlessly elegant, Helena wore the sheer allure of a flaring red dress and Emily swallowed hard. Black leggings contrasted with her dark hair and eyes like a crimson rose and the night sky. Helena chuckled and pulled her into the house.

Emily allowed her to do as she needed, she would have allowed Helena to drag her anywhere and still continue to smile like an idiot. *Gladly.*

Once Helena closed the door, she slowly coaxed her in. Her beautiful mouth opened and claimed Emily's with maddening grace. The taller girl lodged both hands on Helena's waist and brushed torturous lips slowly. The wet feel of Emily's provoking tongue made Helena's stomach tighten; she gave in.

Emily bit Helena's bottom lip, pulling on it softly. Pearl white teeth finally let go of the tempting flesh with a dimpled smile and hooded green eyes. "Hey…" Emily whispered, and Helena batted her lashes gently.

"Hey yourself." she murmured. "Thank you for joining me for dinner tonight," Helena said with gleaming dark eyes, so warm and inviting —Emily loved them. She could look at Helena look at her like that for hours.

"Are you kidding? A night with you and you cooking for me? I'd be an idiot to say no to that."

With an arched brow, Helena looped both arms around Emily's neck. "Well... you, of course, get to have me. However, I did not cook— I ordered something from a place I love; they just delivered it."

Emily smiled and mocked a frown. "Hmm... You didn't even make me cupcakes or something?" she joked with a grin.

Helena laughed, looking enamored. "No... though I am sure I could offer you something more decadent for dessert."

Heat claimed Emily's cheeks; she arched a brow. "Oh?"

Helena blushed intensely and smirked. "Not— *that* kind of decadent."

With a cool smile, Emily looped her arms around Helena's small waist. "What do you have in mind, then?"

Helena rolled her tongue on her lips. "Vielleicht etwas Schokolade..."

Emily bit her lip. "Are you teasing me, Helena?" She was so falling in love.

Helena shook her head and leaned into soft lips. "No."

Emily bore into deep brown eyes with a suggestive grin while gently caressing the small of Helena's back. "I have no idea what you just said, but I am so sure that was German..." she said.

Biting her beautiful lip, Helena's voice turned into the sweetest, most intimate murmur as she smiled. "Du hast Recht, Schätzchen..." she said, and turned with teasing eyes; Emily was left hanging by the edge of madness and want— she shook her head and followed Helena into the kitchen.

They had barely spent an hour together, and Emily only wanted to kiss her into oblivion —to build an entire world around her.

They ate in the kitchen and loved the casual intimacy; the simplicity meant so much more. No place or rules applied to their romance. It was what it was, free and untamed; it was incandescent and gorgeous.

Gazes lingered as they chewed their food, unable to stop themselves from grinning. Between suggestive glances and rushing blood, Emily found herself falling in love with Helena's words. The way she expanded simple subjects into interesting ones, Emily realized just how smart Helena was. She wondered what went on in that bright and stunning mind.

To Helena, Emily felt as effortless and exquisite as she had expressed before. She wanted to discover her and please her; she felt an intense desire to do anything needed to make her smile, because when Emily smiled, Helena was rendered speechless. When Emily smiled, Helena felt complete and satisfied with the joy that spilled from green eyes, simply because Emily made Helena feel like she was more than enough.

They had finished eating, but Emily's taste buds were still on a high, she had never indulged in food alike. With the earlier-promised chocolate treat in hand, Helena turned to look at *her*. "Okay, there is something I'd like to show you," she said.

Emily smiled. "All right."

With entwined hands, Helena guided her through the stunning mansion. Emily's eyes scanned the majestic living room; large windows gave them a priceless view of the bay while the crackling firewood burning in the fireplace made it all cozier. The tasteful chandelier was as perfect as every inch of space and the furniture in it.

"God, your home is just..." Emily said as green eyes

took everything in. "So freaking beautiful."

Helena smiled and squeezed her hand. "Thank you, though I believe you will like what I am about to show you even more." she teased, excited to share the breathtaking balcony view with Emily.

Helena opened a set of doors that revealed a spectacular sight, the dark blue San Francisco sky. Night so deliciously cold, Emily gasped, instantly enthralled. The high location of Helena's home allowed for a clearer and awe-striking angle of their brilliant city.

Emily took in a deep breath. —*It even smells green...* she thought.

Pleased, Helena caressed the back of her hand with a gentle thumb, feeling the cold metal of Emily's thin, almost seamless ring. She took every whispered word she had collected over the years, and allowed them to rush to her throat; Helena pointed to her left.

"See, over there is The Golden Gate, and over there... Do you see those lights in the distance?"

Emily nodded with gleaming eyes.

"I adore to watch them when it's still light and there's fog; the obstructing gray clouds smeared all over every single thing... It's like nothing is unreachable to its grasp, —it moves as it pleases, all with an air of mystery and complete understanding." she finished and turned to find Emily's gaze faithfully stuck on her.

Helena swallowed and grazed their entwined fingertips. With eyes closed, Emily felt it all; the breeze and how every pore on her skin came to life. Green eyes opened. "Are we really all alone here?" she asked. No preconceived notions or hidden plans, Emily simply wanted to spend hours drinking intimate time with Helena.

"Well, Maddison went out hours ago, but my brother is watching a movie —I believe he mentioned something about 'webflick and chill' Helena said with an innocent shrug.

Emily raised a brow and grinned; she scratched the tip of her nose. "Um... did he say he'd be doing that alone?"

"No, a girl joined him upstairs." she said matter of factly.

"Oh, Helena..." Emily said with an endeared chuckle.

"What? Do I have something on my face?" she asked with furrowed brows and touched her cheeks. After all, they had just eaten...

"No, you don't," Emily said, grinning. "You really have no idea, do you?"

Brown eyes stared back in wonder. "Of what?"

"Helena, honey... *'Webflick and chill'* is code for sex."

She deadpanned. "It is?" With confused brows, Helena searched the space. "But that makes absolutely no sense... Where is the correlation?"

Emily laughed and kissed her cheek.

Realization hit Helena like thunder. "So he is having sex upstairs?! Right now?"

Emily bit her lip and nodded with a wince. "I think so..."

"God, he is such a..." Helena chuckled. "I think Maddison was right... he is, in fact, a whore," she said, in amused disbelief.

Emily laughed, and Helena followed. She covered her face with both hands and shook her head once again, slowly falling prey to the infinite view. Organically... Helena looked up at the stars and smiled. She seemed enraptured.

"What do you see?" Emily asked, curious to know what went on inside her.

"The night is so clear," Helena didn't need to point this

time, her eyes said it all and green ones followed.

"Do you see those five stars?" She drew their shape as if touching the night with a fingertip.

"Yeah," Emily nodded, the corner of her lips turned up.

"That is the Cepheus constellation, and that beautiful star shining a little brighter is its pulsating supergiant, it varies in brightness every four-point-five days..."

Sweet dimples pierced Emily's cheeks as she turned to look at Helena, who thoroughly admired the sky. Silver light touched the waters, and Emily felt safer in the warmth of Helena's words. "It's the most celebrated star of the constellation, which is a shame... They are all uniquely beautiful." Helena said, and Mossy eyes glowed intensely.

"You get it..." Emily whispered and blinked softly.

Helena smiled, soulful eyes shone brightly, longingly so. "What's that?" she asked, almost inaudibly.

"I'm a transgender girl who loves soccer and curses like a sailor," Emily said, gently burning Helena with her gaze. She smirked. "I don't wear skirts or dresses, but I'm expected to by others like me. I— have been judged by people who don't get it and also by people who *should* get it." Emily shook her head, green eyes reddened slightly. Was it the wind? Or perhaps the wounding feelings? Maybe the adjacency of pain and relief —pain from old scars, and relief from this new view so peaceful, so vibrant and beautiful. The wind...

Emily inhaled a batch of cool air. "All my life I've been told things ranging from: why become a girl if you're gonna like girls, anyway? —To you're not girly enough." A watery chuckle claimed her lips. "People telling me that there's only one way to be something —I mean, we tear ourselves apart, trying to be heard and wanting to be seen, respected... accepted for who we feel we are and who we want to be, but..." Emily swallowed her tears, and Helena took her hands, she continued to listen. "When something doesn't fit the norm, whatever it is... no matter what circle —it gets trashed." Emily said.

Helena nodded, allowing fresh air into her lungs.

"Anxiety versus society," she said.

"Exactly that... you get it."

The pleasant conversation extended until the silver moon was at its highest and the cold invaded their bones.

***

Helena guided Emily to the intimate warmth of her bedroom. Words had been replaced with gripping gazes and nervous excitement. The soft click of the door closing made Emily swallow hard. She knew this thing with Helena was ardent and beautiful.

The light in her room was dim and warm, the gleam in her gaze so bright. Her scent still clinging to the air like a memory... Like the loneliness in her eyes. Helena inched closer. Her breath was warm and wet against Emily's neck, like a silent whisper. Emily closed her eyes. She moved her head to the side and let go if only for a second, until that familiar tingle invaded her stomach and rushed lower.

"Helena... I..." Emily was nervous. They were alone in her room —they wanted each other shamelessly, and Helena was so, so gently cornering her against the wall. Lips moving on her neck so well, Emily could have sworn she had been doing it for years. Helena's tongue flicked the skin there, and Emily weakened with a shudder.

"Helena... I should go."

Their gazes met, and at that moment Emily saw Helena was no expert, the profound melancholy in dark eyes gave her away. Temptation was raw and new —it was beautiful.

Smiles faded and Helena caressed her cheek softly. "Please stay..."

Emily's heart pounded, her throat went dry. "I... I don't know if I should, I mean, I..." God, she wanted to stay. She wanted to hold Helena in her arms and kiss her; she wanted to feel her, but that insecure part was terrified of scaring her away.

"I would love to sleep next to you tonight... Please?" Gleaming brown pleaded.

—*Damn,* those eyes, those endless eyes. Emily nodded softly. "Okay..."

A brief smile broke from Helena's lips, a smile so grateful and complex. It moved something inside Emily.

"Do you mind if I change?" Helena asked.

"No, not at all."

With a soft kiss on Emily's lips, Helena walked to her closet. After opening the stylish doors, Emily watched her get lost in the large space inside.

—*Shit.* Emily thought. —*Now what?* The idea of sex flashed through her mind; she wanted Helena so much it hurt. Emily shook the thoughts away while wiping two sweaty palms on her jeans; she didn't know what she was doing. She had never gone that far before. She had never slept in a girl's bed before, but she wanted so much with **her**.

Helena walked out in silk pajamas. The garment was dark purple and alluringly short. Emily swallowed a lump —such a perfect view of those enticing, tanned legs. Suddenly aware of her sex and the contact it made with her jeans, the blood in Emily's veins felt like fire.

Helena smiled and handed her a pair of pajamas. Emily simply stood there.

"Em…" Helena said, and chuckled sweetly. "Are you still with me?"

Emily nodded and cleared her throat. Helena locked the door and offered the clothing she had tried to hand her before. "I thought you'd like to change as well," she suggested.

A blushing Emily bowed her head. Helena entwined their fingers while piercing her with unguarded eyes. "Are you okay?"

Emily nodded again and smiled. "Yeah, yeah… I am. I um… it's okay —I can just wear my top and jeans." she said, and shrugged off her leather jacket, revealing softly toned arms and shoulders for the first time.

Helena swallowed hard at the sight, and her nostrils flared slightly. She looked into green eyes again. "Emily, sleeping in your jeans would be far too constricting, unless you don't feel… comfortable with me —I would completely understand—" She looked down.

"No, I do… I mean… I usually sleep in my underwear —is that okay?" Emily asked and found her gaze.

Helena smiled. "Of course… Just make yourself comfortable, whatever feels right to you." she finished honestly, and Emily nodded.

She unbuttoned her jeans and felt a wisp of air as Helena walked away. Mild darkness flooded the room; only a dim, warm glow seeped from her lamp.

Helena snuck under the thick, white covers, and Emily sat on the other side.

"Are you all right?" Helena asked while darkly manicured fingers reached for pale ones.

"Are you sure this isn't gonna feel... weird to you?" Emily responded with a question of her own, almost apologetically, and Helena's heart shrunk.

"Em, of course not... I promise."

Their eyes met. No smiles.

Helena stared with a kind of seriousness that stole the air from Emily's lungs, making the cotton underwear seem like not enough. She too found shelter under the covers stealthily.

Green eyes met brown ones, and Helena leaned in. "Can I kiss you?" Feather-like breaths so close.

"Yeah... of course," Emily muttered softly.

Supple lips parted, and Emily felt like her entire being was breaking in two —this was no joke. She shuddered at the grace of fingertips burning her skin. Helena pulled away with smoldering dark eyes, they stared with a softness and secrecy that died in the source of their intensity. Glassy and vulnerable... so affected. Emily swallowed a knot.

"Whatever you want, Em," Helena whispered.

Restraint thrown out the window, Emily kissed her again. Helena opened her mouth and moaned at the warm feel of their tongues clashing —at Emily's possessiveness. Hands pressed against the mattress, Emily pulled away gently, blonde locks of hair shielded their intimacy. She stared at Helena and wondered what thoughts traversed her mind.

Insecurities roamed Emily's system like chemicals that tainted; her arousal's substance was definite between her thighs... It was growing, and she didn't want to throw her off. But Helena was different, Helena was special and rare; the infinite stars in her gaze kissed it all away.

Brown eyes opened and found Emily staring at her with absolute want. With such intense curiosity and innocence. "Come closer," Helena said, in a ragged whisper. "Please... let me feel you," she pleaded, and Emily nodded.

Emily blinked and took a deep breath. Helena saw hesitation and fear. "Only if you feel okay about it, of course... We don't have to do anything you don't want." She brushed blonde strands of hair and tucked them behind her ear.

Emily had everything she wanted right there, pleading just to let her in. For the first time in her life, Emily *wanted* to let someone in. The feeling at the base of her stomach never so real, things never looked this vivid, life never smelled like this, like them —the heat between her legs never this ready. Emily's hands sneaked under the silky garment and felt her soft abdomen for the first time, shivering under her touch.

Helena closed her eyes... the way her mouth opened... Emily watched every second of the display with furrowed brows while her insides burned and turned on her. "Oh, my God..." Emily's voice broke.

Helena never looked more beautiful. Green eyes observed the way her body trembled and each pore rose, Emily felt it with her fingertips and couldn't help herself anymore. She kissed Helena hard and settled between her thighs so warm.

"Oh, God," Helena whispered as she felt Emily's clothed arousal against hers. With a heaving chest, she opened tanned legs a little wider. She looked up and lost the will to remember the relationship that existed between time and space —Helena had never felt this double-ended demand burn her so intensely. This feeling did not compare to those nights alone with herself; it felt so real, it felt like so much more. She pushed her hips upward, and Emily squeezed her eyes shut.

"Helena..." she moaned and tightly gripped on the sheets. Lean arms on either side of the brunette's head, knuckles on the mattress, Emily began to move her hips grinding herself against *her*. She couldn't believe it.

Helena drowned in shivers as she erotically met Emily's suggestive closeness. Emily allowed herself to fall onto Helena and kissed her hard, just as hard as she had begun to move, leaving no space for air or oxygen between their sexes.

Helena's hands traveled under her lover's soft, white top and ran her fingers down pale skin while the other claimed a round, delicious breast. "Emily..." she moaned hotly. "God..."

The pressure Emily's hard arousal gave Helena was infinitely new and insatiable. Her orgasm began to form deep inside the middle of her body, and she started to move more frantically against Emily's clothed, vulnerable flesh —Helena could almost define the feel of its shape; its size... Oh, the desperation...

They continued to grind against one another desperately, and cheeks grew hot with fever. Emily whimpered as Helena's heat and purchase made her feel inches away from madness —she moaned and quickened her pace; they rocked closer and faster while romancing Helena's sweet nerve.

Helena's jaw fell open, and Emily tried to find those perfect brown eyes. That painfully delicious ache between her legs consumed her. "Oh, Helena..." she panted with clammy cheeks as her wish was granted. Helena's eyes opened, and she looked deeply into them, allowing herself to fall.

"Emily... please..." Helena moaned and pleaded, clenching her jaw while burying the back of her head on the soft pillow and holding on tightly to the sheets. To Emily's white top.

Green gaze never faltered as Helena's glazed with tears that suddenly made her feel a bit too silly and exposed. She rolled them away, and Emily continued to move breathlessly against her. "Look at me," Emily whispered, as the peak started to claim her.

Helena's profound eyes met gleaming ones. Emily leaned down to kiss her; their movements made the contact breathy and warm... messy.

Helena arched her body and shuddered as her lover began to unload herself on the white cotton separating their heat. Emily's small sounds were the ones that brought her over the edge. She whimpered into the shaky kiss, and they broke apart gently; their spent mouths scraped for air —a tear ran down Helena's temple.

They heaved, lips still touching, and Emily didn't dare to move. The last thing she wanted was to make Helena feel exposed. She leaned into her warm neck and brushed soft kisses on it, all the while feeling Helena's sweet breath and tasting the invaluable, tasting salty tears. She gently traced her lips and kissed them.

Helena remained quiet, invested in her willingness to let the other girl see her completely bare. Emily dared to look into brown eyes again, and Helena blinked.

Emily smiled softly. "*You*... are the exquisite one, Helena..." She allowed her body to fall next to Helena's and stared at her for hours until they fell asleep. Until they lost consciousness and drifted away to another place, still anchored to this reality together with the promise of waking up in each other's arms for the first time in their lives. *This* was so much more than enough.

6

HELENA

ETURNING TO CONSCIOUSNESS WAS seamless; Emily's eyes fluttered open with the gentleness of the soft fragrance luring her in. Silence was peaceful, just as the warmth enveloping her side, and *that* delicious smell. Green eyes finally saw blonde and silky black hair smeared on the white pillow they shared. Orange blossom, sweet vanilla, and sandalwood. The scent of Helena's shampoo was non-threatening, just like the rise and fall of her chest.

Emily watched her sleep in silence, she didn't dare move and disturb her. It seemed like possibly creating a ripple on untouched waters —it would be a shame to muddle the image of the sunrise reflected on its calm surface.

She could only hear her breathe. She was still there.

—*She's with me.*

When you stare at a faceless Juliet, all you desire is to listen to your instinct and brush the locks away from her face. You want to get lost in her —admire the perfect work of life's hand on her features unconquered by its absence. Emily would not think of that now. *Not yet.*

She cursed herself in advance for moving a careful hand forward —the sight of a rippling sun could be tolerated if it meant touching her.

Ingenuous green eyes, such young and beautiful eyes followed her fingertips. Flushed lips curled up as daring digits removed strands of dark hair to the side —and oh... the love. The gentle and hushed gleam that crossed mossy green was wondrous, and it was mute.

The flush of Helena's skin was life-giving. She was there, and even though they had not said it, she was already so hers. Emily hoped so dearly Helena was hers.

Brushing her almost ghostly fingertips on Helena's lips; she looked like a girl and also a beautiful woman, each curve of her mouth —the lines they traced on her face in a way that was sensual and enticing. *This* was life's work; this was the time she so badly cursed for being so short. This was time, giving her everything and threatening to claim her. —*No...* She wouldn't think of this. —*Not now.*

Emily was so enthralled with those lips that she missed brown eyes wake and stare at her.

An olive-toned hand brushed Emily's face, and that did the trick. They smiled.

"Hey..." Emily said.

Helena responded softly, "Hey..." She swept strands of blonde hair away from Emily's cheek with care.

Such gleaming eyes and juvenile fervor in their smiles, nothing rawer and closer to truth than the smile of curious and honest souls. This time it had been their turn. They felt lucky.

"Are you okay?" Emily asked.

"I am." Helena continued to look at her like *that*. With love. Helena knew she loved her already, even though it hadn't been said. "Are you?"

Emily's heartstrings pulled hard at her; knowing Helena's hands had touched her skin when it was on fire; that she had moved so suggestively between her thighs, feeling the fever of her divide —Emily never reached through undiscovered depth, but she had so enticingly stroked herself against the wall of Helena's lace-covered axis until she saw stars, until she tasted the warmth breaking from Helena's virtue and out her lips.

Emily blushed. "Yeah…"

Helena gave her a gentle smile, but Emily saw something else in her eyes, a hesitation that scared her frozen as she heard her speak again.

"I'm sorry… I—" Helena said, and averted her eyes.

Emily swallowed dry. She waited for Helena to say something.

Their gazes met. "You're regretting it…" Emily whispered.

Brown eyes widened. "Oh, God, Em, no— of course not."

Emily seemed sad and expecting… she waited for Helena to make herself clear. She hoped.

Helena entwined their fingers and sat, pulling her up, facing her with conviction. "I have absolutely no regrets." Helena smiled. "Emily… Mein Schatz," she said just as sweetly.

Emily looked down. "Are you sure?"

Helena placed two fingers under her chin and searched her eyes. "Emily, listen to me… I swear to you, I don't regret anything we've shared since the day we met." Helena reassured with raw conviction.

Emily bit her lip as they curled up slightly. Hopeful still. "Really?"

"Yes. Really…" Helena said, endeared. "I apologized because, on the contrary, I feel maybe I pushed you and convinced you to stay even though you seemed unsure — maybe I rushed and moved too fast." she said apologetically.

"Oh no, Helena… I…" Emily said, and chuckled incredulously; she felt so lucky. "I wasn't unsure of staying with you. I was nervous shitless, yeah… but —I wanted to stay with you, too," She nodded, looking into suddenly insecure brown eyes. "I wanted that, too." she said.

Helena smiled and blinked, reminding herself that she was the luckiest girl on the planet for having Emily. She appreciated each second they had, her Emily meant so much already. "I…" Helena grew flushed. "I just, you know… I wanted to kiss you and hold you, please don't think I planned what happened, I promise I didn't…"

Emily placed a finger on her insanely beautiful lips. "Shh… It's okay, I know you didn't, I never thought you had."

Appreciative of the fact that Emily was trying to save her from embarrassment, Helena sighed, but had more to say, after all, Helena always spoke with the honesty many lacked. She took Emily's hand from her lips and laced their fingers. "No, please let me say this."

"Okay."

"Last night I…" Helena blushed and looked down, but found courage. "When I'm with you, Emily… I feel…" She sighed, "I've never experienced desire with such intensity before." Helena confessed, looking simpler than ever, simple in the most complicated way.

"I feel that too…" Emily said.

Helena continued, "I mean, I have never —*been* with anyone sexually."

Emily swallowed as her body reacted to flashes of the night before. Chocolate eyes unstained and beautiful; they were honest.

Emily's face fell. "I've never had sex with anyone either... but—"

Helena saw regret in her eyes. She had never expected anything from Emily, but she couldn't help it, the weight of her heart sunk into her stomach.

"I..." Emily looked at her hands entwined with Helena's and shrugged. "I did let someone touch me once... I... touched her..." she confessed.

At that moment envy reached Helena's eyes without mercy. She was jealous. Sadness bled down her throat as she bit the inside of her cheek and looked down.

Emily's breathing quickened. "I regret it every day—" she said in a rush.

Helena looked up, still wounded like a wolf, but seeming more like her understanding and open self; she pushed a smile. "You don't have to say that to make me feel better, Emily —it's okay. I don't know why I—" She shook her head, suddenly feeling a bit stupid. "There's nothing wrong with what you did before."

Emily tasted bitter and bit her lip. "Yes, there is... I didn't... It just didn't feel right." Emily hesitated at the memory and everything that came from it. "After we did that, she wanted— more and I—" she said, and chuckled at herself, feeling relieved. "I didn't."

With furrowed brows, Helena tried to understand. "You didn't?"

Emily shook her head, still chewing on her lip. "I didn't."

"So, what happened after that?" Helena was curious; possession roamed through her system.

"She told everyone on campus about me... It was childish and ridiculous." Emily admitted and looked into

Helena's eyes.

"Em..." Brows knitted together and Helena squeezed Emily's hand tighter. "I am so sorry she did that to you, that's horrible." she said.

A peaceful smile found Emily's lips. She had tried to put the past year in the back of her mind, and she had succeeded. It had been hell, but she had finally found peace. "I don't care about people knowing, but —I felt so exposed and betrayed... I thought I could trust her."

Helena could almost taste Emily's emotions; she had to say something. "What she did was wrong, Em, that truth wasn't hers to tell."

Green eyes reddened, and Emily smiled while studying *her*. It felt good to have her. It felt good to love her —already. She was so ready. So grateful.

And when you have something you cherish, it becomes this decadent exploration of something so divine it seems brief. It is intense and gorgeous, like leaving the breath in your lungs at awe's mercy.

"Thank you." Emily managed.

"What for?"

"For being you and for being here— still." she said, and lowered her eyes.

Helena leaned in and brushed her cheek on Emily's blushed one. She closed her eyes and moved her lips to kiss it, savoring Emily's warmth. Her scent.

"When the word —*time*... became real to me..." Helena murmured, eyes still closed next to Emily's skin. "I began to realize that most people's priorities lie in the wrong place, including my own." Tanned fingers grazed Emily's arm; electricity burned her skin. "Last night you showed me a part of myself I didn't know existed… and it felt beautiful." Helena admitted.

Emily smiled against dark hair while caressing her back gently.

Helena broke away and sought her focus, "I loved feeling every part of you…" she confessed. The ache on her face made Emily want Helena naked in her arms.

Emily swallowed hard and moved into the safety of Helena's neck. She nuzzled the skin there like a promise, and fingertips found a soft, olive-toned thigh. Hands ventured under her silky gown.

With a shaking breath, Helena's head fell back, exposing her neck to wanton green eyes. The moment was like oxygen, perfect in its rawness, but unfortunately broken by the muffled sounds of a female voice echoing in the hallway outside Helena's room.

They gasped, breaths caught in their throats and widened eyes met.

"It's my mother," Helena whispered, and Emily's eyes grew even wider, they were in a pretty compromising half-naked position.

"Shit!" Emily scrambled from the bed and desperately grabbed her jeans and bra loosely scattered on the hardwood floor.

Still sitting on the bed, blushing and heaving, Helena thought quickly. "Go to my bathroom and get dressed there."

Emily disappeared after a nod.

Knock. Knock.

"Helena, dear…" Came from the other side.
She rushed off the bed and opened the 'locked' door.
Katherine smiled. "Helena…"

Looking disheveled, she smiled, and Katherine worried. "Are you feeling okay? Is your heart all right?"

"I am fine... I was... just—" Helena tucked a few strands of messy hair behind her ear. "Talking to Emily," she said, and the girl slowly walked out of the bathroom fully dressed.

A beautifully dimpled and sheepish smile... "Hi,"

Katherine's ease washed with a frown. She wasn't mad. However, in her surprise, she took the time to scan the tall, gorgeous blonde. Those jeans and flimsy top paraded her inviting body, mocking Katherine in the process.

Seconds passed, and she snapped out of her trance. "Hello," Katherine said with a forced smile.

"Emily, this is my mother, Katherine... Mother, this is Emily." Helena introduced them, still wearing her skimpy silk pajamas.

Katherine never stopped smiling; she felt that perhaps holding the sentiment in place was the only way to get through this. —*My baby is not having sex, is she?*

Emily walked closer, and Katherine saw just how beautiful she was; the girl had an edge to her, a charmingly silent presence that was strong and incredibly captivating. —*Fantastic*, Katherine thought, if her daughter wasn't already doing what she dreaded, she soon would be.

Smile pushed frozen in place, Katherine wanted to cry and laugh, or maybe scream? Warm green eyes became more real as Emily leaned in and offered her hand.

"It's a pleasure to finally meet you, Mrs. Millan," Emily studied Helena's mother; she was beautiful. Skin, white like porcelain, brown hair and hazel eyes. The tiny mole Helena had right above her top lip was there, too. So much class and elegance, it was intimidating.

Katherine shook her hand. "Emily, the pleasure is all

123

mine, love," She suddenly remembered what Maddison had said the morning prior at the breakfast table, **'Helena's girlfriend has a penis!'**

"So, Emily is... your girlfriend, Helena?" Katherine asked her daughter.

Emily fidgeted; this woman had *a presence*. Helena didn't know what to say; they hadn't agreed on titles, but given what had happened between them and how they felt... "Mother," she warned.

Emily cleared her throat. "Yes, ma'am, we are together." she dared, hoping Helena didn't think it was out of line.

"We are." Helena repeated, and their eyes met silently.

Emily's heart beat back to life, a new kind of life. She smiled.

Katherine nodded. "Very well, then we should have the talk." A perfect brow arched. "I know you two are of age and I may safely assume you will be having sex."

Emily felt oxygen fail her and turned to Helena.

Oh, Katherine was blunt.

Helena's jaw fell— "Mother, please don't do this!" she managed sternly with wide eyes of her own.

"Helena, I am not judging you girls or telling you to do otherwise. However, if this is the case, I need you two to be careful, and please use protection." Katherine turned to a bright red Emily.

She wanted to run as fast as she could, but leaving Helena alone with this wasn't an option.

Emily's mouth opened and closed as she dissected that last request —*But wait. Does Helena's mom know?*

Katherine didn't know and wasn't sure of anything, though she had the sharp instincts of a physician.

"Mother… I believe we have a pending conversation. A pending *private* conversation."

Katherine sighed. "All right," She nodded politely, "Emily." With a nervous smile, Emily nodded as well.

Katherine left, and Helena closed the door.

Green eyes widened and desperately searched for warm brown ones. "Oh, my God —does she know?!" Emily asked.

"She doesn't —she does… Maybe—" Helena huffed and rolled her eyes. "I don't exactly know what she is thinking… Maddison told her my girlfriend has a penis yesterday morning during a tantrum."

Emily's skin turned vermilion, she ran pale hands over her long blonde tresses and paced back and forth. "Oh, my God." She stopped and looked at Helena with round eyes. "Of course she knows, she said we needed to use protection!"

"Emily, I haven't talked to her. However, both my parents are very open-minded individuals… they see life in a scientific way —they won't judge you." Helena placed a calming hand on her girlfriend's arm. "Are you okay?" she asked, genuinely concerned.

Emily nodded. "I should go, though," she told her lover, hoping she wouldn't misunderstand.

Helena smiled and nodded. "All right… May I see you later?"

Emily smiled. "Yeah… Call me." She leaned in, pecked Helena's lips, and left.

***

Emily walked into her parent's home. Something smelled so good that it made her mouth water and her stomach growl.

"Emily, honey, is that you?" Maureen's voice rang from

the kitchen.

"Yes," Emily casually answered as she walked towards her mother.

Green eyes brightened as Maureen caught sight of her daughter. She smiled. "Good afternoon, sweetheart. Thank you for coming."

"Sure, Mom, so what's the big surprise?" Emily grabbed a muffin from the table and took a shameless, hearty bite. She was starving.

"You're going to spoil your appetite; please put that down, we are having—" Maureen grinned suggestively. "As I said, a very special dinner tonight... —By the way, how's Helena?" She wiggled her brows.

Amused, Emily smirked. "Me, spoil my appetite? Nice one, Mom," She devoured another chunk of the delicious muffin and laughed lightly. "And... Helena's fine." She blushed and quickly changed the subject. "So... special dinner, huh? What's the occasion?" she asked, eyeing over the simmering pot. "Bangers and mash, *yum*." Emily was siked, no one indulged in their Irish roots more than she did.

"Me, of course." the familiar male voice came from behind; green eyes darted as she turned and saw her brother Patrick's confident grin. Arms opened in mid-air.

"Patrick! You're home!" They were the ones with the tighter bond; Emily crashed her body against his and engulfed him in a brief but meaningful hug.

***

Santiago Millan sat in his office, reading the paper as his wife walked in and startled him. The man looked up; his brown eyes followed Katherine until she sat across from him. She seemed strangely agitated.

He examined her over his reading glasses. "Something wrong?" Santiago asked, calmed and collected as always.

Katherine inhaled deeply. "Helena just told me she is dating a transgender girl." she announced.

Santiago put down the paper and focused on his wife. "Are you sure?"

She frowned, annoyed at his silly question. "*Yes,* I am sure, Santiago." She fidgeted. Katherine wasn't one to fidget. Ever.

"Well, just a few days ago you told me Helena was exploring her sexual identity, is this the same girl?" Santiago questioned.

"Yes, I met her today." Katherine said as she continued to play with her wedding band nervously.

The man was taken aback by his wife's unusual demeanor. "Well… How was she?" Santiago took it well.

Katherine contemplated. "She seems… lovely, actually."

"Then what has you so worked up? You are not one to judge others, is she contemporaneous with Helena? I mean, their age—"

Katherine nodded. "Yes, she is, and I am not judging her, but Santiago, I think they are having sex and… and she… Well, she has a penis." she said with furrowed brows.

"Of course she has one, darling…" he said as his mind suddenly caught up with the other part of Katherine's statement. "Wait— is Helena having sex? She's just a girl," Santiago asked, still composed, but not necessarily content with that idea.

Katherine frowned and raised a brow. "Santiago, have you seen your daughter? She does not look her age, and she is not a child, she is an adult... a young woman —a very smart one, and God knows she has more maturity than Caleb and Maddison put together." Katherine continued to play with her ring restlessly.

"I know she is, and that should count for something, that should be a good enough reason for her to make the right decision, and wait until she's older." Santiago could only hope.

"Are you listening to yourself? Helena has a deteriorating heart condition, Santiago; she won't wait for death to start living her life! And she's dating a gorgeous blonde young woman with a penis!" Katherine's eyes wandered everywhere.

"What are you so afraid of, Katherine? Helena knows all about safe sex if it came to that." He furrowed his brows. Something was off about his wife's behavior. There was no doubt.

"Santiago! A young woman with a penis is hovering around your very grown-looking daughter!"

"Darling... What is the real issue for you?" he softened, suddenly concerned.

Katherine's eyes reddened, and she sniffled the stinging in them away, though this was her husband, there was no need to hold back. "She's just so young..." The woman finally allowed her tears to fall. Katherine never cried.

Santiago frowned, taken by the same feeling that haunted his wife. For Katherine, the word sex was a metaphor for death. This conversation wasn't about their smart and responsible daughter having sex, Emily's member, or her differences. This was Katherine finally having a trigger that allowed her to feel her fears openly. She had remained strong thus far. This was her first time voicing that she was afraid of losing her Helena. This was Katherine giving

Helena's condition a fighting chance at winning and taking her away from them forever. It seemed Helena had begun to live her days fully.

Santiago stood from the chair and moved to hold his wife; he held her and allowed her to cry.

***

The evening air was fresh. Emily and Patrick had been playing soccer for the best part of thirty minutes outside their home when the siblings decided to take a break. Patrick went inside for some water.

Emily took a moment to let her head roll on her shoulders and catch her breath. Despite the dew of sweat on beautiful skin, her edge and enticing charm went beyond her athletic and soft anatomy. Her body was still glowing with the after-effects of adrenaline. It felt good.

A beaming Helena shut the door of her sleek car and eyed the Knight home with butterflies in her stomach. Brown eyes caught sight of Emily and walked to her with ease; so ready to kiss those lips again.

She took her breath away, of *that,* Helena was certain.

Emily looked up and found **her** only steps away. She smiled brightly. "Helena,"

Ending the distance between them, Helena smiled back and leaned in for that meeting of lips.

Emily welcomed her with hesitation. "Baby, I'm all gross." She regretted the space between them instantly.

After catching that genuine gleam in green eyes, Helena felt wanted. She felt like part of something beautiful, their intimacy. She smiled and looped her arms around Emily's neck. "I don't care about that; it doesn't bother me." She leaned in for another brief kiss.

Unaware of the two guys approaching them, Emily grinned at her girlfriend and relished the feeling of Helena's warmth —the charming glow in green eyes so captivating.

"HEY! Double pants!" The raspy brash in his voice made their enamored smiles fade instantly. Helena's skin crawled; it was as if somehow her senses had stung her body into full alert. She turned her head in the direction of the obvious offense.

Emily's nostrils flared; she clenched her jaw. It was another voice she *did* recognize, belonging to one of her casual neighborhood bullies. She turned with an unimpressed sigh, immediately facing him and intentionally shielding Helena behind her.

Helena, of course, didn't stand for that. Sensing the theme of the encounter, she bravely took Emily's side.

"I'm not in the mood, Jake." Emily said, face devoid of emotion, though her insides churned with the usual dull belly ache and desire to punch him into silence. The other guy chuckled with derision in his timbre, such mocking demeanor —his desire to lessen, so disturbingly evident.

"You know, you look so fucking ugly playing soccer, I mean, make up your mind, dude,"

—*Ugh.* Helena wanted to vomit.

Emily smirked. "Oh, really? That's so original, Jake. I bet you burned the whole one neuron you have in your head to come up with that."

Jake fake-laughed the soreness off while his buddy punched his arm casually. "It's owning you, man!" Another string of incessant laughter came out of him.

Helena faced forward challengingly. Awed and offended. "Excuse me, did you just refer to her as 'It'?"

"Don't talk to these idiots, Helena, it's not worth it, they are what they talk —trash." Emily said.

"Mmm… Helena," Jake scanned the girl up and down. "Hot name, hot girl. What are you doing with this nasty freak? —Yeah, honey, it's an 'It' I mean, you do know this isn't a girl, right? I went to kindergarten with this… Thing."

Fearless, Emily rushed forward with a tightened jaw and fire in her eyes. "You fucking asshole—" she hissed through gritted teeth ready to jump on him, but Helena held her back.

"Em, don't. You are right. They are not worth it." Brown eyes glared at the two bullies. The argument's vibration was escalating like boiling water, and in the midst of such unfair cruelty, her insides broke for Emily. —*Has she had to endure this all her life?*

They were relentless and so abrasive. Jake mocked a pout and directed his attack towards Helena. "Aw, did I offend you, too? —Oh, dude, wait—" He laughed and snickered, inching towards his friend. "Maybe she's a tranny, too!" They broke in loud, juddering laughter.

The bubbling anger in Emily's veins fueled with their satisfaction. She tightened her fists and could have sworn the adrenaline rushing through her body felt like gasoline. Heat crept up to her face, and she bit tighter; her teeth almost hurting, her brain remembering every crushing memory, her heart swelled with emotion green eyes couldn't hide. Emotion that had branded and taunted her. Emotions… feelings like self-loathing and absolute, undiluted pain. Her hands trembled as she stamped them on his chest and tightly yanked his cotton T-shirt. "I'm gonna break your dirty mouth, you piece of shit!" she hissed between gritted teeth and burned holes right through him.

His mocking gesture soon twisted and turned; it mirrored Emily's anger. His face flushed and his insides overflowed with a corrosive growl that crawled from his chest and out his throat. Consuming frustration propelled him forward as he shoved her back with force. "ArggAAAHHH!! DON'T FUCKING TOUCH ME! YOU FUCKING FAG!!!" The thunderous, grave shout that came out of his mouth was as hateful and resisting as his darkened eyes.

Emily's back crashed into a heaving Helena. "Em," she mumbled, her voice drenched in fear. Emily's eyes were as dark and reddened as her shame. She couldn't believe Helena had been caught in the middle of this because of her.

She launched herself forward and onto him, only to be halted by a solid fist against the right side of her face. "Ungh!" Her lithe body ricocheted the hard set of knuckles that tore her lip open and sent her straight to the ground.

Helena's eyes filled with absolute panic, breathing completely out of control; her insides trembled. "Emily!!!" She rushed to the concrete in aid of her injured lover with tears cascading from emotional brown. The sight of Emily's tearful green eyes juxtaposed to the fresh blood oozing from her lip and stains over her white top was heartbreaking. Blonde tendrils of hair fairly shielded the anger and pain in them.

Called outside by Helena's scream, Patrick slammed the front door and caught sight of the two idiots and both girls on the ground. He saw red.

"EMILY!!!!" he bellowed and rushed to their side with burning feet while two sets of scared eyes looked up, not feeling so strong anymore.

"Shit! It's her brother! —Go, go, go!!!" The sound of their sneakers scraping against the pavement was loud. They shot off and sprinted away. The two guys ran as fast as they could, but Patrick agilely rushed right after them.

"Patrick, NO!!!" Emily shouted and stood from the ground. The last thing she wanted was her brother in jail for breaking their stupid faces in two.

Patrick glanced over his shoulder, and all he could see behind was his little sister. No matter how grown or how old, Emily would always be his only baby sister. He found a spec of reason in a sea of unapologetic vexation but turned to the figures getting further away as he slowed his step.

"YOU BETTER RUN MOTHERFUCKERS!!!" Patrick shouted at the cowardly bullies with popping veins on his flustered face. They soon got lost at the turn of a block.

He rushed to Helena and Emily. "Hey, Em, are you okay?" Patrick worriedly searched her body and face with a heaving chest.

Emily nodded and brought a pale hand to her busted lip. "Yeah, I'm all right." she said.

Helena's eyes were still flooded with tears. She sniffled and sought Emily's face, cupping a hand on her cheek. "Oh, Em, my sweetheart," She caressed her gently. "He cut your lip open," Helena said, needing to ease her lover's pain. "You need to ice it immediately, or it will swell more than it already is."

Emily winced and looked at her hand; blood ran down pale skin. She growled. "Ah! This hurts! Fuck!" she said, still holding her own bravely.

"Shit, I'm so sorry, Em —who were they? I swear I'm gonna go find them and kick their asses all the way to fucking jail." Patrick hissed between gritted teeth with fervent irritation.

Emily shook her head. She knew he would, only the one going to jail would be him for beating them blue. "I don't know... I didn't recognize them." she lied, and soaked brown eyes went from him to her. Helena inhaled her truths back inside. She chose to respect her lover's reasons for keeping this from him.

Emily wiped away Helena's tears and ran the back of her free hand on her busted lip —she wiped the crimson liquid away. "I'm okay, don't worry... You're going to ruin your clothes, Lena,"

All heads turned as Maureen walked out with a frown. "Emily, honey. What happened?!" She rushed to her daughter, face dripping with concern.

Before anyone said anything, Emily found her voice. "Nothing, Mom, it was just an accident. I'm fine... I just busted my lip while playing soccer with Patrick." she said, still holding a hand over her open wound.

Maureen noticed Helena's presence and smiled. "Helena, hi... How are you, sweetheart?" This wasn't the first time Emily played rough with her siblings. Maureen was a pro at patching them up. The woman was so used to it that she didn't even question the lame explanation.

Helena smiled back. "I'm well, Professor Shepherd, thank you for asking." she stalled, feeling ambushed by Maureen's presence.

"Come on, let's go inside, get some ice on that —and Helena, thank you so much for accepting our dinner invitation." Maureen said delightedly.

Helena smiled and looked at Emily. She was still covering her lips with a blood-soaked hand but smiled and winked.

"Oh, it was my pleasure, of course, thank you." she finished, their longing gazes never breaking.

Maureen was happy, she smiled to herself and walked in as the girls followed; Helena placed a protective and caring hand on Emily's back as they entered the Knight home.

7

SAY ANYTHING

THE AIR INSIDE THE Knight's home encompassed something akin to ease and safety; it felt like happiness and safety, aside from the horrible incident they had just endured.

They were in Emily's bedroom. Helena sat on the bed and studied her girlfriend from a short distance while she peeled off the bloody top. Warm eyes grew darker as she took in Emily's beautiful form. Black bra and jeans that clung to her lithe curves, her soft abdomen; breathing in and out. This beautiful human had blinded Helena in the most unforgettable ways, and now, here she was, getting a bitter taste of what Emily had endured her entire life.

Helena stood from the bed and ghostly laced their fingers. "Here, you should sit," she suggested, and turned to find what was needed from the first aid kit next to them.

Emily sat, and green eyes turned up while a concentrated Helena stood between her legs.

Nothing compared to having Helena's entire focus. She gently cleansed Emily's lip with a wet piece of gauze.

"Em, why didn't you—"

"Shhh…" Emily was gentle. She grinned while glistening eyes focused on everything in front of her. The sterile cotton felt cold on her cut lip; the contrast in color with the crimson smeared on it was definite, but Helena's hand on her jaw was soft. She tended to the wound with care; it was captivating.

Brown eyes caught appreciative green shamelessly traveling along her features. Helena blushed and bore into them, curious and disarming —the air between them so thick.

"Does it still hurt?" Helena asked, and Emily shook her head.

"No." she murmured.

Helena's pulse quickened. Emily always made her heart pound, reminding her that it was still beating strong; that she was so very alive. Overcome by her body's commands, she held back, and insecurity flashed her smoldering gaze.

Emily observed her. She bowed her head briefly and then gave Helena a full view of those amazing mossy eyes. They seemed sad and happy —they were raw and open like never before. "I will tell my dad, but not today— I don't wanna mess up my mom's time with my brother, she's pretty excited to have him home, you know?"

So many emotions ambushed Helena, but the loudest one was genuine empathy. She caressed Emily's cheek with the back of her fingers. "Please promise me you will… They can't get away with this, Em, they will just do it again— to you or someone else." Worry etched her face.

Endeared, Emily wished she could show Helena how intensely her heart burned just for her. She smiled softly and brushed strands of dark hair away. "I promise." she murmured with a faint smile.

Pale hands lodged on Helena's hips, and Emily looked up faithfully, never ever taking this girl for granted. "You're so good to me… so beautiful," Emily murmured.

Helena closed her eyes while Emily's touch ran up her sides, gently pulling her down. Palms collided with the mattress and over each side of Emily's head. Their shimmering gazes on each other's lips —only inches away.

With her back now on the bed, Emily brushed her parted lips on a warm neck; pale hands ran up enticing olive-toned thighs —under her dress… pushing it north.

Lips hovering above the other, Helena shuddered, and her sweet tongue moved into Emily's mouth —one delicious stroke was enough to make her moan —their breathing so impatient. Pale hands found two smooth ass cheeks and squeezed them tightly.

Emily swallowed a languid whimper; small sounds were shy and reserved. Only for *her*. "Helena," A pulsating threat invaded her veins.

With exquisite and coaxing delicacy, Helena's beautiful mouth claimed Emily's —her lip stung, but the pain was quickly soothed by Helena's soft muscle.

A wicked throb assaulted Helena's sex, and she moaned. Keeping their hands off of each other was too difficult, or perhaps it was far too easy to get lost in this.

Tanned hips rocked against Emily's. She was apocalyptically soft and delicately strong; her smell was divine… —*I would have chosen Emily Knight as my death over the alternate.* Helena thought.

Emily's scent was unique to Helena, and Helena felt irresistibly drawn to it, to *her*. To that sweet breath and each curve her hands touched.

She ventured and found Emily's denim covered sex

—a soft moan fed to their careful kiss. Helena couldn't stop thinking of how good Emily had felt the night before between her legs; she was curious, and she wanted more. She had been dying to touch Emily.

She continued to rub her hand, and Emily panted desperately, puffs of warm air grazed against Helena's cheek and lips. With a wet sound, she broke their kiss —the ache between her hips grew.

Helena's dark eyes connected to hooded green ones. Desperate breaths on feverish skin. Glistening lips and aching faces. The soft sounds coming out of Emily were the most beautiful and arousing thing she had ever heard; Helena gasped, feeling hardness against her hand. Her desire melted like water.

Helena shivered. "Em..." She saw her usually strong blonde turned into a puddle of vulnerable want. Emily's eyes pleaded for closeness and Helena kissed her ardently.

"Do you want me to stop?" Helena barely managed onto warm lips, tasting the subtle iron in her lover's blood.

Emily bucked her hips into Helena's steady strokes on tight denim. With a whimper, her sweaty forehead sought refuge in Helena's neck. Emily bit back the sounds she knew would be too loud. God, she tried.

"Em, do you want me to stop?" Helena asked again, still stroking her girlfriend's constricted arousal.

"No... no... please —don't stop," Emily managed between hushed shudders.

Helena claimed Emily's mouth; her agile hand still between hot, rocking hips. Rubbing, stroking. Fever flushed through her own face.

Knock. Knock.

Eyes darted to the door, and their steamy make-out session came to a halt. The smacking sound of their breaking kiss was muffled to Patrick who was grinning on the other side of the door. "Em, Mom says dinner is ready —I'm so sorry, guys."

Brown eyes were wide as they scrambled up and sat on the bed. Kiss-marred lips red and gleaming. Emily tried to steady her breathing despite the zealous erection hiding inside jeans. She immediately felt Helena shaking. "Hey... It's okay." she said, and stroked her girlfriend's back gently.

Helena's heart pounded in her ears. Green eyes found brown ones soothingly. "Hey, hey... It's okay, Lena, it's just Patrick..." she reassured softly. Helena clung to the safety she saw in them and slowly settled. Emily placed her hand between her legs and continued to soothe Helena with the other. "It's okay, all right?" she cooed.

With a nod, Helena glanced at the hard arousal threatening to bust out of her girlfriend's jeans. Her brows crashed. She felt terrible. "Em, I am so sorry." Helena tried to touch it, but drew back before making things worse; hands reached for blonde strands of hair instead.

Emily shifted and pushed her legs together. Breaking this heated make-out session was painful, as painful as her erection.

"Are you okay?" Helena asked worriedly. "You look like you're in pain."

"I am." she bit back a moan.

"Oh, Emily —did I hurt you?" Helena was ready to turn the world upside down for her girl —anything to make it better.

Emily pushed a soft smile. "No, you didn't... I've just been holding back too many of these since I met you," She blushed at the admission. "Without —you know...

coming." she finished sheepishly.

"I am so sorry, Em, I didn't mean to…" Helena frowned. "Why have you been holding back?" she questioned.

"What do you mean?" Emily continued to grab her hard parts, knees finding each other.

"I mean, why haven't you given yourself release? It isn't healthy to hold those." she explained.

Emily blushed again. "Because… I…" She shrugged. "I felt bad —I just didn't wanna do it without you knowing; I guess it didn't seem right to get off thinking of you while being just friends."

Helena chuckled. "Oh, Emily…" she bit back amusement.

Emily blushed harder. "What? Are you making fun of me?" she said, and laughed with darting eyes.

"No." Helena tried her best to keep a straight face. "Of course not… I just—"

"What?"

"I wasn't as respectful and thoughtful as you were to me." Helena confessed with a grin.

Green eyes widened. "Are you serious?!" Emily gawked; she couldn't believe her pretty know it all wasn't as innocent as she seemed to be.

A guilt-ridden Helena blushed deeply; Emily's mischievous gleam burned her. "But only once!" she tried.

With a smirk on her lips, Emily brushed a kiss on Helena's cheek. "It's okay. I'm flattered, actually."

"Really?"

"Yeah," Emily winked playfully. "It's hot."

They broke in laughter.

Knock! Knock!

"If you guys don't come down, I swear I'm gonna clean

141

your plates." Patrick said.

***

At the dinner table sat the Knight family and their guest Helena Millan.

Helena got to meet Emily's father, Ben, whom she thought had caring green eyes. He was tall with sandy blonde hair and a captivating aura.

The brother looked like the typical, unapologetic, and magnetic bad boy with dark hair and green eyes, but turned out to be much like Emily; charmingly quiet. Patrick had been particularly thoughtful with Maureen, and in Helena's eyes, any man who showed kindness and respect to his mother was most definitely honorable.

After an exceptionally delicious dinner, warm apple pie and vanilla ice cream melted in each their plates.

Helena sat next to Emily who munched on a perfect scoop of cinnamon-drenched apple and pie crust.

Maureen swallowed. "So, Helena, I heard you mention in class that you would like to go to Medical School —have you always known this is the path you'd like to take?" she asked, glancing between her succulent desert and the sweet girl.

Helena smiled as all eyes fell on her, including her girlfriend's. She cleared her throat. "Yes, I have always loved the idea. However, I believe my parent's influence has played a small part in that decision; I would love to become a neurosurgeon." She smiled and shrugged. "I have been surrounded by doctors all my life, so it feels very organic."

Emily grinned and continued eating her delicious pie. Maureen and Ben smiled as they listened to her. "That's beautiful, Helena, a very honorable profession indeed;

I'm sure the amount of healing you can offer this world is invaluable."

"Thank you." Helena blushed but smiled proudly.

"Emily wants to be a cop." Patrick voiced with mischievous and kind eyes, Helena turned to him, looking surprised. Emily kicked him under the table.

"Detective." she corrected, seemingly annoyed.

With a pleased smile, Maureen and Ben went back to their treats. Helena turned to Emily, the wonder in her eyes, bright and proud.

"Really?" Helena asked.

Emily shrugged. "Yeah... I wanna be a detective like my dad... I plan to major in criminology." she admitted.

The parents couldn't get enough of the way they looked at each other. Maureen squeezed Ben's leg under the table and pouted lightly. She leaned in and whispered, "They are so adorable,"

Both girls realized there was so much they still didn't know. They wanted to know it all.

Helena caressed a pale hand gently. "I am sure you will be amazing at it, Em," she said, smiling while Emily nodded.

"Thanks,"

Patrick smirked to himself, silent joy washed over him. He was happy for his sister. She deserved this.

"Everything was delicious, Professor Shepherd, thank you so much for inviting me," Helena said politely.

Maureen smiled happily. "Aw, thank you, Helena... It was our pleasure having you; you are welcome here anytime."

"Thank you," Helena said.

Patrick cleared his throat and pushed back his chair. "Yeah, Mom, it was great—but if you guys excuse me, I need to make a call."

Maureen watched him stand. "Oh—ok."

Ben chimed in, "I need to go check on that security light in the back of the house," He kissed his wife on the cheek. "It was delicious, honey, thank you." he said, and stood to leave.

Maureen's green eyes followed him up. "Oh... all right." She suddenly looked at the girls. "Is it me or are they avoiding this mess?"

Emily smiled sheepishly, scratching the back of her head. "I um... I forgot I left my cell phone outside."

Helena frowned at her girlfriend. "Emily!"

"What? I'll be right back." She stood and walked away with a smirk on her lips. Helena shook her head.

Maureen scanned the dirty plates and laughed. A slightly gaping Helena joined her in laughter.

While Maureen finished clearing the last dishes and put all leftovers in individual containers, lovely Helena washed the last small pile of plates. The sensation of warm water against her skin was as pleasant as the domesticity of it all; Maureen's delightful company felt genuine. The professor on her part couldn't be happier; Helena was a sight; she was thoughtful, sweet, smart, and she seemed to care deeply for her darling daughter.

Emily, on the other hand, had swiftly escaped, leaving her willing and cooperative girlfriend behind. She went outside to find her cell phone and found Patrick sitting on the front steps. He seemed pensive and off. Emily sat next to him.

"Hey, everything okay?" she asked.

Patrick grinned, trying to seem tough as usual, but thoughts plagued his mind. "Yeah, Em, I'm all right —not as good as you, though." he said with a teasing smirk.

Emily glowed. "She's amazing, isn't she?"

"Definitely a keeper." He looked at her with his squinting, soulful eyes. Emily knew something was going on; she could feel it.

Patrick plucked a shiny green leaf from the bush next to him and fiddled with it. The night was fresh; crickets chimed in.

"Come on, Patrick," Emily nudged his leg with hers gently. "Why are you really here?" she pried.

He turned to her. "Dad wasn't taking it so well, you know... when they pulled him off the case —but after what happened today, I'm glad I came." he said worriedly. "Look, I get it if you don't wanna tell me who hit you, Em —and what you're thinking is right, I'd probably kill them, but you gotta tell Dad."

Emily frowned, knowing all too well the case was about her family getting harassed because of her. She felt guilty, and sadness crossed her eyes —she bowed her head. "I know... I heard them fighting about it the other day, and I will— tell Dad, I mean, I'll tell him tomorrow."

Patrick felt bad for his little sister; she had dealt with enough all through her life... *unfairly*, and so had their parents while trying to protect her; enabling her to grow up as a happy individual, just like everyone else. Humans sometimes had the potential to darken the beautiful.

"I just wanted to make sure you were okay," he confessed, and she gave him a small smile.

"I am."

"I can see that, I'm happy for you, Em."

"Thanks," Emily said, and plucked a small red flower from the bush next to her. They both sat under the stars, feeling the fresh San Francisco evening air.

Patrick fixed his eyes on the leaf in his hand, taking in the green citrus scent oozing from it as he tore it in half. "Tala showed up at my door with a one-year-old kid last week;" he said, and turned to his sister.

Green eyes went round. "What?!" Emily gawked.

Patrick threw the leaves to the ground and nodded. "Yeah…"

"What?!" Emily shook her head. "Wait, you have a kid? …With Tala?" She was shocked, but not surprised; after all, they were high school sweethearts. "But I thought she had broken up with you and moved to L.A."

"Yeah… so did I." he muttered, and gently kicked an imaginary rock on the ground.

"So, um…" Emily didn't want to offend. "Is he… or she yours?" she tried.

Patrick raised a brow and smiled; Emily could have sworn a gleam of pride flickered through his gaze. "He's a boy…" Patrick said, grinning wider.

Emily smiled and nodded; she was trying to make the best out of the situation and support her brother.

"We're waiting on paternity test results," He shrugged knowingly. "But I have no doubts, Em, I mean, she decided to do the test to prove it, I told her it wasn't necessary." He stared at the street lamps in the distance.

Emily sighed and leaned her head on his shoulder, knowing that silent comfort could sometimes soothe the heart.

***

A month passed, and it had proven to be the most amazing month in both Emily's and Helena's life. The excitement of their romance wore the color of their young and eager blood. It had been like floating on cloud nine —a soft dreamy cloud that refused allow either one of them to fall through.

Between Emily's soccer practices and their classes, it seemed they had spent more time on the phone and Math class than alone. Now living on campus with her sister, privacy was nonexistent for Helena, and with Etta in Emily's room, alone time together had become a mission, which meant things had to remain on the other side of what had happened in Emily's room over that busted lip. Things didn't go beyond kissing. *A lot of kissing.*

Lured to the Millan Mansion for a late family lunch, they sat in the living room, holding hands and laughing as they moved between cuddles and rosy confessions to each other's ears. Emily had come to find that there was absolutely nothing in the world she adored more than Helena's smile, the tiny mole, and her lips... that gentle scar —Emily had found the keys to paradise in those sweet sinful lips.

But their haven was disrupted like shattering glass. Helena frowned and rolled her eyes as Maddison's voice found her ears. —*Here we go. Again.*

They turned; an upset Maddison trailed after her collected mother and into the living room. "We are only going to the movie theater, Mother, not Sacramento! Besides, I am nineteen years old, I can do whatever I want —this is ridiculous!" she ranted.

Katherine moved with glamorous ease and found the files she had come looking for laying on the coffee table.

She picked them up. "I told you, Maddison, I don't want you hanging around that young man, and *please,* don't throw the age card in my face unless you want me to throw the living trust one in yours." she finished, looking at her blue-eyed daughter who was a livid mess of fits.

"Arghhhhhh!" She stomped her foot on the floor. Maddison couldn't fight that statement. Two more years and she would have full access to her money; free to do as she pleased. She rolled her eyes.

Emily had to admit that Maddison's ultrasonic voice when having a meltdown took some getting used to, which she was slowly doing. But it was still quite uncomfortable. Helena shifted next to Emily and squeezed her thigh gently. *Apologetically.*

Emily pacified her with a wink. —*It's all right.*

"Mother! He is outside waiting for me." Maddison said with a hint of honest emotion in her voice.

Helena almost felt sorry for her sister.

Katherine flipped through the papers, shrugging with elegance and nonchalance, eyes on the page. "Then tell him to go."

"Please—Mother!" Maddison was at her seams. "Christ! I should have just stayed at the dorm and met him there!" she blurted out with arms crossed.

Helena rolled her eyes. —*That was stupid.* If she were in her sister's shoes, trying to defend a case, **that** would have been the last thing to come out of her mouth.

Katherine arched a brow and eyed her daughter.

Maddison frowned and cursed her mouth a little. "I'm sorry," she muttered.

The woman had to admit that Maddison's interest in this boy seemed sincere, and even though she had prohibited the contact, a change in her was noticeable. Katherine turned to the couch where Helena and Emily sat, looking at them in awkward silence.

She pondered. —*Hmmm.*

"All right, you may go." Katherine gave in, and Maddison's face lit up, blue eyes went round.

"Are you serious?" she shrieked.

"Yes."

Maddison beamed.

"But only if Helena and Emily go with you two." Katherine proposed.

A frown. "What?!" Maddison sputtered.

"What?" Helena added from the sofa, and Emily ran her sweaty palms on her jeans. Things were getting more and more uncomfortable by the second.

"You heard me," Katherine grinned. "If your sister goes, you may go." She kissed both her daughters on the cheek. "Enjoy, my darlings," she said, and left with a smile on her lips.

Maddison rolled her eyes and looked down at Helena. She really wanted to see Leo —this was better than nothing. "So?" Blue eyes stared at brown ones.

Helena was in a tight spot, but she knew that if she said no, her sister would be impossible to deal with. Perhaps a movie wouldn't be so bad. A movie in Emily's arms would definitely be more than not bad. She sighed and turned to Emily. "Would you like to go?" Helena asked.

Emily glanced between the Millan girls. "Yeah… sure, whatever you want is okay with me." she said.

Maddison smiled. "All right, let's go."

Helena raised a brow. "Now?"

"Yes, Helena, didn't you hear me earlier? He's waiting outside. Let's go!" she urged, obviously annoyed.

"Okay, but I am taking my car, Emily and I are not riding with him." Helena added.

Maddison shrugged. "Suit yourself." She couldn't care less.

"Okay, let me get my bag, and I'll meet you two outside." Helena said mostly to her girlfriend, Emily nodded and smiled.

The retreating rays of the setting sun hit the Millan's mansion. The fresh smell of rain threatened to let it fall later that night. Emily walked out the door and saw Maddison rush to greet the smug guy leaning on a sports car —Emily recognized him; they had played against his college's soccer team in the past. Leo Blackwell wore couture and a smirk. Maddison looped her arms around his neck, and his hands found her small waist. They kissed briefly.

At that moment, a soft touch graced Emily's lower back, pulling her out of the trance. Helena stood by her side with a gentle smile. "Are you ready?"

Emily nodded. "Yeah," she said, and gave her girlfriend a small smile.

"Could you please drive?" Helena requested, handing her the car keys.

"Yeah, sure. Are you feeling okay?" Emily was careful with Helena, always making sure she wouldn't exhaust herself into fatigue; Katherine had thoroughly drilled her on how serious Helena's condition was. Emily always watched over her without coddling —Helena hated being treated like a cripple.

"I am." she reassured her with a smile.

"Okay, move it, lovebirds, we don't have all night." Maddison mocked while entwined in her boyfriend's arms.

Tar heat consumed Emily as she silently caught Leo's lewd eyes on Helena. With a clenched jaw, she placed a protective arm around her waist. Both Helena and Maddison were oblivious to Leo's smirk.

Far too consumed in Emily, Helena smiled intimately and entwined their fingers. "Let's go."

Night had indeed fallen spectacularly. Emily held Helena's hand all through the ride as she followed Leo's car. When the bright brake lights flashed, both vehicles gradually stopped. Helena studied her surroundings and recognized the depths of Russian Hill, a neighborhood, no movie theaters in sight. She exhaled and flared her nostrils.

While she hastily unfastened her seatbelt, Emily did the same. "Helena,"

"I should have known." Helena huffed and opened her door determinedly. She slammed it shut and rushed to her sister who was exiting Leo's car.

Emily killed the engine and followed her girlfriend.

"Where are we, Maddison?" Helena demanded with smoldering eyes.

"We, little sister," she said, grinning. "are at a party, and if you say anything, you'll regret it." Maddison threatened with a smirk on her lips.

Helena crossed her arms and glared at her fearlessly. "You are such a child, Maddison, no wonder Mother doesn't trust you —you bring it upon yourself!"

Maddison gave her a dismissive blink. "Save it, Helena. Are you coming or going?"

"I can't go back home without you! Have you lost

your mind?!"

Emily stood next to Helena and placed a calming hand on her arm.

"Well, it's your choice, Helena, you can go and tell on me or come, or stay out here —hell, you can go back to our dorm if you want for all I care..."

The throbbing vein in Helena's neck gushed contained anger; she huffed and took Emily's hand. "Let's go."

"Whatever..." Maddison said, and turned to enter her party alongside Leo. Blue eyes glanced over her shoulder and watched them drive away.

**

After calming Helena down, Emily suggested taking her somewhere if she, of course, allowed. Her secret spot.

The secluded beach shore, surrounded by lush green, was exactly what Helena needed. It was far from everything and everyone. The bay's waters were subtly touched by echoes of lights from the distant city; undertones of the silver moon rippled on them. The immensity of the barely lit Golden Gate Bridge reminded Helena of lasting things, things that resisted the test of time—of longevity and value. She counted herself lucky, so lucky and falling deeper and deeper in love with Emily Knight as each day passed. She hadn't said the words even though she had been dying to let them fall from her mouth.

Strong soft arms around her waist felt warm and safe; Emily's breasts pressed on her back, simply divine. Helena smiled as the wind blew their locks gently. Brown eyes wanted to close and relish the feeling but couldn't. The view was magnetic. Emily nuzzled on Helena's neck and took in her scent, her womanhood, and the thumping flow... echoes of her beating heart. It was happiness.

"I love this, Em..." Helena said, and turned in the embrace; their lips were inches apart. "Thank you for bringing me here."

Emily melted inside; soothing honey ran down her soul. Helena's smile was the verge of a sin and her perfume another excuse. Her warmth and her life were her destinations. "I knew you'd love this place, the tides get pretty high at this time... I love coming here," She looked forward into the dark waters, breathing in the vivid smell of rain narrowing down the window of its arrival. "It's just so beautiful and peaceful."

Helena drew her bottom lip between pearly teeth; gleaming brown canvassed a pale, soft jaw. "You are so beautiful..."

Emily lowered her head and felt *the words* pierce her; so hard to ignore, so good and sweet on the tip of her tongue. The taste wasn't mild. It was strong —oh, so very strong. Those three words meant so much. —*I love you.*

Wanting so badly to speak their truth, eyes moved to lips and then back up. Hands brushed soft cheeks, noses lingered, and they got lost in a kiss.

The sound of crashing waves soon became louder, and a foamy gush of cold water washed their shoe-covered feet with force; unsuspecting eyes opened wide, and their kiss broke.

"Oh, shit!" Emily said as their surprised gazes aimed at the unforgiving ocean while consumed in sudden laughter.

Emily's heart suddenly caught in her throat as she found *her*. Helena had closed her eyes, allowing the cold waves to collide with her skin. *It was everything.* Helena was relishing the taste of love and life.

Seconds later, brown eyes opened, and a mischievous smile painted Helena's face. She slowly lowered her fingertips and dipped them in the freezing water by their feet. Emily's jeans and the flares of her knee-length skirt were effectively soaked.

"What is it, baby?" Emily asked, and a giggling Helena surprised her with a hefty splash of the cold liquid on blonde hair and face.

Emily flinched. "Shit!"

Helena laughed. "Oh, Em, I am so sorry— I aimed for your clothes!"

Emily's eyes matched her big smile. "Oh, yeah? That's how you wanna play?" she said, and rushed down to give her girlfriend a fun taste of her own medicine.

"Emily Knight, not on the hair." she warned, unable to keep a straight face.

"You should have thought about that before you started this, Helena Millan."

Soon, another high wave crashed against them, doing far more soaking damage than what the previous one had.

"Fuck!" Emily laughed and went after her sneaky lover.

Seconds later, Helena let out a high-pitched scream as Emily's wet counterattack found her; she ran towards the car consumed in carefree laughter.

That beautiful sound was music to Emily's ears; she too took off and chased after her Helena.

The sounds of both doors closing and unbound laughter mixing inside the car were a gift. Dry and safe from the roaring waves, they cherished each second as gusts of wind pushed against the glass with force.

Beautiful Helena was drenched; she gawked in absolute bliss. "Oh, my God, I don't think I've ever laughed this much," she said, and their joyful fit died down with ease.

An equally soaked Emily peeled off her sweater, and the cool air hit her skin. Her damp tank top and jeans encouraged a trail of goosebumps all over —tall leather boots, thoroughly soaked.

A lump rolled down Helena's throat as dark, smoldering eyes found an oblivious Emily drying her face with the sweater. "You are stunning..." Helena whispered.

Emily glanced up and into Helena's transfixed gaze.

"Thank you," she murmured honestly, "but you are the stunning one in this relationship."

Gutted, Helena sighed. "You have no idea..." She inched closer despite the armrest between them. "How beautiful you are, Emily —you have no idea of what you do to me." Her longing gaze so raw.

Emily blushed and dared. "Yeah?" Soft lips coaxed Helena into closing her eyes. "Tell me..."

Smiling in the kiss, Helena purred. "You... make me feel crazy... like I lose control of my body's reactions..." She pulled Emily closer, hooded eyes searching for one another. Lips lingered, shivering breaths so imprisoning, fingertips mapped pale skin. "You make me want to be with you every second of every day... so much it hurts." Helena finally claimed Emily's lips and softly pushed her tongue into her mouth.

Green eyes fluttered shut, and Emily grunted as their dueling lips marred lipstick into nothing. "You—taste so good," Helena said.

Smacking sounds and quickening breaths grew desperate; she felt Emily's hands on her thigh and shuddered. They broke the fervent kiss with swollen lips and found each other's eyes smoldering dark. What they saw made their pulses quicken, it made composure want to unravel. Meanwhile, raging winds continued to howl against the windows of Helena's car.

Emily allowed her forehead to fall onto Helena's gently, never breaking eye contact. A tentative hand ran up her tanned, warm thigh, past her skirt and finally made it under her blouse. Piercing breaths claimed Helena's chest, and Emily ached inside. Hot carmine began to spread through her neck and face. "Helena..." she murmured.

Dark eyes closed at the electrifying new pleasure awakening her while a pale hand found the promising softness of a lace cup —black straps brushed Helena's olive-toned shoulders, and Emily wanted more. Fingertips dipped in and found a tightening nipple; pores rose like wildfire on Helena's skin, making her shiver hotly. She weakened at the pressure between her thighs, and her breathing grew desperate; the need to satiate her craving for Emily was as determined as the armrest between them. Poison lips sought more skin to kiss. "Let's go to the back..." Helena coaxed breathlessly to Emily's ear.

Emily whimpered at the feeling on her digits so raw and vivid, at Helena's hushed, intimate sounds so consuming. "Okay."

They clumsily maneuvered their way to the back of the elegant vehicle. The smell of brand new leather mixed with sweet breaths and perfume would become a print they would never forget.

Emily lay on top. Dark shimmering eyes and wanting flushed lips found each other again. The kiss escalated with the thrashing passion of the wind outside.

Helena rocked her hips forward, and Emily ground down into them, meeting deliciously; no air in between, only heat. Their breathing so out of control it fogged the glass; Emily's desire was primal and raw. Her girlfriend was a heaving and aching mess under her — under their bucking hips. "Fuck, Helena..." Emily felt the hyper-aware pressure of her own arousal against the tight denim of her jeans.

Helena arched and felt it push onto her clothed sex, coals of heat burned low in her belly. "Oh, Em..." she said with a breaking voice and kiss-bruised lips that had to express it all.

The sight and sounds drove Emily mad. Hazy green eyes found gleaming and darker ones looking up at her. Completely vulnerable and open.

"I want you so much, Helena," Long strands of blonde hair fell between them as Emily pushed down again, making Helena writhe at the hot friction. She squeezed her eyes shut, and brows drew together.

"I want you, too," Helena said, and clenched her jaw. Eyes dark as the night looked up, nostrils flaring.

Emily's arousal grew harder. The aching reality between her thighs clouded her mind. All she could do was feel, touch... kiss, and love. *Love her so much.* It was as if she had been waiting for permission.

Tanned hands began to push Emily's top north. Emily squeezed her eyes shut and scraped the leather beneath her lover. "Wait." she urged.

Helena froze and gazed into her girlfriend. "What is it?"

Hesitant, Emily nibbled on her lip. "I…"

"We don't have to do anything, Em…" Helena softened lovingly.

"No… It's not that; I want to… I just," she tried.

Helena searched noble green ever deeper and caressed Emily's cheek. "Talk to me," she begged.

"I just… I don't want to hurt you."

Helena smiled, gaze bound to the roof of her car for a moment. —*God, I love her.* "Emily, you're not going to hurt me… I trust you." she reassured.

Emily shook her head again. That wasn't it. "I mean your heart." she finally confessed.

Helena took a pale hand in hers and guided it to her very chest. She penetrated hesitancy with conviction. "Do you feel that?"

Emily sighed almost inaudibly, feeling the wild and strong beat of Helena's heart against her palm.

"You're not going to break me, Em… I am not weak." Helena gave her a watery smile with melancholic, welling eyes. To Emily, it felt more like Helena's plea to be heard and trusted, for her voice to be acknowledged.

"I want you and I trust you with my body." Helena offered openly.

Emily claimed her lips and Helena opened her mouth; Emily had rendered her wet. The tight sensation between her thighs was like a hunger that ran down, leaving behind a perfect gleaming mess. It made demands. She bucked forward into Emily and moaned. The erotic sound echoed in the misty haze inside the car; it encouraged Emily as she pushed off Helena's blouse and discarded it somewhere between the front seats while Helena reached under herself, unhooking her bra. It rolled off her honey skin like a fatal tear, exposing herself to another human for the first time.

Emily gasped at the sight. *The sight* of bare, olive-toned skin was like heat tearing through the chill; the rise and fall from the valley of her chest and shivering abdomen, her longing eyes. Emily swallowed hard while intense craving rooted from the base of her body up into her heart. This wasn't a game; this was a gift.

"Oh, my God, Helena..." Emily weakened as her stinging eyes discovered her with awe. She ran a hand up her trembling abdomen until she found soft and hard flesh, so round and keen grazing her palm, just like the final thrill. Helena closed her eyes, and Emily began to rock herself forward again.

Feeling the push of Emily's defined arousal, Helena whimpered and breathed harder. With rushing fever, she urged Emily's shirt off; her bra so easily discarded. Skirt rolled up around her very own waist.

Emily kneeled between tanned thighs, and the sight of a porcelain-like torso made Helena weaken. Brown eyes welled up as she swallowed back the magnificent taste. The harmony of softness and strength was exquisite; curious eyes caressed the rosy hues on her blinding breasts. "Oh, Emily..." Helena gasped breathlessly as her open hand felt every inch of Emily's abdomen. Darkly manicured nails contrasted so perfectly against white. Just like good and evil, just like life and death.

Helena pulled her lover into a carnal kiss. Emily whimpered, breathing heavily. With flaring nostrils, she caressed Helena's thighs —her shivering legs were like sacrificing everything for love. She pushed a hand between their heated bodies and brushed against Helena's warmest place.

Emily moaned with eager eyes, and Helena threw her head back, biting her lip.

Their naked torsos brushed together like sparks as

Emily lowered herself. She lost her mind and strength; knowing she would forever be a pawn to Helena; a bishop, a rook —*a knight*. Whatever Helena wanted or needed, she would be it. Emily poured herself into a shameless kiss and continued to touch her; she pushed past damp lace and felt Helena's drenched heat for the first time. Emily blushed. "Oh, God... baby, you're so wet," she whispered into trembling lips as a spiraling feeling in her stomach ignited every nerve of her body.

Helena was close, so close to finding bliss; this wouldn't take long for her, she knew that much as she reached down and unzipped Emily's jeans. A tanned hand unbuttoned and pushed them down along with soft underwear, releasing Emily's erection free. Helena felt the flesh exerting pressure on her lace-covered sex and whimpered.

She looked down between their bodies and saw it for the first time, resting on her lower belly. Brown eyes then looked up and met green ones.

"Are you okay?" Emily asked softly. "We don't have to..."

Helena shook her head and bit her lip. "I want to... Do you have a condom?"

"I don't..." she dreaded.

"You can withdraw, right?" Helena tried.

"You mean pull out?" Emily countered, endeared.

Helena nodded with dark gleaming eyes.

"Yeah... of course," she reasoned, "but I can't get you pregnant if that's what you're worried about." she confessed.

Helena's forehead creased. "You can't... Can't you conceive?"

"Not while on my blockers and meds, but it's reversible; for now —I mean, if I stopped them I could. I'm not infertile yet, but I will be in the future." she answered honestly.

Helena swallowed. "I'm so sorry, Em..." She caressed her temple with a gentle thumb.

Green eyes gleamed emotionally. "It's okay..."

Helena's heart broke, it was evident that Emily wasn't okay with the prospect of infertility. "Of course, sweetheart..." she eased and kissed her again.

Their arousal resumed. Helena's hand became brave and touched Emily's sex. Her breathing rushed as she felt the lucidity of it all, just as Emily had when she'd felt her most intimate heat. This was real. This was her beautiful Emily. She stroked, and green eyes closed.

"Fuck..." Emily muttered; her jaw slacked.

Helena looked at her with want and care. She stroked again. "I love the way it feels," she confessed in whispers.

With burning, flushed skin, Emily conquered Helena's lips in a wet kiss. Tanned hands moved to knead on blonde hair while Emily pushed forward, her tight arousal grazing Helena's inner thighs. She rolled lace down olive-toned skin, and Helena moaned as she felt her again. The raw clarity of sensations was irrevocable —God, the way her mouth opened and her body arched off the leather seat... sweet eyes rolled back in ecstasy.

Emily kissed her softly. "Helena..." she tried to pull her beautiful girl out of the trance.

Brown eyes fluttered open; so honest, wanting, daring —yet timid.

One last time before they crossed. "I love you." Emily professed for the first time, caressing her jawline.

Helena's eyes welled up as stinging emotions burned her lids in liquid form. She stroked her girlfriend's cheek and pulled her down till their foreheads touched. "I love you." she gave.

Emily's heart expanded, and never felt more ready to give herself away —to love and to **her**.

Smeared lips, both breathing so close to one another, Emily guided herself to Helena's running heat.

Their breaths faltered as she pushed in slowly. Helena gasped and squeezed her eyes shut while Emily felt her entire world change, brighten so quickly —there was no coming back from this feeling. It was achy and sore, a pain that only penetration could soothe —so deliciously quell.

"Are you okay?" she barely managed.

Helena nodded softly. "It hurts a little."

Emily's heart tore; she frowned. "I don't want to hurt you…" She searched Helena's eyes with knitting brows so honest.

"It's okay… I believe this is completely normal." Helena said, feeling her insides melt and burn with delicious ache.

"Are you sure?" Emily tried again.

Helena nodded. "It's okay, just keep going." she said with hazy eyes.

Emily nodded and continued to push herself into Helena's tight oblivion; into a warm, soft and beautiful oblivion that coated her existence. Helena opened her mouth, and her jaw locked at the fullness while Emily's pelvis pushed against her most sensitive nerve ending. With no space between them, Helena saw the entire universe behind closed lids. "Oh— Oh... God," She trembled.

Emily tensed her grip on the leather seat and began to move her hips. The dull ache returning as she pulled out and so deliciously healing on the way in. "Oh... fuck," Helena's safest place squeezed her tightly.

They heaved and moaned, desperate puffs of breath against the intimacy of flushed necks and lips. Those pretty black nails Emily loved, ranked red marks on a fair back. They burned like fire, and Emily whimpered, lips between teeth.

In and out never looked more beautiful. Helena's teary eyes blinked as she choked on her moans.

Emily's small and intimate sounds were no match for the beauty she was enthralled with. She could die after seeing Helena like this and do so happily. With a thin dew of sweat shimmering on their skin, Emily leaned down to kiss her lips and continued to move.

Ignited by nature, Helena rocked her hips seeking purchase. The more they pushed and pulled the better it felt; until Emily's lower abdomen hit Helena right where she needed her most. "Oh, my God... Please!" Helena cried, desperately rocking forward; her free hand opened on the back of the expensive leather seat.

Helena asked for more and Emily wanted more, she increased the pace, unleashing an onslaught of sensations within their anatomies. Helena's jaw locked midstride as Emily's forehead fell on her sweaty chest.

The smell of arousal and perfume —the rain that had started to fall...They would forever remain.

Emily moaned with each quick push; she squeezed her eyes, "I can't hold it anymore... I have to pull—"

Helena's nails moved to a beautiful ass cheek and kept her in place. She was so close! Seconds later, her body arched and entered nirvana as an electrifying orgasm ripped right through her. Emily was trapped by Helena's relentless hold, trapped while Helena took everything from her. She couldn't stop, she indeed couldn't hold it anymore; she had to let go.

"Oh— Helena—" Emily cried, pushing forward, branding her forever.

Already riding her last wave and seeing stars, Helena swallowed the desire to cry. She had never felt so close to anyone in her life. Decades of loneliness suddenly seemed far... so far away while Emily imprinted on her delicious memories she would never forget. She gave her all; she gave herself until there was no more.

It was Emily's turn to lose herself in space and time. No continuum to keep her in one piece. Her heart and soul were scattered into outer space. She felt whole, so different and new —so in love.

Exhausted, Emily collapsed onto Helena's clammy chest, her sweaty forehead brushing against her girlfriend's olive-toned shoulders with a breathless and thirsty smile.

And so they searched for their breaths, they searched for their lips and eventually their words. Now they were a new kind of us.

8

GREY

MORNING WAS AT ITS peak. Emily and Helena hadn't spent much time together outside of classes since that night in Helena's car. The first game of the season was approaching, and Emily's soccer practices were taking most of her time, while Katherine was taking Helena's.

It had been exactly one week since then, one-week missing each other; still feel each other. This morning, they shared the only class they had in common besides theater, and Emily sat next to Helena.

She had the perfect view, a faultless view of her girlfriend and couldn't ask for more. Looking at Helena was always food for her heart and soul. Watching her color code everything, and pay such close attention to things that seemed so unimportant was everything. Emily had never felt so close to anyone as she did with Helena —Helena was unique; she complemented her. Their eyes were of a different color, their skin of a different shade, their hair, and their minds though similar in some ways, were also uniquely different and that was perfect.

That night they'd shared something beyond anything Emily had ever experienced. Even though their soft, naked bodies dancing against one another felt so similar, they were also different, and to Emily that never felt more beautiful. She couldn't forget her kisses, how they were more intimate and deeper that night; the sounds that came out of Helena... her warmth, the scent of her arousal and exclusive perfume mixed into this addictive concoction —or was it a potion? The way Helena's walls consumed her, how she pulled her in further and further until she was lost. Lost where she was now, feeling like *this*.

Green eyes focused on her beautiful girl. —*I wonder if she feels the same? I wonder what she's thinking.* Emily thought.

Helena though seemingly invested in the class was at an equal loss. She had gladly given herself away to her girlfriend that night, and something of hers had stayed with Emily. Whatever that part was, she could still feel it aching, so deliciously *aching* to return. Emily already had her heart, her thoughts, and now she seemed to have captured her soul.

That night of intense young passion and wet hands printed on cold, foggy glass, Helena had felt her so deeply. Emily had so gently taken her essence and watched it transform. She couldn't stop thinking about her; she couldn't stop wanting her; it was just like phantom limb syndrome. Every time she thought of Emily she could so clearly feel her between her legs and inside her heart, even if she wasn't physically there.

Helena felt Emily's gaze on her skin and turned with a knowing grin. She turned and there she was, ready to make her feel safe as always. Emily was always there if she so wanted it. It was as if Emily understood and didn't hover.

She was there to make her laugh and cover her with kisses; she was there to hold her and make her fly, she was also there when silence was needed. Her best friend and lover. Helena moved her hand and found Emily's. —*I love her.*

***

After their class and a casual lunch under the cherry blossoms, they headed to Helena's dorm room for a heavy Mathematics tutoring session. It seemed this semester Helena's help had dramatically turned Emily's fate with her impossible course.

Consumed in casual laughter and intimacy, Helena turned the key and opened the door with Emily standing right behind her. The place was as tidy as always aside from a fully dressed Maddison smeared on her bed. Helena furrowed her brows and scanned the place while an intense odor hit them.

Emily jerked her head back and blinked at the strong, leafy, sulfurous stench. They walked in.

Helena frowned while brown eyes tried to find the source. "What is that horrid smell?" she asked.

The limp form on the bed started to move. Auburn locks of hair covered Maddison's face. "Mmm... Helena... close the window..." she mumbled lethargically.

Puzzled by her sister's behavior, Helena turned to the window with furrowed brows. "Maddison, *it is* closed." she said.

Loud and sudden laughter erupted from Maddison as she turned on her back and slumped an arm off the bed's edge. Helena arched a brow.

—*Fuck.* Emily sighed and rushed to her girlfriend's sister. "That smell is weed, Helena."

Brown eyes widened. "What?!"

Emily quickly eyed Maddison's body and desperately scanned it for any visible trace of the cannabis. She knew well what would happen if they got caught with it on campus, Clearwater's rules were as ancient as their history.

"Em, what are you doing?" Helena asked.

Startled and on full-on adrenaline mode, Emily's hands patted the bed and spaces around Maddison. "Search her pockets, make sure she doesn't have anything on her." she said, in a rush.

The urgency in Emily's voice alerted Helena; her girlfriend seemed instantly stressed, though in complete control. She nodded and quickly explored her sister's pockets and clothing. Brown eyes couldn't miss the readiness on green ones.

Emily stood and searched the room desperately. "We need to try and mask the smell —shit!" She opened the window. "They don't fuck around with that stuff here, Helena, and they have detectors outside the rooms."

Juddering laughter thundered in the room as Maddison hazily opened her blue eyes. "Helena…" The joyful fit quickly died down, and pale hands reached for her sister's cheeks. All the while, a disconcerted and worried Helena turned to Emily —Maddison's cold hands still on her face. "Open the closet; my perfumes are in there," she suggested hastily.

Emily continued to examine the place for what she needed. "That's not gonna work; we need something stronger —do you have incense?"

Helena shook her head and suddenly felt soft hands caress her face. "Little sister… You are so beautiful, and smart," Maddison cooed in her fuzzy bliss as Helena sighed with emotional brows.

"God, Maddison. Why did you do this?" She felt compassion and absolute anger coursing her system all at once.

Emily opened the closet doors wide and grabbed one of Helena's perfume bottles. "The detectors are in the hallways —hopefully it didn't reach that far." After giving the spraying a standing chance, she hurried to Helena and Maddison's side.

Brown eyes watered with frustrated tears as she clenched her teeth and jerked her sister to sit up —Maddison chuckled. "Woohooo... That was fun! Do it again!"

"Where did you get the marijuana, Maddison? Do you have any more?" Helena demanded with sentiment and contained desire to slap her sister into coherence.

Blue eyes pondered. "Umm... I have some pills Leo gave me, but those are *stronger...*" she sing-sang. "Oops!" she snorted and broke in juddering laughter again.

Worried, sober gazes met. "Fuck, Helena," Emily said.

With an unforgiving jerk and gritted teeth, Helena shouted, "WHERE?!" rage blazing inside. "Maddison!" she tried to meet drifting blue eyes with emotional and red-rimmed ones. Seeing her sister like this was heartbreaking, but the anxiety radiating out of Emily told her that they were in a bad situation.

"In my... —in my handbag —please don't leave me alone, Helena," Maddison murmured; her demeanor had shifted. Blue eyes filled with tears and a sobbing breath pierced her chest. Helena felt ache grip at her heart.

Emily quickly shot up in search of the bag containing the drugs. "Where is it? Which one's hers?"

Helena eyed the room frantically and spotted it. "It's

the one on the loveseat."

With only one thing on her mind, Emily scrambled to it and rushed to the bathroom. The sound of the toilet flushing wasn't grounding enough for Helena to gather the mess of conflicting emotions surging through her system. She gently caressed her sister's hairline with gleaming eyes and a sore heart.

Seconds later, Emily was right next to them again. "They're gone." she said, feeling Helena's ache like it was her own. Brows knitted and a soft hand found Helena's back. "Hey... It's gonna be all right —I promise."

"Why little sister? —Why me?" Maddison wept. The contrasting display of emotions was sharp. They turned to her.

"Maddison, did you take the pills?" Emily asked, troubled.

Maddison shook her head. They could see clarity dying to filter through stunning blue.

Green eyes studied the redhead closely. Pale hands took a limp arm and gently pushed Maddison's short sleeve up. There, Emily found bruising fingermarks on porcelain skin conveniently covered by the soft fabric. "Oh, my God..." Emily murmured, drenched in shock.

Helena's heart shattered, and a tear rolled down her cheek. "Oh, Maddie,"

"Ugh! I swear I'm gonna kick that jerk's ass!" Emily grunted.

Knock! Knock! "Campus safety!" A muffled voice came from outside the room.

Two sets of wide eyes darted to the door. Blue ones blinked softly, finding composure on the parallel of a hazy line. "Helena..." Maddison tried.

"Shhh!" Helena hissed.

"Fuck," Emily muttered between teeth, and quickly thought of a way. Her desperate eyes shot to the closet —she knew what she had to do.

Piercing Helena's gaze with conviction, she placed both hands on her arms. "Helena, listen to me,"

Brown eyes dreaded what they saw in green ones. Her heart slammed against her chest.

Emily immediately saw fear reflected back at her and cupped Helena's cheek. "Hey, baby, it's okay. You two are gonna hide in the closet and no matter what —Helena, don't come out, okay?"

"Emily, don't." she pleaded in murmurs with aching brows and tears bound to fall. "You are going to get in trouble —I'll face him." she said at once, and motioned to stand up with wet, valiant eyes.

"No." Emily didn't waiver and pulled her back. That wasn't an option for her.

Helena opened her mouth to let out what her beautiful eyes already were.

"Shhh... Hey, nothing's gonna happen, but more than likely they'll take me to the dean, so don't freak out, okay? Just stay in there. Please, Helena." Brave green eyes begged, and emotional brown ones gleamed with sadness. She nodded.

"All right." A broken whisper came, and a quick tear ran down Helena's cheek.

KNOCK! KNOCK! KNOCK! It thundered this time. "Open the door!"

They quickly helped Maddison up and hastily found refuge in the darkness of the closet.

Before closing the door, Emily gave Helena another

comforting gaze. Their hands squeezed one last time, and darkness flooded the small space.

Emily glanced around the room, making sure nothing was out of place. She opened the door and smiled. "Hey, sorry I took so long —I was in the shower. What's up?" she asked casually.

Her big white smile and charming dimples weren't enough to turn the suspecting, serious frown of the safety officer at the door. "We got a call —some illegal activity going on in this perimeter." he informed with cutting authority in his timbre.

"What? I mean, I didn't hear anything. Are you sure it was here?" she stalled coolly; her heart pounded hard against her chest.

"It wasn't that kind of disturbance." He scrunched up his nose, and untrusting eyes scanned the seemingly perfect room. "I smell marijuana," He glared at Emily. "Were you smoking marijuana?"

"I don't smoke." she replied honestly.

"Well, it didn't smell like this in the other rooms around yours."

Inside the dark closet, Helena and a more aware Maddison heard the discussion taking place. —*All because of her irresponsible behavior.* Helena thought, and didn't know if she wanted to cry or choke her. She tried to understand her sister, to go back to a time when they were younger, sharing bubble gum while on expensive trips, consoling each other with watery smiles and scraped knees, but couldn't find understanding for this version of her. She couldn't understand why Maddison did the things she did.

Out of her stupor, Maddison found the darkened

shape of her sister's face only inches away from hers. The suffocating lack of echo and reverb in the small place made it easy for her to hear Helena's breathing. She was just becoming aware of what Emily had done. —*What?*

"Wha—…" she whispered.

"Shh! *Be. Quiet.*" Helena hissed, and closed her eyes, trying to collect herself. She was livid.

Outside, Emily continued to defend her case. "You can look around if you want. I'm not hiding anything." She motioned for the man to enter the place, wishing with all her might and twisting stomach he wouldn't —she knew it was a ballsy move since Maddison and Helena were hiding only feet away.

The officer arched his brow, and his square face leaned into the room. He sniffed suspiciously.

—*Fuck.* Emily grew nervous. Maybe her plan had actually backfired. She buried a hand in her jean's back pocket and dragged their lie to the absolute edge. It would either work or explode on their faces —she smiled coolly and motioned with her hand again. "Go ahead." she insisted and shrugged with those angelic green eyes.

The hesitating man eyed the space and stuck his head forward. "That's not necessary, but you have to come with me. I can definitely smell something, so I'm taking you to the dean." he said coldly.

Back in the closet, Helena's stomach sank. She wanted to kill Maddison, yet on her part, Maddison was thrown and taken off guard; *this,* she never expected. *This,* she wasn't used to. —*Why?*

"Okay," Emily said, knowing more than likely she would be tested.

Helena's eyes watered as she heard them walking out

173

followed by the sound of a closing door.

As soon as it was safe, Helena pulled Maddison out of the closet. The auburn-haired girl looked an absolute mess. Mascara ran under her eyes and clammy skin. It seemed the fall from her high hadn't been as pleasant as the rise.

Helena was mad and indignant; she was determined and needed to be heard. "What is your problem?" she demanded.

Maddison stalled, she rarely saw Helena this upset. "What are you talking about?" she said, shrugging off her sister's grip.

"What am I talking about? Are you serious?!" Helena said with anger in her usually collected eyes.

"I didn't ask her to do that." Maddison said, but gleaming blue told a different story. She was consumed by guilt and emotion. However, that's exactly how her brain worked. She had learned to conceal, to pretend the pain away.

Helena cringed. She had never felt blood boil inside her veins this way. "Have you lost your mind, Maddison?! Why would you smoke that here?! And not only that, you had other things with you! Are you trying to get arrested for possession of illegal drugs? —She just took the fall for you —for *us!* —So **you** wouldn't get expelled! And that is what you have to say in your defense?" Helena pressed with darkened eyes, and venom in her voice.

Blue eyes shone as her chest rose and fell desperately. Maddison's face twisted in anger. "You just don't get it; you know nothing! Your life is absolutely perfect, Helena! With your big brain and big stupid words— and in spite of everything... *else*—" she softened at the last statement; they both knew what she'd meant. "At least you have her, okay?!" Maddison shouted on the verge of an honest cry.

Tears stung Helena's eyes. "You say I don't understand, Maddison, try me... Please try me and talk to me, you might be surprised." she dared visibly cross.

Maddison averted her gaze in silence, blocking her sister out. She blinked the weak sentiment burning her eyes away and crossed her arms. "Forget it." she snarled.

Helena sighed, feeling exasperated and stormed out of the room with a slam of their door.

***

The night was dark and cool; a star-filled sky was Emily's shelter as she smiled and her long blonde hair danced along the wind. She held her cell phone to her ear and looked up to Helena's dorm window.

The garden lights of the place were a blessing. The smells of green grass, vines, and flowers were pleasing to the senses, though Emily feared the creepy night bugs as she walked around the outside of the collegiate gothic building. With a free hand inside the pocket of her zipped up soccer jacket, she inspected the side of the vine-covered structure while calculating possible ways to crawl up. "I could totally just climb up your window." she spoke through the device in her hand.

"Absolutely not! Emily, you're not a criminal, and besides, you might fall. Please come to the door." Helena scolded over the phone.

Emily laughed while rolling her eyes at her lovely girlfriend's freak out. "I thought it was supposed to be romantic, you know? Like the whole Romeo and Juliet thing we're doing for the play."

"We are not in the Renaissance. Please don't climb up my window; I am almost at the door," she begged.

Time seemed to go by faster, though Emily felt the stairs that led to Helena's hallway stretch for miles. After a few more minutes of furtive smiles ignited by the thought of soon feeling Helena in her arms, she made it there.

The sounds muffled, the door opened, and they smiled.

Helena crashed her body against Emily's. —*Finally.*

It had been too long; the waiting hours after what'd happened had been excruciating. Helena nuzzled Emily's warm neck and took in her fresh scent —she smelled like love and a soft perfume. Helena's brain began to spin and dissect every tone of that unforgettable fragrance, the one that made her heart and her axis spasm. —*Mmm... A rush of bergamot... juniper and a bright whisk of mint...* she thought while feeling grateful Emily couldn't hear her geeky mind's ramblings.

Helena placed a lethal kiss on her pulse point and pulled back to look into her eyes while gently cupping her jaw. "Em, what happened?" Worry etched her features.

Emily caressed Helena's skin with care. Green eyes gleamed as she smiled. "It's okay, baby —the dean believed me, but I'm sure they're gonna call your parents to warn them —just because it was your room."

Helena inhaled and shook her head. —*So be it.* "I am so sorry you had to go through that."

Emily pulled her into a tight hug. "It's okay, Lena... Let's just forget about it, okay?" Green eyes looked around. "Where's Maddison?"

—That perfume Emily adored grazed the air... Helena's perfume.

"We had a rather tumultuous fight, and she went to spend the night at home." Helena rolled her eyes.

Emily felt bad, knowing just how much Helena cared for her sister even though she almost never spoke about it. "I'm sorry."

"It's all right." Helena pushed the gloomy feeling aside and smiled. "Come here," She pulled her into a devious kiss. The comfort of Emily's arms was unlike anything else in the world. They lay in Helena's bed, bodies entwined as they watched a movie between tongue kisses in the partial dark. Helena broke yet another steamy one and lingered, gently biting Emily's bottom lip.

Discovery had taken a whole new meaning for both of them. Getting acquainted with each other's mouths and bodies; with each other's weak spots was divine. Helena was an avid and curious learner; she always aimed to excel at anything she engaged her focus on, and *this* would be no different. Emily felt the fire at the base of her abdomen and smiled. Helena did, too.

"I love your lips." Helena leaned in again and nuzzled on the warm skin of her girlfriend's neck.

Emily shivered; her eyes fluttered shut. "I love the way you kiss me."

Helena searched Emily's gaze and brushed a thumb on her temple. Brown eyes lingered in their lifeline, profound as always.

"What is it?" Emily asked softly.

"Why did you do it? —Today, I mean... Why did you take the blame?"

Emily's lip curled up as she searched for the right words and sighed. It was Emily's turn to caress some of Helena's exposed skin. "Besides the fact that she is your sister and I love you… I just… I felt bad for her." she confessed.

"Em, sweetheart, you didn't have to do that. I love my sister even though she is so horrible to me and —well— *everyone*— but she needs to learn to take responsibility for her actions."

Emily blinked softly. "I know —I'm not saying otherwise, I just… I guess I just get her."

Confused brows met. "I am not following." Helena said, trying to understand Emily's perspective.

"I've been where your sister is —emotionally, and…" She chewed on her lip, piercing brown eyes honestly. "It sucks." Emily confided.

Sadness clouded Helena's features; fixed loving eyes tried to discern.

Emily inhaled deeply and tried to elaborate. "When you are in that place… where you feel like you don't fit in or belong anywhere —like nobody gets you…"

"Emily, we've all been there —that is no excuse to behave the way she does, so careless and reckless." Helena added.

With a tender grin, Emily caressed Helena's cheek; she attempted once more. "Baby, I'm not trying to undermine what you went through, because I know it was tough for you, but… Helena, at the end of the day you had so much to fall back on —you are strong, insanely smart and you have your parents trust… you have your brother's friendship; you have everything she wants. Maddison isn't careless or reckless…I don't think she does it on purpose, at least."

Helena contemplated the resonance of those words and recognition dawned on her in the form of a deep sigh.

"She's desperate…" Emily said.

"But… You had your parents, your brothers— I thought

you said they had always supported you." Confusion rooted on Helena's face.

"At first, I was stuck inside —behind a name and body that weren't mine. That kind of loneliness tears you apart because you feel like no one can understand you, no one gets what you feel... like something is inherently wrong with you," she said, and pressed her lips, a perfect dimple pierced her cheek. "When you reach that point... Just knowing someone has your back no matter what —it really helps, that's what my family did. It was how everything started to change for me, and even though I know you love her, and I'm sure your family does, too..." Emily said, and smiled sheepishly— "I don't think she gets it yet."

Helena wanted to cry. She swallowed a hard lump and blinked back the tears. What could she say?

She caressed Emily's sinfully soft jawline, dipping a delicate hand behind her pale neck and pressed their lips with a searing breath leaving her chest, eyes squeezed shut. Helena's sudden emotion held the intensity of a sad song. —How could someone ever not want you? —How could others be so cruel to you?

A beautiful and unrelenting soul so free and so trapped all at once —Emily always held it all in and bore too much in silence. Helena wanted to convey with her lips what no combination of words inside her brain could. The silent ache swelling inside her chest was contained. Some things simply couldn't be turned into an element of speech; they traveled to Emily's heart with each brush of Helena's tongue. A thick silence fell upon them, and both pulled back gently.

Wet lips still touching, chests heaving, in and out.

Eyes.

Raw, longing eyes met. Gleaming brown and green. Hot breaths tickled their lips smooth and unguarded; they crashed again. Oh, the sound of their collision.

Emily went inside herself.

'I wasn't sure whose tongue entered whose mouth first, but it was wet and invasive. Helena's touch on my skin was wicked and beautiful.

That night we made out for hours. We kissed so hard that the healing cut on my lip started to burn again, but Helena... she made everything around me blur; she made the pain I always felt inside go away.

We kissed each other everywhere until it got so hot between us, like there was no space —until our clothes were on the way.

Then there was a moment.

That moment when she tugged at my shirt and bit my lip, she pulled it back between her teeth and looked into me with her bright brown eyes... I knew. I felt the whisper slide right out of me. "Fuck... Helena..." I was so in love with her.

I closed my eyes, and she pushed a hand between us. I was crumbling inside. Helena made me feel so weak and strong. She undid my button and pushed the zipper of my jeans down —I can even remember the sound.

I snuck my hand under her blouse; her small breast was soft against my palm; she shook and swallowed... The way her throat moved, God, I felt lucky to have seen it so close. I brushed my lips against it. The sensitive skin on her breast hardened to my touch, and she threw her head back on the pillow. My Helena was so beautiful that night... I undressed her top and straddled her hips —I took off my T-shirt, and my hair fell on the side of my face until it tickled my chest. It was all so vivid; she touched my hips and took my heart. I lost my bra, and I swear I'll never forget the way she looked at me... Helena made me feel like I made sense to myself... In her arms, I started to feel beautiful, something I had never felt before. Ever.

Helena's hands caressed my back; everything was hazy, but I know she said my name and touched my breasts.

"Oh, Emily..."

*Her eyes were so dark, sweet and predatory —my entire body cramped, I wanted her so much. Still lingering above her, I knew I would never know what it felt like for her to be turned on, but I was so aware of what she made **me** feel. "Are you still sore?" I asked her as softly as I could, remembering a conversation we'd had —Helena had told me how she could still feel me inside. Just thinking about her words made me need her more.*

She shook her head, pushing my jeans and underwear down until I felt the waist of them below my ass.

I was so hard. When I felt the numbing pain and the cold air hit me, I pulled out the condom from my pocket and finally pushed my jeans completely off.

Emily's provoking arousal had broken free from repression, almost touching her soft lower abdomen.

Helena's walls twisted and tightened as Emily sex grazed her inner thighs —she knew just how beautifully blinding it was. She remembered the phantom limb comparison and opened those brown eyes to find Emily moving south.

Green eyes followed as pale hands removed Helena's

jeans and lacy black underwear —smearing kisses on her tanned stomach and hip bones. She caressed smooth, olive-toned thighs gently.

Helena's knees weakened; smoldered desire between her thighs dripped down. She bit back a moan and shivered at the feel of Emily tasting and licking a path down her body. "Oh, Em..."

Emily was drunk in love; she was so high on Helena's love it drove her straight into madness, a head-on collision she chose so fucking gladly. She continued with her steady attention, transfixed in the deadly darkness of Helena's thighs... so warm and wet. She kissed the flesh there with blushed lips. Finally...

Helena's mouth fell open. "Scheiße..." She shuddered and buried her head deeper into the pillow.

Sinking in the viciously erotic sound of Helena cursing in German, Emily's taste buds found a new kind of sweetness there; she had fallen in love with Helena all over again. Inside wet shelter, where rapture and chemistry made something so beautiful it kindled every cell inside Emily's body like flames, she smelled the faint trace left behind by the sex they were making. Her aching arousal rubbing casually against the cold sheets felt like glory, but nothing like *this* newfound glory.

Arms looped around her hips tighter and warm a tongue delved in deeper. Helena shivered; the pleasure that fell from her lips was the most beautiful sound Emily had heard her give yet.

"Emily..." Helena trembled, and so did her thighs, so did her stomach as she opened brown eyes and looked down to find green, loving ones looking up —Helena placed a hand on soft blonde hair and encouraged her.

So, Emily kissed deeper, knitting a blanket of stars and all those pretty things that came with love. She kissed wider and wetter. She made shapes and intrinsic knots... new patterns and forms.

"Oh... Em— Oh, please... God, please don't stop..." Helena's eyes rolled back shut, and her chest became hollow. Legs opened wider, and heels rolled on sheets.

Emily moaned loudly into her; telling sounds reverberated deep inside Helena, buzzing under her skin; her erection begging for purchase, having a torrid affair with the comforter. Both Emily's hands far too occupied holding her lover's stunning pelvis to bother with giving her longing dick any attention.

Helena melted into Emily's mouth, and those gorgeous sounds persuaded her —she stopped.

Helena's tongue rolled on her slightly dry lips, and puzzled eyes opened, revealing the night sky to a smitten Emily hovering right above her. Helena pulled her down and into a grasping kiss —a kiss where she tasted new flavors brought on by their untamed romance. She tasted Emily and herself for the first time... she tasted herself and fell in love with love —Helena fell madly in love with what they had made together, and never wanted life more... The purest form of lust for life radiated inside her chest. Emily on her part, was addicted, her knuckles ghostly brushed against wetness as she slipped on the rubber.

With eyes closed, Helena braced herself as she knew what to expect. The initial ache was there, but it quickly turned into the most beautiful and paradoxical kind of pain.

Emily flew high as Helena pulled her in so perfectly. The sight of parted lips and jaw fixed in place was liberating. Helena's brows found each other as she felt

Emily's searing end meet her —the craving inside; definite, absolute and sated.

"Oh, my God..." Helena's moan was devastating.

It made Emily tremble as she began to move. "Are you okay, baby?" Emily breathed out, the frail wisp of a broken voice so vulnerable.

"God, yes..." Consumed, Helena nodded and turned her head towards the nightstand. Lightly tanned hands gripped tightly on the sheets. While in a dreamy haze of satisfaction and ache, she saw one of the candles flicker — move within its own self-consumption. As Emily left slow and came back fast, the electrifying jolt hit the edge of her. Each time. Hot, wet, and easy strokes of a love red-colored and transcending.

"You feel so good..." she said, and breathed out as Emily's flawless movement seduced her will.

"You too, baby, you're so tight," Emily said, and heard her react. Helena's soft sounds were beautiful; they were all Emily needed to survive. Her breath was sweet, warm and tempting. Emily wanted to kiss her so badly, but *this* was transporting her straight into a state of no-self, simply watching *her*... The ins and outs of Helena's breaths grazing her lips just as they met in a kiss were binding. Emily's hands held onto those wicked curves and squeezed tighter.

Green eyes looked magical; maybe it was the night... the tightening arousal of the coming and going between their sweaty bodies or maybe it was just love. Emily wanted to keep this moment engraved to her memory until her last good day and beyond. She watched how right before her eyes, Helena became the most beautiful woman ever to walk the earth, the love of her life —she knew she would love her forever; there was no doubt.

Helena moaned on Emily's lips, and Emily couldn't hold herself anymore. The ardor in her heart and sex lured her into that exquisite mouth, and so she claimed it, she kissed Helena so hard that night. She kissed her like she was about to lose her.

That was how Emily's heart began to break at her mind's wandering. Thoughts of loss unraveled and she felt it all. Helena rocked her hips faster and grasped a fist on white sheets, Emily felt her tighten —but Emily's young heart was fracturing, it was rupturing wide open by the most beautiful and blinding love.

"God, Helena..." she moaned desperately and bruised her lips with a messy kiss.

Helena's orgasm began to extend; it seemed to have stopped mid-stride, only to turn into something more, something more intense and intimate. Her time-starved lover continued to move with frantic passion and speed. Legs opened wider, and Helena dragged red lines on Emily's back. The sound of their bodies colliding was confining.

Relentless... Once, twice, thrice... Helena's body tensed. She got lost in a mixture of Emily's lips and her definite presence inside. Emily took her to the peak of lust and showed her new constellations behind closed eyes. "Oh... God... Emily..." Helena suddered as she swallowed and choked back on love. She opened her mouth and locked it in place as she felt her lover catch up to her. Emily moaned and came.

The aching and pulling in... Helena was happily waiting to watch stars with her. A gift to her forever. She was lost in a haze while Emily's hopes, dreams, and love, were collected by the rubber.

Pale body shivered, and a heartbreaking sob escaped her lips. Emily sniffled, and Helena's smile turned into a frown, a worried frown. She quickly searched for Emily's face hidden in the safety of her neck.

Brown eyes found green ones bloodshot and soaked in tears; Emily was bawling in silence —her beautiful face flushed and broken.

"Emily," Panic overtook Helena's face. "What happened, love?" She desperately caressed Emily's wet cheeks and sought an answer.

Emily stalled with a small chuckle. She was swollen and embarrassed. "I'm okay... I'm such a girl, I'm sorry." she said, sniffing.

"Why are you crying?" Helena asked.

"It just got to me... the moment." Emily wasn't lying... technically, but saddening Helena with gripping fears of losing her wasn't an option.

Helena melted and kissed her softly. *Deeply.* "I love you."

Emily smiled again and nodded. "I love you, too." she said, and kissed Helena's forehead as she parted from her gently.

....

"Shit..." Emily muttered.

"What it is?" Helena asked, looking down at her lover's sex.

"The condom broke..." Emily said, and found brown eyes. "I'm so sorry."

"It's all right; those things happen, I believe... don't worry." Helena said, smiling, she brushed her thumb on Emily's lips.

"I'm sorry... maybe I— I was too rough, I am so sorry, did I hurt you?" Emily was frantically falling into desperation and guilt at the mere thought.

Helena sat up. "Em… look at me," She caressed her cheek. Emily eased down and complied.

"You didn't hurt me… I really loved it." Helena said with a small smile and confident eyes, glistening sweat damped her dark hairline.

Emily nodded and moved to help Helena with her clothes —a hand stopped her.

"It's all right, love—I need to shower anyway." Helena said, and grinned softly.

"Okay." Emily murmured, and Helena's lips pressed on hers.

"I will be right out... Will you please stay with me tonight?" she begged, and how could Emily say no?

"Of course…" she said, and watched Helena disappear into the bathroom as she turned over her shoulder with *that* smile...

Emily felt whole. Helena always looked back when she walked away.

Always.

She couldn't stand the thought of watching her walk away forever.

***

The warmth of early morning came without fail; it filtered through leafy trees and Helena's dorm window. The chimes of her cell phone's alarm tainted their all-consuming REM. Sleepy brown eyes awoke to the familiar beeping patterns and opened slowly.

Helena smiled. Emily was tangled with her in the most beautiful mess of blonde and black strands of hair, white sheets, and soft skin; they had apparently lost their clothes the night before, yet again.

Helena trailed soft kisses on her girlfriend's neck and shoulders. "Love... wake up." she said tenderly between smooth lines drawn by the tip of her nose on Emily's skin —she adored those sweet freckles.

"Hmm..." Emily muttered, eyes still stuck together.

Helena giggled and pressed her lips deeper into the crook of her neck. "Emily, you have to wake up; we need to shower and get dressed; I have an appointment with my cardiologist." Another warm kiss. —*Perhaps the use of my hands might be more effective.* Helena thought, and brushed gentle caresses on soft flesh under their warm sheets.

Another kiss.

Hands grazed her abdomen... Helena shifted closer to Emily and felt substance —she arched a brow.

In a sudden fit of chuckles, green eyes finally opened. "Mmmm... Oh, my God. What are you doing...?" Emily said with her groggy and raspy morning voice while those charming dimples appeared.

The happiest smile spread on Helena's lips as she captured Emily's.

"Mmm... I need to wake up like this every day of my life." Emily said whileHelena moved to her neck.

"I agree, but..."

Emily frowned. "Ugh."

"I know, I'm sorry." Helena apologized. "We have to get out of bed." Her lips found the tip of Emily's nose and pulled her in. "Come on, love, or I will be rudely late for my doctor's appointment."

Completely bare, Helena openly stood from the bed. Emily lost her access to oxygen as the soft rays of sun hit olive-toned skin; her warm chocolate eyes… her soft dark hair parading on her back, the wisps of its ends brushed her mid-spine.

With a coaxing grin, Helena pulled her enthralled girlfriend out of bed and dragged her towards the bathroom. She bit her lip, and enamored eyes gleamed as Emily's equally naked body came into full view.

Deep dimples pierced her cheeks. …There it was, that smile Helena adored.

Once inside the spotless bathroom, Emily pushed Helena against the cold tiles, bodies flush against one another. Helena smiled and looked into mossy, magical green.

"I am so in love with you," Emily whispered, and Helena's eyes shone brightly, their edges reddened as tears threatened.

"I love you, Emily," she said, and swallowed hard.

Smiles faded.

It was real. *They were real.*

***

They had spent longer than anticipated in the shower, though both Emily and Helena managed to get dressed on time. Sitting on her girlfriend's bed, Emily's damp hair fell forward as she tied the laces of her red chucks while Helena was lost in the bathroom, drying her hair and putting on makeup.

The muffled sound of heels clicking on the floor came from the hallway outside. Emily turned casually and saw their shadow stop right on the thin line under Helena's door.

Knock. Knock.

It was soft, but Emily's eyes went wide, those heels

sounded awfully familiar. "Shit. Shit. Shit!" she whispered as she rushed into the bathroom and dragged Helena out by the arm.

With perfectly contoured eyes and no lipstick, Helena's riveting lips parted and brows furrowed. "What is it?" she asked confusedly.

"Someone just—" she muttered. Emily was freaking the fuck out. *Indeed.*

Knock. Knock. Knock. This time steadier. "**Helena, dear, are you ready? We have to get going soon.**"

Green eyes almost jumped out of Emily's face. "Fuck! It's your mom," she whispered with mortified brows. "Why is she here? Oh, my God!"

Helena sighed and kissed Emily's lips. "It's okay." she tried.

"No, it's not! Oh, my God—I can't believe this is happening to me again." She searched the room with dread.

Helena walked away, and Emily wanted to die. —*Maybe if I jumped out the window? Yeah, that should work.*

The door opened, and Katherine's smile faded with the ease of vapor.

"Hello, Mother… I am almost ready —though I thought we had agreed to meet there." Helena arched a brow.

Collected and scrutinizing hazel eyes spotted the tall, gorgeous girl. This felt all too familiar.

A sheepish smile and shrug of two shoulders. "Hi,"

"Emily, hello, love. How are you?"

"I… I'm fine, thank you and you?" —*Fuck, that sounded so lame!*

"I am fine. Thank you for asking…" Katherine said while she scanned her daughter's dorm room. The disheveled white comforter... Helena's clothes scattered on the floor.

Tiny drops of sweat sprouted from Emily's pores. They may have been invisible, but she sure as hell felt them.

Katherine spotted jeans... a bra... a shirt... **a condom wrapper?** — "Not as well as you two it seems." She smirked sorely and found their eyes.

"Mother, I—"

—*God!* Emily wanted to bury her vermilion-colored face in her hands.

"So you will finally admit that you two *are* indeed having sex?" Katherine questioned coolly.

"Mother... I... We..." Helena grew flushed and frustrated. —*Ugh! I can't believe she's doing this again!*

"I love your daughter." Emily blurted out, and green eyes darted to Helena.

Hazel and brown ones fell on Emily, and she met Katherine's stare. "Yes— we did— have—"

....

"Sex." Katherine said what Emily couldn't push out.

"Yes." Emily confirmed.

"And you just said you love my daughter."

"I do, and I would never hurt her, I—"

Katherine exhaled deeply. "I knew this was bound to happen... at least you are using protection."

Brown eyes found her mother's hazel firmly, yet a faint spark of hesitation glowed brightly, Helena turned to Emily and then back to Katherine.

Oh, Katherine knew that expression... Her eyes grew large. "Helena, you *are* using protection, right?"

Emily blushed. —*Oh —my God.*

"We— we had an issue but managed, Mother," Helena

admitted, and Katherine glared at Emily.

She really, *really* wanted to jump out the window. "We had condoms, I— we—" Emily stammered.

Helena locked her jaw. Nostrils flared as her veins filled with suppressed exasperation. "Mother, this is none of your business!"

Katherine shook her head and sighed while rubbing her temples. "Are you ready for your appointment?"

Regal Helena found her center and nodded with dignity. "I am, I just need to finish my makeup."

Helena saw the longing in Emily's eyes. —*I'm sorry*. It was unspoken.

—*I'll be okay*. A wisp of a smile grazed Helena's lips.

Emily wanted nothing but hold Helena. To face whatever followed this next to her. Maybe even accompany them to her appointment, though she knew all too well about Helena's apprehension to seem weak in front of others because of her condition —including her. With a deep sigh, Emily faced Katherine— "I'm sorry Mrs. Millan..." she said, and found Helena's eyes. "Would you like me to stay?" Emily asked. Leaving her didn't feel right.

Helena smiled and adored her more. "It's all right, love. I will be okay."

Emily nodded. "Okay." She kissed her cheek and turned to Helena's mother. "I'm very sorry about all this... Bye, Mrs. Millan," she said earnestly.

"Thank you. Goodbye, Emily..." Katherine said in acceptance of her apology.

"I will call you later." Helena said with a soft smile.

***

As Emily made it to the bottom of the stairs outside, the blinding sun and chirping of the birds told her that it certainly was a new day; a gentle morning breeze blew her locks with peace, but squinted eyes rose and found Maddison right there.

"Hello, Emily," Maddison said.

Emily deadpanned. "Hey,"

Blue found green, and Maddison pointed over her shoulder. "I saw your motorcycle and tried to stall, but you know my mother." she said, and smiled casually.

Maddison's unusually soft and friendly tone threw Emily off her tracks. "Thanks..." Emily said.

"No... um..." Maddison averted her gaze, but eventually found words, "about yesterday... I heard you didn't get in trouble—I'm glad, and I'm sorry —I don't do drugs, you know?" she said honestly.

Emily looked down at her chucks and bit her lip with a ghost of a nod.

"Thank you... I won't forget it." Maddison said.

Emily shrugged softly. "Sure. You're welcome."

Helena's sister pointed at the stairs. "I should go help her out."

Emily's smile was a grateful one. "Thank you."

Maddison nodded genuinely, and Emily felt the shift. She turned and watched the auburn-haired girl get lost up the stairs.

9

STAKES

THE RIDE TO THE doctor's office had most definitely been quite the trip. When Helena entered her mother's sleek, elegant car, she was still blushing due to Katherine's newfound knowledge of her recently active sex life. It was embarrassing. She felt exposed. Not ashamed, but incredibly exposed. This was hers and Emily's only. Now it was Katherine's as well.

After a few provoking comments from Katherine, Helena spoke her mind, her words. This was her life, but it didn't end there. By the time they had arrived at the glass-covered, tall building in the middle of downtown San Francisco, Katherine Millan had mentioned Emily's penis twelve times — Helena had counted, and her patience was wearing thin.

The elevator ride up was calm, since there were other people joining mother and daughter. Silence was broken by those soft sounds from the moving metal box. The welling churns in Helena's stomach each time she rode an elevator made her sick. She hated elevators, they made her feel claustrophobic, and after the debacle she'd had with her mother for the past forty minutes, this just wasn't helping.

Ding!

Bold red numbers told them they had arrived at Doctor Rossi's office. With a releasing breath, Helena pushed the last tumultuous hour to the back of her mind, knowing it would be rude of her to enter her cardiologist's office in such a mood —which was rare for the usually sweet young woman. She was lucky, and she reminded herself of that fact every chance she got. If it weren't for this man, she'd be dead, and in all honesty, not many had the opportunities she did.

Doctor Rossi was a close family friend who flew across the world once a month to meet with Helena and check her progress. She knew he had other patients in the U.S, but still; the least he deserved was her full and collected focus.

Helena and Katherine walked into the contemporary office. Clean lines and neutral colors dressed the space surrounded by glass windows and a postcard-like view of the skyline. Doctor Rossi's tall and beautiful assistant greeted mother and daughter with kind poise. While in Zurich, Helena had had the biggest crush on the woman, mesmerized by her long dark hair, bronze-kissed skin, and sharp amber eyes. This time? She didn't look twice.

"Hello, Mrs. Millan... Helena..." the woman said with a thick German accent and smiled. "Doctor Rossi is ready for you ladies."

After the door was opened for them, a tall, handsome man in his mid-forties smiled as he stood from his desk with pleased brown eyes. He hugged Katherine.

"Michael, dear. How was your flight?" she asked.

"It was great, Katherine, thank you. Working through the jet lag, but it's nothing a good glass of wine can't cure." he said, smiling casually at his colleague and friend. "How's Santiago?"

While the pair spoke, an unconscious smile broke from Helena's lips. Brown eyes got lost as they fixed on the distant view of the city. She thought of Emily and missed her; intense feelings roamed her system like potent chemicals. They seemed to have grown after such intimacy. Beauty stretched inside Helena's chest, or was it love?

"Helena?"

She snapped out of her trance with blinking eyes and a kind smile. "Hello, Doctor, it is lovely to see you… Thank you for coming, of course."

Michael Rossi had to admit that Helena was his favorite patient. She was sweet, polite, considerate, kind, smart, and she was definitely Katherine Millan's daughter. Helena had her mother's confidence and charisma.

"Well, thank you, Helena, it is good to see you as well," He smiled brightly. "You look fantastic."

"Thank you." she said with a swift blush on her cheeks.

Katherine cleared her throat; she had a very good idea as to why her daughter was glowing this morning.

Helena glanced at her mother from the corner of her eye and tried her best to ignore the silent taunt. She knew Katherine was playful and incredibly open, but there were parts of her life she liked respected. Helena wasn't five anymore.

"Let's check you up and see if everything is working as wonderfully inside as it seems to be on the outside," he said, and Helena pushed a smile.

***

They sat across Doctor Rossi while the man examined several sheets of paper in his hands. "Helena, your EKG is beautiful... whatever it is you have been doing; please continue to do so." the man praised, unable to take his eyes off the test results.

Katherine raised a brow, and Helena blushed. Certainly her mother thought of sex, but the truth was that Emily entering her life had been the most amazing thing ever to happen, sex or not.

Helena's glare threw daggers at her mother.

"Your blood work was taken how long ago?" he asked.

"Two days ago, Michael. I did it myself, at the hospital, and sent it to my most trusted lab technician." Katherine said.

"This is stunning, simply perfect; everything is exactly where and how it should be." Rossi looked at Helena. "Have you been adhering to the meal plans I gave you last month?"

"I have, Doctor Rossi."

Helena was tremendously organized, a rare quality in someone her age. However, she was almost like the perfect patient for a cardiologist aside from the unfortunate obvious. Doctor Rossi wished she didn't have to be a patient at all.

"Your heart is the strongest it's been since I saw you in Zurich. I am very pleased." he praised.

A calming wave of relief washed over Helena. This meant more time alive, more chances to enjoy life... breathing, being... It also meant more time with Emily.

"However, I need you to maintain our strict regimen;

please continue taking the medications, diet, and exercise." He didn't say it, though Helena knew those words were code for *'you're still sick, there is no cure for you'*.

Helena never allowed herself to have hope, at least she always tried. However, ever since she had met Emily, it was the only thing she was unwilling to let go of. Doctor Rossi's heart cracked at the silent but obvious shift in Helena's telling eyes.

Something inside her moved at his reminder. Be it sooner or later, but she was still on her merry way to death. —*Emily...* she thought of her lover as a sad gleam welled up brown eyes. Helena pushed a smile and nodded. "Of course."

"Oh, dear..." Katherine's insides bruised, the walls in her chest narrowed, they squeezed her heart blue as she held Helena's hand. "You heard Michael, honey, you are doing great, and he is still working hard on developing a way, my love... you're healthy, and the present is all that matters... My beautiful girl," Katherine's hazel pierced her daughter with sentiment. "I know how great she has been to you and for you, but Helena, darling, think of *the now*... That is all any of us have. You. Are. Okay." Her usually steady and poised voice faltered. Katherine gathered herself and smiled. She turned to her friend. "Helena met someone in college, Michael..."

"That's just fantastic, Helena, who is the lucky fella?" He was pleased.

"It's a girl, Doctor Rossi... Her name is Emily." Helena said.

"Oh, well, that's just as great! I see now why the sudden change, it makes sense... Young love," he said, and looked at Katherine. "Just like puppy love, it seems to have magical healing properties." he added casually.

Katherine crossed her legs with graceful ease. "Well, this is not puppy love, Michael, this is full-blown, Wuthering Heights, raging and *hormonal* love." she admitted.

With a sharp turn of her head, Helena's eyes went round. —*Oh, she didn't.*

"Oh… well, okay," he said evenly.

"And that is exactly what I would like to talk to you about next…" Katherine added coolly.

Helena's mortified eyes couldn't possibly grow wider… Oh, but they could. "Mother!"

"Oh, no, no. Helena… we must have this conversation with him; it affects your condition."

Helena's face grew hot. "Please, Mother, this is not necessary."

"On the contrary, dear, it is." Katherine smiled. "Michael, it has recently come to my attention, that my daughter's girlfriend is a transgender girl."

Doctor Rossi shifted in his leather chair. He felt uncomfortable not because of the admission, but for a flushed Helena and the embarrassment radiating from her. It was certainly unusual and unexpected. However, he nodded and listened to Katherine attentively.

"She is this… tall, gorgeous girl, I mean, you should see her —simply stunning." Katherine mused and sighed. "I saw it coming…"

"You saw what coming?" he asked.

"Please don't!" Helena tried.

"They are having sex…" Katherine informed.

"Oh…" he said. This was none of his business, really, not as a friend, but as a doctor, yes.

"They are having *unprotected* sex."

The man opened and closed his mouth a few times as

Helena's jaw fell. She was indignant.

"Mother! Are you really doing this to me?! I already told you what happened!"

Katherine faced her daughter with stern brows. "Helena, I need for Michael to explain to you just how *risky*... what you two are doing can be!"

"I am not pregnant! She can't get me pregnant; she is on puberty blockers and hormones right now!" Helena defended passionately.

Michael tried to speak, "I—"

"It doesn't matter!" Katherine bit right back. "Your girlfriend has a penis! A penis and you have a vagina! You must use protection, Helena! I know you are smarter than that, dear, not only a pregnancy could kill you, but sexually transmitted diseases are a very real thing." her speech was passionate.

The man's mouth opened and closed some more. The situation was highly uncomfortable as this was a girl he had held in his arms when she was a baby.

An unrelenting Helena shot up from her chair. All of a sudden, smoldering coals in her veins burned brightly. Helena had grown tired of hearing the word penis fall from her mother's mouth so seamlessly. More now that it was her girlfriend's penis she spoke about. Exposed and tired, Helena's eternal patience had run low. "Yes! Mother. My girlfriend *is* gorgeous, and she has a gorgeous penis!"

Katherine's eyes grew large while Michael blushed and cleared his throat.

"Yes! *It is* beautiful, and I love it —I enjoy it and not because it's a penis, Mother... but because it is part of the woman *I. Love!* —Yes! I know we were irresponsible those two times—"

"Two times?!" Katherine interrupted, obviously shocked.

"Yes. Mother. *Two*. *Times* —we technically had unprotected sex twice, and I know the risks, I am not stupid, but the chances of Emily getting me pregnant are incredibly slim to almost none!" Helena's chest rose and fell ardently.

"That is not necessarily true, Helena. No, no, dear, science is very advanced. However, since you seem to know so much about this... tell me, what drugs is she currently on? You said she was on trial medications while we were in the car— besides the blockers and the hormones, what is her physician trying to achieve?" Katherine questioned.

Silence permeated the office; a more collected Helena exhaled and turned to her mother. "I am... not sure," she admitted.

"Exactly, dear, for all you know she has already impregnated you."

"Katherine... calm down —would you two like some water? Something to drink?" the poor man offered in kind spirits.

Katherine pushed a polite smile. "No, thank you, Michael... I am sorry about this."

A gush of frustrated air flared Helena's nostrils. She sat back in her chair, crossed her arms and stared at the wall behind her doctor. She turned to Katherine. "And for your information, I had never had sexual intercourse before, neither had Emily —she doesn't have sexually transmitted diseases, and we are committed to each other—she wouldn't do that to me." Helena said with bright, emotional eyes.

Katherine softened; she had hurt her daughter's feelings and probably bruised her pride. "Sweetheart, I didn't say she had, I am simply stating the facts of life, Helena —these things are a reality… and if you plan to maintain an active sex life with your girlfriend, I need you two to be a little more responsible and *careful*."

"Your mother is right…" Doctor Rossi said.

Helena's tight face softened. "I know… we will."

The man sighed and addressed his lovely patient with different eyes; he regarded her as an adult. "Now that you will have an active sex life, you *must,* Helena, please… you ought to be very careful. In your condition you could carry a pregnancy to term but—"

Katherine's piercing glare cut right through the doctor's words; he raised a hand in mid-air to the woman, never taking his scoping eyes from Helena. "I will be honest with her… she is an adult, and since she's living like one, this is now an adult conversation." he added, and surprise transformed Helena's face.

Katherine cleared her throat and crossed her long legs elegantly.

"Could I carry a child to term with my condition?" Helena asked, looking confused. Surely her mother hadn't lied. She eyed Katherine defensively.

"You would have to stop your medications— for the child's sake, and we would have to place you on a different treatment. You could survive a delivery. However, the risk of you dying is exponentially high. It would be ill-advised for you to conceive."

Helena exhaled through her nose with a deflating shudder. Emotion shadowed her gaze. Life was beautiful and awful. It collected chances others took for granted and crammed them into her soul like some stuffed baggage; life suffocated her, but at the same time smeared such stunning things in the mess. She never felt more used and wanted by fate.

A stealthily affected Katherine took a painful breath and gracefully scratched an eyebrow. She averted her eyes as they reddened with silent tears.

The sadness in Helena's gaze was heart-shattering. She wasn't planning on becoming pregnant, but she would love nothing more than to have the chance to be a mother someday, a day when her anatomy wasn't mocking her. Helena was silently drowning in the absolute cry inside, but after a second, she reclaimed her strength and painfully let go of that idea. Having that choice... Having *a* choice had meaning.

Her choice.

A certainty of control over her body —a body that was currently ruling and willing over her; she would love to have a choice —if she were to live, of course.

Rossi's heart fractured at the profound defeat in her eyes. Helena was on the verge of tears she held back like a pro. "Helena, I promise you... I am working so, so very hard to find a way around your condition. Nothing is set in stone, absolutely nothing. Please remember that." he said with care.

Helena swallowed back tears that burned their path down her throat; she nodded and pushed a smile.

"Before you go, Katherine... Please run new blood tests on her, and we will meet again before I go back to Switzerland —I will stay in San Francisco for another week, then we can retake the test."

"Very well, Michael. Thank you." Katherine said.

Eyeing her mother and cardiologist, Helena interjected, "Doctor Rossi, you don't have to do that... I am not pregnant— I'd hate for you to delay your trip because of me."

"It is no trouble at all, Helena… I am doing this gladly, and because it is very necessary, I'd rather be safe and leave everything running smoothly until next month." he said, and gave them a smile.

There was no point in fighting them, Helena sighed. "All right."

Doctor Rossi scribbled on a piece of paper with his shiny pen. "Helena… When was the last time you had unprotected sex?"

She shifted in her seat uncomfortably. "Last night."

"Very well. Then the timing is perfect. Katherine, please execute these tests for me, and we will remain in touch." He signed the paper and handed it to Katherine with a smile.

***

In the comfort and solitude of her dorm room, a downcast Helena sat on her bed, staring at the cornucopia of condom packets next to her. The doorknob turned with the jingling sound of keys.

Maddison walked in and caught sight of her little sister's mood. Brows crashed.

Helena met her eyes from across the room in silence. The air was thick with awkwardness and genuine, *contained* concern. Maddison narrowed the distance and sat on the other side of the bed.

"I am not in the mood, Maddison." Helena's voice was soft. The blue-eyed girl acknowledged her sister's sadness.

"I come in peace," Maddison said honestly.

Brown eyes found familiar blue and studied her unusual behavior.

"What is it, Helena? Why do you look so down? Did Emily do—"

"No. She didn't do anything." Helena shook her head. "I saw Doctor Rossi today."

Maddison's face contorted with worry. "Is something wrong?"

With a soft, silent gleam in brown eyes, Helena contemplated Maddison's words and reaction —the sensations in her chest, she hadn't felt since they were probably ten years old. She smiled. "No. Actually, everything seems to be surprisingly well."

"Okay... Good. Then what is it?"

"We... touched a subject that has just —it made me a little sad, that's all." Helena finished softly, and pushed a furtive smile.

"Oh... Would you like to talk about it?" Maddison offered.

Helena shook her head, still smiling. This very conversation permeated her heart with happiness and confusion. She instantly thought of Emily and the obviously beautiful consequences of her actions. She had shown her sister kindness and compassion, and what a stunning ripple effect this was —Maddison hadn't spoken to her this way in many years. "Thank you." Helena said.

Maddison nodded. Expressing care wasn't her forte and a very strange place for her to be at, but there she sat. Blue eyes lowered and focused on the out of place mess on Helena's bed. She gawked at the small mountain of condoms all over the mattress—a chuckle escaped her lips. "What?" Maddison looked at her sister.

Helena sighed and rolled her eyes. "Please, don't, okay? I've heard enough about these today."

"She bought you condoms? Oh, Mother..." Maddison

said, inspecting the brightly-colored packets. Her jaw dropped as she zeroed in on the sealed wrappers. "Bloody hell!" she let out and ogled.

"What is it?" Helena asked confusedly.

Maddison's gaping mouth cradled a grin. "Nice color." She winked deviously, "If you know what I mean."

A defeated eye roll aided Helena's amused scoff. Her cheeks turned a brighter shade of red. This was far too much awkwardness in one day with her family so openly discussing her girlfriend's privates as if they spoke of the weather. Helena rubbed her temples and bit back a smile. "That is— none of your business."

Maddison chuckled. "Oh, my God... You always get the longer end of the stick, don't you little sister?" she joked genuinely, "Pun, of course, so intended."

An involuntary chuckle fell from Helena's lips as she joined Maddison in the brief fit of laughter. It was as if for a few seconds both girls had forgotten about the last ten years of bickering, bruised feelings, and involuntary distance.

Their moment died down softly, gently. *Effortlessly.* Glowing, organic smiles transformed into content expressions. After a brief silence had fallen upon them, Maddison spoke up. "Well, I should go get ready, I have a date." she said in the midst of returning awkwardness — they hadn't spoken this way in so long. She stood from the bed and walked to the bathroom door.

"Maddison..." Helena voiced, and her sister turned to find honest eyes gleaming warmly at her. "I can't tell you who to date, but please be careful... Don't give that horrible guy your time."

"Oh, I won't see him again. He's a jerk. It's someone else."

A subtle smile brushed Helena's lips. She felt proud.

"Thank you."

Maddison nodded, nibbling on her lip. The smile that broke from her was just as authentic as Helena's; she looked down and gently patted the doorframe. It was altering. It was brief. It was *progress*. She got lost in the bathroom and shut the door.

Emily had certainly done a very wonderful thing; she seemed to have set something precious and once seemingly unreachable into motion.

***

Evening had arrived entwined with rain. Grey clouds dispersed in the sky like smoke smeared in dark blue. They opened way for a clearer aftermath. Only a chill and its signature earthy smell were left, bringing forth the untamable San Francisco vibe —the most peaceful and gray of all wet evenings. The lights reflecting on the tar, black pavement promised the night would turn out to be just as uniquely worthy.

The day had exhausted Helena, leaving her with only one desire; to crash in bed and enfold herself in the safety of those arms she loved.

There was a soft knock on the door and Emily's stomach filled with that familiar full emptiness. She knew it was Helena.

Emily rushed to the door and smiled at the sight.

—*Finally...*

Ever since she'd had to leave her girlfriend earlier that morning, she had only cursed herself for not staying. Regret ate at Emily all day, and having **her** right there was everything. "Hey," she said, and crashed into Helena's body.

Green eyes squeezed shut. —*Her perfume... her warmth.*

"Hello, darling," Helena looked tired and happy; she pushed an honest smile and closed the door behind, the distance between them narrowed at the need of Emily's soft lips on hers.

Emily's dorm room wasn't as immaculate as Helena's and Maddison's, but it was free of large messes. The place was relaxed and cozy —a more typical college student's lair indeed. Emily was grateful Etta had given them some space for the night.

Helena's dazzling lips claimed ready and expecting ones with ardent ambition; the kiss was slow, and even though completely uninvited, it was welcomed. Emily's tongue and her longing hands on Helena's small waist encouraged it inside.

As their warm, glistening lips broke apart, an exhausted Helena pressed her forehead against Emily's; she sighed with unguarded eyes. "Em..." she whispered, and basked in life. Helena inhaled the irrevocable vivid clarity of Emily's existence. The rise and fall of her chest. She pressed an open palm on it... It was warm —it was real. It was strong and fragile... It was all a gift.

The pleasant texture of Emily's wool sweater and those dim lights entwined on their headboards. Helena thought about the invisible flow of electric charge traveling through the wires they were attached to... A simple yet abstract interpretation of how something as fickle and powerful as electricity interacted with her surroundings. Perhaps the stories that clung to the walls... The countless stories they had watched unfold. Helena was orgasmically enthralled with the simplicity life offered —to everyone... anytime, anywhere. It was a deliberate taste of something missing, so ardently there and still so absent.

Emily moved her lips to Helena's forehead and continued to hold her. "I'm so sorry I left you... I should have stayed with you." she said, resting her cheek on Helena's.

Helena pulled back and out of her high gently. "You don't have to apologize —it wasn't a big deal, I just..." She pushed fatigue out with a sigh while longing eyes got stuck on the comfortable looking bed. Brows furrowed as she almost begged, "Can we just...?"

It was easy to see just how exhausted Helena was. "Of course we can," Emily said, their hands entwined as they walked deeper into the room.

Helena sat on the mattress, and Emily stood right there, exquisite hip bones covered in washed denim, green eyes looking down. Pleasant dimples grazed blushed cheeks as she admired *her*, completely lost in lust and love, but her lust would have to wait; there was no way she would even attempt to make a move on Helena while she felt this tired.

Helena looked up with gripping eyes and placed both hands on Emily's thighs while Emily ran the back of her fingers on a smooth cheek and tucked a couple of dark locks away —hypnotizing fascination and love, indeed.

Darkly manicured fingers hooked on the loops of Emily's jeans, Helena pulled her in and rested her forehead right in the alluring valley between Emily's hips. Mossy green squeezed shut as a soft hand caressed Helena's head. Emily could have sworn that was the ultimate test to her strength.

A tanned hand traveled underneath the fabric of Emily's top; nails tantalized warm skin as brown eyes looked up again and found a darkening gaze. "Kiss me, please..." Helena whispered.

Emily caressed the side of her girlfriend's face and

guided her down on the bed. She slowly lowered herself on Helena's body and claimed her lips with sweet infatuation. Soft kisses moved to Helena's neck —the warmth and lingering scent of Helena's perfume were enslaving. "I love you so much..." Emily murmured, still consumed in her haze, hands running up her girlfriend's sides slowly.

Helena cradled her hands on Emily's cheeks, locking their gleaming eyes.

—*God, she looks so tired and so beautiful.* Emily thought, realizing she had never seen this much conviction in Helena's eyes. She would never get tired of admiring every single inch of Helena's face. How could you want so badly to live and die for the very same thing all at once?

"I adore you, Emily Knight." Helena's thumb caressed her jawline

A light yawn sprouted from Helena and Emily was endeared. "Let's rest, beautiful..."

Dark lashes fluttered as Helena tried to shake off slumber. "It's only seven..."

Emily rolled off of her and lay next to that familiar warm body; she kept a protective and gentle hand on Helena's abdomen. "You look exhausted, Lena..."

With a pleased smile, Helena shifted to face Emily, all while her eyes focused on a leather-covered notebook resting on the nightstand. A wondering brow arched; it wasn't a notebook... It was a journal.

"What is it?" Emily asked, caressing her. She turned to see what had caught Helena's attention and tensed at the sight of secret pages that knew it all. Emily sighed and the tight muscles on her back relaxed; this was Helena. It was okay.

"You write?" she asked with a sweet smile.

Emily shrugged. "It's just a journal my therapist makes me keep."

"Makes you?"

"Well, I'm not obligated, but... I guess it does help." Emily said.

"It's beautiful..." Helena reached for it, and her fingers brushed the thick leather that enveloped it. It felt like time and raw confessions, even though this was only the surface of a deeper part of Emily Knight. Helena then realized she didn't know it all. —*I know I love her.*

Ever since their day of confessions, Emily had been patiently waiting, desiring and expecting for Helena to invite her into the side she kept sheltered. Helena was open, though a profound and intimate part of her stayed locked in. It was the side that always made her eyes look so... *moving.*

Emily had never desired to delve in others as she did with Helena. She was usually practical... used to her loneliness, just as Helena had grown scarily comfortable in hers. But this time, Emily wanted the weakness and pain, the unrehearsed, absolute and vivid emotions surrounding the thing that hovered above her. Helena was always so private and particular about her illness being displayed to others, but just now, looking into those sweet eyes, Emily realized that there were so many unlit places inside her own self. Small corners where the light was dim, and how in some of them, it was simply nonexistent.

How could she ask for what she hadn't offered? Emily took the journal from her girlfriend and opened it.

"What are you doing?" Helena asked with more awakened eyes.

"There is something I want to show you."

"You don't have to do that, Emily... those are private; so intimate —I didn't mean to make you think I expected—"

"I know you didn't... but I want you to..." The corner of Emily's lips curled up. "Your name found a home in this thing since I met you, so..." she said, and shrugged earnestly.

"Are you sure?" Helena asked.

"I am, yeah..."

With a complacent nod, Helena sat against the headboard of Emily's bed, feeling the warmth of the string lights on her back.

Focusing on the fabric of Helena's designer jeans, Emily grinned shyly; she zeroed in on the clarity of her warmth while pale fingers caressed her hips. She shifted and rested her blonde head on Helena's thighs. Long strands of hair smeared like a melting sun. Green eyes sought north as Helena read the page she had guided her to. Watching the rise and fall of her chest, and then watching her smile. Emily wondered which combination of words had brought Helena joy. Pale fingers brushed sweet olive-toned skin. Emily then saw warm brown eyes fill with tears that had to be blinding —her heart shattered; it shattered a thousand times, but she knew those weren't sad tears.

A smile broke free from those sweet lips... Helena was happy, and her tears were falling. And so, she continued reading while Emily caressed her like they had no time to repeat it all.

Helena later made a confession—Helena gave more, and Emily held her close all night long. At that moment and in that light, this was them, and it was so much more than enough.

10

EMILY

THE PASSING OF FIFTEEN days had culminated with Helena's second set of test results being negative for pregnancy. Katherine was relieved, and Helena had gotten confirmation of something she already knew; she had done her research and believed in her conviction —Emily couldn't get her pregnant.

At Clearwater, morning had flowed with normalcy; both Emily and Helena agreed to meet at The Vine for lunch since they hadn't run into each other all day.

Helena made her way into the open space filled with people who were still strangers; they had somehow become familiar faces that she knew nothing about. The rich smell of freshly ground coffee hit her pleased nostrils, and soft experimental music washed her ears.

As brown eyes searched the vibrant cafe, Helena spotted two very familiar blondes standing in the food line. A smile broke free, and she made her way to Emily and Etta.

While narrowing the distance between her and them, Helena realized Emily's clothing was slightly different than usual. The soccer jacket had been replaced by her black

213

leather one, it hugged her perfectly, just as the slightly loose jeans that flirted with her lower hips —those beautiful hips Helena loved and knew so well. A thin chain hooked on denim and a back pocket. Emily's slightly differing look was most certainly provocative.

Helena placed a soft hand on her lower back, slipping it right under the jacket.

Unknowing, Emily turned and found the smile that had absorbed her entire universe. Her face lit up.

"Hey," Helena said, and claimed Emily's lips.

Pale hands found a small waist and welcomed the kiss. "Hey,"

"Hi, Helena," Etta said with a casual smile as she took a red apple from the tempting food display.

"Hello, Etta," Helena replied, and eyed the bright palette of appetizing colors; leafy greens... strawberry reds —not at all the section where Emily's eyes were on.

Seconds later, Helena ran an intimate hand on Emily's lower back. "You look..." Delicious lips met. "Different today. Stunning... yet a little different —we match." she said with a pleased smile.

"Oh, yeah?" Emily arched a playful brow.

"Yes." Helena winked and took a step back with coquettish open arms.

Loving every inch of displayed beauty, Emily's heart filled with revitalizing crimson. Helena resembled a dark ballerina. White dress and black leggings —her petite torso wrapped around a killer, black leather jacket.

"You look gorgeous, baby... always." Emily said with a grin and turned to the food display; her pale hand grabbed a perfectly wrapped cheeseburger —then another.

"Are you ready for your game this afternoon?" Helena

asked, and chose a bright-green salad.

Emily smiled and took a bag of cookies. Helena's eyes followed her food choices the entire time. "Yeah, I can't wait to kick their asses." she joked and grinned. A pale hand claimed the last piece of a perfectly contained slice of apple pie.

"That's not very nice, Em," Helena arched a brow.

"That's Leo's team we're playing against —I maintain my words." Emily boosted.

Helena took in the new information, but couldn't hold her tongue any longer, "Emily, your calorie intake is very alarming."

Green eyes glanced at her beautiful tray, and her stomach growled, so very happy to know it would devour the contents in a few minutes. "What?"

"There is an average of three hundred and three calories in a cheeseburger; you have two. I haven't counted your pie, cookies, and drink yet. That is an excessive amount of empty calories, Em." Helena lectured.

Eager to defend her stance, Emily opened her mouth to speak, but instead, she watched as her girlfriend's delicate hand took one of the burgers away and replaced it with a salad. She frowned.

"But…" Emily whined as she continued to watch an olive-toned hand put the other —oh, so lovely half of her lunch back on the food display.

Helena smirked and placed a shiny red apple next to her salad, Emily's furrowed brows and gaping mouth were endearing.

"But I need my empty calories, and besides, I'll burn them all later today—I have a game, remember?" she sassed.

"Emily, you eat two cheeseburgers almost every day,

regardless of your continued physical activity, it is bound to catch up with you eventually."

Deep dimples and a smirk appeared, "Yes, I eat them every day because they are delicious, and I'm fine."

Helena arched a warning brow.

Emily huffed and moved to pay.

"You are so whipped." Etta murmured under her breath, and chuckled.

Emily deadpanned.

Handing a bill to the cashier, Etta caught her best friend's glare. "What? You are," she mouthed and shrugged. "She's right, though."

Emily looked at her tray and then caught a wink from Helena. —*God, I am whipped, fuck!*

***

The day had culminated with the start of the first official soccer game of the season, and they would be playing against East Valley College.

Emily was known as the star forward and captain of the team. Therefore, the anticipation and expectations were running high for many. While some reactionary spectators awaited her failure, others eagerly expected a worthwhile game.

Etta and Helena sat next to each other among the sea of people and looked around the large field. Emily was still not in sight, though the hyperactive crowd was more than ready for the players to come out. Thank God for front row seats.

"I'm glad you could make it, Helena, I know how much it means to her to see you here... I..." Etta blushed, no one knew of Emily's prior loneliness more than she did. "I'm so happy she found you."

Helena saw tears well up in Etta's eyes and felt the meaning behind them claim her very own with stinging sentiment. "I wouldn't miss this —I adore her, Etta... Thank *you* for being by her side all these years."

With a brief bow of her head, Etta's smile turned into a half concerned frown and Helena didn't miss it. "I've noticed she's been acting a little weird these past few days... Is everything okay between you guys?" Etta inquired.

Helena knew exactly what Emily's best friend meant. Though the behavior she had gotten from her girlfriend hadn't been weird —they were far too close for that. However, Emily had become more withdrawn towards other people, frustrated with college assignments, and slightly short tempered with anyone who looked at them the wrong way; this was indeed very out of character for the usually relaxed and quiet girl.

"We are okay, but I have also noticed a change in Emily's behavior lately." Helena added.

With a deep sigh, Etta shielded her eyes from the setting sun —she pushed a smile. "Maybe I am overreacting; maybe it's just the pressure of the tests and the demands from the team." —*It has to be that, of course.* Etta thought and shook it off.

Helena favored her with a brief smile. She accepted Etta's answer but knew something was going on inside her girlfriend. The blonde's hesitation was telling. Sometimes it is far too easy to lie to ourselves and pretend everything into normalcy —into something that feels good. Helena wasn't keen on stroking denial's ego; she would most definitely keep a close eye on Emily.

The sudden roaring of the crowd around them broke her trance.

"There they are..." Etta pointed, and Helena spotted Clearwater's team walking out from a distance, including player number 7, her beautiful Emily. She smiled and felt an unwavering sense of pride from watching her girlfriend stand out in the group of males. Her talents prevailing over the tedious gender lines.

Back on the green field, Emily's gaze rose to the crowd and caught sight of Helena and her childhood friend, proudly smiling as they cheered her on.

Emily thought it was impossible to find new ways to love *her*, but each day that passed, more and more of Helena encompassed her world, extending its edges. Expanding and stretching her beating heart to be able to fit in more, so much more. She would do anything for Helena... she adored her so.

Emily reached for her foot and pushed it back as she began her non-negotiable routine of stretches; she worked on her muscles and breathing while the opposing team made its way out, ending up right across from them one by one.

The testosterone in the air was bold and inevitable; behind the heated line of war, they eyed each other competitively.

Sitting in the front row, Helena's attention was focused on her girlfriend and brother, of course.

All the while, Emily couldn't peel her menacing glare from one of the players. Her nostrils flared as she caught sight of Leo Blackwell's mocking grin, it taunted her composure. Some sort of conflicting energy lingered between them ever since the day he had so lewdly stared at

Helena like she was something to eat —after what he had done to Maddison.

His reasons still obscured in Emily's brain; she could only pin his jeering and lecherous interest in Helena to juvenile idiocy, though she had to admit that the twisting knot in her stomach only made her want to give into violence. She clenched her fists. Leo Blackwell was a cocky bastard, and every inch of his demeanor was drenched with exactly that. Emily didn't know much about him, but his interest annoyed her; he obviously lived for the thrill of a chase. In fact, at that very moment, Leo turned to the crowd, as if searching for someone.

Suspicious green eyes traveled from him to his target. It was, of course, Helena. The beautiful girl wasn't hard to find. He grinned shamelessly, and a growl birthed at the base of Emily's stomach, coals burned through every vein. It was officially on.

She turned and locked gazes with Helena, who simply had no eyes or joy for any other. Emily smiled back at her.

On the field, challenging eyes met again. Emily wasn't one to use the word hate, though every fiber of her being told her that the little prick deserved to have his ass kicked. None of the words her mind concocted spoke of restraint. Fire raced through her body as she clenched her jaw and fists so tightly that every muscle in her arm was strained sore, her bite locked, her glare darkened. —*Breathe, Emily... the fucking asshole is just trying to piss you off... just... breathe.* She tried her very best to remain calm as the game's start was announced through the speakers.

***

The match was at its peak. Sweaty players ran freely through the field, executing their moves with passion and concentration. The score was tied, and the crowd on edge, waiting for the other shoe to drop.

2 - 2 and only a few minutes left; the winning goal rested on the shoulders of their star forward, Emily Knight.

An anxious Etta fidgeted as restless blue eyes followed her best friend's agile moves, all the while refraining from indulging in the nagging desire to munch on her nails.

Emily readied herself and ran towards her designated spot. Their coach, of course, eyed them like a hawk; the man was a fantastic trainer; he had faith in all his players and team, but his hopes to execute this last play were set on Emily's talent.

Etta and Helena held on tightly to one another, literally on the edge of their seats. The tension in the crowd could be cut with a knife; many cheered on and singled out player's names, some whistled, and others shouted as they clapped with anticipation.

Caleb passed the ball to a midfielder with smooth ease, player 2 caught it with agile feet and ran with it, only to be intercepted by Blackwell a few steps away.

—*Fuck!* Emily cursed between her teeth as she watched the checkered ball get stolen from her teammate. They had been working on that play for the past fifteen minutes and didn't have much time to spare.

The ball rolled further and further away from Emily, passing from one set of opposing feet to the other. "Fuck!" she hissed and scowled; blood boiled inside her.

Emily's eyes followed the rolling ball, only to watch it end at the little bastard's feet.

—*Fuck it!* She left her position.

In a moment of temporary madness and personal rage, Emily went after what she wanted —herself.

Back in the crowd of shouts and whistles, Helena furrowed her brows. "What is she doing?"

Etta frowned, submerged in absolute confusion as she watched her friend break the established dynamic of the game. "I... I don't know," she muttered.

Emily's teammates looked at each other with heaving chests and sweat running down their faces —they shrugged. With no other choice, they ran towards her, trying to defend whatever move she was planning to make.

A thick vein popped from the coach's temple as he watched his star forward tear the play to pieces. "What the hell are you doing, Knight?!" his flushed shout was drowned by the sinking sounds of the excited crowd.

Emily's darkening eyes zeroed in on her prey, everything around her completely blurred and gone. The only things she felt were adrenaline in her veins and the royal desire to break his stupid face.

The vexed coach chewed on his gum tightly and contained his urge to break something —the board in his hands slammed and bounced on the grass as he threw it frustratedly. "Damn it! KNIIIIIGHHTTT!" his roaring shout merged with the louder noise of the passionate crowd.

Leo ran away with the ball and Emily ran faster, she pushed her athletic body to the limit. Completely aware of her senses, she swept him with a foot and pushed him; the sweaty guy winced as he plummeted to the ground and cried in pain —he cradled himself like a baby and clung to his shin.

The crowd went wild as the loud sound of the whistle brought the game to a halt.

Helena's jaw hit the ground, and Etta covered her mouth in disbelief.

A red card was flashed on Emily's face by the referee as he blew on the whistle and motioned out of the field.

Emily sneered at the idiot on the ground; she couldn't find the will to care, part of her felt a rush of satisfaction. She wiped her sweaty face and walked off the field, soon finding the disappointed and lost faces of her teammates in her passing. Their frowns hit hard and reminded her of what she had done; they would have to go to playoffs without her; she had probably cost them the win.

Helena moved through the crowd as she excused herself and rushed to the field. "Emily!"

Once there, avoiding a couple of bodies on the way wasn't difficult, she spotted Emily and jogged to her. "Emily!" Helena shouted once again and noticed the large man's flushed and screwed up frame barking at her girlfriend.

Emily turned at her name being called and ignored the scolding words of the bellowing man.

"WHAT THE HELL WAS THAT KNIGHT?!" he thundered out while tiny drops of spit aided his fiery speech.

With a tight frown, Helena interjected, "Okay. That is enough! You are a horrible man for abusing your position of power this way! This is completely unnecessary!" she managed in her most intimidating and paradoxically enough, respectful tone.

"It's okay, Helena," Emily murmured, she felt deserving of the verbal vomit for letting her impulses get the best of her.

"No, it is not!" Helena looked up and challenged the towering coach defensively.

The man looked down as if a tiny fly had landed on his robust frame; he chewed on his gum tightly and turned to Emily. "Who da hell's this pretty little thing?" he asked, almost endeared.

Helena inspected him and picked up on his thick, New Yorker accent.

"She's my girlfriend, Coach... Look, I'm sorry, I'm really sorry, I don't know what happened—" Emily apologized honestly.

"All right, whatever's going on, I need you to get it in check. We have a heavy season ahead. No more of what happened today, got it?" he warned, seeming more calmed.

"Yes, sir." Emily said with broken spirits. She really did feel like shit, not only had she let her team down, but also thrown weeks of practice and careful planning down the drain.

He turned to look at Helena, and a hint of a smile found his lips. Her face was tight, crossed arms on her chest and an arched brow. "She's real cute, Knight... Don't piss her off, though."

The coach walked away, and Helena rushed to search her girlfriend's gaze. "Oh, Em... sweetheart. Are you all right?" she asked.

With a nod, Emily met devoted brown eyes. She pushed a cheerless smile. "I am, baby, don't worry."

"What happened? I know that guy is an idiot, but you've worked so hard for this." Helena said.

Emily stalled, not wanting to worry Helena with how off she had felt lately. "I know... I just misjudged my distance; that's all." she said with a small smile.

Even though Emily's intentions were in the right place, Helena knew what she had seen her girlfriend do, but decided to let it go, *for now...* "Okay. Do you still want to go out for dinner? I made reservations earlier, but we don't have to go, love..."

Emily brought Helena's hand to her lips with exquisite gentleness. "I have to shower first… give me a few minutes and then we can go, all right?" Green eyes were back to their natural soft light.

Helena nodded.

***

Their intimate dinner turned out to be exactly what Emily needed after such unsettling turn of events. A couple of hours later, both girls walked towards Emily's dorm room tangled in casual and joyful chuckles.

Steps were easy and unworried, but in truth, nothing could have prepared them for what they found as their feet came to a halt. Helena was the first one to catch a wide open door and two policemen exiting Emily's and Etta's room. Slack-jawed, brown eyes watched them walk by as green ones widened.

"What the hell?" Emily said, and rushed into her room with Helena in tow.

As they stepped inside, sight of an absolute and horrid mess collided with their disconcerted eyes. *A mess*, her childhood friend, and her father.

"Dad?"

"Emily!" Ben took a deep breath as he saw his daughter. "Honey, I came as soon as I could —are you two okay?" he asked as worried eyes went from Emily to Helena.

His question was answered with a stunned nod.

It was more than disheveled sheets, actually. Emily's and Etta's dorm room had been heartlessly trashed and turned upside down.

Still unable to form another word, Emily and Helena scanned the place with unsettled insides. Books were torn and scattered all over, mattresses turned, years of memories captured in childhood photos ripped to pieces amongst shattered glass. Every piece of furniture either flipped or brutally busted... and sadly enough, a nasty arrangement of words Emily was used to being called or seeing written over her parents home was spray painted on the wall. She clenched her jaw and took a deep, seething breath.

Brown eyes reddened and filled with unshed tears, Helena couldn't believe what she was witnessing.

Emily's broken gaze found Etta's equally shattered one. "What happened? I'm so sorr—" —*Ugh...* Emily sighed as embarrassment filled her anatomy. She was so sick of others having to suffer the aftermath of what was clearly aimed at her.

Red-rimmed blue eyes softened. "Em, don't. This is not your fault." Etta said.

"Of course it is." Emily replied with a sullen chest, but Helena's faithful hand squeezed hers.

"Em, love... Etta is right; don't do this to yourself."

Soft pale hands ran through blonde hair in frustration. "Grr! This is so fucking ridiculous!" Emily gritted her teeth as she walked toward a small pile of books on the floor, and leaned down to pick up a busted picture frame. It was a photo of her and Helena smiling at the camera. Another priceless moment disregarded amongst broken glass as if it didn't matter.

"Motherfuckers... I bet that asshole had something to

do with this!" Emily said, and kicked an already busted night table.

With a sore and frustrated heart, Ben's loving hand found his daughter's arm. "We are already onto them, Em... Whoever it was, was sloppy —we found a busted bat, and I have an officer running it for prints as we speak. They already collected what they needed from here... we should go home. I've already spoken to Doctor Andersen."

Confused, Emily shook her head. "Wait. What? Why do we have to leave?"

"Emily, it isn't safe for either of you to stay here after this... at least not until we find out who did this."

Sad green eyes met her father's.

"I'm so sorry, honey —Helena, you should go home as well... It just isn't safe; you would be an easy target if they were to do this again."

Emily's stomach turned, she wanted to vomit. Helena nodded and reached for her cell phone.

"Of course, Mr. Knight... I will call my sister immediately." She turned to find those eyes she adored dressed with threatening tears and endless, silent apologies.

A gentle smile grazed Helena's lips. "It's okay, my love... Everything will be okay. I am here, Em..."

It wasn't fair.

11

VIOLET SHADOWS

OCTOBER WAS ENDING, AND even though autumn leaves weren't burning California's concrete walks, San Francisco was still beautiful, so was this night and her intentions.

Helena walked into her father's office, the familiar fragrance of his musky, woody cologne and mint made her smile. It reminded her of warmth and cherished hugs from the man she loved most. She had missed her father greatly while studying in Europe; a strange sense of regret filled her heart for a moment; she had barely shared with Santiago since her arrival. Gentle and strong chocolate eyes peaked over reading glasses as his dear daughter approached him.

"Helena, cariño... ¿Como estás?" It was always nice to see his youngest.

Always.

She smiled and brightened his world a little more. "Hola, Papi. Muy bien ¿y tú?."

"Muy bien, Mija... Gracias. What can I do for you? Is

everything okay?" Santiago asked.

Helena tucked the back of her dress with grace and sat across from him. "Yes, there is something I would like to talk to you about... well, more like I need your authorization for something." she hinted.

The man listened attentively. "Okay, what is it, dear?"

"It regards my living trust. I know that I am not supposed to touch it until I'm twenty-one, but..." She glanced down at her pristine, black nail polish. "let's face it, I may never see twenty-one." An awkward chuckle in these types of uncomfortable situations should always help, right?

Santiago felt a dagger pierce right through but contained himself, his next breath was stealthy and painful, but Helena would not notice. He made sure of it.

"I would like to make a withdrawal for twenty-five thousand dollars."

With furrowed brows, a collected Santiago pondered on her words. "That is a rather significant figure, Helena. What do you need that costs this much?" he inquired.

"Well, it's not for me. I need it to buy Emily's Christmas gift."

"Have you talked to Katherine about this?"

"I have... she said it was okay by her, but that I needed your approval as well, so this means you have the last word." Helena finished, hoping for that yes.

Santiago removed his reading glasses and contained amusement, because even though she was selling her idea with enviable charm, she seemed a little nervous.

Compared to Helena's living trust and their wealth, the amount she asked for seemed minimal, and it would be like a cat losing a hair. If Katherine had agreed, it meant the woman had given it plenty of thought and judged it properly. He trusted her rationale. "And what are you planning on buying Emily with this money?" he questioned.

Helena smiled. "I wanted to give her something of meaning to her. After some extensive research, I have found this organization —they help families with transgender children who can't afford puberty blockers. This amount would be enough to provide treatment for one of them in Emily's name." she was concise. The soft gleam in her eyes and knitting brows melted Santiago's resolve into a pool of nothing.

"That is a very thoughtful and life-altering gesture, sweetheart." Santiago voiced with great affection for his girl. He felt proud. "I have absolutely no objections to this. I will authorize the withdrawal."

Helena's eyes were as dark and bright as the starry night outside, warm and full of life, so full of joy and good things. Santiago felt satisfied; he felt lucky to have put that smile on her face.

"Thank you, Daddy," Her next batch of oxygen caught in her throat as she stood and rushed to him.

Santiago wrapped his arms around her and smiled. In one unforgiving stroke, the effect of his love for her consumed him; losing Helena would stain his soul like a cut from the sharpest blade. When his strong hands were at their gentlest, caressing her black hair was like holding on for the longest night —the smell of orange blossom and the sweetest love of all. Helena was unforgettable and unique; he cherished her now. He hoped for an again, he always did.

Just as Helena parted from the embrace and motioned

to leave, Santiago's mind wandered. "Helena, dear..."

With a swift turn, brown eyes met her father's again. "Yes?"

"Have they found the person who vandalized Emily's room?"

A deep breath that was both painful and slow, surged into Helena. "Nothing yet... We have an idea of who it was, but the surveillance videos show two people with masks... Emily's dad is still looking."

"I can't believe that sweet girl is being targeted by such unspeakable hate... It is not fair."

"No, Daddy, it isn't." Helena said with newfound wisdom on just how terrible people could be. Her Emily didn't deserve such horror. No one did.

***

With the end of October, of course, came Halloween and Etta's signature party. Emily loved the all hallows eve because people got the chance to free their minds and souls, becoming anything their imagination desired. While in her younger years, Emily was always first to thrive in the horror, costumes, candy-apple-colored lights and a ton of gore to go around, she loved it all, but no one loved the tradition for the departed more than Etta.

Even though in most places fall was a season of sweaters, pumpkin lattes and earthy variations of the color orange, living in California had huge perks; the weather was still fresh and quite fantastic. Both best friends sat under one of the many cherry blossoms dressing their green campus. Emily casually hovered over her burger while Etta's wheat sandwich had been completely forgotten; her entire focus was on the cell phone in her hands and the text she was typing.

Emily bit on a crispy fry and observed her friend with a smirk on her lips.

Etta sighed frustratedly, and big blue eyes finally rose. "Ugh!!! Stupid blizzard!"

Emily chuckled. "What the hell are you talking about?"

"It's the kick-ass band I booked for my party;" Etta huffed, obviously disappointed. "They might be stuck in Toronto due to some crazy winter storm."

"Oh, I'm sorry, Etta..." Emily said, and once again smirked as she chewed. "You can always retract yourself and claim temporary insanity. What if it turns out like your birthday party last year? —And are you sure your parents are okay with that big of a party? I mean, you hired a freaking band."

Emily grinned, she wasn't sure if Etta's glare was because of her words or the fact that her party plans were crumbling.

"Yes... they are, and I am sure you will be pleased to know that I booked Violet Shadows." Etta said matter of factly. "*And* I made the guest list very carefully; I didn't tell many people from here..." she finished, and went back to the checklist on her lap.

Slack-jawed Emily couldn't believe her ears. "Violet Shadows? Etta, that's Helena's favorite band—" She beamed.

"Oh, I know." Etta winked.

Just as Emily opened her mouth to thank her for the thought, she gasped and furrowed her brows. "Wait. Why would you book Violet Shadows? —I smell a bullshit plan." Emily suspected.

Etta arched a devious brow. She so had a plan, a wicked one at that.

"Fine. I'm not putting on a costume, though." Emily smirked and took another bite.

Etta's mouth fell open. "You have to, Emily!" She dropped her sandwich.

"Nope... I don't."

"You can't abandon me like this!"

"You're so dramatic." Emily said with a chuckle.

Arched brows sheltered blue eyes as they spotted Helena approaching their tree —Etta grinned. "Oh, you will put on a costume, my friend... *that... you... will...*" she finished, and stared at the beautiful brunette getting closer.

With a screwed face, Emily scouted over her shoulder and saw what had caught Etta's complete attention. Wide green eyes turned to glare at her friend. "Don't you dare manipulate my girlfriend into making me put on a costume!" she hissed.

"Oh, Em... I so will... Violet Shadows, remember?"

Emily curled a vengeful lip and watched her gloat. "You are such a—" she couldn't say the words and searched her brain for better ones, less insulting adjectives for her good friend.

"Such a what?" Etta challened playfully.

"You're evil."

Etta shrugged smugly. "Well... that is not news my friend, of course I am. It's Halloween, what did you expect?" she said, grinning with a devilish glint in blue eyes.

"Ugh! I swear..."

Soft arms wrapped around Emily and a gentle kiss grazed her neck. "Hello, gorgeous," A kneeled Helena said, and sat next to her girlfriend. "Hello, Etta," she added with a casual smile.

"Hey, baby," Emily said with a smile as her insides melted.

"You're so dressing up," Etta muttered as she bit back

amusement. Green eyes bore through her in warning.

"Will you stop it with that? No, I am not!" she countered.

Completely lost, Helena reached for one of Emily's fries. "What do you mean by she's dressing up?" she asked, and put the crispy treat in her mouth.

Emily arched a confused brow and observed her girlfriend.

"Well… remember my party is this Friday, and I was just telling Em that a costume is mandatory *and* that I booked Violet Shadows." Etta stated, eyeing her friend suggestively.

Helena's face brightened. "Oh, I love them!"

Etta smirked and winked at an unamused Emily. She was so gloating.

"The costume theme sounds incredibly exciting; I have never even been trick or treating." Helena added.

"Seriously?" Emily asked.

"Very…" Helena nodded. "When we were younger and still lived here in San Francisco, my parents never had time for those sorts of things; we were always with nannies… their schedules were very hectic. However, I have always wanted to dress up for Halloween." she said with an unknowing and excited smile that dissolved Emily's 'no costume' rule.

A shameless Etta winked at Emily.

"I can't believe you."

With a gentle hand on Emily's thigh, Helena sought her gaze. "What is it, Em?"

"Nothing… I'm just not really into costumes, that's all." Emily softened.

"Oh… Really?" The mild disappointment in Helena's tone shrunk Emily's heart.

Etta raised a pleased brow. —*Mission accomplished.*

Pale fingers laced with tanned ones. "But since you've

never had the chance to experience Halloween, then I'll dress up with you."

Etta grinned victoriously, while Emily wanted nothing more than to kick her shin; it was so close to her foot.

"Oh, Em... you don't have to do that." Helena voiced, and Etta frowned, her hopes deflated.

With folded fingers on Helena's cheek, Emily smiled. "It's okay... I want to do it with you." Anything for Helena.

Emily's intentions reshaped a corner of Helena's heart; she always had soul-bending intentions. "Thank you..." Helena kissed her.

While Etta smiled and took a bite of her sandwich, Helena reached for Emily's burger and took a small bite herself, Emily deadpanned.

"Mmm... This is so delicious." Helena savored and chewed on that juicy bite, placing it back on the foil wrapper as she stood.

A pair of stunned green eyes blinked. —*What?*

"However, I have a class to catch," Helena said, and kissed Emily's cheek. "I'll see you later, okay?"

Emily nodded, her mouth agape and brows knitting purposefully.

"Bye, Etta... thank you for the invitation, we will be there." She smiled, and so did Etta.

"Bye, Helena."

***

The next couple of days were uneventful, aside from the fact that both Emily and Helena had barely managed to share a night of slumber in each other's company. Time together was always precious; it was always invaluable and simple; though what they felt was far from simple.

Separation meant ardor and exciting expectation for the day they would meet again. Now that privacy was a thing of the past, most nights were spent in the warmth of each other's arms, indulging only in sleep and that was enough.

Watching Helena sleep had no definition and had thousands at the same time; it was captivating delicacy.

This night, though, would be a different one because it was Halloween, which meant Etta's party was only a mere thirty minutes away from starting, and Helena was —oh, so ready. Back in the familiar walls of her bedroom at the mansion, she turned her attention away from her reflection in the mirror as a knock came from the door. "Come in…" Helena said, and Emily entered.

Breaths were lost, and oxygen left their lungs, but a smile came first. Awe transformed Emily's face —Helena was just so beautiful in that black dress, her face… so different, the edge of youth and adulthood, so defined… her essence smeared towards the latter. Helena was the most beautiful woman she had ever laid eyes on.

An annihilating smile broke from Helena's crimson red lips while brown eyes gleamed eternally. Her costume was exquisite and dark, in other words, it was most fitting. It was simple.

A frozen Emily shook herself out of the haze. "You look so beautiful…"

Helena took the time to revere Emily in contrast. Her strong edge still reigned. She wore ripped white jeans, white chucks, and a white muscle t-shirt that was as milky as a waving peace flag. The soft lines of her stunning arms and sides were on display, only relying on her black bra for discretion. Emily looked down at herself with carmine cheeks and scratched the back of her head. She had no idea what Etta had done.

Helena's eyes were on a high... mossy ones, light and hypnotizing —blonde hair fell freely... wildly... beautifully. They drew each other in and Emily wrapped her hands around Helena's small waist while Helena looped both arms around Emily's neck.

"You look stunning, Em... I love it." Helena cooed intimately.

Emily blushed and shrugged. "Really?" she asked.

Helena grinned. "Oh yes."

"Thank you, but you... you are the one who looks stunning... I still don't know what you are —hell, I don't even know what I am— but I fucking love it." Emily brushed her infatuated fingers on crimson lips, completely in love with this new side of them. "God, and here I thought your lips couldn't look any sexier..." she said with exquisite fascination in her voice.

Helena blushed. "Are you sure? Isn't it a bit too much?"

"Oh, my God, no. You look..." Emily would have given anything to kiss them. She moved her fingers under Helena's chin and inched into alluring blood red. "Can I?"

"Do as you please." Helena said with a delicious grin.

And so Emily did, she tried to satisfy the need in her heart. What words couldn't convey, this touch of lips would try to say.

They parted, and Helena smiled. "And to clear your doubts, I am oblivion..."

"Oblivion?" Emily asked.

"Precisely." Helena winked. "It's from a book I am reading, Coalesce. An incognizant state; no craving or loss, no search for meaning... No pain?" Helena ventured. "Absolute and magnificent nothingness." she explained with a smile.

"Sounds grim," Emily said.

"Perhaps... or conveniently freeing."

Emily scanned herself. "Well, this was all Etta... she said it was supposed to compliment your costume, so..." Emily shrugged, and Helena smiled.

"It does, love. You are my contrasting state... awareness, recognition... realization. **Knowledge**."

With a smirk, Emily tightened their intimate embrace. "Then maybe I'm supposed to save your soul." she teased.

Helena arched a brow and grinned. "To save *my* soul?"

Emily nodded and kissed her lips again. "Mmhm..."

"Love looks not with the eyes, but with the mind, and therefore is winged Cupid painted blind. Nor hath love's mind of any judgment taste; wings, and no eyes, figure unheedy haste. So I say... may both our souls collide, my love..." Helena finished softly and claimed Emily's lips with her red rouge ones. She opened them with arousing grace.

And so oblivion and awareness met, their tongues embraced provokingly. It was far from mathematical, no parametric equation of cycloid or hypocycloid... It was far from existential. It was simply human.

As warm lips parted, gleaming brown studied her girlfriend. "There is only one thing missing," she pointed out.

Emily watched while Helena took the thin necklace chain she always wore from the nightstand and looped it around her neck.

"What are you doing, Lena?" Emily asked.

Helena secured the delicate piece of jewelry and tucked

it inside her lover's white tee. "Now you truly are my awareness."

"Helena, this looks expensive… I'd hate to lose it." Emily touched the almost seamless loops of precious metal with soft fingers.

"You won't." Helena said, and entwined their hands. "Now… we should really go."

Emily swallowed down another attempt to convince Helena. As her gaping mouth shut and digits lingered on the necklace, she was guided out of the room and down the grand staircase.

Minutes later they found Helena's brother sporting a ripped bloodied shirt and jeans, the snow-pale face screamed: **Zombie!** He sat on the luxurious sofa with slouched shoulders and a fallen face.

"Caleb, are you all right?" Helena asked, and sat next to him.

He pushed a smile. "Yeah… aside from the fact that my date for tonight just stood me up, and now I'm just an idiot in a costume." he mumbled.

"Oh, Caleb… I'm so sorry." Helena looked up at Emily and then back at him. "Where were you going?" She felt terrible; he looked like the cutest, most depressed zombie she had ever seen.

He shrugged. "Just some party downtown, I think— It was her thing."

Emily interjected, "Well, why don't you come with us to Etta's party?"

"Naw… it's okay. I'd hate to crash; she didn't invite me."

"She won't mind, I promise. Just come with us." Emily insisted.

With dark shadows under his eyes, Caleb looked up at Emily and then at his sister, who gently rubbed comforting circles on his back. "Are you guys sure?" he asked sheepishly.

"We are… come on, let's go." Emily nodded coolly.

Helena stood from the sofa and squeezed his hand. "Cai…"

Caleb smiled and rose.

Just as they had reached the refined doors of the mansion, an all too familiar voice and accent came from the stairs; they turned.

"Aren't you all a bit too old for trick or treating?" Maddison asked as she eased herself down the staircase, wearing a black dress.

Helena bit her lip and turned to Emily.

Caleb smirked. Any chance was good to taunt his sister. "*We* are going to a party." he teased.

"Oh…" Maddison said as she reached the last step and faced the disguised trio. Emily and Helena didn't miss the disappointment in her voice.

"Would you like to come?" Emily asked, and surprised blue eyes rose. Maddison tried to hide her excitement but failed miserably. "All right." She shrugged coolly… seemingly unimpressed. *Right*.

"All right… Let's go." Emily beckoned.

"Wait!" Helena halted.

"What is it?" Emily questioned.

"She isn't wearing a costume; Etta said it was mandatory."

Emily rolled her eyes. "Etta's crazy, Helena."

"No. This is her party, and if she says costumes are mandatory, then they are." Helena added and thought quickly. "Wait here… I won't be long."

After a time-lapse, Maddison was wearing a black witch hat and sat in the back of Helena's car along with Caleb.

Emily drove through the beautifully lit San Francisco streets while an increasingly irked Helena settled on the passenger seat, she glared over her shoulder. Caleb and Maddison had been annoyingly changing the radio station for the past fifteen minutes, and Helena was losing her mind.

Maddison reached to the front and changed it again; the thumping bass of an 808 echoed through the car.

Caleb's arm reached over. "Grr! Stop! How can you listen to this crap on Halloween? It totally ruins the mood, Maddison!" He changed it back to his station, and the electric sounds of a rock song filtered through the speakers of Helena's elegant car.

"Joel Jett is not crap, you log..." Maddison reached over and changed it again.

"He sucks! —Oh, my God, *you* suck!" Caleb bit back.

Emily cleared her throat and shifted in her seat as she continued to drive while Helena rubbed her temples. Emily couldn't help but think she looked just like Katherine. She smiled, and green eyes went back to the road.

"All right— please *stop!* You two are acting like a couple of brats, and it's driving me insane, okay?! —And if you touch this radio again, I swear you will have to walk the rest of the way." Helena scolded the adult babies on the backseat as she glanced over her shoulder.

Maddison arched a brow and crossed her arms while Caleb simply sneered at the auburn-haired girl and sat back. They had to admit that Helena's costume helped on the scolding, she looked fucking intimidating.

Helena changed the radio station to something softer

and less mainstream.

Emily smiled, feeling incredibly turned on, kinda morbid... but hey, whatever.

Once they had finally arrived at Etta's party, the foursome was immediately taken. Etta had turned her parent's garden into something from another dimension. Straight out of a book could better describe the purple and hot pink lights, the 'smoke' and all the 'blood' splattered on white fabrics dancing with the night wind. Dancing, just like many of the people in disguise while others spoke freely and mingled, holding different colored drinks in their hands. The pool had been turned into a vapor-oozing glacier filled with dry ice.

"Not bad, Etta..." Emily muttered and grinned.

Helena gasped. "Oh, I love it, Em..." She was irrevocably enthralled.

Thoroughly pleased, Emily smiled and placed a hand on Helena's waist. "Come on, guys, I—" Emily tried to lure her girlfriend's siblings, but they had already fled.

"I am so sorry." An embarrassed Helena huffed.

"What? Why?"

"Because they are behaving so rudely... when you truly didn't have to invite them in the first place."

Emily shrugged. "I'm sure they'll manage, and as long as I have my oblivion, quite frankly... I can't care less about anything else." she said, smiling, and inched closer to crimson lips.

Helena simpered and welcomed that mouth she adored. "Mmm... so charming..."

"Naw... it must be the dimples." Emily joked, and stole another kiss from delicious red lips.

Helena laughed and looped both arms around her girlfriend. "Would you dance with me?"

Heated carmine conquered Emily's cheeks. "Lena, I can't dance for shit." she admitted sheepishly.

Dark eyes gleamed with an enticing flare that easily incinerated Emily's soul each time—it made her fly, and it made her want. Helena had mastered persuasion and tenderness. She had a look... *that* look. "If you let me lead... I'll show you it isn't so scary. Besides, it's a relatively slow song..."

Emily, of course, caved in. Helena led her to where a few other couples danced engulfed in the lights and that fresh night wind.

Once facing each other, Helena looped her arms around her awareness, and Emily held her oblivion tight, she allowed Helena to sway their bodies from side to side slowly.

Getting lost took no time for either one, their loving gazes engaged in devastating magic's hold, and even though most eyes were on them, they didn't notice or care. Just as their mouths met so did the force of their romance.

At that very moment, Emily loved her more—she held Helena and had no choice but to breathe her in, to get lost inside, again... Nothing ever hurt more than missing her and she hadn't even lost her.

The kiss broke, gleaming lips lingered close.

—*Stay.*

Safe in Emily's arms, not even the woe of a fallen star's song could bring tears to Helena's eyes; those eyes that looked as black as the night igniting everything inside. They made Emily feel closer to Helena than ever before; it was something so primal and beautiful she couldn't attempt to explain. She felt a new connection to her lover and its nature seemed unbreakable. However, Emily was painfully aware of just how fragile everything truly was.

—*Please stay with me.* Emily continued to yearn.

Love never hurt like this.

***

The spooky night lived on. Etta and Helena were deep in conversation about Violet Shadows while watching them play another song. Emily on her part, had retreated to get them a couple of those cool-colored drinks —little did she know that her night was about to take a violent turn.

Once at the food-filled table, a hand reached for the same drink in her aim. They clashed, and Emily turned.

Every tiny hair on the back of her neck stood, not with fear, but with the tempting pushes of rage.

Absolute rage.

Deep breaths claimed her chest as the soft line on her jaw flared. Beautifully defined, tightly clenched. It was Leo Blackwell.

"Ah, the freak strikes again, nice show you and your hot little girlfriend gave everyone," he taunted her and coolly bit on a carrot. "It was almost as good as the one you gave on the field when you tripped me." He grinned derisively.

Emily's lungs expanded and deflated. With a menacing glare, she inched forward and faced him like a rabid dog. "What the hell are you doing here, asshole? Didn't you have enough with trashing my room and hurting Maddison?" The anger in Emily's voice was as sharp as the tempting grip of violence seething inside her.

"Maddison... she's a sad bag of mommy and daddy issues —it's a shame really; I had to dump the little whore.... and your room? What the hell are you talking about?"

Leo smirked, and something inside Emily shattered, patience maybe. She'd had the douche bag between two eyes for the past two months, and it seemed like she would finally get to wipe the smugness off his face. "Don't fuck with me, Blackwell or I swear to god—" Nostrils flared as she tightened her fists, fingernails almost piercing through her skin.

"Or what, you stupid bitch?" A shadow crossed his glare. Two open hands beckoned her. "Come on, tranny... just because you're fucking a girl, doesn't mean you're not a revolting little faggot —you're fucking disgusting, and so is Helena for mixing with you." He hissed with absolute detestation.

Emily's face burned, a savage snarl found her lips as she charged forward and launched a solid fist against his rock hard jaw. She shoved him against the table, knocking down a couple of bottles in the process. Eyes completely blank, Emily rammed a numb fist into his gut and a splitting last blow to his cheek. "Ugh!" He stumbled.

Knuckles raw, Emily winced and shook her hand; eyes dark and focused, her breathing out of control.

The band stopped playing, and the murmuring, curious crowd surrounded the commotion.

"You fucking piece of shit! I swear I'll break your face if you even look at Helena again!" Emily threatened as her lungs screamed for air; every single head turned towards the scuffle. It was venom, pure venom, and unadulterated rage.

There was a nagging... devious glint in his bloody grin.

He spat crimson and laughed, predatory eyes shot a glare at all the surrounding faces. "You're gonna regret this, Knight! You're so fucking dead!" he warned and launched himself at Emily, but was jerked back as Caleb agilely gripped on his shirt, clumsily stretching it back.

"Stop! What the hell, man? Are you really about to hit a girl?" He locked an arm around Leo's chest and struggled.

"That's no girl! —Argh! Fucking— let go of me, Millan!" he spat, and continued to bleed from his broken lip as he desperately tried to flee from Caleb's strong grip. Irate eyes so threatening, he aimed to jump at Emily again, though this time another guest moved in and helped Helena's brother restrain the unwanted party crasher. "Hey, man!—" They wrestled with a seething Leo.

Emily's chest rose and fell as a mortified Helena rushed to her side. Both Etta and Helena had missed the entire fight.

"Who the hell is this?" Etta asked as Helena's hands frantically searched her girlfriend for injuries.

"I'm okay." Emily murmured, never taking her eyes away from a bleeding and cross Leo.

Consumed with worry, Helena could only see the blood splattered on Emily's white shirt and pants... her hand; "Emily, you're bleeding... What happened?!" Helena asked, on the verge of tears.

"This isn't my blood... I'm okay, I promise." Emily tried to reassure her girlfriend while still catching her breath.

Helena shook her head. "What happened, Emily?" she demanded.

Etta was quick to confront the unknown guest. "Ok! You, whoever you are, get the hell out of my house or I'm calling the police!" she warned.

Leo sneered at her and everyone else, including a shocked and offended Maddison. Her ears had caught his horrid words before the fight.

He had nothing else to look for; with a sore ego, Leo Blackwell jerked himself off Caleb's grip and left.

Etta turned to her murmuring guests. "And you guys... come on, back to the party, there's nothing to see here." she tried to ease her friends.

Soon, the hi-hat of the drums was heard, then came the soothing synth line, and finally the electric guitars, announcing the start of another song. Everyone turned to Helena's beloved band —a neverending imagery of cute and evil.

Etta searched for her best friend's eyes. "Are you okay?"

With a sore hand, Emily winced and nodded. "Yeah, he didn't touch me."

Helena took Emily's wounded limb and regarded Etta. "Could you please find some ice for Emily? The pain will be unbearable tomorrow if she doesn't treat this now."

"Yeah, sure. I'll be right back." Etta said, and turned to leave.

"Emily... What happened?! Why are you acting this way? This is so unlike you..." Sentiment stung Helena's red-rimmed eyes as the words left her lips.

It killed Emily to see her cry. With a sick stomach, she took a deep breath and shook her head. "I don't know... I just— I couldn't contain myself, he—" She refrained from repeating Leo's disgusting words. "He's just an asshole, okay?"

"Emily... please talk to me, love... I am here." Helena tried softly this time as she searched for her adored girlfriend, and she, of course, found her there, hiding behind wounded green eyes.

A flushed Emily tried to hold back, but tears blurred her vision. "I don't know what's happening to me... I just—" She swallowed hard and inhaled deeply. "I feel different, and it's driving me crazy, Helena," she confessed with a sob, and her tears finally fell.

Desperate hands cradled Emily's soaked cheeks. "But why? What is making you feel this way?"

Emily bit her lip as it quivered; she placed both hands on her hips and looked down, trying to hide the embarrassing cry. Wet green eyes found brown ones. "I don't know..."

"Is it me?" Helena asked with knitting brows.

"No! God, no... of course not, Helena... you're the best thing that's ever happened to me."

Loving arms wrapped around Emily and held her tightly. With bloodshot eyes and hot wet cheeks, Helena found shelter against the thumping skin on her girlfriend's neck.

Emily closed her eyes and drowned herself in the only person who made her feel found.

It wasn't remotely close to the lover's end, but it was goodnight.

They would never end.

12

ROMEO

WEEKS HAD CONTINUED TO move along. —That's the funny thing about time… it doesn't stop. All measures of time derive from cosmic rhythms, Helena wished to be able to move backward in time or forever freeze a moment.

"The more I fell in love with her, the clearer it all became. We are all prisoners of time; we are stuck in time with no ability to move to a past that we know or a future that is uncertain. We are all hostages of a now that doesn't stop. Of something designed to keep schedules and meet deadlines. I hated time, and I craved for it..."

While cooler winds roared outside, the grand theater walls sheltered them. Emily was sure Shakespeare was twisting in knots inside his grave. Even though she loved the thought of being Helena's Romeo, *this* was turning more and more into a tragedy.

Emily exhaled deeply and clenched her jaw with frustration. It was the fifth time Professor Silverstein in all her sweetness had made her repeat the lines.

Helena lay on a small cot while Emily hovered above

her. Emily's frustration radiated in the form of heat. Helena caressed her forearm. Warm eyes softened her soul with just one stroke of gentleness.

"Em... it's all right, don't frustrate yourself," she whispered.

"How can I not? I don't understand eighty percent of this stuff."

The patient professor spoke up from the comfort of a velvety red chair. "Emily, darling... here, he believes her to be dead... I need you to feel it, don't repeat the words you've learned by heart... *feel it.*" She nodded, trying to convey meaning and Emily nodded as well; a gleam of sadness shone in noble green eyes.

Emily's intellect was far from challenged; she understood what she had been saying perfectly well. How couldn't she? Those were the very things she feared in real life. The lie protected her mind and heart from complete insanity.

She swallowed hard and took a deep breath; Emily had tried to avoid going there because that place always tore her heart in ways she couldn't stand.

With one last smile, Helena closed her eyes. The air grew thick, and even the professor shifted in her seat while other students stared at the couple in silence —almost as if they shouldn't.

Emily admired her love and gently caressed soft strands of dark hair. Her eyes roamed Helena with adoration and ache. "Dear Juliet... Why art thou yet so fair? ...Shall I believe that unsubstantial death is amorous and that the lean abhorred monster keeps thee here in dark to be his paramour?" Emily's voice was soft, only loud enough to bounce on hollow theater walls and find everyone else's ears. Helena was indeed so beautiful. How could she blame death for falling in love with her?

The rise and fall of Helena's chest was the only thing keeping her sane, keeping those emotions from devouring her whole, but for a small moment, Emily slipped off the edge. The silence around was too thick and real. Too violent for her heart's sake.

"For fear of that, I still will stay with thee..." Pale fingers caressed her cheek as green eyes welled up. "And never from this palace of dim night depart again." Emily could never leave Helena, not even in death.

The professor was on the edge of her seat with a wrinkled heart while the others were glued to the scene, sinking in the heaviness of what unfolded before them.

A thick glow pooled in Emily's eyes until hot tears fell free, and with a sick stomach, she rested her head on Helena's belly. Fingers folded tight on the soft fabric of her dress. "Here..." She sniffled and found the next words in her closing throat, "here will I remain with worms that are thy chamber maids. Oh, here... will I set up my everlasting rest," Wet lips blushed a deeper shade, they quivered, and green eyes squeezed out a fresh batch of tears. Fists tightened the hold on Helena's dress while teeth gritted with frustration. "And shake the yoke of inauspicious stars from this world-wearied flesh!" Emily cried.

The woman directing them was lost in the pit of her own emotions, while the students were feeling further beyond their reach. No one this new to adulthood should be expected to have felt such tormenting heartbreak in their short life. They simply stared in a kind of silence that spoke of respect for something they didn't yet understand, but still, their human hearts were not immune to.

Empathy.

Emily broke the heartbreaking embrace and looked down at her lover. "Eyes look your last. Arms, take your last embrace." She leaned down and held her sweet Helena close —she felt so warm and alive... A flood of relief surged back into Emily's veins.

So they stayed there, cheek to cheek as the salty wet of Emily's tears spilled upon Helena's faulty heart. She then realized just how much Emily had been keeping inside. It all made sense... That's why she had broken down while they made love; Helena's insides twisted. She was causing Emily incredible pain —pain Emily had decided to bare alone.

Pale fingertips caressed the portal to that glorious mouth. "And lips... Oh, you the doors of breath, seal with a righteous kiss... a dateless bargain to an engrossing death." Warm lips met Helena's still ones, and gave Professor Silverstein something beyond any expectation.

"Oh, Emily... that was breathtaking, honey,"

As the kiss broke, Emily sniffled, and Helena opened her eyes.

Hearty claps broke the silence, and the students joined in, some with smiles, others with awkward teary eyes.

Emily and Helena felt exposed. Emily wiped away her tears, feeling as if she had just woken up from a bad dream, while Helena more aware of their vivid clarity, sat and shielded Emily's privacy.

"Professor, could we please take a small break?"

"Of course! After that, anything..." She looked down at her watch. "Okay, guys, let's take ten minutes, Tony and Raaj, you two will be next."

Helena took Emily's hand and walked her to the back of the curtains; backstage, where all masks were removed and the strings of puppeteers were visible —the place where lights lost their glow.

Delicate hands cupped Emily's cheeks and perfect brows furrowed. "Em... Are you okay?"

Bloodshot green met wounded brown. "I am... That was some acting, huh?" Emily pushed a chuckle and tried to stall.

Helena's insides were in pieces; she didn't buy it; "Em..." she whispered, "I am so sorry, love —I didn't— I just—" Helena tried. Very few times in her life had she struggled to find words.

"What is it?" Emily pushed a smile.

With no time to explain, Helena sighed. "Would you be able to spend the afternoon with me?"

Emily nodded. "I can, yeah... I have practice in thirty minutes, but I should be done by the time your last class is over."

Helena pressed a soft kiss on Emily's lips and smiled. "All right, don't worry about showering... please meet me by my car as soon as you finish, okay?"

"But Lena, I'm gonna be all sweaty and gross."

"Just trust me, please? I really need to spend some time with you... *alone*, without someone barging in." Helena missed the furtive taste of privacy they'd had in the dorms.

"Okay, I'll be there."

The truth was that something inside Helena had been raging like fire, and the lack of intimacy was driving her crazy. In all honesty, she couldn't explain the hunger she felt for Emily. It was primitive and undeniable; it was a craving that needed to be sated. With blushed cheeks, Helena smiled internally and told her brain that she couldn't take her there. That she had to wait; that there needed to be reason somewhere in her need.

She laced their hands. "Are you ready to go back out there?"

In calmer spirits, Emily nodded. "Yeah, let's go."

They returned to the stage and continued with their practice. Gladly, it was someone else's turn. Somewhere along listening to Tybalt and Mercutio's lines, Emily felt grateful, she wouldn't have to dive into her emotions again. —*At least not today.*

***

Emily tried to catch her breath as they walked into the tall, exclusive building. Still wearing long training pants and her soccer jacket, she peered at the concierge from the corner of her eye as they walked past him. Helena, of course, impeccable and collected as always, regarded the man with a polite smile. He nodded.

"Are you sure this is okay?" Emily asked while being led to the elevator.

Her girlfriend's nervousness was endearing; Helena smiled. "It is, love. My aunt is out of town."

Emily's face fell. "Your aunt? Are you serious?" She gawked awkwardly.

Helena chuckled. "Yes, my mother's youngest sister, she just turned thirty... we get along very well, and she knows we are here. I told her that we would be coming together..." Helena assured her with a grin, a delicious juxtaposition of accuracy and endearing mischievousness. Helena had impeccable charm, and somehow always managed to make it feel as if she knew exactly what she was doing, *and* that it was always right.

While Helena maneuvered the lock, Emily brushed a small kiss on her shoulder. "I wish I could thank your aunt for this..."

Helena smiled and opened the thick, wooden door, revealing an exquisite apartment. Emily's jaw dropped, but it made sense; the rest of the building looked too luxurious to have an ugly corner. "Oh... my... God."

Pleased to see Emily so happy, Helena closed the door. "Do you like it?"

Emily's jaw was still hanging. "Are you kidding? This place is amazing..." Green eyes took in the tasteful contrast between contemporary grays and whites transposed with rich, dark woods. She rushed to the large windows. "Holy shit..." she said.

San Francisco was covered by the falling evening, glowing city lights survived the thick stir of gray fog and a dark blue sky.

Helena looped her arms around Emily's waist and kissed the back of her neck.

"Baby, I'm all gross..." She blushed and turned in safe arms.

Helena adored Emily's natural scent, and even though she had been running for an hour, the result was enticing. She smiled and grazed her lips on Emily's throat. "Mmm... No, you are not. I love the way you smell..."

Cheeks blushed deeper, and Emily smiled brighter, those sweet dimples in full view. "Ew... no... Lena, please, let me shower first." She shyly shriveled away from her lover.

With lingering lips and a soft smile, Helena gave space. "All right... I have a phone call to make; you can take your shower or a bath if you'd like," She winked. "There's a very nice tub in there." Helena pointed to the neat guest bedroom.

Emily smiled wider. "Seriously?"

"Seriously." Helena said, chuckling.

"Okay… I'll be yours soon." Emily unzipped her jacket and shrugged it off.

Helena bit her lip as Emily walked away, exposing herself. Taken by the provocative sight, Helena shook her head and took a deep breath. —*Phone call… Right.*

She searched for the device in her bag and dialed a recent number. The sound of water cascading and softly crashing on tiles meant she could speak freely.

'Camilla Young,' Came from the receiver.

"Hello, Mrs. Young, this is Helena Millan… we spoke yesterday regarding a donation." Helena said, and smiled earnestly.

'Oh, yes! Helena, thank you for returning my call. I simply wanted to let you know that we have received your kind gift… Words cannot express how much this means to Leah and her parents.'

"I am so very happy for them, though remember, I did not make this donation." Helena glanced at the open bathroom door, and could still hear the sounds of Emily moving in the shower.

'Oh, worry not. We have the paperwork you filled out with the correct information; you will receive a copy of everything as soon as tomorrow. Thank you, again.'

"On the contrary, thank you for your guidance in the matter and, of course, your help." Helena nibbled on her bottom lip. "Thanks again…" She nodded at something the woman said. "Of course… Goodbye, Mrs. Young," She ended the call.

With the passing of several minutes, Helena made herself comfortable in the guest bedroom and waited for Emily. She thought of the conversation they needed to have; speaking of death and loss wasn't easy, but Emily's silent pain was something Helena would never forgive herself for.

Emily walked out wrapped in a thick white robe; long strands of damp blonde hair and blushed cheeks contrasted perfectly with light green eyes. "Oh, my God, that shower is amazing," She skimmed over her shoulder and into the fantastic washroom she wished she could steal.

With a smoldering gaze, Helena still sat on the edge of the bed; her wounded heart skipped a beat as she admired Emily in silence. A wild and lethal combination of want and melancholy surged through her blood.

"And this robe... it's so perfect," Emily added but lost her breath as she turned and found dark shameless eyes exploring her; that sad longing gleam made them shimmer.

Helena stood and reached back to unzip her dress.

Emily's smile died —a thick lump rolled down her throat.

In a delicate woosh, Helena's dress fell and pooled around her ankles; she immediately unhooked her bra, never taking lustful eyes away from *her*. She wanted her —oh, so much.

Quickening breaths claimed Emily's chest; blood flowed faster and warmer. Long lashes blinked as nervous green canvassed Helena's beautiful breasts, her soft abdomen, and curvy hips. The most beautiful woman.

Two tanned, unapologetic, and delicate thumbs hooked on black lace, only to push her panties down.

Emily gasped; so very glad to have a sustaining wall

behind —she leaned further on it for support.

Olive-toned legs walked closer; Helena had one goal in her eyes. Only warm brushing inches from Emily's lips, and gleaming brown took her in. "Are you comfortable?" she murmured and moved her delicious torture to that fair neck. Emily's print had been washed away and replaced with the fresh smell of soap.

"Yeah... I am." Eyes fluttered shut as Helena's tongue licked a sweet path on the soft contour of Emily's neck, igniting with it a shivering trail of goosebumps.

Helena pulled back with a piercing stare and brushed Emily's robe off her body; olive-toned fingers mapped the gentlest touch against her trembling abdomen. Helena moved in and pressed their naked bodies together, pinning Emily to the wall with a searing, but slow and sensual kiss.

Needy mouths melted in a warm and sweet merging of tongues they had perfected over the months; it was languid, untamed and inside the edges. Helena drew Emily in between pearly teeth with a wet sound. Bruised lips gleamed like their smoldering eyes. They stared at each other as contained breaths finally fled from their moving chests.

Helena's exploring hand crept between their agitated bodies and found unguarded flesh; its sturdy touch made the heat between her legs tighten and Emily shiver.

A choking moan escaped Emily's throat as she threw her head back against the wall. Green eyes faltered; they broke the gaze Helena maintained and stared north, not into a starry sky, but Emily found patterns on the ceiling above —blinding lights behind her eyes. Helena's lips had made a path of wet streaks and sweet kisses on Emily's supple round breasts; she found a hardening peak and entwined her daring tongue on it. They were so perfectly small and full... Helena adored how they favored Emily's athletic body. "You are so beautiful..." Helena whispered in a haze. The heat of her breath against a wet nipple wrecked havoc inside her girlfriend.

With parted lips and closed eyes, Emily leaned further on the wall keeping her steady. Breaths grew desperate at Helena's ministrations; she licked the contour of a sweet breast with such care... so wet and tentative—never neglecting the other as she rolled her fingers on responsive hardened skin. Green eyes flew open.

"Oh, God," A shuddering breath escaped Emily's lungs while her fingernails scraped on the wall. Helena's lips were on her trembling belly. She moved lower and lower as heaving breaths rushed out of Emily's open mouth; green eyes risked a glance. Helena was doing what she thought she was doing. —*Oh...*

Emily pressed her lips together as Helena continued to kiss south; her nostrils flared as the contained whimper burning her vocals chords escaped. "Helena..." she said, in a broken whimper.

With knees on cold Italian marble, Helena whispered kisses on Emily's exquisite hip bones. Dark eyes looked up and dipped in thick lashes as she pressed alluring lips on the smooth base of Emily's beautiful sex. "Can I?" Helena whispered.

Their gleaming eyes met as Emily nodded. Helena felt her axis tighten and grow wet so fucking quickly. The provoking arousal near her lips promised her so much.

Brows crashed, and Emily struggled to find her voice, "Baby... you don't —have to if you don't wan—" she stuttered and gasped as Helena licked the flesh and wrapped her hand around it.

Emily swallowed her suggestive sounds and tightened her fists on each side of her body.

"My love, just relax..." Helena whispered, near the hardening that had her melting in the middle. She looked up, and their gazes met again. "Are you sure this is okay?"

"Yes... I want you to." Emily nodded, and Helena's warm tongue found the aching arousal. She licked its entirety from beginning to end.

Emily's lungs scraped for air, as she threw her head back on the wall. After a few seconds, she found an ounce of composure and looked down at Helena; she stared at her doing what she was doing... Emily caressed dark locks softly as that addicting mouth opened and slowly consumed her —a soft hand stroked the other half of the beautiful dick.

Green eyes welled up as her mouth fell open. Emily's tear-blurred gaze found the ceiling, and her body collided with stunning new sensations. She moaned and moaned; she whimpered and whined. Her lungs were like a black hole—Emily prayed for oxygen as the woman she loved took her to the edge of forever with each tempting, all-consuming stroke of hand and tongue... her mouth. —*Oh, God...*

Helena found a rhythm as she inexpertly explored Emily, caressing her sides and thighs, making her shiver —pale hand still on dark hair. "Oh, Helena, baby... Oh... my—God, Helena..." Emily moaned, mouth locked open and eyes closed as she trembled with pleasure.

Emily had finally spoken, and confidence soothed Helena's insecurities; her own arousal ignited the ache that ran down her thighs like water and thoughts... Helena thought of love, she felt it in her heart. Love felt red, and it tasted beautiful.

After a wet sound, Emily's eyes opened —she immediately missed the most sublime rush of sensations she had ever experienced. Stunning Helena stood with tousled hair, a hooded gaze, and maddening lips that a pale thumb brushed and smeared. "Em..." Helena whispered. Brown eyes welled up as her heart caught up with the binding intimacy of what she had just done.

"You are so beautiful... I love you so much, Helena." Emily whispered to her lover's lips, caressing her immaculate jawline... the small scar on her lip.

"Please let me make love to you." Helena whispered as careful digits touched that beautiful constellation mapped on fair skin with tiny moles.

Emotion stung Emily's eyes, she blinked and realized Helena was right there, equally moved and exposed. She nodded with an unguarded gleam in her gaze. "Okay..."

Anticipation burned brightly in the center of their crimson-colored hearts, it felt volatile inside, yet quiet and longing on the outside. Helena lowered Emily on white bed sheets as pale thighs adjusted to the cool rush of the fabric against them. Gazes never breaking, Helena pushed her upwards with ease and reached for the condom packet she had placed on the nightstand.

As a bare Helena maneuvered the rubber, Emily reached between her legs and felt what was there just for her. The conflict in her eyes prickled like tears... she couldn't convey the intensity of what broke her inside. "Oh, Helena... you're drenched..." She stroked gently, and that sweet sticky sound provoking their need was the final catalyst. Helena closed her eyes with a whimper, echoes of their breathing mixed with the thick silence and bounced against the walls. "Are you ready?" Helena asked, and Emily nodded.

Helena leaned into warm lips and eased herself down as she favored a kiss. Gleaming eyes closed while she took Emily in completely. Helena shuddered as the fullness consumed her and the craving in her axis hit that searing end. "God, yes..." she whispered, opening her eyes once again.

Throwing her head back in ecstasy, Helena's hips moved and melted with Emily's. Pale hands on her hips squeezed as their heaving sounds made the tightening ache a culprit of madness. One of Helena's hands discovered her very own body while the other clung to the sheets as her insides crumbled. Emily looked so raw, bare and beautiful in her desperation, she propped herself up.

Between hushed whimpers and intimate sounds, they both knew it wouldn't last long—gasping, brushing lips felt their sweet demise just around the corner.

The small dew on sweaty skin made magic. Emily moved her hips like her dizzy mind moved inside her head; and found the deepest parts of Helena; she unknowingly coaxed her sweetest spot into agony. Helena became desperate...

"Fuck— Helena!" Emily pulled her into a kiss. Short rushed breaths grazed their blushed lips as they moved faster and faster, messier and closer. Gleaming eyes were so eternally green and in love —they found more in brown ones. The wanting became unbearably painful to hold back.

Helena squeezed her eyes shut; sounds were drowning in the back of her throat with each short thrust. Kiss-bruised lips, absolutely open, while a claiming fire burned her from within. "Em!" Helena cried as her clenched thighs shook in convulsing waves. Dark strands of hair fell forward and shielded the aesthetically beautiful mess they had made. Right then, Helena thought to have found something beyond the scientific. She flew freely to the top of her love for Emily and saw beyond their next lifetimes.

Still consumed in the trappings of Helena's walls, Emily began to fall apart.

"Helena!" Shameless hips arched and collided with devastating euphoria, finding a home inside the woman she loved and adored. Electricity consumed every single inch of her flesh as she fell back on the bed. Emily sold her soul to love right through Helena's veins. If only she could keep her... The prospect of death wasn't a formidable foe. It towered over, and the thought of it gutted her. But Helena was special, so if death were to walk behind them so be it. She wouldn't leave her... she could never run. Emily hoped to keep every beautiful bruise Helena had left inside her heart forever.

"I love you, my sweetheart," Helena whispered with sleepy eyes and calming breaths.

A silent tear rolled down Emily's temple as a spent Helena kissed her sweaty forehead and fell next to her gently. Completely drained and unaware of Emily's conflict, she drifted right into her very own oblivion. Sleep.

"I love *you*, Helena..." Emily whispered, and brushed her soft, dark hairline. A gentle thumb caressed her temple. Emily watched Helena sleep until she allowed herself to let go as well.

***

After an hour of slumber, night had fallen. Emily shifted in the comfortable bed and quickly realized she wasn't in her room. Sleepy eyes tried to focus in the dark; enthralling shadows and moonlight filtered through the tall glass windows, but Helena's warmth brought her back. The smell of her delicious perfume all over her own skin, all over the sheets; Emily smiled.

She didn't even care to check the time. Green eyes canvassed a sleeping Helena touched by the silver light and those distant glows of the stunning city outside. Emily brushed her lips on Helena's shoulder.

"God… I love you," she whispered.

The signature fragrance lingered on her skin mixed with the salty taste of sweat from their previous lovemaking; Emily's taste buds were in heaven. Longing touches grew more intimate and unrushed; she rubbed softly on Helena's lower belly and nuzzled her neck.

A delighted purr birthed in Helena's throat and tickled Emily's lips. The pleasure in her sounds was definite. She was smiling.

Emily grinned. "Welcome back, sleepyhead."

"Mmm… How long did we sleep for?" Helena asked without turning; she was far too comfortable feeling all of Emily pressed against her back, unadulterated delight.

"I have no idea." Emily murmured, and continued to kiss Helena's neck. She moved a hand lower; fingertips were on the warm skin of olive-toned thighs, gently drawing long, intimate touches.

Love's fever fluttered inside Helena's heart; that sensual grin that crossed her lips Emily would have loved to see, and perhaps put it in her precious collection of all the ways her beautiful Helena could express delight. This one smile was given to the dark.

Helena entwined their fingers and brought them to her

lips as she stretched towards a costly lamp. A bit of light was in order; it was easy to feel torn by the move because it meant looking for one of their phones and taking note of time... of remembering that soon, they would have to break this spectacular cocoon and go back to reality.

Just as dim intimate light flooded their bed and half of the room, Emily contemplated Helena's back. A deep breath found its way into her lungs; green eyes had become the perfect target for awe to seep in through. Pale fingers reached for it without hesitation and brushed tanned flesh gently down the longing valley of her spine. Oh, the love...

Emily's heart lit up as Helena turned with the vulnerability of a constellation in dark eyes; cell phone in hand —they still had some time. She pressed a soft and ambitious kiss on Emily's lips; careful and determined, it moved inch by inch like pure water until it found a defining, soft jawline.

A swollen breath hurt Helena's lungs as she smiled and stared at green eyes; she remembered how much Emily had been suffering in silence because of her disease. A conversation about death and fears could go in many ways, but all Helena wanted... **needed,** was to give Emily some peace, to give her a set of truths she had never shared with anyone.

Delicate pale fingers moved dark strands of hair away. Helena was unforgettable, just like her fragrance, just like a memory that refused to ever leave and come back suddenly —even when uninvited.

"I love you..." Emily said; the honesty in her voice broke right through Helena.

Affected brown eyes relished the one person in the world who had stolen her heart and soul. Helena's thumb brushed soft lips with cruel wanting, the wanting of more time. "I love you, too, Emily... so much."

"I don't want to go..." Emily whispered with a burning and lonely star in green eyes.

Helena sighed. "I know... neither do I." She wished for more time... she always did. "I wish we could stay here forever."

"That would be perfect... Let's." Emily said, smiling, her dimples painted charm on blushed cheeks.

With a beaming smile of her own, Helena kissed one of them. "One day we will, my love." she spoke words that sounded so true, almost like another promise.

"Really?" Emily wanted to believe.

"I have hope..." Helena nodded and smiled softly; sentiment reddened her eyes.

At that moment, when Helena sat on the bed and urged Emily to join her, she knew this would be difficult, but it was time to speak about it.

"You know..." Their honest gazes connected. "Before I met you... I perceived life differently."

Another level of raw honesty is reached when you sit face to face with the one you love, completely naked and allow your heart to fall to your wrist.

"You did?" Emily's brows knitted softly, and Helena nodded.

"I did..." She ran a finger over Emily's chest until it found the valley between her soft breasts. "Before I met you, the word hope seemed like a lie —a way to make my days easier until death came; I never allowed myself to have hope." Helena confessed.

With wounded eyes, Emily bowed her head. Death... five letters that held the weight of oceans.

Helena rushed her fingertips to Emily's chin and searched for her gaze with the burning desire to explain.

"I don't feel that way anymore," she said with unwavering eyes. "You have given me so much more than I thought could ever exist, Emily— you gave me a friend, the best one I could ever ask for… an honest and gentle lover,"

A silent tear ran down Emily's cheek, and its twin soon followed, warm and unheard.

"Before you, I was afraid of dying, but now," Helena swallowed, some words tasted bitter before they came out, a sigh choked her and tears blurred her vision. "Now, I am terrified." she whispered with soaked eyes.

Emily shook her head. "I don't want to talk about this."

Full of regret, gleaming brown engaged emerald eyes, and Helena grazed a gentle thumb on Emily's cheek. "My love, we have to." It broke her in two, but this had to be done.

Emily tried to keep her lips in check as a deeper form of crying threatened her. She failed and shook her head once again, trying to hide away the embarrassment that came with such kind of cry. Helena had always been the strongest one —Maybe Emily was slightly taller and could kick a guy's ass, but Helena had a different type of courage inside her.

"Please look at me," Helena begged softly, and Emily complied; bloodshot green gave in without hesitation.

"Ever since I learned about my condition, I have only thought of my own fears and early regrets… with thinking of —what would my family do with me after it happened? To be honest, it's an eerie thought;" Helena felt sick to her stomach each time her mind drifted there.

"Wondering… Had I done enough? What kind of print was I leaving behind me? —I… I fear there is nothing more, no awareness, no you —only sleep." Helena's soaked lashes blinked, and more hot liquid fell. She sniffled and took Emily's hands, pale and cold —brushing them against her swollen lips felt good. Helena smiled and looked at Emily, because looking at her was always like looking at the moon.

Emily sniffled and felt the warmth of Helena's tears on her skin, her breath. Even when submerged in the sadness of it all, she still felt it was a gift. Emily listened.

"I had been left with assuming thoughts— death is a very complex concept to dissect." In hopes to ease something so obscure to the heart, Helena smiled, but Emily didn't. Sad eyes focused on the sheets and her girlfriend's tanned abdomen, a true frown of the soul.

Helena gently placed a finger under Emily's chin and sought her gaze; she smiled again, hoping Emily would see it this time. It was a small smile full of early apologies.

"Emily, I had not thought of your part, of your side, and I am so sorry," Helena said; honest ache etched her face.

Soaked lashes met and Emily chewed on her lip. Her face, flushed and silent. Even in sorrow, Helena thought she was the most stunning human on earth.

"You have been swallowing your feelings and your pain, your fears —and I am *so sorry.*" She wiped away warm tears from her Emily's skin. "I know this is unfair, and it hurts, but I need you to know that it's okay to be afraid, Em… you have made me understand the beauty that exists in vulnerability."

Emily continued to listen faithfully; Helena had never spoken so openly about her illness before; this honesty was something Emily had once craved, she treasured it now, but God, it was hard. Those words were just words when they weren't put together in that order. In that specific combination they hurt; her insides felt sore; she couldn't imagine what it was like for Helena to live with them taunting her mind.

"The prospect of putting so much on the line is terrifying, but sometimes it is so worth it," Helena confessed with a longing whisper and wet eyes. "You are so worth it, and now that I have you; all that intense fear has found the loveliest companion, Em… hope —Emily, you make me feel it and believe it, believe that I can have more —that we *will* have more, just you and I… someday."

Entwined fingers brushed on each other tenderly. That intimate human link was grounding.

"It isn't just me anymore, and I need you to please let me help you carry this. I now understand that this disease isn't only mine, it belongs to those who are left to pick up the pieces of its disasters, and for this, I am so sorry, Emily— but I am not sorry we met." A watery smile interrupted Helena's stance, but she continued even if it meant more tears would fall.

"I am not sorry I love you so much it hurts, I am not sorry that my fears have grown to the size of monsters—I would do it all again so gladly if it meant I get to have you like this…" Helena said with gleaming eyes.

"I need you to know that you have a choice now, and you will have a choice tomorrow and the next day… you can walk away from this, and I would never blame you or judge you. *Ever*. Because I know this isn't easy." Helena offered honestly.

Brows crashed together, and Emily frowned. "What?"
"Emily…"
"No! Helena —I don't want that choice —I don't need

it. Please don't say that, ever!" Emily spoke passionately as her breathing made her hostage of its lunacy.

Brown eyes softened, and Helena nodded. "All right, all right, sweetheart," she tried to ease Emily with intent. "I didn't ask you to. I just wanted you to know..." she finished with a small smile and reddened eyes.

Feeling prey of desperation, Emily launched herself against Helena and held her tightly. Lips brushed a tanned shoulder... she kissed it.

A soft hand soothed Emily's back. "My sweetheart... please remember... I am fine," she whispered on Emily's shoulder and grazed her lips against the contour of her beautiful bones... her skin.

Sniffing away her tears, Emily pulled back to look at brown eyes. "Are you sure?"

Helena smiled. "I am." She hooked their fingers and thought of how beautiful the contrast of their skin tones was. Juxtaposed, like their love.

"Do you remember that day in your room when you showed me your journal?" Helena asked.

In all her swollen beauty, Emily nodded, seeming more calmed. To Helena she looked so flushed and adorable, the way her skin reacted every time she cried was like watching a drop of ink being poured into water.

Helena smiled. "The first thing you thought when you saw me that day we ran into each other, and you helped me with my books..."

A chuckle fell from Emily's lips as she wiped wet streaks away. "I do... it was silly and weird, I know." She felt sheepish and embarrassed.

"You wrote that you saw me years down the line, that you saw yourself by my side... It was the most beautiful thing you could have written about me, Emily —about us. It's not silly or weird." If only she knew the impact of those words.

Emily blushed and studied their entwined fingers with a bowed head.

Even through messy blonde strands of hair, Helena saw a sweet dimple.

"That very thought makes me smile every morning, it makes me feel I'll be okay, and I swear to you, I believe it because I can only see life when I venture that far, I see us." Helena confessed.

Their gazes met.

"Please believe with me?" Helena begged with bright, optimistic eyes.

With a gentle nod and gaze that gleamed again, Emily tried a smile. "Anything for you."

"For us." Helena corrected, "Together."

Emily nodded. "Together." she said.

"Thank you." A smile broke from Helena's lips while a growling sound echoed between them. Emily jerked back with a smirk. "Lena… Are you hungry?"

Helena arched a tempting brow and grinned.

"Famished."

An amused chuckle fell from Emily's lips; Helena had her ways. She had ways to shift everything and make the shit go away if only for a while. They laughed.

"Then let's get up, get dressed and get you whatever you want," Emily suggested. "What do you feel like eating?"

Helena sighed. With squinted eyes, she pondered on her cravings. "Mmm… I'd kill for a burger right now… *with* bacon."

Emily's face twisted. "What?! Are you serious?"

Helena smiled. "I am very serious. Please?" she whined

charmingly. *Successfully.*

"I don't think I've ever seen you eat a burger before—are you okay?"

"Em, of course I've eaten a burger before, it isn't something I would usually choose, but there is nothing wrong with enjoying one once in awhile."

Still thrown, Emily stared at her. "Okay…"

With heavy efforts, they finally got out of bed and got dressed. Emily threw on her jeans and a flimsy, long-sleeved t-shirt while Helena zipped up her dress.

Standing inches away, Emily watched as olive-toned fingers tamed beautiful strands of dark hair in front of a mirror. Helena was certainly exquisite. Emily bit a blushed smile and walked towards her, looping both arms around a small waist.

Feeling Emily's hands on her, Helena relaxed and smiled; she turned in the embrace. "Are you ready?"

Emily felt like a big baby in advance, but she didn't care; with whiny brows, she stomped her foot lightly. "I don't wanna go…"

"Neither do I, love… but I promise we can do it again soon." Kiss… "And maybe next time we could take a bath if you'd like."

—*Ugh…* Emily slouched. "Okay…"

"Yes?" Helena said, smiling.

"Of course… I would love that, never have I wished to be thirty and completely independent so I could have you all to myself, **all the time.**"

Helena giggled. "I am already all yours. However, I could never object to the 'all the time' part."

"Where do I sign?" Emily said with deep dimples on

her cheeks.

"There's no need for that, though we could if you wanted." Helena added.

A passionate gleam flashed through mossy green. "Of course I do! We have to; I will do everything the right way with you." Emily suddenly heard the imposing words out loud and blushed. "If you want... I mean,"

Helena smiled. "There is no wrong or right way, love… but —do you really think about that?"

"Marrying you someday? …Hell yes, I can't wait." Emily blurted out and remembered they were merely in college. —*Shit, nice one, Idiot...* she scolded herself mentally.

Endeared by Emily's sudden embarrassment, Helena smiled and pressed her lips on warm ones. "Good… neither can I." She winked.

The past few hours had been powerful and painful, but also so very beautiful. Emily relaxed, it felt good to dream freely and have long-term expectations. Just like most people could, they could, too. Couldn't they?

**

After satisfying every craving Helena had, both made their way back to Emily's parent's house. They walked towards the Knight's door, laughing and holding each other.

"How could you find watching me eat a burger arousing?" Helena asked between chuckles, and Emily, of course, joined her.

"I don't know," Emily shrugged. "Lately everything you do looks sexy to me, I guess eating a burger is no different." —*God, I'm so whipped.* Emily thought.

Under the warm light outside the Knight's house,

Helena's hands found their way under Emily's top and pulled her into a kiss. "Really?" she asked and searched for that clear mossy gaze.

"Yeah," Emily responded and smiled. "It's like I feel this perpetual desire to just —*make love*— to you all the time." she said, and rolled her eyes at the mushy term. "and I just... I want to protect you." Emily finished with honest and sweet dimples.

With an arched brow, Helena grinned in the comfort of her arms. "Very primitive of you, Em…" she joked with a small laugh in her throat, though Emily's recent sweetness and attention had been endearing.

"I am not a caveman." Emily corrected with a scrunched up face.

"I never said you were…" Helena sassed. "I love the way you've been spoiling me these past few weeks; it makes me feel special." she confessed as joyful arms looped around Emily's neck.

Emily's lips curled up. "Good, because you are." she smiled softly when suddenly, realization hit her; a dulled expression washed her face. "When did we become this mushy?"

Helena laughed. "I think we've always been excessively sentimental, though I must agree, it seems to be growing. Does it bother you?" she asked.

—*Well, fuck it.* "I'm whipped remember?"

Helena winked. "I believe we established that the third time we had intercourse, yes."

Emily's face disjointed like a crooked frame. "Why do you have to call it that?" she teased.

"Call it what?" Helena asked with a spur of geeky aloofness.

273

"Intercourse. What happened to fucking?" Emily's teasing grew inches.

Helena frowned, mortified. "Em—"

Contained laughter spilled out, but Emily spoke before Helena killed her dead. "I'm kidding!" She laughed some more, thoroughly amused by Helena's reaction. "Lena, I promise, I was just joking." She kissed her cheek.

Helena arched a warning brow, and Emily shrugged sheepishly as she pulled out her keys. She held the door open, allowing Helena to go in first and closed it behind them.

The immediate sound to hit their ears was that of a male voice echoing through the answering machine. The strength of his tone wasn't as horrible as the words he spoke. Both Emily and Helena searched for the source and realized it came from the kitchen.

Emily knew what it was all about and took her girlfriend's hand; looking into her eyes wasn't easy when fear and embarrassment twisted her insides. Emily hung her head, and Helena listened; the longer she did, the clearer the man's intent became to her.

'You people are sick, living the way you do... you're all going to hell, including that sick, sick boy... or whatever it is. Only death will wash your sins.'

—*How dare they?* Tears pooled in Helena's eyes as bile burned her throat, she felt sick and horrified. A shadow cast Emily fixed her expression; embarrassed green avoided brown with a subtle wince, and Helena immediately squeezed Emily's hand tighter.

The replay of the message was stopped, and Maureen's voice came through first.

"I can't believe the nerve this guy has... even with

the police on his trail, he doesn't stop!" Emily's mother protested, baffled.

"I swear, Maureen if I find him I'm gonna kill him—" It was Ben's frustrated warning to an unknown and elusive threat.

"Ben, they removed you from the case because of this, you need to control yourself, honey," she tried to ease him.

Emily inhaled deeply and filled her chest with something lighter than pain. She walked toward the kitchen with Helena in hand.

Green eyes reddened and hid with shame. Emily hated that her family was repeatedly put in this position because of her. Helena caressed their laced fingers.

Wide-eyed, the parents turned to the presence by the kitchen entrance and lost their words.

"Emily —sweetheart..." Maureen tried and rushed to them.

"It's all right, Mom... I'm sorry that bastard keeps calling the house." Emily said; sadness stained her shame. Helena's heart broke as pain and anger tore right through. Not knowing what to say burned her —it vexed her. She had seen the fights, the blood, and trashed room, the name-calling, the looks. *Her pain.* Helena shook her head and blinked away hot tears.

"Sweetheart, you have nothing to apologize for." Maureen squeezed Emily's arm and sought those loving eyes she would so gladly die for.

"Your mother's right, Em... that man is obviously sick." Helena offered with knitting brows and a bruised heart. She cupped Emily's cheek in one hand and pierced her emerald eyes.

Broken, Maureen tried again. "Yes, baby, you are

beautiful inside and out —my sweet girl, never let anyone make you think or feel otherwise." Her daughter's silent pain cut her. Maureen knew Emily... she knew her tough exterior and her soft inside; she had felt only what her daughter had allowed her to see and it had been too much. There was still so much Maureen hadn't seen or knew about, and Emily wouldn't have had it any other way. She would never put her mother through that kind of pain.

Emily sighed and ran her frustrated fingers through blonde hair. It was hard for words to erase the way she felt and she hated that Helena had to witness it.

Helena took her hands. "Emily... please look at me,"

Sadness flickered in green when they rose and met love.

"Your existence gives mine purpose... you are the most stunning human being I've ever encountered in my life, Emily... you and I both know that people can be so cruel, baby, but it doesn't mean that they are right." Helena's conviction was like a perfectly aligned spine, the backbone of a hero with soulful and profound eyes that looked like the starriest of nights.

Emily pushed a smile, and an annoyed huff swirled in her chest. "I know... it just kills me that everyone around me has to suffer because of me. You guys don't deserve this..." She found all their faces.

"Em, neither do you. No one does!" Helena sighed. "I know how that feels, love, but this isn't your fault. Together... remember?" she tried a hopeful smile and caressed her jawline with gentle fingertips; a vivid touch as loud as her gleaming eyes.

Emily's lip turned up, Helena was right.

"Together..." she murmured and felt a surge of red in her heart. "Now it's my turn to tell you that you have a choice, too… Life with me will be filled with crap like this— all the time," Emily added as the hurt inside juxtaposed itself onto the exasperated edges of her current mood.

"I don't want that choice." It was Helena's turn to use Emily's words, "*you* are my choice."

Emily's joy was shy, and felt unseen; almost like disbelief… so honest. "I love you…"

"And I love you." Helena said.

It was simple.

Emily embraced Helena and held her tightly. She loved her more. Just when you think it isn't possible, there is so much more.

Maureen walked towards her husband and held onto him while he looped his strong arm around her. It was the most beautiful way to end such bitter turn of events. They had endured much in the past fifteen years but never felt happier and more satisfied with having supported Emily at such a young age. The result was more than enough.

Witnessing what love could do was worth it all.

13

HER WINTER

ECEMBER IN SAN FRANCISCO was beautiful. Helena had forgotten how much she loved Christmas in her city as a child, though she missed the thick, white and captivating German winters she had grown up with.

When your mind is that sharp and young, even a drop of rain is enough to capture you forever. It was Helena's turn right before she left for boarding school... Her last night in San Francisco twelve years prior.

Living in an eternal moment of complete bliss and happiness was as easy as opening her arms into the cold night. With rosy cheeks, gleaming eyes, and a tender smile made of milk teeth—*and* a few half-grown permanent ones— a young Helena gazed up so unknowing of what was to come twelve years into the future. She smiled at the sky while invigorating and unique drops of water fell from the deepest night onto her sweet face. The smart and awkward little girl with no friends had no idea that years later, a grown version of herself would find love and happiness. Helena would meet that lonely, sweet and shy blonde girl a few miles away. The one who lived inside herself and her dreams, looking at the rain outside with elbows on a foggy windowsill. Maybe one day she would get to be a princess on a horse —Emily always wanted to be a different kind of princess; the one who was brave and fair, the one who would find a princess of her very own.

But that was then, and this was now. Their stars had aligned, and so had their hearts. This night was cold and equally beautiful under that same sky. They were the same and yet so different; they felt like women —rebels of life who ached for independence and a little more, because they felt more than capable of handling life... because they were more mature than what they were given credit for.

It was December 23rd —which meant they were off campus and enjoying their winter break.

Emily waited outside the Millan's door; blonde hair danced in the cold wind.

After ringing the bell, she shielded her freezing hands from the chill. Thank God for pockets in jackets and jeans —though the weather didn't matter because she was happy, she was so happy and eager to have her girlfriend in her arms; if only she could wait a few more minutes, she would.

'Helena! It's for you.'

Emily heard Maddison shout from the other side of the door and grinned. Her girlfriend's sister opened the large, wooden barrier a few seconds later.

"Hey," Maddison was pleasant.

"Hey," Emily gave her a shivering smile.

"Come in," Maddison offered and stepped aside.

"Thanks." The cozy warmth of the home was heaven sent.

"I don't think she's ready yet..." Maddison said, and turned to look up the grand staircase. "Helena!" she shouted.

"It's okay; I can wait for her." Emily offered, holding a hand behind her back faithfully.

Maddison shrugged. "All right. So, where are you taking her?" Blue eyes were curious.

Emily glanced at her boots, trying not to make a mess on the immaculate floor. She looked up. "Oh, um, she wanted to watch a movie and then I'm taking her to—"

Maddison arched an expecting brow.

Emily blushed and scratched her forehead. "There's a place I wanna show her." She shrugged.

"Nice."

"Yeah…" Emily still wasn't comfortable around Helena's family without her being present to keep them in check. They loved to interrogate and ask incredibly invasive questions at times, but this was okay. She smiled awkwardly, and so did Maddison.

"I um…" Emily tried, "I'm sorry about what happened with Blackwell, but I can't —you know… I won't apologize for what I did; he crossed a line when he made it about Helena."

Maddison pushed contentment and Emily could have sworn she saw a flash of disappointment in her. "Oh, I know. He is a gross bastard —we were over anyway." she said honestly.

With pursed lips, Emily nodded. "I'm sure the right guy will come along… you deserve better, you know?"

Maddison's icy blue rose in surprise and blinked; she smiled softly. "Thank you."

Emily nodded and looked around uncomfortably, wishing so hard for Helena to walk down the stairs.

Aware of Emily's awkward state, Maddison gave her a break and turned to the staircase with a huff. "Ugh! Are blind monks sewing her dress on? HELENA!" she shouted again.

Seconds later, Helena popped out from the top of the stairs, and Emily felt like she could breathe again. She watched her girlfriend bicker with her sister as she walked down each step, unaware of her presence.

"God! Maddison, would you please stop yelli—"

Emily smiled, and Helena stopped her blabbing as she reached the last step and saw *her*.

Helena smiled. "Em, I didn't know you had arrived."

Maddison scoffed as blue eyes found the ceiling. "Why do you think I've been shouting at you for the past few minutes?" She smirked. "Dimples here was about to explode from awkward tension overload." She winked at the pair and walked away. "Have fun, star-crossed lovers and *please,* misbehave!" she shouted freely while walking up the grand stairs.

Helena smirked and shook her head. "She is impossible; I am sorry."

"I think she's hilarious." Emily said, grinning, she welcomed her girlfriend in. "You look beautiful,"

Helena dove into the scent of that soft, clean perfume as always and savored the safety in their embrace. She eased a kiss on blushed lips, and Emily maneuvered the rare flower she had been hiding right into view. It was a cosmos atrosanguineus.

"This is for you... it's supposed to smell like chocolate." Clear green eyes shone brightly. The way Emily looked at Helena melted even the coldest of hearts.

Catching sight of the silky dark flower, Helena beamed. "Oh, Emily..." She took it in her hands and smelled it. "It's perfect; I love it. Thank you."

Their eyes met and glowed as if meteor showers fell across

them. Emily bit her lip and nodded. "I'm glad you like it."

Helena smiled, and Emily laced their fingers.

"Are you ready?" she asked.

"I am, let me just get my coat, and we can go."

***

An hour deep into the movie and the smell of popcorn was driving Helena insane, but not as insane as the delicious scent of Emily's perfume on her neck. The darkness of the theater was spectacularly convenient as was Emily's idea of sitting in the last row. While Helena's hand caressed her girlfriend's thigh, she felt thankful the foreign movie with subtitles had attracted an almost minimal audience. Helena's lipstick was long gone; she imprinted intimate kisses on Emily's jaw and then her irresistible mouth. Their lips melted together as their passion bruised and concocted a signature brew of their most secret warmth.

Emily's senses were on edge; Helena had been all over her for the past forty-five minutes, and blood felt torrid inside her veins. Addictive curvy lips opened wider, and Helena's tongue coaxed Emily into doing things they shouldn't have been doing in a public place.

Pale fingers ran up Helena's thigh with hitching breaths, and soft hands started to tempt hidden places she loved to pay reverence to. Emily broke the kiss, only to smear love on Helena's olive-toned neck fervently. "Baby, don't make me hard here..." she whispered, immediately regretting the words.

Helena whimpered as Emily's hands sneaked under her cardigan and found feverish skin aching for her touch. "I want you so badly, Emily... I feel like I can't control myself." Helena whispered hotly in her ear. She pulled back and found green eyes in the faint light from the screen reflecting on Emily's face.

The darkened desire on Helena's expression made Emily want to break all existing rules, perhaps even make new ones and break those as well. Her chest rose and fell as she launched forward for a bruising kiss. A pale hand found intimate purchase between the warmth of Helena's thighs, cupping her clothed sex and gifting her every hungry nerve ending with some friction and pressure. Helena bit back a moan and shivered near Emily's ear.

"Fuck." Emily whimpered and pulled her shameless hand away. "Helena, I don't want to put you in this vulnerable position —not here."

"Can we please go?" Helena begged. "Just please take me to someplace else... I want to be alone with you."

They weren't animals; Helena knew that in spite of her raging hormones there had to be some sort of control deep down inside, but she was having a very hard time finding it. It was like she was a hunter and Emily was her prey.

Emily nodded, and they got the hell out of there.

The drive was difficult. Helena had stained sinful kisses all over Emily's neck and used her beautiful hands to bring her closer to something more sincere than any restriction. There was nothing more honest than the bright spark in dark and green eyes. Nothing more real than who they were and what they felt.

As the miles grew, Helena got a better hold of herself and her blinding desire —she felt embarrassed for rushing their date. Emily parked the car at Clearwater's deserted lot. The action lost to Helena. Fallen eyes were fixed on her lap and kneading hands.

Emily knew something was bothering her. "Hey, baby, what's wrong?" Pale hands caressed Helena's cheek.

"I am sorry, Em."

"Why are you sorry?" Emily sought her gaze.

"Because, I was unable to control my greedy lust, and I broke our date."

"Lena, please don't think that. I didn't care about leaving," She smiled. "We weren't even watching the movie, and I swear I just wanted to take you right there." Emily said with a chuckle.

Helena looked so ashamed that Emily's heart overflowed with empathy. "Please, don't feel bad… It's okay, I promise."

With brighter eyes, Helena pushed a smile, and Emily claimed her lips.

The intimate sounds of the deepening kiss ignited Emily's blood and Helena's hunger; she moaned. Emily adored Helena's kisses; they were arousing to her body, but also to her heart and soul. Helena stimulated her mind just as she did her desire, and that was invaluable.

A wet sound echoed in the elegant car as they gently broke apart with eyes closed and heaving chests. Helena felt sex-starved, and that very thought made her laugh at herself. It was as if her body had been playing a very pleasant, but inconvenient joke on her as of late. It all felt quite perpetual.

Helena sighed and just as she opened her mouth to speak, brown eyes caught sight of the familiar buildings surrounding them. Clearwater's parking lot was empty. Lamp posts illuminated the once filled spaces, and soft gusts of wind whistled around the safety of Helena's car.

Her brows crashed; she deadpanned. "Em, what are we doing here?" she asked.

"I have something I want to show you..." Emily said, and grinned with bright excitement.

"What is it?"

Green eyes were like deep, calm waters. They shone eternally on the surface, but beneath something vast lost its name. It was grand... How could something so beautiful feel like an ache in the heart? It was vibrant and blinding; it seduced Helena like shadows and glowing red. It was love. She swallowed.

The softest smile broke from Emily's lips. "Come with me..." she said

As they walked towards the very center of Clearwater's lawn, gushes of wind stamped their clothes even closer to shivering skin. The tall, collegiate gothic buildings were barely lit. They stood guard, but the cherry blossoms and their falling petals gave the main show.

Helena lost her breath and looked up with a beaming smile. "Oh, Em..."

Emily smiled in return and took Helena's hands. "Do you like it?"

The roaring wind grew wilder and louder, seamlessly dismembering the white petals off the branches and making them fall just like globs of snow.

"It's winter..." Helena's enamored eyes gleamed like the night above them. Tears blurred her vision as a wet chuckle crossed her stunning lips. "I love it..."

Emily knew how much Helena missed snowy winters. Ever since that night in bed while holding her warm body tightly, Helena's fleeting confession never left Emily's mind. She had to find a way to give her a winter.

"Good, because I have something else for you." Emily said with a grin, and Helena chuckled as she wiped away a fallen tear.

"There is more? This is magnificent, Em... so much more than enough."

"Well, this is supposed to be your Christmas gift, but I wanted to give it to you in private, you know... since I'll be spending half of Christmas Eve with you." She blushed. "Doing this in front of your family would have been a lot of pressure..."

Ambushed by happiness and love, Helena smiled. She was beaming and hadn't even gotten the gift yet. "Em... you didn't have to get me anything, love... I—"

Emily's stomach was a mess, a beautiful mess that made her want to vomit. She shivered and smiled. "I wanted to." Emily had no doubt that Helena was her one. Her nobility and sweetness were always muting. She searched her jacket's pocket and pulled out a small black box.

Emotional brown eyes grew wide.

"Please don't freak out..." Emily said with the most adorable and nervous smile. "My mom gave me this when I turned fifteen, and I want you to have it..." She opened the box, and Helena gasped. It was a platinum ring with a light purple stone on it.

"Emily..." Slack-jawed, Helena's heart melted into her bloodstream like sweet honey.

"This is my promise to you... I want you forever, Helena, and if you have me one day... I'd love to give you everything you deserve."

Brown eyes reddened and pooled with warm tears that rolled down with ease. Helena smiled as her girlfriend placed the meaningful piece of jewelry on her finger.

"Oh, my love... This... You didn't have to, Emily." She looked into those perfect eyes. "This means so much —are you sure?"

"I am."

"But your mom— she—"

"She was more excited than you when I told her. My dad gave it to her when they were our age, and now I'm giving it to you..."

Without immediate access to matching words, Helena chuckled and cried; she launched herself into Emily's arms and pressed their lips together. Emily felt wet streaks on her cheeks and tasted the salty essence of her girlfriend's emotions. Helena placed a delicate hand —now adorned with Emily's promise on her fair neck.

More cherry blossom petals fell and covered the green grounds of the deserted place.

It was Helena's very own winter.

***

Waking up the next day meant Christmas had arrived. Just as planned, Emily would spend half the eve with the Millans and Helena would then go with her to the Knights and finish the night there.

Helena refused to wait until midnight to give Emily her present, and well, Emily had planned for Maddison to help her with another surprise she had for Helena.

They sat on Helena's bed. "When I pondered on what to get for you... the impulse was sudden and inalterable. I delved into my memories with you, of you... and I realized that when we first met, what struck me most was

287

how beautifully brave and giving you are, your will to stand up to injustice," Brown eyes glowed with emotion. Helena gave her a ghostly chuckle. "You are so thoughtful, Emily Knight."

Green eyes blinked softly as Emily listened to her irreplaceable lover speak. They welled up, and Helena laced their hands.

She sighed. "You are so beautifully thoughtful... So I gave this my entire focus in hopes to give you back the same." she said, and handed Emily a folder. "Please open it."

Emily did, and green eyes took in those words neatly typed on paper.

"Thanks to you, a little girl named Leah will have access to puberty blockers," Helena said, smiling and sniffled as she sneaked a brief glance at the folder. "I believe she wrote you a letter; it should be in there."

Their eyes met.

"Helena…" Mossy green were angelic and wounded all at once; they gleamed. A tear fell so rapidly that Helena almost missed it. "This is…" Where were all the words?

Perhaps inside, still unconveyed. But they were in there, radiating love. More of the undiscovered good things that could be felt.

Helena smiled and squeezed their hold. "You deserve everything…" She gently wiped away the salty emotion on Emily's cheeks.

Enamored arms looped around Helena and held her. Warm lips and sobbing whispers against her neck; Emily closed green eyes and relished everything. *Her* soft skin… the flow of blood under it, pumping. Helena's unique scent taking her higher and making her fall deeper. She encompassed Helena's beautiful existence and everything that made her invaluable. Everything that made her… **Her**.

"Thank you so much, Helena…" Gentle lips pressed on her neck. "I love you."

Helena smiled and held Emily. "I love you, too, my sweetheart."

They pulled back gently. Emily's face was wet with drying tears.

***

Once downstairs, Helena sat on the elegant sofa with eyes closed. Maddison had been the culprit who had kept her sister's gift unseen. **Unheard**.

An expectant smile broke from Helena's lips. "Em?" Behind the darkness of her eyelids, she wondered if she was alone.

Emily smiled. "I'm here, baby, but don't open your eyes yet."

Helena's gift wiggled in Maddison's stretched out arms. With a wrinkled nose, she handed Emily the cutest, fluffiest most adorable puppy —Emily had found him at the shelter the day before, completely alone and overlooked because of a bad paw. He shook his light brown fur and looked around with the gentlest dark eyes. Helena's dog for sure. Emily knew she would love him.

A grin crossed Emily's lips as she saw Helena, still patiently waiting with eyes closed. She approached her softly. "Okay, baby, open your eyes…"

Bright brown melted, and her mouth fell open. "Oh, Em,"

Her new furry friend was perfect and adorable. "For me?"

"Yeah… It's a boy." Deep dimples pierced her cheeks and adoration her heart.

The puppy whined, and Helena took him; she held

his shivering little body in her arms. "Oh, Em, he is gorgeous... Thank you."

Emily smiled, completely satisfied to have brought Helena such happiness.

***

Christmas day continued. Katherine had arranged an extravagant banquet and was over the moon to have her family home for the holidays. Caleb had spent most of the afternoon playing video games while Santiago helped Katherine and escaped to his book whenever he could. Emily and Helena, of course, glued to the hip, stealing kisses and holding hands. Maddison casually searched the cornucopia of goods on the table for her favorite; passion fruit pie.

Blue eyes failed to locate the treat; Maddison huffed. "Mother, where is the passion fruit pie?" she asked.

Katherine's voice rang from the kitchen, "It should be on the table, dear."

From the corner of her eyes, Helena glanced at Maddison and then Emily, who sat right next to her on the sofa; she caressed the sweet puppy on her lap. "I ate that..." she whispered, and green eyes widened.

"All of it?"

Helena felt like a pig; she bit her lip and gave Emily a sheepish shrug. "Maybe?"

"Lena... Are you serious?"

Helena drew back with a tightened face. "There were only two pieces left... I didn't eat the whole pie."

Emily bit back laughter and Helena arched a brow. "What?"

"My little glutton;" Emily said, the contained chuckle

fell from blushed lips.

Mortified brown eyes widened. "Excuse me?"

Emily tried to censor the amusement tickling her throat. "Baby… It's okay; there's nothing wrong with eating a little —I, for one, love it. I'm not judging." she said. "I just think it's adorable that you've been stuffing your face so shamelessly lately." she added and laughed. "I mean, you are usually the picture of decorum, but now you're like Barney Bornholdt."

Helena wasn't amused, confusion etched her face and brows furrowed. "Who?"

"Barney Bornholdt… you know, the kid that ate three pounds of ice cream in the movie Amelia."

Helena had no idea who Barney and Amelia were, but she drew back in offense. "Emily!"

Shit, she really couldn't stop laughing. "Baby, don't be mad…"

Helena was far from amused. "Are you calling me fat?"

Green eyes widened. "No! Helena, you are gorgeous, and your body is stunning —not that I wouldn't love you in any shape or form, because you know I would— I—" Emily rambled, and Helena maintained her arched brow in place.

Emily pressed her lips together and decided to stop talking.

Maddison approached them with a hand on her hip. "Did you eat the last of the passion fruit pie?" she asked.

Helena looked up, visibly annoyed. "What if I had?" She gently placed her puppy on the sofa.

"It wouldn't surprise me as you've been inhaling everything in your path lately… You're starting to look a little chunky, you know?" Maddison said.

Emily's eyes widened; she rushed a silencing finger to

her lips in hopes Maddison's blue eyes would catch it.

Helena's jaw fell. "Okay, that is enough of you two calling me fat!" she said, and stood in a huff.

"I didn't say you were fat! I said you were chunky; there's a difference, Helena."

Once on the other side of the elegant sofa, Helena faced her sister. "Well, I'd rather be chunky than a complete and total bitch!"

Icy blue eyes widened, and so did Emily's green ones. Called by the growing argument between her daughters, Katherine walked into the living room, thoroughly mortified. "Helena!"

Not feeling an ounce of regret, Helena crossed her arms while a hurt Maddison's concealed her disappointment; they had been getting along so well; this outburst was very out of character.

"I am not fat!" Helena said, and Katherine scanned her daughter from head to toe; she wasn't, though the doctor had to admit that the dress she was wearing fit her a little tighter than usual.

"I didn't call her fat, Mom." Maddison defended honestly while Emily's eyes silently darted between three fierce women exchanging. —*Fuck*.

"I only said she was chunky; even a blind man could notice she's been eating like a starved homeless hobo lately."

"Maddison!" Katherine scolded, "both of you ease it with the insults and name-calling, we have guests, and it's Christmas, so *please*, behave like the adults you are."

Maddison huffed and walked off murmuring, "Whatever."

The thing about Helena was the eyes; they left her bare before the world around her; it was like witnessing profound alchemy. Her anger had turned into guilt.

"Helena, darling, are you all right?" Katherine asked.

Emily stood and rushed to her side. Helena nodded. "I am… I shouldn't have called her that horrible word; I don't know what came over me, I just—"

The physician in Katherine observed her daughter in silence; she considered Maddison's statement. It was true, Helena had been eating a lot more lately, her clothes fit a little tighter, and her emotions had been too flaky for her usually even and collected moods. "Helena, when was your last period?" Katherine asked.

"Mother?!" A wide-eyed Helena blushed at the intrusive question.

Emily grew nervous; sudden heat rushed to her cheeks as she ran a sweaty palm on her jeans. Katherine had that effect on her when she got inquisitive.

"Well?"

While Helena's sharp brain narrowed the numeric answer in seconds, she tried to convince herself that it couldn't be. A deep breath found her lungs. "Eight weeks ago." she said. How could she have missed it? She had been so distracted and happy...

"What?!" Hazel eyes almost popped out of Katherine's face.

Emily's pounding heart slammed against her chest. She eyed them both and almost felt it stop beating when Katherine's dark glare stabbed her. —*Shit.*

"Okay, you are taking a pregnancy test, right now! Let's go." Katherine grabbed her daughter by the arm and pulled her along.

The jerk was sudden, and Helena's face hardened. The way her mother invaded the most intimate parts of her life bothered her greatly, she felt exposed and now like a five-year-old child her mommy dragged by the wrist. "Mother!" she protested.

Katherine pierced Emily's eyes. "And you are coming, too."

A thick gulp rolled down Emily's throat, and she nodded in a rush.

A silent promise flashed through their meeting gazes just as Katherine pulled Helena towards the staircase. The speed of it all seemed unreal. "Mother, stop!" Helena tried, but Katherine was determined, blinded perhaps.

Emily followed in a hurry. "Mrs. Millan, please— you are hurting her!" she begged, trailing behind them.

As they reached the equally grand second floor, Helena's chest felt close to exploding. —*Ugh!* She yanked her arm away. "I can walk on my own, Mother! You don't need to treat me like a child." Helena said, feeling violated and hating every minute of it. "And what? Do you now happen to have pregnancy tests stocked up in safe keeping?"

Katherine opened the door to her pristine room and motioned for them to enter. Helena went in first as she rolled her eyes and Emily followed, flushed and deeply embarrassed. Not only was her mind running wild, but being in the middle of her girlfriend's parent's bedroom was awkward. The way they were being treated...

"Yes, Helena, ever since you started your sex escapades I needed to be prepared, though I hoped this day would not come... I thought you two were using protection!" she scolded.

"We have been!" Helena bit back with clenched fists.

"Yes, ma'am, we have— I swear." Emily said bravely, swallowing her fear.

The doctor searched a rich wooden drawer and handed

her daughter a small packet. "Please go take this."

She couldn't be pregnant... Helena took it and walked towards her mother's bathroom. The chances of a pregnancy were incredibly rare. Not only was Emily on blockers, but they had also been safe every time.

Emily felt almost uncomfortable to even breathe; Katherine pinched the bridge of her nose, dreading what she felt was now a reality.

The scattered mess in Emily's mind was anticlimactic; she was confused because her treatment and blockers would make a pregnancy a very slim possibility. Helena being pregnant meant testosterone was roaming through her body, and that was anything but good. That meant something wasn't right and not only that; it meant her body could start changing. Emily felt like panicking as that thought barged into her mind. She shook it off, at least for now. A baby with Helena would be the most beautiful thing she could imagine. Emily didn't think about her age or plans. Altering emotions blindsided her, absolute love and her biggest fear... becoming a man. With shaky hands she shoved in her pockets, Emily swallowed bitter dread.

Helena walked out of the bathroom with a blank face and welling sentiment in her reddened eyes; they spoke volumes. The liquid rolled down after a blink. "I'm pregnant." Came a wisp of a broken murmur.

Tears pooled in Emily's eyes, and Katherine's heart tore wide open. The woman sat on a chair as the foundation of her world trembled. It felt like defeat.

At the fall of hot tears, green and brown eyes met. Emily's chest was bursting with something that suffocated her; she dared a few hesitant steps while trying to read Helena. She would die on the spot if Helena rejected her nearness. She felt scared and guilty, but she loved her so much. "Lena— I—" Emily sobbed with heavy lungs, but Helena rushed into her arms.

There were no words only the tightness of their embrace and the love they had made; Helena didn't feel death, she felt life. Warm breaths and salty tears found shelter in each other's shoulders. A baby of their blood and flesh. What were they going to do now?

14

LUCKY

AFTER FINDING OUT ABOUT Helena's pregnancy, a seething and disappointed Katherine tried her best to remain calm and collected. The doctor feared what would be of her daughter's health. She asked Emily to go home and allow them some time to speak to Helena's father.

It was the hardest thing Emily had done yet, leaving Helena alone didn't feel right, and it wasn't what she wanted. With shattered hearts they said their intimate goodbyes, promising each other to call. Emily pleaded and Helena, of course, gave her what she needed to hear —she would pick up the phone as soon as they were finished talking to Santiago.

Emily rode her motorcycle and sped home. She felt alive and scared. Fear tore through her without compassion as thoughts of everything that was happening ambushed her. There were so many scenarios, so many voices in her head... left and right. A baby, a little baby she had made with Helena, a child of their flesh and blood... of their love and most intimate moments. She smiled inside the shielding plastic of the motorcycle helmet; tiny whips of raindrops hit her as she rode through the cold evening. It was still light outside, and for that, she was grateful. Emily didn't have enough mental focus to ride and think while having to watch out for things unseen.

Fear crept in as adrenaline left her body; she had absolutely nothing to offer Helena and their baby. —*I don't care... I can find a job and take care of them.* she thought, while her heart and mind said goodbye to dreams of entering the force and eventually becoming a detective, at least for now. —*It doesn't matter; she is everything.*

All Emily wanted was to get home and talk to Helena; hell, in truth what she really wanted was to turn around and be with her. The need was at its most intense. She suddenly understood many things they had been feeling, nature's way of strengthening their bond. Maybe it was the little person inside her girlfriend.

Emily didn't understand how she had managed to get Helena pregnant. Something had gone wrong. Her young heart pounded, and tears washed down shielded cheeks as she rushed home and ran to her mother; the one person who had been there all along, her constant support and the one who understood the magnitude of what was happening. Emily tried to calm herself, but only cried harder; she couldn't turn into a man, she just couldn't. Not only had her thoughts ambushed her, but so had her body. This baby, she already loved, but whatever was changing inside her needed to be stopped, or she would go mad. Emily couldn't fathom the thought of being trapped inside a body that didn't belong to her.

Once home, she closed the door and found support on it.

Emily wiped tears from her soaked cheeks with a flimsy cotton sleeve and felt absolute guilt. How could she be thinking about herself and her fears while Helena was out there facing her parents alone? It was their baby, not only Helena's. —*I should be there.*

"Em, sweetheart, I'm in the kitchen." Maureen's chipper voice rang through the house while the grounding smell of pumpkin spice and pine cones entered Emily's lungs.

She walked to her mother and hovered by the doorframe with hesitant, bloodshot eyes. Maureen's smile turned into a frown; something was *very* wrong.

"Emily, honey, what is it?" she asked, searching her child's eyes worriedly. Those lovely eyes that mirrored hers so perfectly were so broken.

With a bowed head, Emily finally found valor and the strangled confession fell from her quivering lips, "Helena is pregnant." she said, crashing into her mother's arms.

Slack-jawed, Maureen held her shaking daughter and searched for words inside her eloquent mind; she needed to be a mother... Mothers were supposed to have the right words; she couldn't find any but soothed blonde locks. "Emily..." Maureen broke the embrace gently and sought her gaze. "How can she be pregnant? You have your blockers implant —were you not using protection?" she asked.

Still swollen from crying, Emily nodded. "I know... I don't understand —and yeah, we were safe... not at first, but yeah,"

"Something must be going on..." Maureen said, feeling dread. She quickly untied her apron, food completely abandoned. "We have to see Doctor Andersen, *now*." She took her cell phone from the table; Emily observed her as she swallowed and sniffled.

"But Mom, it's Christmas Eve... Etta told me they had plans with her grandma." she said.

Their eyes met; Maureen worriedly waited for the ring on the other side of the line. "I don't care, Emily... this can't wait." It seemed she was only preoccupied with Emily's hormonal issue, but in truth, Maureen couldn't believe her young daughter was going to be a mother. Life had just changed abruptly, not only for them but for the Millans as well.

It was pointless to try and convince her mother. Emily wiped away a few more tears and pulled out her cell phone. All she could do was think about Helena and their baby. She just wanted to be with her, facing things together. No message or phone call yet.

***

Katherine felt absolute vexation brought on by completely justified reasons. The elegant woman paced in short spans while she and Helena waited for Santiago to come to the living room. Helena's blushed cheeks were stained with watery streaks; suddenly her hands became the target of intense focus. Inches away, Maddison brushed compassionate circles on her back. She didn't dare ask what was happening but had an adamant feeling of what was causing this tense and thick silence.

Caleb's brows knitted together as he observed his mother and sisters. He knew something was terribly wrong, the stress radiating from Katherine was starting to take hold of him when Santiago finally joined them with a peaceful and unsuspecting smile.

"I am sorry it took me so long, it was the hospital on

the phone... It's incredible how people choose the holidays to behave so stupidly," he said, and quickly caught on everyone's frowns, his smile faded. "What's wrong? Why the long faces?" he asked worriedly.

Helena's warm and soaked eyes released new tears, head hung in shame. Maddison's heart shrunk, Helena was shaking like a wet puppy. She looped a protective arm around her little sister's small body.

Katherine stopped pacing and stiffened. She let out a harsh breath, giving part of her load to Santiago. "Helena is pregnant." she said at once, her voice cold and firm.

More tears ran silently down Helena's face while both her sibling's eyes widened. Maddison tightened her reassuring hold, Helena needed the support.

Heartbreak clouded Santiago's face. He knew what this meant for his daughter's health and also that he needed to remain calm. Helena was just too young, her possible bright future... plans of burning stages in a healthy and timely manner slipped through her fingers, but right now his little girl looked just as broken as he felt —Helena looked so ashamed.

Wet brown eyes fought the inability to meet his, but she finally did. Helena stood and approached her father.

Santiago felt his existence bruise in thousands of ways, the look on her face was soul-wrenching. A trembling chin was followed by a hand over pretty lips, trying to hold back a cry.

"Daddy... I'm so sorry, please don't hate me." she managed and broke down.

Santiago held her shivering body in his arms. "Oh, Helena, I could never hate you, cariño..." he said, and comforted her as she cried against the soft material of his crisp shirt. He always smelled like Polo and mint; his embrace so strong and gentle.

"Please, don't make yourself sick... it isn't good for your condition." Santiago added while leading her to sit, he pulled out a fresh handkerchief from his pocket. "Here, darling, I need you to please calm down."

Helena sobbed and complied. She took the soft fabric and dried her tears.

Katherine's eyes pierced him, how could he be so calm and compliant? He needed a wake-up call. "This pregnancy is what isn't good for her condition!"

"Katherine..." Collected brown eyes found his wife's and warned.

"No! Do not Katherine me..." she bit back at Santiago and looked down at her daughter. "Helena, there is absolutely no going around this, you need to have an abortion as soon as possible!"

Helena winced as fear ravaged her stomach. She was petrified because this would be her mother's word over hers; it would be a difficult battle to win —but something she had never felt before burned her veins, an instinct that went far beyond her strength.

She jolted from the sofa with clenched fists. "Mother! How can you say that?!" Helena challenged.

"Katherine, please stop, you are going to upset her." Santiago tried.

"Oh, upset her? If her heart can take the agitation brought on by sexual activity, she can take this, too!"

Helena cringed and shrunk as Santiago's eyes grew darker and he became angrier. "Katherine! I SAID STOP!" His strong voice thundered so loudly that even Maddison and Caleb sank in their seats.

Completely unfazed by Santiago's passionate defense

of Helena, Katherine inched forward. "She *will* have an abortion, Santiago, if she doesn't this is going to kill her! Is that what you want? To gently guide your daughter to her death?! —No! I refuse— you and I both understand that this is a risk far too high to take!" she pointed at the man accusingly.

"I know exactly what this means, Katherine, but you need to calm down! We need to gather ourselves; we will call Michael and see how we can best approach this." the man tried with a milder voice as their progenies watched in silence.

A wounded Helena shriveled away from her father. Her eyes filled with ache and betrayal. "I will not kill my baby… this is my body not yours to govern over!" she shouted with tear soaked eyes.

"Helena, darling…" he tried gently.

"No! I know you see this from a scientific perspective and I know exactly what this means to you both."

"It means *that* is a *fetus*, Helena, not a baby." Katherine pointed.

With a heaving chest, Helena felt cornered and alone. —*Emily…* She needed Emily to hold her hand and help her face this, to help her fight. Gleaming eyes shone; more tears broke free, and Maddison stormed to her side.

"Okay, both of you, stop! Stop making choices for her; she is not a child! Mother, you are suffocating, God!" Maddison shouted, blue eyes so wide unloaded even her own frustrations.

"Well, she sure has behaved like one! We gave you all the tools, Helena! A thousand times I asked you to be careful and be safe! Michael told you, practically begged this of you and what did you do? You swiftly ignored everything!" Katherine shouted.

"We were careful! After the tests came back negative, we always used protection!" she threw back as Maddison stood guard.

Katherine rubbed her temples and closed her eyes in frustration.

"I won't have an abortion!" she shouted at her parents. "I won't!" Heat crept up Helena's beautiful face.

***

Anxiety was killing Emily. A frantic leg trembled as she eyed the door. Her doctor was supposed to return with the rushed test results, and Helena hadn't called. She was losing her mind.

Aware of her daughter's frustration, Maureen placed a gentle hand on her thigh. "Em, calm down... try to breathe and relax a little."

Emily nibbled on a nail. "How can I relax, Mom? I may be turning into a man, and my girlfriend is pregnant, facing her parents completely alone... I should be with her."

"Honey, I understand, but you won't accomplish anything by beating yourself up, you have to do this now... I'm sure Helena's parents will want to speak with her in private."

Emily shifted in her seat as her best friend's father walked into the office, holding her test results.

Both sets of eyes followed him to his chair on the other side of the desk.

"Well, Emily, it seems your implant is wearing off, this has caused the irregular levels of testosterone in your system, it explains the emotional instability, the aggressiveness your mother spoke about and unfortunately, this incident with your girlfriend."

Maureen interjected, "Well, if it's wearing off then we need to replace it, right?" she asked.

"Not quite, Maureen; the blockers would not be an option for Emily anymore; she's too old already. Remember this was a viable way to help her transition so that she could feel comfortable in her body as she aged into a young woman, this wasn't a permanent solution, reason why I suggested she should start visiting a therapist. It was a prelude if you will —a chance for Emily to truly grow into herself physically, mentally and emotionally. A way to prepare her for the full transition."

Emily's heart choked her, but she continued to listen.

"You will not have to undergo heavy and painful surgeries to soften your features —I know this isn't a rule to go by, of course, but I am speaking about your case specifically since I know how you feel about certain things..." he said, and gave her a soft smile. "Your voice, for example, has a beautiful non-threatening tone; no Adam's apple and the list goes on. All that is thanks to the early attention your parents gave to this —that was part of the blockers job, but now we must move forward, if we don't, your body will start to change into that of a male."

Emily swallowed hard as heartbeats pulsated in her ears. All the words... the terms were so familiar to her, yet she didn't know what was about to come out of his mouth and that scared her deeply.

Maureen inhaled a sharp breath and glanced at her shrinking daughter.

"You mean the sex reassignment surgery and the hormones replacement therapy?" Emily asked.

"Yes... However, we do have other options, I know you're not comfortable with the sex reassignment surgery, and that is very normal... not everyone is. We could perform an orchiectomy which would consist of removing the testicles to reduce the levels of testosterone your body is actively producing."

"And what are the risks of this other surgery?" Maureen asked, lacing her fingers with her daughter's.

"Potentially, loss of sexual desire, mood swings, loss of sensation in the genitals, erectile dysfunction... you would, of course, become completely infertile. However, we can preserve your sperm in case you decide to have children down the line." he was honest, and while Maureen's heart broke into pieces, Emily ran a trembling hand through her blonde hair.

Her world was sinking, and her chest felt hollow. How could she face the loss of something she had just discovered? —It was unfair. A stubborn tear escaped her eye.

"Emily... You don't have to undergo surgical procedures; though we need to move forward with the HRT, which alone... has virtually the same possible side effects, excluding the risks of invasive methods."

Sentiment prickled at Maureen's eyes; her little girl had already endured so much.

"In the years I've been practicing medicine, the number of patients who suffer from dysphoria towards their genitals is rather great; the levels of anxiety vary, but there's also a high number of those who, like you, Emily, don't. You don't have to opt for surgery to fully transition into a woman; with the hormone replacement therapy, you would be able to lead a normal and healthy life with the genitals you feel comfortable with. Of course... you can always opt for surgeries later if you choose."

"What's the catch?" Emily asked, chewing on her bottom lip; her brain leaned towards the latter outlet.

"Well, you would have to take this for the rest of your life which in the other two cases you'd also be taking aiding treatment. However, you will keep your penis and testicles."

Maureen gave her daughter an infinite gaze and squeezed her hand. She wasn't alone.

"Honestly, I like those odds better; at least for now." Emily said. "So, do you really think we could freeze my sperm?"

"Of course we could." Doctor Andersen reassured.

While a torn Emily fought between the thought of her girlfriend and her mental sanity, things at Helena's home were silent. Not because everything was suddenly okay or because they had all reached a mutual understanding, no. Things were far from okay between Helena and her mother. She felt betrayed by her father, and even though the man never agreed with Katherine's resolve, Helena knew he would rather keep her alive at all costs than risk allowing her baby to live.

Christmas was officially ruined as everyone had fled to their rooms. Helena frantically packed a small bag with a few pieces of clothing and scribbled a quick note. She needed to get away from her parents and their intentions. She pushed the note under Maddison's door and rushed out of the mansion.

Exhausted and still crying, she drove through the dimly lit San Francisco streets. Everything she wanted and needed was Emily. She needed space.

***

A shivering Emily patiently waited for her girlfriend outside her parent's house. As the headlights of Helena's car appeared in the distance, relief washed over her lungs letting out a smoky puff of breath —she was freezing her ass off. Emily rushed to the car as Helena fled the driver side and ran to her in tears. Their bodies collided; safe arms held her tightly.

"Baby, what's wrong? Why are you crying like this?" she spoke in the tight embrace, feeling Helena's trembling body and sobs. "Come on, let's get in the car..." Emily urged.

She opened the passenger door for Helena and ran over to the driver side. The warmth of the vehicle was delightful. Emily took Helena's hands with a shattered heart. Wet streaks married her cheeks while bloodshot eyes seemed lost. "Baby, please talk to me, Helena... What's wrong? We should go inside the house—"

Helena sobbed. "No! Please— please, Emily, just drive; get me away from everyone."

"But where?"

"I don't care... they want to kill our baby, Em!" Helena cried. The words gutted Emily.

"What?! Who?" Knitting brows sheltered desperate eyes.

"My mother wants me to have an abortion —please just drive away from here, I don't care where... just get me out of San Francisco."

"But Helena... I don't have much money, what—"

"I do. Don't worry about that, just drive, please!" Helena urged and tried to find calm within herself, knowing they would run away from it all, at least for a few days.

Emily's mind was a mess, but she nodded and began to drive. She drove off and away from everything they knew.

***

After a couple of hours on the road, Emily was exhausted. The day had certainly taken everything from everyone, but she rubbed her stiff eyes and continued driving. Only the silent night had witnessed their escape. She turned and saw her beautiful Helena fast asleep. A gentle hand on her thigh felt grounding; she seemed so broken and tired. How did she manage to still look so beautiful?

Emily glanced at the gauges and the GPS screen. They still had many hours of long roads ahead. As white lines painted on black pavement were consumed, Emily took better hold of the wheel and drained a few of her frustrations on the tighter grip. She was mad, happy... confused and afraid. Life had just jerked her awake from a dream —because that's how her old life felt like, a dream. She had never tasted adulthood this vividly, reality this bitterly, but it didn't matter, she had *her*, and now, they had a tiny baby growing inside. Inside the woman she loved more than anything in the world.

Hours were unforgiving, Emily yawned and rolled her head on tight shoulders. Watching the quiet sunrise in the horizon paled in comparison to watching Helena asleep and juxtaposed to it. A brunette head rested near the clear glass window as peaceful hues of blue and peach gifted Emily's tired sight.

They were finally cruising the captivating Seattle streets. She was bone-tired, and before even attempting to look for her brother, she knew Helena needed to rest properly and eat.

"Baby..." Emily murmured, caressing Helena's thigh,

"wake up."

Helena dragged a long breath and squinted her sleepy eyes. Bright light; *daylight*.

She shifted in the comfortable seat and scanned her surroundings, tall buildings and vibrantly-colored lights seeped through falling globs of white snow. "Em, where are we?"

"Seattle." Emily said, and managed a tired smile; she knew how much Helena missed snowy winters and wanted to give her some happiness. Loud sirens faintly rushed nearby as they waited for the light to change from red to green. Helena jolted and rubbed her eyes.

"Oh, Em... I'm sorry, I slept all through, and you had to drive alone."

"It's okay, that's what I'm here for, don't worry about that —but I woke you because I didn't know which hotel you'd wanna go to."

With a gentle pop of her sore neck, Helena cocked her head to the side. "When we come here we usually stay at The Elysium."

Green eyes widened. "Helena, that's like a month's worth of tuition. Are you nuts?"

"It's okay, Emily... they would know who my parents are."

"What if they call them?"

"I honestly don't care about what they do... they will know once we use my card anyway, I'm sure they are already looking for us." Helena said, and took Emily's hand. "I just want to take a shower and eat a gigantic piece of meat."

A prickling laugh escaped Emily's lips —damn, her baby had turned Helena upside down.

"We will deal with them later, love... I just can't care right now." Helena added.

"All right, The Elysium..."

***

The sound of water falling on tiles was tempting; Emily stretched out on the wonderful bed as she spoke to her mother on the phone. "Mom... we're fine, just please tell Helena's mom to give her some space right now —I'll talk to her, and we'll go back to San Francisco, but we need to talk, too... we need our space, please..."

'All right, Emily, but you two make sure to come back here after you sort things out, and please, call your brother; I'll let him know you are there.'

"Okay, Mom, thanks..."

'Em, sweetheart, I trust you to be responsible... please take care of her and call me as soon as you find Patrick.'

"Of course, Mom... I promise. I love you... —Bye." Emily ended the call and huffed.

She sighed and caught sight of Helena exiting the lavish bathroom in a white robe. Damp hair; black like the night, sleek and fresh, her smooth olive-toned skin glowed flawlessly. Helena was always a sight for sore eyes.

"Hey..." Emily said, and sat by the edge of the bed.

Helena walked towards her with a soft smile on her lips. "You look exhausted, Em," She tucked away blonde strands of hair. Emily opened her legs and allowed Helena to stand between them.

"I am... but that's okay; I'll take a shower and eat something, maybe get some coffee..." she said, and pale hands found Helena's hips. Sweet green looked up.

Helena graced Emily's cheek with careful fingertips, gazing into the mossy wilderness she adored so much. Warm lips inched forward and melted.

"Thank you..." Helena murmured against the parting kiss.

"What for?"

"For being you..." Helena said, smiling, brown eyes shone again.

Emily chuckled. "Well, you're welcome, but I didn't do much."

They stared at each other, letting it all sink in. A thick emotional mood fell upon them. The realization of what now lived between their bodies was grand.

"I can't believe it, Em..." Helena whispered.

"I know, neither can I." Emily murmured, grazing an open palm on Helena's cloth covered abdomen.

Tanned hands reached down and untied the robe. Gleaming green followed the movement; Emily swallowed hard, filling her lungs with air and her heart with love. The robe fell to the floor, leaving Helena's beautifully bare body on display. Emily wanted to cry; a lump got stuck in her throat while Helena took pale hands and brought them to her warm belly. It was still flat but had changed... their baby was growing, and Helena's body was indeed delightfully curvier.

Emily choked on a sob and minced a timid cheek against her girlfriend's abdomen. She held her tight enough to make her feel just how much she loved her, but gently enough not to hurt her. Helena caressed blonde locks, and Emily cried.

Helena knew she had to come clean; she had omitted

some painful truths because she never thought this day would come. Emily had no idea of what keeping their baby alive entailed. Helena held her love tightly, and warm tears fell.

Their intimate silence was love. It was happiness and sadness; it was their life unfolding.

15

RUNAWAY

EELING THIS CONNECTION WITH Helena was unlike anything Emily had experienced before. The more she got to know her, the more she realized just how deep her emotions ran. Helena was the embodiment of sweetness and kindness, but also had a side that seduced her in different heights and levels. She was this strong girl who'd had a flirting affair with death and seduced her way out of it, while the aftertaste of it had led her to where she now was... looking into green eyes with tranquility and ease. As they lay on the bed, Helena completely naked and Emily still wearing her jeans and top, they gazed at each other.

Emily brushed and tucked dark locks behind her girlfriend's ear. "I love you so much, Helena..." she said with an honest smile.

With an irrevocable kiss to blushed lips, Helena murmured; "I love you, too, Em... I..."

Emily saw hesitation in dark eyes. "Is something wrong?" she asked, and caressed a rosy cheek, the tiny mole on her top lip... Her scar. —*I love it.*

"Do you want our baby?" Helena answered with a

question.

Emily felt hyper-aware of her heart, Helena's wonder was so warm and true.

"Of course I do. I know we didn't plan this, but..." Emily's smile was timid and enchanting; just like a blushing secret. "We made a little baby, you and I —I love you, Lena. How could I not want it?"

Helena relaxed, and relief gushed out of her chest.

"My mother wants me to have an abortion." Dark eyes averted and found solace in the ring wrapped around her finger. Helena played with it when she felt uneasy.

Irritation claimed Emily; brows crashed together in a scowl. "Why...? I mean, I can understand her disappointment, but how can she suggest something like that so lightly?"

Helena swallowed her omissions. She needed to come clean with Emily about the dangers this pregnancy could bring to her health. "Actually... there is something I need to talk to you about;" Star-like eyes were still as deep as the night.

Emily's stomach sank, stress took over her even though she didn't know what Helena would say, maybe it was the tone of her voice. "Tell me —you can tell me anything."

A faint nervous smile tempted Helena's lips. She brushed her fingertips on the hem of Emily's shirt; perhaps to keep herself anchored to something before she tore right through her girlfriend's peace of mind. "A few months ago... my cardiologist told me it was ill-advised for me to conceive." she finally confessed and looked up into unknowing green.

"Wait... What?" Emily's calm began to dissipate, each breath desperate to catch the other.

"Because of my heart;" Helena said, and blinked softly, averting her eyes momentarily. She knew this would break Emily. "It is very risky for me to carry this baby to term and have a successful delivery..." Helena said, looking elsewhere yet again; she had done a lot of that in the past twenty-four hours. "I could..."

Emily's world caved in while she realized what Helena's sorrowful face said. Helena couldn't push the words, so Emily did. "Die..." she whispered with reddened eyes. Emptiness invaded her, the space in her chest, torn and wounded.

Helena's brows knitted compassion, she had made peace with her decision, but Emily's broken state spoke of the story unfolding inside her. She swallowed hard again and nodded.

"Helena..." Emily whispered with dread. Sadness flooded her eyes as she sat up and buried her face in her hands.

A naked Helena rose with urgency. She noticed pale fingers trembling and laced them with hers. "My love... I am so sorry," Bad conscience broke her voice and welled up tears in brown eyes.

Bitter fears ran down Emily's throat like venom while her salt-flooded gaze looked away. Helena placed two delicate fingers under a trembling chin and sought her.

Green met brown, and liquid sentiment fell from Emily's broken eyes. Helena drew in a deep, heart swelling breath that branded her with new heights of guilt. Her silent tears broke free. "I know I should have told you this before, but I didn't think it was a possibility —I..." Her chin quivered. "I read so much about your blockers and the medications you were on, I... I didn't think... I don't—" Helena tried as heat claimed her face and more tears choked her.

Emily wept in silence.

"Em, my love," she said with a sniff. Helena took her lover's hands; those tender, beautiful hands she loved so much felt so soft against her lips, she kissed them.

Bloodshot green finally turned.

"I want to have this baby." Helena said, and Emily's heart twisted inside.

"Helena…" she whispered brokenly.

"Baby…" Helena said, and pushed a wet smile through her cascading tears. Olive-toned fingers caressed Emily's face and hair. "Please… try to understand me."

"Helena, I can't lose you… I— how could I live without you?" she finally spoke between sobs. Emily saw fear in dark eyes, but she also found conviction there. Helena was now a mother, and this had somehow changed her. Of course it had.

"I'm alive, Em, and I feel fine." she said as loving hands cupped Emily's cheeks. "You make me feel alive and brave. I have to do this; I am choosing this, not because I think it is wrong or right to have an abortion —love, I have my reasons, and I want you to know that you are not obliged to do this with me if you don't want to." she finished evenly, honestly, *lovingly*.

In a moment of clarity, something so vivid flared between them. Perhaps it was the reality of it all, maybe the stunning gleam in Helena's eyes or the raw knowing of possibly losing it all. Emily was petrified of the love she felt; it was so profound. She swallowed hard.

Helena squeezed her hand. "We will take this one day at a time; I am sure Doctor Rossi is already on his way to San Francisco —life is also a possibility, Em, we can both talk to him. Together, remember?"

Emily never felt so torn. She adored their baby already, but Helena was everything —she felt sick to her stomach from thinking that maybe Katherine was right. She felt selfish, and like the worst mother; Helena was already willing to lose everything, and here she was, feeling like she could lose anything, but not Helena.

"I…"

If anyone in this world understood the importance of respecting someone's desires and body, it was Emily Knight. This wasn't only their innocent baby that hadn't asked to be conceived; this was the consequence of their choices, and even though it was a beautiful one, it could become the ultimate price to pay. But this was Helena's body… It was her baby as well; this was the love of her life asking so bravely for support, having already given everything to this child. How could Emily say no? Deep down she knew she wanted their baby.

She finally looked up and found Helena waiting for the other end of that promise they had made. She nodded. "Together…"

Helena's face contorted into the most honest form of crying; she could breathe again, but she also never felt so afraid. Emily's support was all she had asked for; though she would do what she had to even if without it. "Thank you…" Helena whispered.

She tucked blonde strands of hair behind Emily's ears and leaned in for a meaningful kiss. The salt in their tears mixed into one, just like their DNA and their love.

After the warm and messy kiss had broken with ease, Helena pulled Emily into a tight embrace. Green eyes looked at some elegant piece of furniture in their hotel room and wondered where the hell Helena got so much strength from, because at the moment; she felt stripped and lost.

Helena drew back and took pale hands in hers. "Em…" she said with candid sniff. "What did your endocrinologist say? What happened? You told me over the phone there was something wrong with your blockers."

Emily nodded. "Yeah, it's wearing off —the implant in my arm, I mean,"

Tanned fingers caressed the skin there; Helena knew exactly where it was, though no one else could see if they didn't. She was gentle. Always.

"How do you feel about that? I mean; what now?" Helena asked, obviously concerned.

Emily sighed and wondered how it was that life had turned on them in a matter of hours. "My doctor told me I couldn't have another implant because I'm too old, and not a candidate since the blockers are a reversible option for younger people who go through puberty… like a way to figure out what you want and feel comfortable in your body. He said I have to complete my transition, but I don't want sex reassignment surgery…" Emily shrugged honestly. "I don't know, that surgery scares me."

Helena squeezed her hand and listened faithfully. Dark eyes radiated fierce, uncompromising support and intelligence.

Emily observed and cherished her focus. She adored Helena, her lover, and absolute best friend.

"Are there any other options?" she asked.

"Removing my testicles…" Emily said, and ran her hands through sun-kissed hair. "But the aftermath of that surgery is fucking horrible, Helena…"

"An orchidectomy." The term fell from geeky lips, and Emily remembered this was her medicine buff. A wisp of a smile brushed Emily's face.

"Yeah... but with all this —I feel selfish by even telling you; it's nothing compared to what you're going through."

A sharp crease formed between Helena's brows. "What? Emily, no. This is as important to me, I know what this means to you, my love, how could your gender identity and everything that makes you feel comfortable be any less important?"

"Don't worry about that now, you and the baby are all that matters."

"No! Emily, if your blockers are wearing off, that means your body will change —are you okay with that?" Helena asked.

—Honestly?

"No..." Emily whispered with a bowed head.

Helena's sought her with compassion. "Em... please look at me."

Emily did.

"Please... don't devalue how important this is; I love you inside and out; I need you to know that I support you no matter what, but be honest with me, please —I know you're holding back."

"Without the blockers, my body will resume its natural course, and it'll be entirely male... I'll change —my voice... have hair all over my body, my features would change completely, I..." Emily's voice broke as she looked into Helena's eyes with fear. "Helena, I can't, I just... I couldn't —who I am today would be lost if I don't finish my transition as an adult, but if they remove my testicles I could suffer from everything ranging between erectile dysfunction to freaking loss of sensation —I'll be completely infertile." Tears fell again; "I'm... How could I... You —I mean, we couldn't—" she tried, her anxiety was strenuous.

"Emily, darling, I know how serious this is, but I need you to know that I am here, okay?" Helena said, wiping away a couple of warm tears from Emily's flushed cheeks. "It is scary, but I would never love you any less, sex or not... there are other ways to have intercourse, sweetheart —I would be more than fine with whatever you choose."

A sheepish shrug hunched Emily. "I like sex— I mean, I love what we have, and I just—"

Helena smiled as they both blushed. Emily was adorable. "I know you do; I do, too, that is normal —Em, dealing with all these possibilities at nineteen is incredibly scary and unfair, but regardless of sex you'd still be the same —most amazing, smart, sailor-mouth—"

They chuckled between tears. "Gorgeous woman you are today... Love, you already have me, don't worry about that." Perfect brows furrowed as Helena delivered passionately.

With a hint of a smile, Emily loved her even more, so much more.

"He suggested I could just transition without losing my bits."

Helena chuckled, and said, "Still with the bits?"

Emily blushed. "They are my bits." she replied, and shrugged honestly, Helena did, too. The terminology gave Emily a personal sense of comfort.

"Of course, love," Helena said, caressing her hands. "What are the risks?"

"They aren't as scary, but I mean, there are more uncommon serious risks like with any medication, blood clots, heart disease..."

"Em..."

"I know... I know, Helena, but this is good! Those are rare; it doesn't mean they'll happen, besides, I really don't feel like having my balls cut off if you know what I mean... if I do that, I could still suffer from scarier side effects anyway —I might change my mind later; I don't know... but right now, I don't want surgery."

"I see what you mean... so, what do you want to do?" Helena asked.

"I want to start the HRT; I want to keep my whole penis, I'm okay with that, but I can't turn into a man, Helena... I just couldn't; it may sound selfish to others —but I don't know how to explain it, I— I just—"

"Darling, how could it be selfish? This is your identity, the core of how your brain defines itself and *you*... this is your body, Emily, no one else's —your life."

Emily's aching heart smiled, how did she get this lucky? How could she indeed live without this magnificent girl? Green eyes filled with unshed tears. "Thank you, Helena..."

Those killer lips birthed an unforgettable smile, and Helena tightened their hold. "Always, my love."

Helena was always so tender and strong. Emily would often seem to be smiling at nothing, but in truth, she was smiling at everything.

Those perfect and mischievous brows arched in a way that spoke to Emily of something brewing inside Helena's beautiful mind.

Emily blushed and bit her lip. "Tell me..." she said.

Helena gave her one of those longing and sensual smiles of hers while leaning in. Emily felt like losing her mind and any shred of composure she had as a naked

Helena erased the distance between them inch by inch.

Emily's breathing quickened, and her lungs became hollow. Pale hands found Helena's waist while hooded green eyes sought her mouth. "Baby…"

"Hmm…" Helena soothed the ache with a smoldering meeting of lips. Lightly tanned fingers tangled on the hem of Emily's top and pushed it up north.

They broke the kiss and Emily allowed Helena to peel the flimsy shirt from her body.

Lusty green admired her lover while the restrained numbing inside her jeans longed for more.

Helena straddled Emily and enticed her neck with stimulating kisses while undressing her topless. Emily moaned and softly caressed her smooth, lightly tanned ass. "God…" she whispered.

Helena smirked against a delicious warm neck and unbuttoned her lover's jeans. The sound of the zipper pierced through the thick reverb of silence and their breathing.

Emily's hands ran up Helena's curves and found two small, but fuller breasts; she claimed them; one wet with the heat of her soft tongue, the other aroused by the faint touch of fingers. Feeling Helena react to her caresses was glorious. Emily moaned when a tanned hand dipped into her pants, between denim and hot wanting —cotton bypassed.

The erotic way Helena undressed Emily while flaunting her beautiful naked body was intoxicating. Her hand opened on the delicate valley of Emily's chest and pushed her onto the mattress, Helena then rolled washed jeans down smooth legs —Emily wanted nothing more than to kiss that smoldering smirk away... If Helena was so dark and irresistible at almost nineteen, she could only imagine what the passage of time could accomplish. —*Years down the road when she's my wife, the mother of our baby.* Emily bit her lip allowing her mind and heart to soar without fear. —*When we have our own home; she will be the most amazing wife, mother, and whatever she wants to be. God, I love her.*

With an untamed grin, Helena removed the soft underwear that was so constricting to Emily. She swung a leg over and slowly straddled her. Tempting lips trailed a warm exposed neck, and Emily swallowed hard —that suggestive sweet scent of Helena's arousal drove her mad.

"Let's get you in the shower…" Helena whispered as the tip of her nose traced the length of Emily's neck.

Green eyes screwed shut in delight. God, it felt so fucking good, she was in heaven.

It was so easy to forget.

A soft kiss, "So that…" A kiss, lower… on her clavicle. "We can…"

"Mmm… yeah…" A breathy moan vibrated in Emily's throat, and Helena smirked against her skin, feeling the need between them.

"Go and eat." she finished.

"Mmhm…" Green eyes suddenly darted open—"Wait, what?" Emily asked, suddenly confused.

Helena pulled back and smiled. "I am craving an entire cow —your child wants food… a lot of it, covered in melted cheese," she said.

Emily's brows crashed. "But…" She looked down at herself, knowing Helena was smoldering wet —Emily's mind whined. "I…" Her mouth opened and closed while Helena laughed lightheartedly.

She tried to bite back her amusement. "I promise

you, we can do this later, Em, but right now I **need** food; I need animal protein, and quite frankly the thought of that makes me want to eat myself into a coma and cry at the same time... Why couldn't he want soy meat or lentil sausage?! Something healthy!"

Emily shook her head confusedly. "Wait, he?"

A smile curled in Helena's lips. "I feel it's a boy." she said with a shrug, and Emily beamed.

"Really?"

"Yes..."

Pride radiated inside Emily's chest, but soon her brows furrowed, assimilating the rest of Helena's sentence. "What the hell is lentil sausage?" she asked.

Helena chuckled. "It is a sinfully delicious alternative to animal protein."

"Oh..."

"But our baby wants entire farms of fat-filled innocent little animals, not only shouldn't I eat that, Emily, it's horrible! I don't eat meat!" she whined.

Emily chuckled, and feathered light caresses on Helena's skin. "I'm sorry, baby, but I mean, maybe you could eat a little bit of meat and fool him? Then eat your healthy stuff?" she suggested with a sheepish half shrug.

Helena smiled. —He... Emily had just taken her gut feeling as a fact. "We don't know if it is a boy... I may be wrong." she proposed.

"It doesn't matter to me... I just want—" A thick lump that wouldn't move down got stuck in Emily's throat, so hard to swallow... she remembered and frowned. "I just want you both to be okay." It was a murmur.

Helena sought her gaze with intent. "Em, I refuse to lie to you and tell you that I know everything will be okay, but... I feel that we will be." she said, and smiled earnestly, for a moment it looked just like the sun... it felt right in Emily's chest, maybe Helena was right.

"We can't live like this for the next few months... please? We will take it one day at a time like we said."

Emily pushed a smile. "Together..."

Helena's lips turned up. "Together." she whispered.

"You know... I was thinking; maybe I should just drop out of college and get a job." Emily said, and Helena's wide eyes objected.

"Absolutely not, Emily!"

"But Helena... I need money to provide for you and our baby." she said sweetly and rubbed Helena's belly.

"Em, I think you are the noblest person I know, and I adore you for it, but there is no way I am letting you do that —you will finish college and go to the academy as you wanted, I will, too, we need to —now more than ever."

Emily sighed. "Lena, I can just go to the academy right away then."

"What about your dream and plan of becoming a detective? You are so close to graduating!"

Emily shrugged. "I'll try to finish the associate's degree, but I'm definitely getting a job as soon as we get back home —if I just go to the academy and become a cop, I can be out there making a living to take care of my kid. You, for example, are cut out for the complete college experience, and that's great, I get it —you're so smart, Helena... I want you to do anything you want." she said with a caress on tanned skin and a proud smile.

Helena arched a brow, unamused.

"Right, so, it's settled... you'll go to college, and I'll become a cop, then I'll get a job to take care of you and our baby." Emily tried, smiling.

"No, it is *not* settled," Helena protested. "You need to focus on your studies, Emily —a job, the team… and now us and the baby? No! You will exhaust yourself, and your grades will suffer."

Emily rolled her eyes. "Helena…"

"No." she pressed, unwavering.

Emily deadpanned and grinned. "Oh, my God, you're bossy,"

"Excuse me?"

"In the sweetest, most sexy and determined way… I mean," she said, and beamed earnestly. "It's hot."

Helena snorted in disbelief and chuckled. "You're kidding,"

"Absolutely not, and getting back on topic, I have a baby on the way —I need money."

Helena took Emily's hands. "Sweetheart, you don't have to worry about that." she said.

"How the hell not? Babies are cute and expensive."

"Because I have my living trust, don't worry about money, Em; once I'm twenty-one, I can have full access to it —in the meantime, I have access to some of it." Helena responded.

"Okay, first of all… I have to provide for our kid, too —I think it's awesome that you were blessed with so much, but I need to do this. You can't expect me to let you support us, I— What?! No."

"Emily, that is retrograde. Besides, I never said that, though I would gladly take care of our family, I meant while we get ourselves through college; once we are both working and comfortable in our careers then you may do as you please." she compromised. "However, I still think you should *not* drop out."

327

Emily gushed out a mildly defeated sigh. This wasn't quite flying, but she would let it go for now. "What about moving in together? I don't wanna be away from you... now more than ever." she said longingly.

Helena smiled and melted; she cupped a rosy cheek in her beautiful hand and caressed it. Her brown eyes shone. "Em, love; I want us to be together as well, but right now we can't move out, darling —not while I'm pregnant and dealing with this condition."

Emily lowered her head and looked at her hands. "I know..." she said.

Helena smiled and placed a kiss on her lips. "What if... after the baby is born, we move in together, would you like that?"

Emily's eyes flooded with unshed sentiment. "Of course, I'd love that." she murmured with a small, honest smile.

"Now..." Helena said as she parted and crawled out of the comfortable bed, leaving Emily sitting there completely aroused and naked.

She walked towards the bathroom and turned. Green eyes were, of course, glued to her every inch. "Follow me?" Helena asked as her brow arched suggestively.

Emily smiled and followed her into the immaculate bathroom. "But you just took a shower," she said, grinning and gently cornered a very naked Helena against the wall —cold, expensive tiles flush against her olive-toned back.

"I won't melt if I take another one."

Hypnotized, Emily leaned in and brushed their lips. "Then who am I to deny you?" she said, grinning charmingly.

Helena reached down and ever so gently ran her fingers

on Emily's thigh. Pearly teeth claimed her own bottom lip —brown eyes never left green ones. "There is something else I am craving." she murmured.

Emily raised a brow. "Oh?"

With a slow, sexy smile, Helena nodded.

"And what would that be, Miss Millan?"

Helena opened the glass doors and pulled a more than willing Emily into the shower.

She turned the handle, and a delicious spring of water fell on them. Emily squealed and laughed. The echo of their voices mixed inside the private space that was only theirs; they made memories, they simply lived. Soon, their laughing died down as Helena pushed her blonde against the wall with a smoldering look —the serious kind that burned and made stomachs revolve around their own axis.

Eyes fell on lips, breaths raced, and mouths crashed.

Emily quickly trapped Helena's hips with loving hands and pushed her tongue in. Tanned fingers felt their way to the soap and began to run sudsy hands on Emily's body. A wet blonde head fell back on the tiles as she felt Helena all over. Her kisses, her tongue, her hands. "God… I love you." Emily said.

Helena's smoldering kiss was excruciatingly slow, erotic... She licked slightly open and welcoming lips, pulling Emily's bottom one between provoking teeth. Brown eyes coaxed green ones into giving their focus. "I love you, my beautiful girl," Helena whispered softly.

The words reached Emily's heart, not only because they came from *her*, but because she knew exactly what Helena was doing. She felt her girlfriend's gentle and meaningful words deeply because at the moment, her womanhood was trying to flee from her grasp, not internally, but physically.

Helena made her feel truly like the most beautiful girl in the world.

Bruised lips left a sinful trail of open-mouthed kisses all over Emily's neck, shoulders... Helena's curious tongue glided between the valley of her soaked breasts, tasted its way down her torso lower and lower until she found the soft skin at the base of Emily's beautiful sex. She placed an open-mouthed, wet kiss on it, and Emily shuddered —she almost crumbled against cold tiles.

Finger's kneaded through Helena's wet hair and Emily looked down. Her warm, loving eyes gazed up without fail, piercing her existence. Emily knew in her heart that she would be incapable of life after Helena, she could not see beyond the line they dreaded.

Helena opened her mouth and claimed her. Emily's jaw fell with a shiver as she watched the love of her life indulge in one of the most mouthwatering forms of pleasure she had ever experienced.

It was heart and soul; it was more than sex —it was more than defining, and it was transcending adoration.

16

HOLD ON

AFTER THEIR SHOWER, EMILY decided to find the best place where Helena could indulge in food that tasted like what she craved. Meat. Something healthy, exactly what she needed to aid her heart condition, and boy... had she delivered.

Helena tore through the most delicious mock meat burger she had ever indulged in. Seattle now had a special place in her heart.

Brown eyes grew with delight, and green ones followed. Emily beamed.

Helena chewed with impeccable manners, though the pleasure on her face was divine.

"Mmm... Oh, my God," She licked her tempting lips.

"Ah, see, I told you... awesome, right?" Emily ventured.

Helena swallowed. "That was spectacular."

Emily smiled with raised brows; she had never seen her girlfriend eat this much before. She munched on a sweet potato fry. "I'm glad you liked it, baby. Do you feel better?" she asked.

Helena rolled her eyes with the utmost satisfaction and smiled. "So much better..."

"Good." She smiled, reaching for Helena's hand. Brown eyes gleamed, and Emily felt full —nothing made her feel better than to see Helena happy and satisfied.

Suddenly overcome with excitement, brown eyes darted over Emily's shoulder and across the intimate restaurant. "Uh!" she urged, and waved her hand towards someone in the distance.

Emily turned to find the waiter looking back at Helena. "Baby, are you still hungry?" she asked, under her breath.

Helena grinned. "Apple pie... I saw it on the menu earlier; it looked delicious." she said.

"Are you sure?" Emily tried. "How about just the apples?"

Helena arched a sly brow. "Why? What is wrong with me eating the pie?"

Emily raised both hands in mid-air. "I... I mean, I just thought," she tried.

"Are you calling me fat?" Helena said, edging closer.

Green eyes widened. "What? No! Of course not, Helena, I... but you said you shouldn't be eating a lot of the things the baby is making you crave,"

After a settling breath, the pained and confused look on Emily's face told Helena that her pregnancy hormones were getting the best of her. She didn't deserve her mood swings... Helena entwined their fingers and gave her an apologetic look. "I'm sorry, Em... I didn't mean to be a grouch."

Emily blinked softly as she caressed her hand. "It's okay, baby, don't worry..." she eased, and at that moment, crossed gazes with the man approaching their table.

"Ladies, can I get you something else?" he asked.

Emily looked up. "How high is the sugar content in your apple pie?"

A secret burst of joy curled Helena's lips into a tiny

smile, her usually careless eater was suddenly worried about hers and the baby's health. Helena felt weightless and optimistic... The organic moment infused her with a surge of absolute hope. It is the tiniest things about life... the moments and instants we miss.

The way unaware green eyes gleamed as they rolled further up into her beautiful lashes and waited for an answer from the pleasant man lingering above them. Helena sighed and smiled in silent acknowledgment of another beautiful second of their life.

The hazy instant dissolved as the sound of the waiter's voice zoomed in, he smiled.

"Oh, there is zero refined sugar in our apple pie... we use coconut palm sugar, so the glycemic content is far lower than the regular one, but the crust is completely fat-free, and it is *fantastic.*" The eager waiter explained. Emily nodded and turned to find Helena looking at her with pure love.

"Do you still want it?" Emily asked softly.

Helena smiled and looked up at the man holding the small notepad. "We'll take it to go, please." she said.

"Perfect; I'll go get that for you."

"Could you also bring the check, please?" Helena added, and the man nodded as he left.

While the casual words effortlessly fell from Helena's beautiful lips, Emily shifted in her seat uncomfortably, but brown eyes caught the change.

"What is it, Em?" Helena asked, caressing her hand.

Two shoulders rose in a mild shrug. "Nothing— I just..." she barely said, and chewed on her lip while staring at their entwined hands on the table. "I feel useless."

"What? Why do you feel that way?"

"Because every two seconds I remember that real life is just— hard! And I have nothing to give you two."

A mix of embarrassing defeat and sadness loomed over Emily's stiffened frame. Money had always been the last thing on Helena's mind, but she couldn't be insensitive to Emily's feelings or concerns about it.

She knew Emily had a gigantic heart and an equally large sense of pride that was quite hard to penetrate, but Helena understood. It was Emily's baby as well, the need to feel capable was natural. She was a college student who didn't get to have things handed to her, she was still young and now an expectant mother. An expectant mother with a sick girlfriend begging for support on her decision to have their baby. An expectant mother whose body changes were creating a set of terrifying possible outcomes for her future as an individual. Emily had a lot on her mind, and Helena knew how much she tended to carry everything alone and in silence.

With a gentle thumb, Helena brushed the soft skin there and begged with warm eyes. "I know, Em, but it's okay, I promise... Please don't let that worry you right now, you don't have to provide for me, darling, and I told you, I can do it for both of us until you can, okay?"

Emily inhaled a batch of air that bruised her ego; she forced a dull smile and nodded. Helena knew it wouldn't be the last she would see of this, but also understood Emily's stance.

Minutes after, Helena got her pie to go, and Emily arranged to meet her brother at Kerry Park. She knew Helena hadn't slept well and dragging her all over the city wasn't an option. This way was perfect; they would get to see her brother, and then just go to the hotel right after for some well-deserved rest.

Finding a place to park had been easy, and so was breathing the cold air of that beautiful place. Apparently, winter was quite stunning in Seattle; it was no German frost-coated wonderland, but living it while walking hand in hand with Emily Knight, was nothing short of extraordinary.

Pale fingers feathered over tanned skin as heat crept up cold cheeks; consumed with thoughts that stretched for miles, Emily turned to find chocolate eyes.

Helena smiled, and said, "What is it?"

"I can't believe I'm here with you," Emily responded and shrugged, feeling content.

Easy steps guided them to the breathtaking view of Seattle's skyline. The wind was crisp and gentle; a light shade of carmine blushed Helena's cheeks, and Emily thought she looked just so beautiful. Face to face, pale hands tucked a few strands of dark hair away. The more Emily experienced how good life could feel, the more she dreaded Helena's possible fate.

"Talk to me, Em..."

"I just love you so much, Helena, I'm —this feels like a dream, and even though things seem so difficult right now, somehow your presence in my life helps me breathe easier. You mean everything... If I had to die tomorrow so you could live happy— I would, in a second, but the way I love you makes me feel so selfish —I'd rather cling to you and burn with you than lose you." Emily confessed as wet warmth blurred her vision. "I don't want to lose you; I'm so scared."

Helena's eyes reddened as she noticed green ones shine

with unshed tears. "Oh, Em..." She untucked a hand from the pocket of her expensive coat and cupped Emily's cheek.

Helena knew. She knew *her*, but having Emily openly express words that sprouted fresh from her beautiful heart was something she had rarely gotten the chance to witness. Emily was loving; she was sweet and usually showed it in silent ways that were so loud to Helena. She often spoke of her love and sometimes of her wants, but this was Emily showing her just how she had been torn open. Life had been hard, and it had made her turn inwards, but Helena had gently and lovingly changed that.

Emily sniffled and wiped away her tears with the back of her hand. "I know we're not supposed to think about it, but I feel like I'm choking..." she said as the cold wind blew blonde strands of hair freely.

With a wet smile, Helena too wiped away her own sentiment. She realized just how much her decision to carry their baby to term was affecting Emily. Right then and there she understood how much Emily loved her. Emily was willing to ache and drown in sadness that was so heavy inside just to give her what she wanted —even if it meant losing her.

Helena's chin quivered as she swallowed her crying. "My beautiful Emily..." A darkly manicured thumb grazed over a flushed, wet cheek. "I wish I could show you how your words alter me..." she said.

Emily blinked rapidly and looked up at the grand sky. It was so big and steady, even if they were to fade, it would remain there. She laughed between tears. "God! I'm so tired of crying!" she said, and stomped her foot on the ground, feeling frustrated with herself.

Helena broke in laughter and sobbed away the last few

drops of her split emotions. "Me too…" She glanced at her boots or maybe the concrete, searching for excuses, but knew there weren't any. There could be none. "Emily…" she finally said, looking at her.

"I know that what I'm asking of you is… just so difficult, and I honestly don't know how to put it into words that make sense, but… I *need* to do this, I hope… maybe not now, but someday you can understand why." Helena said with raw intent in gleaming eyes.

"I know…" Emily murmured, a tiny smile brushed her lips.

Helena pressed a kiss against them; the harshness of the wind became more real. Emily hid her face in the warmth of Helena's neck and held her tightly; right there, in the middle of a landmark that had witnessed countless other confessions and circumstances —this was life unfolding; this was their story. Both could only hope for a happy ending.

A few minutes into the warm embrace and a familiar male voice startled them —it sounded like a smirk. "You girls are so corny."

Emily broke away and turned —she smiled and excitedly said, "Patrick!"

"Hey, sis," Patrick threw a charming grin and looped his arms around her. Emily's smile froze as the sight she found over his shoulder melted her. A sweet baby boy in Tala's arms. He looked about one year old, had tanned skin like Patrick's High School sweetheart and Maureen's green eyes.

"Oh, my God, Patrick…" Smitten, Emily pulled back. "Is that him?" she asked but knew that had to be her nephew, and he was perfect.

Tala smiled and nudged him gently. "Look, Noah… That's Emily, say hi to Emily," The beautiful brunette woman smiled. "Hi, Em," she said.

Emily walked closer with happiness on her lips; she could hear Helena and Patrick exchanging their hellos behind her.

"Hey, Tala... Can I hold him?" Emily asked.

"Sure."

Emily smiled at the baby and offered both arms to him. He observed her with almost identical eyes; it was surreal. "Come on, Noah..." Emily encouraged him softly, but the boy tucked his face into his mother's neck.

"Aw... He's just a little shy." Tala said, and Emily turned to Helena with a smirk.

"This doesn't bode well for us."

"Don't be silly, Em," Helena said, inching towards the baby and smiled at Patrick's girlfriend. "You tend to have that effect on people; I can vouch for that. He's just smitten." she finished, giving her gracious attention to the boy. "Hi, baby," she cooed.

Patrick interjected, "Helena, this is Tala —Tala this is Emily's girlfriend, Helena."

"Hi," Helena offered kindly. "It's nice to finally meet you."

"Me too, I've heard so much about you," Tala said to Helena and winked at Emily.

"Good things, I hope."

Tala seemed genuine. "Of course..."

Charming Helena lowered herself and laced a finger with Noah's tiny ones. She smiled and noticed familiar and vast mossy green. "Oh, Em... He has yours and your mother's eyes."

Emily and Patrick smiled.

"He's gorgeous, Tala." Helena offered honestly.

"Thank you." Tala said.

After a few seconds of showering him with baby talk

and that amazing smile, Noah threw his arms and tiny body at Helena.

"Oh!" she said, suddenly surprised by his move while leaping forward to catch him.

"He knows what's up," Patrick said with a grin, and they all broke in laughter.

Emily lingered in silent bliss and stared at their possible future —Helena looked stunning holding baby Noah. Emily then knew she would be an amazing mother, it seemed to come so naturally regardless of the unfortunate circumstances, it simply fit. Her beautiful hands gently touching his tiny body, the way they took an immediate liking to each other —it was magical.

Helena was giving away what she had always craved. Emily knew then that Helena wouldn't be a distant mother; she would give their baby exactly what she'd had with Maureen, and for that, she counted herself lucky —their baby so, so lucky. How could someone who'd had so little of her parents turn out to be this in tune with such nurturing energy? So loving and easy.

We are born ourselves, but we're also shaped by our experiences and how we allow them to affect us. When Helena confessed she could die because of the baby, Emily's mind raced between taking Katherine's side and offering her girlfriend the support she desperately needed and begged for —but this had changed everything. There was no choice to be made anymore. Anything for her.

Their afternoon together flowed with ease, even though Emily wanted to tell Patrick what was happening, she decided to bask in the happy moment instead. Watching Helena engage with her nephew was beyond any dream.

Faint rays of sun filtered through wintery clouds and found a way to warm their glowing skin. A few feet away, Helena held the boy, and Tala sat next to them. Emily and Patrick sat close enough to see them clearly, but far enough to be able to have some privacy as they caught up.

Patrick focused on the color of some nearby tree and squinted his eyes at the seeping flares of sunshine. "So, what's going on, Em?" he asked, and turned his head to meet her gaze.

"What do you mean? Nothing's going on." she lied.

"What are you guys doing here on Christmas Day?" he said, smiling coolly. "Aren't you supposed to be at home stuffing your face with mom's food and watching the game with Dad and Rhys? I figured Helena would be with her family..."

Emily pushed a sad smile. "They had a bit of a fight, so, she needed to get away..." she said.

"Oh... Damn, I'm sorry."

Emily gave him yet another lazy smile. "What about you? When are you gonna tell Mom and Dad about Noah? They missed you last night, mom was sad you didn't show." she told her brother.

Patrick took a deep breath and thought of how much his life had changed in the past few months. "I'm gonna go home next week and talk to them." He shrugged. "We're gonna move back to California." he confessed.

"What? What about college?" Emily asked.

That was a funny one.

He let out a contemplative and tired sigh. "I can't keep living here, Em, when Tala showed up at my door I had to move out of the frat house... put in more hours at work, classes, the team —it's just too much." he said, shaking his head, Emily saw a gleam of sadness and desperation in his usually relaxed eyes. "Living here is just too expensive; raising a kid even worse."

Emily's brows knitted, she felt for her brother and saw herself reflected in his current state. "What about Tala? I mean, are you guys back together?"

He smiled and said, "Yeah, she's been helping, too; she got a job, but Noah is still so little; we have to leave him at this dump of a place every day —I mean, some of the teachers are nice, and they try… but it's a mess, Em —I don't want that for him. Besides, Tala's mom is gonna rent us her guest house." Patrick confessed, taking in his surroundings as he felt the vivid clarity of how life now was.

"It's hard, I mean… being a parent changes everything; life as you know it, suddenly fucking evaporates —I love him, don't get me wrong… that kid is my life, but it's no walk in the park."

A hard lump rolled down Emily's throat. Even though Patrick had no idea Helena was pregnant or sick for that matter, everything he said hit her right in the middle of her life. She looked towards the other bench and saw Helena still playing with the baby boy in her arms. She felt absolute love and numbing fear.

***

Their time in Seattle and their little bubble was coming to an end. Both girls knew they had to go back to San Francisco and face reality, face Katherine —though Emily knew that going home was the last thing Helena wanted to do.

When they held each other in bed, Emily usually searched for shelter in Helena's arms like a little girl; she was her haven, her refuge. This time, it was Helena seeking safety for her heart and mind.

Beautiful hands played with the soft and flimsy fabric of Emily's top; a brunette head rested on Emily's shoulder as her exquisite olive-toned arm curled around that small waist. "This feels so good, Em; I don't want to go back... I wish things were different." Helena confessed, and even though Emily couldn't see her face, she heard regret in her voice.

Emily caressed dark locks gently, wishing she could change things for them. "I know, baby, but we have to; you need to see your doctor as soon as possible... we need to do this right."

A warm thumb feathered over Helena's smooth hairline seamlessly. Every touch they shared embraced Helena's soul in ways that couldn't be described with words. She didn't have any recollection of ever reading a book that explained just how fated Emily felt. Helena smiled against the familiar scented warmth of her girlfriend's clothes. She then shifted in her arms and looked up into green eyes. "No more crying..." Helena said.

Emily pushed a grin. "No more crying." she agreed.

"I mean, it is normal to feel our emotions... we were designed to feel them and work through them... this doesn't mean I want us to withhold our thoughts or feelings, Em..."

Emily grazed a kiss on Helena's forehead. "Of course not. I promise. I agree with you; we should focus on the good things."

"Good..." Helena said. "You know... If my calculations are correct, our baby should be approximately four millimeters long, and his heart should be beating at this stage." she shared with a hopeful smile while looking into gleaming green.

Emily beamed. "Really?"

"Yes… only if my calculations are correct; I think we conceived him our second time... Do you remember?"

"Yeah… I remember," Emily's heart fluttered; she could never forget her moments with Helena. "The condom broke…"

And now here they were.

Helena nodded and bit her lip. "I can't believe it, Em, we made a little person… It's so surreal yet at the same time absolutely beautiful."

The honest gleam in Emily's eye was captivating; her lips curled upwards. "We should call him something, I mean, he is a person, so calling him 'The baby' is a little impersonal."

Helena's heart warmed. "I think you are right, though I might be wrong about his sex."

Emily shrugged as she rubbed circles on Helena's shoulder. "It doesn't matter, I mean, we could choose something unisex for now, or do you have any names already picked for your hypothetical babies since childhood?" Emily joked softly.

"I don't… Do you?"

"Not at all —I never let myself dream that far and get excited about something I thought I'd never have, regardless of the fact that I never opposed the idea of having kids in the future," She shrugged. "I never thought I'd get to have one." Emily confessed.

The cruel reality of that statement hit Helena; she could only imagine how cruel people must have been to Emily throughout her life. She smiled and fingertips feathered her girlfriend's jawline. "What if we call him or her Winter… for now, until we can both agree on a name, what do you think?"

Green eyes gleamed. "Winter…" She turned to look out the window; it was perfect. Helena adored the season. "Yeah, I like that…"

"Yes?" Helena asked excitedly.

Emily nodded. "Yeah…" She leaned into Helena's face and claimed her lips —Helena giggled against the kiss; that soft feeling of their breaths mixing as one was always so imminent for the other; binding and freeing all at once.

17

TWO HEARTS

A S SOON AS BOTH girls woke up, they dove deep into their last few moments of privacy and kissed until their lips were bruised. After an invigorating shower, Helena demanded breakfast —in large quantities. Emily thought it was adorable how her usually disciplined girlfriend had been eating like this, all because of their little one and the changes occurring inside her.

The drive back to San Francisco had been less peaceful and undoubtedly fun this time, since Helena had stayed awake keeping Emily company. It was roughly 5:00 pm by the time they had arrived home. Helena begged Emily to drive straight to Outer Sunset, avoiding Katherine at all costs. She wasn't ready, not yet. She wanted to rest; her body begged for sleep even though night-time was still far.

Emily complied and drove them back to her house where Maureen happily welcomed them with loving hugs to spare. Relief washed over Emily; she felt an odd mixture of contentment and worry. Contentment because they were now in San Francisco, and regardless of anything, being so far away from Helena's parents —the people who knew her condition best, was stressful. At least here they could aid her if she were to need it, but not knowing what Helena's cardiologist would say was tearing through her sanity.

The man was on a plane bound for the U.S and was scheduled to meet with them the next day. Emily didn't know what to think anymore; her mind raced —it flew upwards and forward. Green eyes focused on the sinking sunlight seeping through the window. She found some ease on the familiar scent imprinted on her fresh sheets now mixing with that delicious one belonging to a sleeping Helena pressed against her.

Tranquility engulfed the room as they lay in bed. Helena's head rested on Emily's shoulder much like it had the night before at the hotel. Soft lips grazed her silky dark hair —it smelled like fresh orange blossoms and some exclusive perfume. Emily couldn't stop her thoughts and worry; it was like they were wild creatures, similar to the butterflies in her stomach that had mutated into birds or something much bigger than that. *Those bastards.*

Only the soft and steady sounds of Helena's breathing kept her sane. Her mind felt full and busy, but knowing Helena was content and free in deep sleep gave Emily peace. Their baby was really a tiny Knight, big eater, big sleeper, no doubt a Knight.

As more reflections resonated in Emily's mind, so did the sound of two distant voices merging in conversation. Two very familiar voices that after a while became a little louder, thankfully not loud enough to wake Helena.

Emily caressed her arm; brows rose in pure curiosity and wonder. The muffled sounds of her mother begging the other woman to please lower her voice became clearer —she was barely able to decode the words.

It was Katherine.

In the gentlest, stealthiest move, Emily shifted her body and protected Helena's sleep at all costs, disturbing her tired lover wasn't an option. She placed a soft kiss on the bridge of her nose and silently minced out of the bedroom.

Walking down the stairs slowly, Emily's ears were attentive. From the sounds of it, they had moved to the kitchen. She bit her lip and curiously scanned the living room. Nothing.

They were most definitely in the kitchen. She continued to listen in silence and walked closer.

"Please have a seat, Mrs. Millan," Maureen said, and Emily stood behind a nearby wall.

Katherine didn't speak, but Emily heard the moving sound of a chair. She figured Helena's mother had accepted the invitation.

"Okay, Mrs. Knight, I have done as you requested... I apologize for being so forward before. However, I need to see Helena."

Emily swallowed a knot and searching eyes focused on a nearby object. She needed an anchor, so she stared at a photo of herself, resting on a stand among others. Emily was eight; long blonde hair up in a ponytail, the girl wore her little league soccer uniform and held a ball on her side. Life seemed so difficult then. Even though she was smiling brightly; she remembered the endless teasing and name-calling; life was as hard as she thought it could be. That was then; this was now.

Maureen's voice was as soothing as usual. "I understand

your concerns, and you are, of course, in all your right to see Helena, but I'm sorry... she is sleeping as I told you before, Mrs. Millan. Can I offer you some tea?"

Emily heard a polite smile at the end of her mother's sentence. The smell of some timeless and delicate perfume hit her nostrils. It belonged to Helena's mother.

"Thank you."

Katherine must have nodded, because a few seconds later, Maureen began to move around the kitchen as quietly as she could.

"I don't understand why she didn't come home as soon as they arrived." Katherine said.

Another chair dragged softly on the hardwood floor. "She was so exhausted, and to be honest; she seemed scared." Maureen replied.

"Scared? Did she say she was?" Katherine asked defensively.

"She didn't, but it wasn't hard to see. With all due respect, Katherine... as Helena's professor, I can say with certainty that she is just so bright, but in the little time I've had the pleasure of knowing her, I have seen that her emotions run as deeply as her strength and her maturity..."

The doctor interrupted and said, "Well, thank you, Mrs. Knight, though I already knew this; she is my daughter after all."

"Of course she is, and I am not trying to imply that you don't know her, but Katherine... what she is going through isn't easy at her age, that is difficult enough. I feel that she needs to know you understand and support her—"

"Support her? That is the last thing I plan to do —Helena cannot have that child! Don't you people understand that she can die?!"

"*Please, lower your voice.*" Maureen hissed.

Emily swallowed hard again and felt warm tears prickle in her reddened eyes.

"I am well aware, they spoke to me while in Seattle and told me of this, but Katherine, are *you* aware that Helena doesn't want to have an abortion?" Maureen asked.

The doctor huffed. "Of course I am. Tell me, Mrs. Knight—"

"Maureen…" she offered.

"*Maureen*… If it were *your* daughter circling the edge of death because of a stupid and sentimental desire to keep a fetus alive —what would *you* do?"

"A fetus? I'm sorry, Katherine, but that is a baby… hers and my daughter's baby." Maureen's emotions poured through her voice.

A silent tear escaped Emily's eye and ran down her flushed cheek. She was breaking her promise to Helena; they had said no more crying —she tried to bite them back, to blink them away. She needed to walk in and fight for their baby —speak to Katherine.

"Nonsense, they are not ready to have a child at this age, not only would it ruin their lives, it could cost my daughter hers!" Katherine defended passionately, her voice trembled with emotion and Emily clenched her fists, tears blurred her vision.

"*Katherine… Please...*" Urgency transformed Maureen's murmur.

The elegant woman sniffled her tears away. "I need to speak to Emily before Helena wakes then…"

Full of courage, Emily came out from hiding and stepped forward. Both women turned to the presence entering the kitchen. Wet streaks marred Emily's cheeks, but she was more than ready to face her girlfriend's mother. If she wanted to talk, they would talk.

"Honey…" Maureen whispered with a broken heart while Katherine's discrete hand wiped away a tear from the corner of her eye. The strong woman took a deep, dignifying breath.

Emily found her voice, though hoarse, "I'm here, Mrs. Millan."

Katherine stood. "Emily, I need you to please talk some sense into Helena, she will not listen to me or anyone… However, I am confident she will listen to you."

Emily's expression closed up. *That wasn't an option.* "I can't… we both want our baby." she said.

Disdain contorted Katherine's face. "Have you lost your mind?!" she said, and barged forward, but Emily didn't move a muscle. She stood her ground. Eye to eye. However, Maureen inched a hand between them.

"Katherine, please! This is my daughter you're speaking to." Maureen said, and the energy quickly shifted into that of each mother out to protect her own. Katherine Helena, Maureen Emily, and Emily Winter.

—*Winter*. With shaken heartstrings, Emily swallowed hard. How could she forget the past hours? So intimately falling in love with their baby and even more with Helena. How could she advocate to end their little Winter's chance? She wouldn't.

Ignoring Maureen's divisive hand, Katherine inched closer to Emily until their unwavering gazes were mere breaths away; the look plastered on the doctor's face told Emily that she was fuming.

"*You* did this to my daughter! This is all your fault, Emily Knight. *You* fix it!" Katherine shouted with fire in her eyes; so ready to rip Emily's heart out if she could. A blaming finger sharply pointed at her.

A silent tear ran down Emily's face; she remained expressionless, though the sadness in smoldering eyes was loud, the redness in her cheeks spoke of her repressed stress. It didn't matter; she could take it. —*I deserve it.* she thought. The guilt of being so careless and irresponsible mocked Emily's mind and heart. Even if unknowing of the risks for Helena, she felt guilty, **so guilty**. Her chin quivered, a sign of the weakening cracks rupturing a dam inside her chest. More tears fell.

In a rush of instinct, Maureen cut between them, her usually loving face mirrored Katherine's in intensity and determination. "Okay, you need to stop harassing my daughter, right now! It took two to make that child! Not one —how dare you blame this entirely on her?" Maureen said at once.

Emily couldn't stop the effortless tears, but somehow that spark of composure surged back into Katherine's darkened eyes. A deep breath washed the woman's lungs with calm while she stepped back and pinched the bridge of her nose.

"I… you're right, Helena is as responsible as you are, Emily; I apologize for losing my temper like that," Katherine's regal posture returned. "I…"

Emily felt her mother's support in the form of a gentle touch. "We won't kill Winter." she said, and swallowed hard in her stance.

Winter?

Both Katherine and Maureen wondered, yet quickly assumed of the baby's name.

"It's Helena's body... It's our baby, and I support whatever she decides." Emily bore into Katherine's eyes. "I'm not insensitive to the risks..." she choked. "In fact, I'd trade my life for hers —to make this right for them," Emily shook her head. "If I take your side, I'd have to betray her, and that I'll never do... so I beg you, *please* stop pushing her and making her feel so stressed —you're only making it worse for her."

That arrangement of words didn't sit well with Katherine, but the woman remained silent. She took in Emily's statement and knew that *yes*, stressing Helena could be counterproductive. A settling breath surged into her as frustrated hands turned into fists.

While minutes ticked away, the peaceful silence was slowly turning uncomfortable. No one had said another word.

"Mother..." Helena's voice came, and three heads turned.

Emily studied her face and behavior. She seemed more confused and nervous than upset, which meant nothing of what Katherine had said made it to Helena's ears. Emily sighed in relief.

"Helena, dear," Katherine rushed forward, but Helena shriveled away from her touch like she had been burned.

A silent crack fractured Katherine's heart. She gasped and retreated her extended hands with gleaming eyes.

In a defiant stance, Helena's chest rose and fell as she stared at her mother. Emily took her hand and caressed it reassuringly.

"Helena, my love... Please, I..." Katherine tried.

"No, Mother, I won't do what you want." Helena exclaimed with sullen eyes. "That is why you're here, right? Please go!" she finished, erupting into tears.

Emily curled her arms around Helena's shaking body

while Maureen's brows bumped in compassion. It was a painful thing to witness.

Katherine's eyes reddened as warm sentiment pooled in them. "You're afraid of me…" she whispered, soaked in dread and bold pain.

Emily held her trembling girlfriend tighter. "Hey, it's okay… Shh, I'm here," The whisper was so intimate to Helena's ear that everyone else missed it.

Maureen's gentle touch aimed to soothe her —that motherly warmth Helena had always craved from Katherine, unconditional affection. "Helena, sweetheart, your mom only came to speak to you, you don't have to go anywhere if you don't want to." Maureen said, locking eyes with Katherine and begging for her understanding. It was a silent plea.

Katherine swallowed her tears and sniffled. "She's right, my love, I just wanted to see you and make sure you are all right… Could we talk? Please?" Katherine begged in a way Helena had never seen.

Brown eyes bore deeply into the woman she adored in spite of her constant absence. There, in her mother's gaze, she found honesty.

"I won't hurt your baby… I promise." Katherine raised both hands in mid-air as a sign of peace.

Reluctance rolled down Helena's throat as she swallowed and loosened the tight grip on Emily's clothing. A wisp of a smile birthed from Katherine's lips.

"I give you my word, Helena." she reassured her daughter, looking into frightened and tear soaked eyes. At that moment, Katherine felt like a horrible mother. She had failed Helena as a parent and felt like she was betraying her entire belief system by agreeing to allow her sick daughter to endanger herself. She felt torn —at a true crossroads.

Katherine found Emily's eyes and saw the love and loyalty sprouting from them. Emily was genuine and fierce. Inside her lived a kind of silent and noble bravery.

The moment was heavy and light all at once. Maureen felt the need to speak up, "Helena, sweetie, you two should go to the living room so you can have some privacy."

Emily nodded, searching for her lover's eyes. "Yeah, baby… you two should talk." she said.

"It's quite all right; I don't want to disturb... I simply needed to make sure she is okay." Katherine told them and regarded Helena, "How are you feeling, dear? Have you been taking care of yourself?" she asked.

"I feel fine, Mother, aside from increased appetite and particular cravings, I feel... fine."

"You were sleeping, and it is merely evening —are you feeling any fatigue?"

Helena shook her head. "No, but I have been sleeping more, not fatigued, simply tired."

Katherine took in the information and a deep breath. This could mean many things, but for her mind's sake she chose to believe it was the pregnancy; these symptoms were completely normal. The woman nodded, pushing a gentle smile as she tried to touch Helena's arm, this time Helena didn't jerk away. "Maybe we should go to the hospital... I could check you up properly, or your father could, dear, whatever you choose."

"I am *fine*, Mother, please," Helena said calmly and marked her boundaries. "I will be staying with Emily tonight."

Unsure and weighed down by her instincts, Katherine

found Maureen's gaze and the pleasant woman bobbed her head rapidly. "Of course… she can stay as long as she wants, this is her home, too." Emily's mother said.

Ever since Katherine's offer to check up on Helena, Emily's lips itched to intervene. "Helena, maybe your mom is right, a checkup wouldn't hurt, baby."

"When is Doctor Rossi coming?" Helena asked.

"He should arrive at Atlantic Aviation tonight; he flew in a charter… I could ask him to check you up if you'd like, I'll ask him to come to the house,"

"No, Mother, that would be abusive; I am sure he'll be tired. We can wait until my appointment tomorrow." Helena took Emily's hand in hers and smiled softly, Emily, of course, returned the loving sentiment. "We will meet you at his office as I am sure you would like to be there."

Another stinging breath burned Katherine, so she pushed a smile. She had to conform and accept the fact that Emily had the right to be there as well. The doctor wasn't happy about them acting like a married couple, but she understood the kind of binding force that was now growing inside her daughter. She had always adored Helena's strength, her will, and intelligence, but Katherine felt awed at her daughter's ability to love —to love and fight for her ideals so ferociously; without acting like a child in the process. She had to respect that.

"Very well," she said, and looked at Emily. "I will meet you both there at 8:00 am, sharp."

Emily nodded and Helena bit her lip, the doctor couldn't help but simply *know* her daughter had more to say.

"What is it, dear?" she tried softly.

"You can… examine me if you'd like." Helena said, knowing her mother always carried her medical bag in her car.

Katherine smiled, and a soft gleam crossed her eyes. "Thank you, darling... I will go to my car and return shortly." The elegant woman said.

The ambiance had softened in a matter of seconds, and for that, Maureen was grateful.

After checking up on her daughter, Katherine left with the satisfaction that as of now Helena's vitals were completely normal. There was only so much she could do with what she had and her knowledge, but was able to leave the Knight residence knowing that Michael Rossi would thoroughly assess her state and suggest the best course of action. Just a few more hours.

***

Night had fallen upon them. While in the comforting warmth of her sweatpants and tank top, Emily lay in bed as Helena exited her bathroom with damp hair and a skimpy little silk piece.

"Baby, aren't you cold? It's freezing outside." Emily asked with a grin and curious brows.

"Outside, Em, I am not cold, *at all...* on the contrary, I am hot." Helena sat on the plush bed, and Emily chuckled.

"Winter has really thrown your body for a loop."

A longing sigh lit up brown eyes; Helena found happiness. She felt it so deeply.

"What?" Emily asked, wondering what had made her glow like that.

"I love how you say his name, well, his temporary name at least," Helena said, smiling. "It feels so beautiful and real."

"He *is* beautiful and real." Emily cooed. She already

loved her kid, and even though she would gladly die to keep them both alive, Emily hadn't engaged in intimate touching of Helena's belly or spoken to the baby like most parents so mushily would —aside from that one time while in Seattle.

Helena allowed Emily to open herself up to this new side of their relationship at her own pace. She on the other hand, constantly caressed her own belly and tried to enjoy each moment in its entirety.

Green eyes stayed on Helena as she turned off the lamp and joined her under the sheets.

"I love your home, Em,"

With a charming grin, Emily looped her arm around her. "Really?"

Helena's eyes gleamed like the silver moonlight that crept through the window and brushed her features.

Emily saw it clearly. Her happiness.

"Yes, I love the sounds... The scent of lemons and fresh wood."

Emily laughed softly. "The sounds must be the squeaky old floors, Lena, and I'm glad you smell lemons and not Rhys' room." she joked.

Helena nudged Emily's ribs playfully and laughed. "Emily Knight! I am serious!"

Deep dimples pierced Emily's cheeks as she joined Helena. "I know what you mean; I love the scents and the sounds, too." she admitted with honesty flaring from her eyes even though it was partially dark. "It's home." Emily said.

Helena nodded softly, and her smile faded. "Exactly..." she whispered.

The instant was seamless; effortlessly organic. Emily's smile had fled, and a serious look on both their faces had replaced the outer show of inner bliss. The smoldering gleam in Helena's eyes was that of pure lust, and the one in Emily's sparkled like magic. They stared at each other, only silence and breathing. *Feeling.*

Helena inched closer and grazed the heat of her breath on Emily's jaw. Green eyes fluttered closed as gripping electricity rushed inside.

Indulging in the clean smell of soap and some other delicious scent, Helena engulfed herself in those warm surges of arousing breaths that came in and out of their mouths. She sunk graceful fingertips under Emily's flimsy top and made her shiver. Her taut abdomen weakened at the mercy of Helena's seductive ways and lips —the erotic curve of their aesthetically beautiful form, juxtaposed onto Emily's ear... No composure, only persuasion. Such sweet and warm coaxing.

"Helena..." Emily whispered, still with eyes closed.

The wet tip of Helena's tongue misbehaved in the most stunning of ways; she painted a needy trail on Emily's earlobe, raising an onslaught of fire on pale skin. "I need you, Em, please kiss me," Helena begged in whispers.

Emily propped herself up on one elbow and leaned down to kiss Helena's lips. Blonde locks fell forward, and Helena gently tucked them back. Emily found exposed eyes. She stared at them for what seemed an eternity and Helena let her.

"That night, Helena opened herself up to me completely. I don't know how to explain it, but what she gave me through her eyes meant more than anything and everything; it's when I knew she'd be mine forever. She put her arms around my neck and kissed me. Her lips were so soft and addictive; tasting her was unlike anything in

this world. In my haze, I felt her soft fingers caressing the back of my neck when she opened her mouth. I moved my tongue against hers, softly at first, but kissing Helena was almost never tame... Even though I was the only person she'd ever kissed, her lips and tongue moved in a way that could trap anyone; I was so far in and deeply gone for her. She moaned, and we pulled away, needing some air.

I'll never forget the sound, her glistening lips. —Her eyes —the depth of Helena's soul always made me want to cry; they were so dark and beautiful, but they were also so profound. It was like I could see into her heart.

What I saw the first time we met made me fall for her almost instantly, even though I waited so long to tell her. Helena was like a drug; I could always see the woman I wanted to spend the rest of my life with. Now, there was a baby between us. Our baby.

She closed her eyes and pushed her hips into mine; I never told her, but every time she touched me, I felt so much it physically hurt. I looked down and saw her small body arching into me, like she needed me, just as much as I needed her. I kissed her harder, and we made out.

She pushed my top up, and we broke the kiss —she pulled it over my head.

Her gaze on me made me shiver. I always loved the way Helena made me feel beautiful, I never felt beautiful until I met her —until she looked at me with her unforgettable eyes.

She moved both hands to my cheeks and whispered something; I think it sounded like...

"You're so beautiful..." She was as desperate as I was, I felt it when I caressed the skin between her thighs, her underwear was soaked.

I choked on my words, on her name, "Helena," I think I moaned… or said, maybe she was the one who moaned, I couldn't really tell. I was always struggling to find words, to coordinate them. Helena was so smart, and even though I knew she didn't care about any of that, I never found the way to really let her hear what I felt for her.

She was on her back and under me like we were most times. She looked so open and vulnerable, and it scared me to feel this much, but I felt brave enough to feel that scared. I knew I would do anything for her.

Everything was so hot; our skin, my lips were on her pulse point. It always calmed me to feel her heart beating —it meant she was okay. I licked her neck, and she made that quiet, desperate sound, I was breaking inside. I began to move, and she opened her legs a little more. I was breathing and moaning against her lips as quietly as I could, but Helena was going faster, and her brows were almost touching each other, it was like she was in pain, but I knew she wasn't. She looked stunning when she was like this, letting go in my arms.

I took off her short silk gown, and I pulled it over her head, she fell back on the pillow, and my eyes got lost on her body. Helena was stunning. Her breasts were small, so soft, so perfect and somehow each time I saw them they looked a little fuller. The shades of her skin and her nipples were exquisite. That was her word, it was a word she loved to use on me, but I felt the definition of it was her. Helena's body and heart were memorable.

I leaned down and began to kiss her. I tasted every inch of her body until her hips began to lose control against my lips. I had to close my eyes tightly and find focus on something inside myself. Ever since we found out about

Winter, I hadn't touched her like this, and I was going insane.

I kissed her belly, and with the tip of my nose I caressed lower; there, I gave my heart to Winter. I left a kiss for our baby. Helena was shaking so much, I looked up, and saw her face with eyes closed, she looked so perfect like this, I still couldn't believe I was the one doing that to her.

I moved lower until my lips felt the lacy material of her panties. I smelled her, fuck... she smelled so good; she was so wet, she was so mine, but she looked so free. She was so free, and I wouldn't have had it any other way.

"Emily..." I heard my name. I always wondered what her voice would sound like when she grew older; it was so sweet now; I couldn't help but dream about our future.

The pull of her fingers on my hair drew me back to the moment. My lips found a little bit of her flesh through the soaked black panties; I licked what I could reach, and she shivered. "Oh, Emily..." she whispered, and opened her legs wider —I pulled her underwear down her thighs.

I leaned in and got lost so fast. Helena's moans became more intense when I kissed her, but she kept them all low and intimate —just for us. Right there with my head between her thighs, I teased her with wet kisses until I heard her whisper to me again.

"Please, Emily... please, baby," Her hand was on the back of my head. She almost never called me baby... I loved it when she did.

She looked like she was crumbling. I pushed my tongue inside her as much as I could, and she began to grind against my mouth. I looked up, and she was drowning in herself, she was touching her trembling belly, and her mouth was open wide. I was so self-conscious about many *things, but she made me feel better about myself; her reactions... her sounds —she made me feel so strong.*

Helena made me feel special. Like I wasn't broken inside, she made me feel like my existence made sense, like there had been no mistake —like I was part of this world... like I actually mattered.

I continued to kiss and touch her; my lips felt so soft and wet on her; I found that when I kissed her harder, she looked like how I felt inside, so I did it again and again until her whimpers turned into words.

"God, Emily..." she choked on my name, and from where I was it seemed like she wanted to scream but we couldn't. Her thighs were shaking, and I knew she was close.

I pulled away, and she immediately opened her eyes, but before she could complain I moved up to her mouth and kissed her, I wanted to show her how good she tasted... She moved more desperately when I pushed my hips between her legs. I know she could feel me against her, I was about to crumble. I wanted to make love to her so bad; I needed to be inside her again. It had been so long.

Before I took off my pants, Helena had already pushed them down enough to uncover me. Her hand was around me, and that's when I felt her suck me into her world again. I was helpless... but I didn't care; I loved it there. In our alternate world. There, we were one, and we loved to watch stars like only books or movies could show.

I heard myself moaning against her lips; she was sobbing desperately; it sounded so beautiful that I had to pull back and look at her. "Look at me;" I whispered as gently and sweetly as I could, and she opened her warm eyes for me. I was almost all the way inside her —she always closed her eyes through this part, but I wanted her to know… I needed to show her or at least try. So I gently pushed into her, and she opened her mouth. I stayed there without moving, I looked into her eyes and smiled. Her breathing was rushed, and her dark eyes looked so vulnerable. I hoped she could see the same in mine. I was letting everything go for her.

So I caressed her face with my fingertips. "I am so in love with you…" I said, and opened up completely, just like she had. I wanted to show her the broken soul she had healed. Meeting Helena Millan had been my salvation. She had saved me from myself.

She just smiled, and a tear fell down her temple, it broke me and made me feel alive at the same time. She sobbed and pulled me into a kiss.

That night was the night Helena opened up to me completely, and I did the same. I made love to her, and she made love to me. We forgot about the world and about tomorrow. It was just the three of us now, and that was enough."

18

MOVIE

APPOINTMENT TIME HAD ARRIVED. Earlier that day, Helena had experienced her first episode of morning sickness, somewhere between stealing kisses with Emily before the sun had even risen, she abruptly scrambled off the bed and into the bathroom.

Emily rushed right behind her but was left with two palms against the wooden door.

"Helena! Let me in, baby..."

"Absolutely not!" Came the muffled response from the other side.

Oh, the sound that came after... Emily's face was torn between disgust, empathy, and happiness. It was real... it was happening.

***

Katherine couldn't complain; both girls had arrived at WSF Medical Center fifteen minutes before the set time. Emily got to meet Doctor Rossi; he seemed kind, centered and definitely spoke like a cardio eminence.

They sat in Katherine's office, and while Helena seemed comfortable —she had probably been in her mother's office hundreds of times— Emily dealt with the awkward feeling. Green eyes noticed pictures of her girlfriend, Caleb, and Maddison resting on the desk. It was rather surreal.

Doctor Rossi sat on Katherine's throne, and she had taken a chair across from him, Helena sat next to her while Emily settled for a small sofa bench nearby.

Nerves nagged at Emily; the man had spent the past two hours with her pregnant girlfriend, performing all kinds of tests while she hung out on her own —*with her thoughts*.

"Well, Helena, it seems you are eight weeks along," he said, scanning the papers in his hands.

Helena turned to Emily; absolute happiness engaged them in a silent lifeline. —*Two months...*

Katherine shifted slightly but remained calm and collected.

"Everything looks good aside from a bit of iron deficiency which is rather normal. However, we need to fix that." he finished, reading the tests and raised his eyes to meet Helena's.

Emily took notes in her mind, but sharp Katherine didn't like the way her colleague sighed.

"What is it, Michael?" Katherine asked.

Helena tensed, and so did Emily.

"Well… as I mentioned when we had this conversation, Helena, I told you that if you were to conceive you would have to be taken off your medication for the baby's sake, which will affect your condition irreversibly."

That, Katherine knew. Dread washed her face, and with a shake of the head, she couldn't believe this was happening.

Helena remembered this well and was ready to take a chance for her baby —Emily, on the other hand, shrank on the small elegant sofa. She swallowed hard and bitter.

"*However,* there is alternative treatment you could take, but I would also have to perform a series of tests with machinery that quite frankly isn't available here." he informed confidently.

Those words not only made Katherine's eyes radiate fierce intent, but they made her lean forward. He had her full attention. "What are you saying, Michael?" she asked.

Helena observed them in silence.

"I am saying with confidence that we need to take alternate measures to ensure that Helena's health doesn't deteriorate, this is crucial… I will need to keep a very close eye on her, aside from the fact that the medication I am suggesting hasn't been approved here." He paused with a shrug. "I still don't understand why; it has been in circulation in Europe for years with impressively high rates of success… It is the only thing I can think of that we could try to replace her current treatment without harming the fetus."

Helena's heart split in two; she knew where this was going —she didn't want to be away from her. —*Em…* She dreaded and looked at Emily who was intensely focused on the conversation.

"Are you suggesting that we move Helena to Zurich?" Katherine inferred.

Doctor Rossi nodded. "Yes, I am."

At the sound of those words, Emily choked on a deep breath, and finally realized that sad brown eyes were stuck on her. Helena looked broken, perhaps the saddest she had ever seen her. Tears stung Emily's eyes, but she blinked them away and tried to stay strong for both; she needed to be.

Emily dug inside the deepest parts of herself and

smiled for Helena. —*It's gonna be okay...*

A knot in Helena's throat made it hard to swallow; she turned to Doctor Rossi. "Is that the only option?" she asked worriedly; the pain in her voice made Katherine's heart tremble.

Michael felt for Helena, as he was aware of a possible separation from her girlfriend. "I am afraid so, Helena... It isn't a cure; as I mentioned, it is simply a way to replace what your heart needs to try and stay healthy. However, anything could happen, dear, as I told you before, there are, of course, chances you could carry your baby to term as there are chances you couldn't... but Helena, I need to keep your progress and try to maintain momentum —it is crucial." he finished softly, as softly as he could manage for the obviously affected girl.

Helena turned to find Emily with red-rimmed eyes and a quivering chin; seeing Helena so distraught ruptured her like nothing else on earth managed to do. She rushed to her side and kneeled down. "Helena, baby..." Emily swallowed her tears and laced their fingers. "This sucks, I know, but..." She brought soft hands to her lips and kissed them. "It's for Winter and for you —we have to do the right thing." Emily pleaded bravely.

Heat crawled up Helena's cheeks, she sniffled, and a single tear fell. She nodded and whispered, "For Winter..."

Emily swallowed another batch of tears she refused to shed. "For Winter..." she said, and pushed a soft smile. "I promise I'll do whatever it takes to go see you," Emily had no idea how the fuck she was going to manage that, though she sure as hell would try. "But— we have to do this right."

Emily was already dreading the words; the truth was

that while away, Helena could still die. It meant she would miss watching her pregnancy develop; she would miss watching Winter grow inside her.

"How long would she have to leave for?" It was the first question or intervention Emily had managed all morning.

"It's hard to say... for as long as necessary, more than likely the entire pregnancy and up to delivery." Doctor Rossi addressed.

Withered gazes met; Helena's breathing was so faint, she looked silent and defeated. At that moment, both felt the unforgiving heat of the consequences, though in their innocence and love, they'd never meant harm. Ever.

"It is settled then," Katherine spoke up, "I will prepare everything here at the hospital for my absence and arrange the trip."

Doctor Michael smiled and nodded softly.

—*It sounded so easy, but it wasn't.* Helena thought. Katherine made it sound so simple, and in reality, for them it was. They had the means to engage in such sudden move. Zurich was lovely, and she understood that moving there for a few months was necessary to give her baby his best chance, but Emily... How could she leave Emily? How could she live without Emily?

After finishing the appointment, Helena had finally agreed to go back home. However, Emily had spent the entire day by her side while Katherine made call after call in Santiago's office.

They had shared with Maddison and gotten to hear about Helena's new puppy's adventures. When Helena left a few days prior, she had commended her new furry friend to her sister with a note. Maddison was mortified when she found and read what her little sister had asked of her, but had to admit that hanging out with the little mutt was all right and even fun. The puppy wasn't a mutt, but well, Maddison was… Maddison.

The news given by Doctor Rossi had been unforeseen at best. Emily didn't know what to expect when they met with the talented man, but this… *this* was something she hadn't even considered as a possibility. Her little family was about to be taken away from her, and it hurt.

They spent the day planning and coming up with ways, dates… visits, time off, and possibilities. Emily didn't care about college anymore, but she couldn't afford to think or feel that way, now more than ever she needed to be responsible, now more than ever she needed to focus on getting through college and remain sane while the love of her life and her baby were gone.

Time passed by them quicker than expected, night had fallen, and Helena suggested showing Emily a secret place, a part of her home that she adored. She led her to a hidden spiral staircase on the second floor; Emily felt like she was inside some magical chapter of a fantasy book. The hidden steps led to a floor higher. Silver rays of moonlight filtered through a tall, stained glass window. With clasped hands, Helena guided her up the spiral.

Green eyes were smitten with the kaleidoscope of moon-exalted colors. While the muscles on the back of her neck cramped, Emily realized the mesmerizing window was a door —double doors that led to the highest balcony located on the back of the mansion. They were beautiful but not as beautiful as what was out there.

Emily gasped as the cold wind crept in, it swept inside

the place and into their souls. She turned to look at Helena and loved what she found there; bright endless eyes that loved her and *that* smile. Helena was simply happy to see her happy. Emily felt so lucky.

"Do you like it?" Helena asked.

"Like it? Helena, this is amazing... I had never seen this part of San Francisco... not like this... Wow."

They stood under a dark starry night. Blonde and brunette strands of hair were free against the wind. Emily inhaled deeply and blinked back the sting of sentiment in her eyes. The lights, the rooftops... all the other beautiful houses surrounding the upscale neighborhood. Emily was a true believer that the most beautiful things in the world were free, but she then realized that money could also arrange a series of fantastic things and make magic. Small streets were paved with bricks and stones, charming gas lamps scattered afar. Historically well-preserved mansions spoke of the rich story of their old, old city.

With a sad smile, Helena gazed at the star-filled sky and caressed the back of Emily's hand with her thumb.

Things were about to change, but Helena felt strong. Perhaps it was all Winter's doing. Their hearts burned and finally understood why parents were indeed capable of doing anything for a child. Sudden relatability to others washed their minds with new cognizance.

Helena turned to watch Emily stare at the sky. A peaceful silence permeated everything except the thing they couldn't control, nature. How could the wind of a dark and bright night sound different from any other wind? Helena realized that if she truly listened and felt, it could. How could a person feel so beautiful? To Helena... Emily did.

'I will never forget the day I got to read my favorite book on my own; the first time it wasn't recited to me. I had gotten to feel its soft pages and indulge in that unique smell... A Boy and His Moon; it spoke about a boy, his desire to touch the moon and a million things to learn about unconditional love. Three hundred and sixty-four books in between then and now, I was reminded of how my lovely Emily had given meaning to the simple words of my first favorite tale.

'I am the moon, and you are just a boy. It may seem as if distance is real, but it's not; you can't touch me, and I can't touch you, but if you look up I'll always be there looking at you, and if you need me I will forever need you.' *The little boy had a story in his hands, something he could hold and call his own, something no one could take away. He could see himself reflected on the pages the writer had given him. The moon had finally spoken to him even if only through ink.*

Emily had taken a piece of my heart with her that first day we stumbled upon each other, and now, here we were... saying goodbye in order to keep our baby alive.

As I caressed her hand and stared at the night above us, the wind felt cold as it entered me; the stars looked majestic. Unmistakably perfect. The universe could be partially credited to the accuracy of numbers, but I always fell short when trying to analyze the missing element.

Mathematics were tasteful to me; you could always rely on a predictable outcome; regardless of the path's length, its precise culmination was always so elegantly pure, just like her... The symmetry of Emily transcended the gorgeous trappings of any painting or appoggiatura. I then knew the missing element had to be what I felt inside. It left me breathless... My love for our baby was stronger than my desire to live, yet at the same time, I never wanted life more. It was a paradox. Interminable and unapologetic... just like that missing element.

I felt her arms surround me and I wished for time to stop. Leaving her behind was killing me, I adored Emily, she was not only my best friend but my love. I closed my eyes because I felt her lips on my neck; so leaned my head to the side so that I could feel her closer. Emily was my safety and the purest expression of strength and honesty I had ever witnessed. What her simple touch or the scent of her perfume did to my body surpassed any logic —logic be damned, I refused to credit our prime need to procreate for the rush of life that surged through me when she was near me, inside me. Emily and Winter were everything to me.

That night, the smooth strokes of her tongue against my skin were all I wanted to feel aside from the cold wind around us. We did just that, we admired the beauty of it all and felt in silence because somehow, we both knew and agreed on the same thing; we had to do this for our baby. I knew deep down that Emily was doing it also for me... I knew my decision to keep Winter was a contradictory concept that caused her incredible pain; I knew it was difficult for her. I, to this date, have not forgiven myself for being the cause of that. I finally understood that only integrity would make good once you have broken someone or something into complete vulnerability. It is where decency and consciousness mark the difference.

How could I get through the next few months without my love and my best friend? I was lost in thought, but her touch guided me back. Her hands were on my lower abdomen; her caresses were always so gentle; Emily always touched me as if I were the last thing left in the world. I gasped... A sob had fallen from her warm lips on my neck; she was crying. I had been so concentrated on her that I hadn't realized I was crying as well; she whispered something and sniffled.

"I won't drop out..." she said.

I turned in her embrace and saw myself reflected in her current state; her beautiful eyes were soaked with tears, I reached and tried to wipe some away.

"What are you talking about, love?" I asked.

Emily looked absolutely shattered and determined. "I will finish college; I've been thinking about it,"

She wiped her cheeks with the back of her hand and sniffled again, her chest rose and fell so quickly, I placed a hand on it and tried to appease her. There was so much conviction in her eyes.

"I can go to the academy as soon as I finish my associates and become a cop, and get my bachelor's as I work too, I figured that by the time I get my degree, I could have better chances of becoming a detective faster. I won't give up on my dream."

I wasn't surprised. I was so proud of her. "What changed your mind, Em?" I smiled and caressed her cheek; I loved doing that, her jawline was stunning.

She looked around and then back at me. "After we talked in Seattle, I just... I researched, and I found out that most detectives have degrees. I want the best for our baby..."

"Em..." I barely said, right before she leaned in and kissed me. Emily's lips were my weakness. It was always difficult for me to let her go. I was drunk in the sensations *coursing through my lower body. Ever since Winter my desire for her had intensified. Many times I thought I could never want her more... I was wrong.*

I was lost in my own pleasure when I felt her body shaking. At first, I thought she was cold, but then she broke the kiss and held me tighter than ever. She was crying again; she was hiding in my neck... sobbing.

"I want to go with you... please take me with you," she was begging in tears, I had never seen her cry that way. I was falling apart.

"Please, don't cry, love..." I broke down as well and held her tightly.

At that moment, I remembered when the writer had warned the little boy; **'Tears will seem endless once you've truly loved... Are you sure this is what you want?'** *I had chosen the same fate as the little boy... Without hesitation.*

My mother and I would be flying to Zurich with Doctor Rossi the following day. The quickness of it all infuriated me. I hated this disease... I always tried to ignore it and not think of it, but it always found a way to bleed through my days and sometimes nights. It had managed to bleed through my pregnancy, my relationship, and my entire world. My mother's determination and affectivity in arranging everything within a matter of hours didn't surprise me. Her refusal to give me more days with Emily didn't surprise me either.

That night before Emily left, it was nearly four in the morning. She had watched me pack my bags and helped me; she almost didn't let me do anything... that is the kind of person my Emily was; she was everything and much... so much more than that.

We kissed until we ran out of air and said the word outside the door of my parent's house. I had never felt so somber and fragmented in my life; I couldn't find the will to let her go from my arms. She wanted to take me to the airport, but I refused. It was unacceptable for me to leave her broken and alone in the middle of a crowded airport. It had to be this way, and that is what we did. We said goodbye."

***

Daylight found Emily awake and laying on her bed. Staring at the window in some distant state of spirit and mind, she couldn't cry anymore, she had no more energy... she was just there. Still wearing the same clothes, tall boots on her feet and up to her knees, thinking about how the day before she had watched that same sunrise with Helena in her arms.

Maureen had been knocking on the door for the past two minutes and decided to enter her daughter's room after not getting an answer. What she saw shattered her. Maureen had to take a deep breath and remember why she was there. The heaviness in her chest would have to wait.

"Okay, sweetie, please get up." Maureen urged and patted Emily's leg as she strolled by her bed.

Emily sighed and blinked. "Not now, Mom, my girlfriend and my baby must be about to take off to the other side of the ocean in a few minutes."

While opening Emily's closet, Maureen looked at the watch on her wrist. "Actually, no... they must be about to leave for the airport, so, you better get moving and start packing, baby." Maureen said.

Emily's confused brows crashed as she propped herself

on two elbows. Green eyes followed her mother from one side of the room to the other. Maureen took a suitcase and opened it on the hardwood floor. The sound of the zipper echoed through.

"Mom, what are you doing? If this is a joke, it isn't funny." Emily said with bloodshot eyes.

Maureen stopped and smiled. She bit her lower lip.

"Where's your passport?"

"What?" Emily asked, still confused.

"Well, I just bought your return ticket from Switzerland... and, honey, you *will* need your passport," Equally green eyes gleamed with excitement. "You're going with Helena!"

Wide-eyed, Emily's heart dropped to her stomach; she swallowed hard and hurled off the bed, her gaze fixed on Maureen's. "Mom... Are you serious?!" Her smile was so bright, just like that fresh morning.

It was nice to see Emily happy. It had been a while. Maureen nodded and pulled out a prescription bottle from her back pocket and handed it over. "I got your medication... Please, don't forget to take it and call me... every day." she ordered with love.

Emily was still dwelling on disbelief and ready to dive into excitement; she took the orange bottle and looked at her mother again. "But... I mean, how? What?"

"I spoke to Katherine... apparently, Helena is equally devastated, and well, we came to an agreement. You are allowed to go and be with her—" Maureen started.

Startled eyes almost jumped out of Emily's face, and her smile grew wider.

"*Until*... classes start. I want you here in two weeks, Emily Knight, you hear me?" Maureen said, looking into her only daughter's eyes. "I know you are an adult, but no tricky games and trying to stay there… you need to graduate, Em, I am serious," she warned, feeling the magnitude of it all, feeling her daughter's adulthood creep up on her.

Wired and excited, Emily jumped up and down, yanking her mother with no mercy; a gorgeous dimpled beam on her face. "Oh, my God, Mom! Are you serious?!!!"

Maureen smiled and nodded. "I am very serious."

Her mother certainly was the very best. In a sudden gush of sentiment, Emily's eyes welled up; she couldn't help it. "Why this gift?" she whispered.

Maureen caressed the tears away from her girl and looked at her. "No, sweetheart… it's not a gift; this is a small way of saying thank you."

"What for?" Emily didn't understand.

The gentlest smile broke from Maureen's lips; she saw herself reflected in those beautiful eyes… in her beautiful daughter. "You have taught me so much, Em, ever since you were a baby… You make me better every day by showing me new levels of strength, love, and bravery… you deserve to be with her and *your* baby, come to terms with the distance —this was too abrupt and unfair."

Emily sobbed as her sullen gaze filled with more hot liquid.

"You are my greatest teacher, sweetheart…" Maureen joined her daughter in the weeping fall of truths.

Emily's body collided with her mother's and held her tightly. "Thank you, Mom…" she sobbed as green eyes glazed over with endless liquid transparency. They focused on some blurry object as she felt life return to her chest.

Pale fingers touched the screen of her phone, and beaming happiness sprouted from her very heart to every inch of her face; she was ready to share the news with her love, she could almost taste more time... more **her**.

After a couple of rings....

"Helena..."

ALL THROUGH THE NIGHT

TAKE A PEEK AT

THE CAPTIVATING AND HEART—ALTERING SEQUEL

∞

THEY WERE FOUR HOURS into the long flight to Switzerland, and Emily felt as if she was the only one awake in the entire private plane. However, she knew that Doctor Rossi and Katherine sat somewhere in the back.

Peaceful silence.

Only the faint sounds of the engine, and what she thought was normal of the plane found her ears. —*Was that the sound of air? Maybe it was the sound of clouds.* Green eyes focused on the tranquil and soft looking sky. No water… no land… only white and soft shades of blue, yellow and pink afar. The sun was close to setting, and Emily's lips softly rested on Helena's forehead. She loved doing this while Helena slept, and hopefully dreamt right against her. Emily thought of nothing and everything; she contemplated the astonishing sight. This way she could always protect them both, love them both and live them both with no distance in between.

Emily had absolutely no idea of what to expect. She had never been to Europe; hell, she had barely been out of San Francisco, knowing that the furthest she had traveled was to Canada. Once.

But Emily was sure of one thing; she had never flown in such comfort before. It was intimidating to see just how much the Millans had and could afford. She didn't dare imagine the totality of their monetary reach, but while in the middle of all this, Emily understood why Helena seemed so at ease when it came to money and spending large quantities of it. It made sense. However, the thing that stroke her most was realizing that she felt relieved. She was relieved to know that there was nothing Katherine Millan wouldn't do for her daughter, this made Emily bask in a sense of safety and appreciation. She couldn't imagine just how different the picture would be for someone who didn't have the means.

It wasn't fair.

Something twisted in Emily's stomach and she pulled Helena closer, she brushed a soft kiss on her temple. She felt grateful.

***

"Ever since Helena's doctor said the words that changed everything, things had been like the weirdest most vivid blur. I was so fucking scared of losing Helena and Winter, but at the same time, I had so much hope and faith in this man's conviction. He spoke like he had invented hearts. Literally. He was always so calm, like one of those people who made you feel better by just being in the same room with you. Those people who seemed like they knew something you didn't. I allowed myself to feel excited between all the worry and stress.

Helena and I were so tired of crying, we had agreed on that fact about a thousand times, there was even a point when we started to laugh about it. Guilt still ate at me, though. I felt responsible for her being in this position, which made me feel even worse, because every time I felt guilt for Helena, I felt guilty for thinking that way since I already loved my kid. Many times I felt like I was going insane, and burdening her with that wasn't an option for me. I could take it, after all, it was just me and my loud mind going at it again.

The second we landed in Zurich, I was blown away. That place was just unreal. I don't know if it was the crazy jet lag or the fact that everything around us was so foreign and beautiful. The city not only looked but also felt like some-thing completely new to me; the white Alps made me feel so small in a world I ignored before.

The house was beyond anything I'd expected, and by then, I knew the Millans were big on luxury, maybe it was the fact that we were in the city of money. The place looked like a small castle; it overlooked Lake Zurich, and I never felt more like a pop out figure in a fairytale book. It was classy and elegant like all of them, it all felt like a dream.

Helena held my hand and squeezed it; I smiled and turned to look at her. She got more and more beautiful by the hour, she looked so beautiful and tired. I caressed her cheek with my free hand and looked into her brown eyes.

"Maybe you should rest, you look exhausted." I told her, and she smiled sleepily back at me. I heard the sound of Katherine's stilettos echoing in the distance; she was on the phone with someone... I barely caught some words; 'We made it safely, dear,' and then my complete attention went

back to Helena.

"I'm okay, Em, I slept all through the flight. Besides, I wanted to show you the city," She looked so excited.

The intrusive voice zeroed in from behind me. "Absolutely not, Helena." It was Katherine.

She scared the shit out of me, so I turned, but I couldn't miss Helena's annoyance. I felt terrible for her because I knew once my two weeks in Zurich were over, her mother would drive her insane. I had to agree with Katherine on this one, though, but the last thing I wanted was for Helena to feel like I was taking her mother's side. I had been doing too much of that, and I knew just how sensitive she was about her condition. I smiled at her and Katherine quickly blurred out of my view.

I cupped her soft cheeks with my hands, looking into her eyes. "How about we get settled and eat something? I'm starving, Lena." I made it about me, and she immediately nodded, not even a hint of selfishness in her eyes. It was so easy to fall in love with her more and more, whoever didn't, was a fucking blind idiot.

Katherine started to speak again, and I turned to look at her. "I have already ordered lunch, girls, going to the city right now is nonsense. Helena, you can't strain yourself like that."

I noticed Helena ignored her mother and part of me felt like shit. I didn't want to be rude; I was trapped in the middle of whatever was going on between them. So awkward. For me, it was always easier to sink my hands into whatever pockets I could reach.

Helena was still saying nothing.

"Um… Thank you so much." I told her and smiled; my face was on fire. Helena took me by the hand and pulled

me away. It was so fucking uncomfortable; I smiled at Katherine again as my girlfriend dragged me further away. "Thank you, ma'am."

Shit.

In a matter of seconds, we were inside a bedroom, and I was smitten again, the place was incredible. Helena seemed to make her way around so easily that it made me think it wasn't her first time there. I had barely turned my focus from the killer windows when I felt her lips on mine, and I moaned. I put my hands on her hips and kissed her.

"Mmm... I needed that," she told me and pecked my lips again. It felt like she was melting on me.

I smiled and caressed her soft hair. "I needed it too..." I kissed her again.

"Baby, I feel bad, leaving your mom like that... What's going on? It's not like you to act that way." I needed to at least try to smooth things a little before I left, I knew how intense Katherine Millan could be, and I really didn't want that to make Helena feel worse when I went back to San Francisco.

She sighed, and I could tell that something was indeed bothering her. "I hate the way she keeps treating me like a child. First, she made this decision without even consulting me, then she decided to leave with no warning and refused to listen to me, even though I practically begged her to give me a couple of days with you."

"But Helena, baby, I'm here... I know everything was very sudden, but she loves you; she's just trying to help, you know?" I caressed the warm skin on her neck.

I knew that whole deal between them went deeper than that, but at the moment my focus was on trying to make her *feel better, I caressed her, and she gave me a tired smile.*

"My mother is relentless, Emily —what bothers me most is the fact that she makes these harsh decisions —she has been making them since I was diagnosed... I understand she's my mother and that she's afraid, but I have not been included in any of them." Helena sighed, frustrated; I could safely say I had never seen her like that. I nodded and tried to make her feel I was behind her as much as I possibly could.

"I have just been dragged around and, Emily, I get it! Trust me, now more than ever I want to live, but all she had to do was include me— acknowledge me! Instead, she treats me like I am twelve! I'm just... I'm tired, and I won't stand for it anymore."

It was amazing to see her; not only her, I think it was both of us. I knew I felt different and I then confirmed that so did she. Circumstances had pushed us to the edge, Helena and I had been taking shit from life and people for years, and it felt like we were finally ready to stand up for ourselves and who we were. My sweet girl was still there, but honestly, my sweet girl acted and looked more like a woman every day. "I know, baby... I know."

I held her —because what else could I do? She was right.

She clung to me, and I felt her cheek on my shoulder, I caressed her hair and inhaled... I loved her scent. I needed to start collecting every inch and every smell.

"I can't forget about the fact that she wanted to kill Winter..." I heard her say that and I pulled back to search for her eyes. She wanted to cry.

"Helena... I..." What the fuck was I supposed to say? Defend Katherine? God, she looked so sad and alone, that just broke me inside.

Suddenly, she smiled almost to herself and looked me in

the eye. "You know... she wanted to do the same to me..."

I felt every drop of blood in my body rush to my feet.
—What?

"She didn't because my father begged her not to... To this date, she has no idea that I know, and for years it really hurt to know that she didn't want me, I eventually got over it... I forgave her, but I don't think I can forgive her for wanting to do the same to my baby. I am an advocate of freedom and choice, Em, but... when you find out you weren't wanted, it just..."

I could feel my mouth was agape, I was stunned, and I was so mad but more than anything I was hurting for her. I couldn't fathom. I had no words. "I... I'm so sorry, baby— Oh, my God... I... I don't know what to say,"

My stuttering sounded so lame to my ears. God, I wanted to kick myself, but what do you say to that? I couldn't imagine a world without her. Katherine's cold ability to dictate who lived and who didn't bothered me, even though I didn't know her story or her reasons then, in my mind and my heart nothing would ever justify robbing Helena of her chance at life, of robbing our Winter of the same. A world without Helena in it would have been incomplete and bleak; she was wonderful and special, she had an amazing mind and an even more beautiful heart. Winter was new and made of our love, our flesh, and blood —no matter how irresponsible I felt for how things happened. Helena was a fighter and a fierce mother. I felt relieved of having chosen to listen to her. That was when I really understood.

I took her hand, and we sat on the bed. I needed her to understand what I wanted to say, and even though it was usually so hard for me to convey meaning, this time I really had to try. I caressed her soft cheek and tucked a few strands of hair behind her ear. She looked at me with those gorgeous and deep brown eyes, God! I couldn't understand... I just didn't get why someone as sweet and good-hearted as Helena had to suffer so much —how did she manage to remain so kind?

"Listen to me, you are amazing, Helena Millan," I squeezed her hands gently, and she nodded, looking into me with reddened eyes. She wanted to cry, and it broke my heart.

"Your existence has made mine worth living —you are a gift, please never forget that. I love you with all my heart, and I promise you that I will never let anyone hurt you or our baby. Ever." By then I felt tears on my cheeks, but I didn't care. She smiled, and a tear fell from her eyes. It wasn't fair, we were sick of crying, but maybe it was because we had both held too much for too long.

"You are going to be an incredible mother, Helena, and I do believe with you, I feel that same hope you feel, too." I was always so insecure of my words, but I knew she understood what I needed her to understand. She crashed her lips on mine and kissed me.

We cried, and we kissed, I caressed her lower back softly, and then we parted. Our foreheads touched, and she wiped away my tears. "Thank you, Emily... Before I found you, I felt so alone... I don't want this to end," she whispered so close to my lips, and I felt like dying. I felt everything.

"It won't end, sweetheart..." My fingers got lost on her skin, whatever skin I could find. She was so soft and so mine. "You're not alone, Helena, not anymore... I promise, please believe me."

"I do believe you," she said, and then let out the most adorable yawn.

"You're tired, baby," I smiled because she rolled her eyes.

"All Winter wants me to do is sleep and eat." She touched her belly with so much love and care. Helena already was the best mother. I, on the other hand, felt like I could be better.

"That's definitely my kid."

She smiled and looked at me with the same amount of love and then I finally found some courage.

"Would you mind if I..." Shit, my cheeks felt hot, what I was feeling was new and strange, but it felt so right.

"What is it, love?" She searched my eyes kindly as always. Open as ever. I knew that whatever I asked of her I'd get. Helena always made me feel that way. I gently pointed at her belly. "Can I see it?"

She smiled brightly and stood. "Of course you can."

Helena never pushed me or made me feel like a bad mom, I rarely touched her belly, and I had never spoken to Winter. She walked to the door and locked it, my eyes followed her steps. When she was back in front of me, she turned.

"Could you please unzip me?"

I did, and her pretty dress fell to the floor. I couldn't help myself, so I leaned in and kissed her beautiful back, my hands had a mind of their own, I caressed her softly.

Her body was exquisite, and when she turned, I lost my breath. She was barely showing, but she was showing. I saw a small bump, Our baby Winter was growing. Her stomach wasn't completely flat anymore; tears choked me as she guided my hands to her belly.

"Oh, my God..." I could barely speak.

I caressed the love of my life and hoped that the gentle touch of my open hand on her skin would be enough to catch Winter's attention. I leaned forward. "Hi, baby... I know that maybe you can't hear me yet, but I just want you to know that I love you so much... we... both love you, and we want you. You have the best and most beautiful mommy, so please be gentle with her, okay?"

When I looked up, I saw her unforgettable smile and more tears. She was looking down at us, but those tears were happy ones.

How could it be wrong?

I was so in love.

We were so in love.

Next thing I knew, her hands were cupping my cheeks, and she was leaning down kissing me; it was soft and perfect. Her sweet tongue touched mine; she was so tender, it was impossible to realize when she broke the kiss. We were so connected, and it felt so easy; her lips lingered on mine, and she whispered, "Can we please take a nap?"

I kissed her. "Of course, baby, come on... Let's sleep."

When we were under the covers, she put her head on my shoulder, and I held her until she fell asleep.

I didn't sleep. I couldn't. All I could do was look out the window and notice that the sun was still out, all I could do was think... and think. I didn't know it then, but my eight-hour sleeping nights were over, or so they would be for a long time.

***

Two hours passed and Helena was still asleep. Part of me was afraid that she was sleeping so much. I had no idea of how normal it was... I felt torn between my fears and letting her rest. I decided not to wake her since she seemed so comfortable. I knew that Katherine would soon come knocking on the door; so I tried to beat her to it. I carefully parted from Helena; kissed her forehead, and left.

I walked down the stairs of the ridiculously gorgeous mini castle and was actually glad I didn't get lost. I was relieved that even though the place was very elegant, it was still warm and cozy. I searched the living room, but Katherine wasn't there, I walked to the dining room, and noticed the table was set for three; candles were lit, the arrangement of expensive-looking china and glass cups was precise and impeccable, the delicious smell of food almost killed me, my stomach growled. I looked up and noticed it was getting dark —the huge glass windows gave me a perfect view of the garden. I could see lights adorning the trees outside. The place was incredible... I wondered if it was theirs, too.

"Emily, darling," I heard Katherine and turned around. Without Helena, being around Katherine was always so fucking uncomfortable for me, she was intimidating even though she had always been nice to me. This time things were different, something had definitely shifted inside me. I didn't know if it was my desire to defend and protect my family or the fact that Helena's confession had really thrown me off.

I liked Katherine... I knew she loved Helena very much; I also knew that she wanted the best for her and she always seemed to strive to give her nothing but. I knew that she was a woman that thought in a very scientific way. God, I repeated that to myself over and over that night as I clenched my fists and forced a smile. I kept telling myself she must have had her reasons for not wanting a baby, and that was okay, but shit, that wasn't just any baby, that was my Helena.

I took a deep breath through my nose, trying not to let it show. I couldn't betray Helena's trust even though I wanted to confront her. I wouldn't.

I didn't. But I definitely needed to speak to her and vouch for my girlfriend and my kid. I needed to make sure they would be okay when I left. I didn't want to leave them, it was killing me, and I had just arrived; I knew Helena was afraid... She didn't say it, but I knew. My day to go was still weeks away, but somehow my brain was operating in a different mode. All I could think about was Helena and Winter. They were everything.

I cleared my throat, and honestly, I felt proud of myself, it was the first time I was in front of Katherine Millan, and I wasn't intimidated. I felt strong, and I felt ready, for the first time, I felt like an adult.

"Helena is still asleep, and I didn't want to wake her."

She smiled, it was small. "Well, then it will just be us for dinner, I suppose;"

I nodded. "I suppose, yeah."

It was still so fucking awkward, but it got easier as the minutes passed. We sat, and she offered me a glass of wine. With them being of European mindset I figured it was okay. Hell, a glass couldn't hurt. It definitely didn't. It helped me relax; I was hoping for my irritation to go away, too, but that didn't happen. I had to swallow it and have a civilized conversation with my girlfriend's mother. Not about her decision to not have a baby, but about my baby's best chance at life.

"I'd hate to assume; however, I feel there is something weighing on your mind, Emily,"

I put the glass on the wooden table and clenched the fist

I was hiding under it.

"Yeah, actually, there is..." I cleared my throat, and she looked right into me, not at me. Right into me. "I know my time here is limited and to be honest, I hate it. It breaks me in two to have to leave them... I don't want to, but I know my invitation to stay was temporary."

Katherine nodded in silence.

My blood was boiling because it was so unfair. "And I also need to graduate, my priorities have changed, and I want you to know I will take care of them."

She opened her mouth to speak, and I knew what she was going to say...

"I know Helena has no need of it and that I couldn't offer her the same lifestyle she's always had, but I can offer her my unconditional love and my presence." I knew that last one was gonna sting her, but I didn't care; it was the truth. It was our truth.

She shifted in her seat; she was indeed bothered by what I had just said. She tried to hide it, but it was obvious.

"Helena and I have talked about it, and she has made it clear that she doesn't need me or expects me to take care of her monetarily, but Winter is a different story... In truth, they both are my responsibility somehow, just like she feels I am her responsibility, too."

"That is where my problem lies, Emily."

My stomach twisted, I had no idea of what she'd say, but I was ready to hear it.

"I don't understand what you mean;" I said.

She was so calm and collected; no one would have thought the conversation was in fact so serious. She was straight to the point, and she didn't budge. "On how you two have suddenly started acting like a married couple, need I remind you... you aren't, and honestly, dear, to me this has never been about money. This is about the fact that both my daughter's health and her future have been compromised by this child."

At least she wasn't calling Winter a fetus anymore... Still, I was bothered.

"Look... I know you love Helena, I know that you're not a bad person. It would be incredibly unfair to judge people in a black and white scale, but Helena is just so hurt by the fact that you wanted her to have an abortion —I'm honestly afraid of leaving because she is just so nervous and afraid to be alone with you."

Her eyes widened, and I knew I had hit her right in the heart.

"Has she told you this?"

She was honest and blunt? I was, too.

I nodded. "She has, and frankly this isn't about playing house... I love your daughter, Katherine." That was straightforward, I had never called her that, but I didn't take it back. "I will respect your house and your rules, but please understand that things have changed. Helena and I want to be together; we want our kid... we are a family now, I know it's hard to hear, I get it... and I am so sorry that things happened this way. —For Helena's sake if I could turn back time and do things differently I would, but... I love my kid, and I'm about to spend the next few months away from the person I love and our baby —I'm gonna miss everything, and even though that's so not all right—" I could feel tears starting to sting my eyes, but I refused to cry in front of her again. "I'm willing to do it for her sake because I have to. So,

I will respect your rules, and I'll go in two weeks, but you need to know that— yes, Helena is afraid of you and she is stressed, that worries me, so, I need you to please fix that."

By then I could see she was very shaken. Her eyes were glassy and red, her ability to conceal emotion was really good, but I saw then that she truly did love Helena. A lot. I never thought I'd see her cry, but that night, I did, a single tear fell down her cheek.

Just as easily as it rolled down, she sniffed and wiped it off with poise. That woman was strong and elegant. Always. I couldn't take that away.

"Very well. Thank you, Emily, for letting me know where you stand, and also for being honest with me about Helena's state. I will speak to her and try to mend this."

I nodded, I could tell she meant it.

"I believe it goes unsaid that I have no intentions of forcing Helena to have an abortion, it is why we are here after all... to ensure that they both get the best treatment available."

"Yes, ma'am, and I am very grateful, I could never thank you enough."

"She is my daughter; I would do anything for her."

"I understand you, and so would I."

"Given the obvious circumstances, it would be useless to have you sleep in separate rooms. However, I have arranged for you to have the one next to Helena's... It is Maddison's room; I hope you find it suitable." she said, and I realized that it actually was their house, too. —Damn.

I nodded. "Thank you... really; it means so much to me to be able to be here with her."

"I know, Emily," she said, and even gave me a small smile.

We had barely eaten anything and frankly my appetite

was gone. I kept surprising myself, which meant that either things were really changing or that the world was ending.

After our talk I felt better, I knew there was more to be said between us, but it would come in time. I felt like I could breathe easier.

While minutes passed and we had a few more sips of wine, her cell rang, and she excused herself. I was almost sure it was local since she started speaking German.

She got lost in the living room, and I took the chance to get out. It wasn't like she needed help with the dishes. I had barely pushed the chair back when the kind woman, whose name I didn't know yet began to clean up.

I smiled at her and left.

I went upstairs and found Maddison's room. I noticed my luggage was there, so I decided to take a shower, hoping it would help.

***

About four hours passed and I was still wide awake —like a fucking owl. After my shower I put on a pair of loose sweatpants and a hoodie, it was so cold. I fell on the bed and crossed my arms behind my head. I lay in the dark for four whole hours, until the door opened slowly and I heard her sweet voice say my name.

"Emily... Are you awake?"

I got up quickly and sat on the bed. "Hey, beautiful... Yeah, I'm awake."

I reached to turn on the lamp, and saw that she had come closer to me. I cupped her face with my hands and kissed her. "How do you feel?" I asked, and she smiled.

"Very well rested and famished."

I laughed a little and caressed her cheek. "I'm sorry I didn't wake you for dinner, you looked so comfortable I just couldn't bring myself to bother you."

Her brown eyes widened. "You had dinner with my mother? Alone?"

I smiled and nodded. "Yeah..."

"Oh, God, Em, I'm so sorry... I know you don't like to be alone with her."

"It's okay, don't worry about that, it wasn't so bad... why don't we go downstairs and get you something to eat?"

She smiled, and her eyes lit up. I was happy. She made me so happy. Helena was the center of my world.

***

I was glad it was late; the mansion was quiet and deserted. We made it to the kitchen between hushed giggles and our hands holding. The options were varied; the freaking fridge was so loaded, it was ke a cornucopia. Out of everything in it, Helena insisted I'd make her a honey and cheese sandwich, it sounded so fucking gross, but whatever my girl wanted she got. Winter was really messing with her.

She sat on the counter, and I stood between her legs, she looked so happy with her food. She smiled, and I did, too. I loved just looking at her... Helena was incredibly beautiful. She looked adorable wearing my pajama pants and soccer jersey. When she finished her weird sandwich, she leaned in and kissed me; her lips were sweet, they tasted like honey.

My hands instinctively went to her lower back and under her t-shirt. She deepened the kiss and moaned into my mouth. Next thing I knew her hands were under my sweater and she was reaching into my pants. "Baby... What are you doing?" *I said, still on her lips.*

She moved her kiss to my neck and grabbed me. I shivered and gently wiggled my way out of the kiss to look at her. I saw pure lust. She wanted me, and I knew she wasn't gonna back down.

"Helena, baby, not here… What if someone comes?"

She went back to my neck. "They won't… I need you," *she whispered the last with her voice like that. I almost lost my mind.*

Almost.

I took her in my arms, and she looped her legs around my hips. She giggled and broke away from my lips. "I'm impressed," *she said.*

I held her tightly and made sure she was secure enough for me to carry her to the room. She buried her hands in my hair and kissed me again. We laughed and kissed as we left.

ABOUT THE AUTHOR

K.R Prince fell in love with stories at the tender age of five and has been unable to put away her ink and quill since then.

Made in the USA
Coppell, TX
31 January 2024

28457232R00246